THE INQUEST

MICHAEL MANSFIELD QC
TONY WARDLE

The Inquest – first published in Great Britain 2014 by
Michael Mansfield QC & Tony Wardle.

A CIP catalogue record for this title is available from the British Library

ISBN 978-0-9571874-3-6

Cover design and layout: The Ethical Graphic Design Company Ltd.

DEDICATIONS

This book is dedicated to the courage and tenacity of the families of the Marchioness disaster on the Thames and especially to the tireless pursuit of justice by Jim Swire in relation to the Lockerbie disaster.
(Michael Mansfield QC).

for Sue
(Tony Wardle)

EDITOR'S NOTE – FORESIGHT NOT HINDSIGHT

I have been contributing ideas to *The Inquest* since its inception in 1990 and editing the various incarnations of the novel since the first draft was produced by Tony Wardle in 1991. The reason it has taken so long is all the fault of Michael Mansfield, whose original idea it was. He has been rather busy with some highly significant inquiries and inquests, which have had ramifications for our criminal justice system for over forty years...

- Bloody Sunday, Derry, North of Ireland, January 30, 1972. 14 shot dead by British Army soldiers, 14 injured.
- Dublin/Monaghan bombings/unlawful killing, Republic of Ireland, May 17, 1974; 33 civilians and an unborn child killed, 258 injured.
- Lockerbie air disaster, Scotland, December 21, 1988. 270 died.
- Hillsborough football disaster, Sheffield, April 15, 1989. 96 died, 776 injured.
- Marchioness river boat disaster/unlawful killing, London, August 20, 1989. 51 died, 80 injured.
- Stephen Lawrence racist murder/unlawful killing, London, April 22, 1993.
- Dodi Fayed & Diana, Princess of Wales/unlawful killing, Paris, France, August 31, 1997.
- Ricky Reel, racist murder/open verdict, Kingston on Thames, October 14, 1997.

- Omagh bombing, County Tyrone/unlawful killing, August 15, 1998. 29 and 2 unborn children killed, 220 injured.
- James Miller, May 2, 2003 and Tom Hurndall, January 13, 2004. Journalists shot dead by Israeli soldiers in Palestine/unlawful killing.
- Jean Charles da Silva e de Menezes, shot dead by police/open verdict, London, July 22, 2005.
- Mark Duggan, shot dead by police, London, August 4, 2011.
- Dr Abbas Khan, "deliberately and intentionally killed" in a Syrian prison, December 2013.

Michael has contributed to a greater or lesser extent in all the hearings associated with these momentous cases in the period between 1990 and the present.

Despite the pressure of time, *The Inquest* has been revisited and revised as windows of opportunity have opened. Without Tony Wardle's commitment and immense talent and my tenacity in keeping the project alive, it would not have been finished. Importantly most of the book has been written in real time with foresight, not with the benefit of hindsight.

Finally, almost 25 years later, it is finished. Tony has meanwhile written another thrilling novel, *POD*, and I have become a professional artist, with three recent successful exhibitions. Michael, needless to say, continues to work on many high profile cases, pursuing his quest for justice and adherence to the rule of law.

Yvette Vanson, Editor
www.yvettevanson.com

CHAPTER ONE

Friday, December 7th, 1990, 4.50 p.m. It was arrogance that killed Eric Lloyd. Most people who knew him thought it might lead to his downfall but death was an unexpected bonus.

Flying back to Edgware from a late City lunch, Lloyd insisted on taking control of his Bell Jet Ranger despite having had a glass or two. He concentrated intently on the compass in front of him, determined to hold his course so that there would be no criticism, no patronising advice from his pilot alongside him – a pilot whose wages he paid and who he resented for his superior knowledge of flying. The lights of West London were already twinkling and sparkling from the black carpet beneath him and as he whirred his way over them he felt a quiet satisfaction with his skill as the nose of the helicopter remained pointing steadily at the correct compass heading.

The words: "I have control," spoken firmly and suddenly by Peter Thornton, his pilot in the adjacent seat, angered him. "Your heading's good but you're on an upwards trajectory, constantly increasing your height." He felt the control column and foot controls develop a life of their own as Thornton's hands and feet began to take charge.

"No," shouted Lloyd, "leave it!" and refused to relinquish his grip. In that one refusal, he broke the fundamental rule of flying that anyone under instruction immediately obeys the command of his instructor – and no one was more aware of it than Thornton. He was angry but bit back a retort.

There was no immediate urgency, Thornton rationalised. They had drifted two thousand feet above the ceiling stipulated by West Drayton control at the time he had lodged his flight plan. But that in itself was only a precaution as their route took them through a no-fly area for fixed-wing aircraft and they were certainly above the ceiling that any other helicopters would be using. They were not in immediate danger and he allowed Lloyd to continue flying while he decided the best course of action. He was fairly certain that, having made his stand, his boss would shortly do what he was asked.

Thornton glanced at Lloyd with a sideways look which could only be interpreted as contemptuous. He realised he had rarely seen this sombre, arrogant man smile.

For Lloyd, life was about image – face, and how to avoid loss of it – and a smile might reveal a chink in his facade. The East End accent hadn't quite been erased, the suit was just too sharp to be tasteful and his inability ever to say sorry said more about his weakness than his strength.

Thornton knew he was being outrageously snobbish and he was also uncomfortably aware that one of his reasons for allowing Lloyd to continue flying might have been fear of losing his job. He hoped it wasn't but if it was, then it was nothing short of an abrogation of his responsibility and ran counter to all he had learnt and practised over years of safe flying, both in combat and as a rich man's chauffeur. It stung him with embarrassment. The altimeter showed that the aircraft had barely descended despite Lloyd's rigid concentration.

"I have control," Peter Thornton said again and this time his hands and feet worked quickly and firmly, allowing no room for argument. Lloyd surrendered without resistance and Thornton felt an immediate sense of relief – partly because he now had control and could begin the descent back on to his approved course but mostly because his judgement had been entirely vindicated.

He was unable to consider the situation further as a thunderous roar engulfed the helicopter and the wingtip of a P11 passenger aircraft sliced through its rear fuselage, carrying away the tail rotor. Rather than the main rotor spinning above the helicopter, the helicopter now began to revolve round the rotor like some sickening fairground ride.

4.55 p.m. Winter darkness had already erased the last vestiges of light from a depressing and overcast, grey day. Vicky Denton drew the curtains over the French doors of her neat and not inexpensive house in Mount Park Road and switched on another light. Before sliding into the VCR probably the tenth cassette of the afternoon, she went through to the adjoining kitchen and switched on the kettle.

She returned with tea, bread, butter and Marmite and continued trying to cast the play which currently occupied her. She had already decided that there would be no cooking tonight and David would have to get a takeaway when he came home.

Another actor in another production sprang into electronic life on the monitor. The peace and quiet of working from home – no jangling telephones and no pointless interruptions – made her twice as productive, she felt.

Vicky turned up the volume on grainy footage shot with a cheap camcorder from the auditorium of a regional theatre. The sound quality was poor and she flipped the volume button again, which increased the background hiss to a point where it was almost unbearable.

When her tea cup and saucer began to rattle she reduced the volume but the crockery continued its chattering. It then began to skip about on the highly polished surface of the occasional table, slopping tea in all directions.

The hiss became a roar which engulfed the house and every moveable object joined in the vibrato performance. Vicky could feel the tremble through to her bones and froze in terror. And then, as quickly as it arrived, the all-enveloping wall of sound departed and the furnishings gradually ceased their erratic performance.

4.55 p.m. "Roots aren't funny, Mr Harrison, they're very damaging, very dangerous!" Mrs Millie Arthur leant forward with irritation and confronted Tom Harrison in his unprepossessing office. "They're undermining my house, the whole thing could collapse around my ears and what have you done about it? Nothing, that's what!"

Tom Harrison tried unsuccessfully not to smile. At this precise moment he could not care less if a sycamore root snaked its way across Mrs Arthur's back garden, wormed its way up the bathroom waste pipe, popped out through the lavatory pan and strangled her while she was performing her morning ablutions.

"You're not listening to me, Mr Harrison," snapped Millie Arthur, as she re-crossed her ankles with a display of irritation. Thick, lisle stockings hung down her stick-thin legs like Austrian window blinds. "I didn't come here to be laughed at!"

As she spoke, her perfectly white teeth peeked at Tom, the top row having a habit of clacking down on to the bottom, revealing the half-inch or so of pink plastic to which they were attached.

"Excuse me a second," Tom said and smiled at Millie Arthur as he stabbed a number on the telephone keypad. "Oh good, you're in. Anyone with you at the moment? No? Excellent! I have a client with me who would value a second opinion," he said, before replacing the handset.

"It's time you saw our top man, Mrs Arthur – our roots expert. Needs must when the Devil rides." He towered over the wiry little frame and placed his hand under her elbow to help her up.

"Drives," corrected Millie Arthur, as she rose, holding her bag in both hands. "When the Devil drives."

"Exactly," replied Tom. "Exactly!"

Millie followed him nimbly down the stairs and past reception, her thin little legs as sturdy and agile as any mountain goat's. Tom knocked on and opened a panelled door which bore the gilded inscription, Senior Partner, but remained outside in the corridor. "Mr Harrison Senior," he whispered confidentially to Millie and ushered her in. "Mrs Arthur has an uncaring neighbour and a particularly bad root problem," Tom announced to his father, his head protruding into the room only marginally while his body remained rigidly outside.

Tom withdrew his head and closed the door quickly – but not quickly enough to drown his father's voice as he shouted Tom's name. The word was swallowed by a thunderous, reverberating sound which, for a split second, Tom thought was a product of his father's annoyance but it soon assumed such terrifying proportions that Tom was frozen to the spot, momentarily grasping at the belief that it was an earthquake. As the noise subsided, Tom could hear Miss Rush sobbing with fear at her reception desk.

"It's all right, Miss Rush, it's gone," he shouted over his shoulder as he ran out into the road and was engulfed by the stench of burnt paraffin from a jet's exhaust.

4.56 p.m. Harrow School Library was always particularly quiet at around five o'clock as groups of very privileged young boys had their heads bent low over evening prep, watched disinterestedly by the duty master.

The sudden onslaught of noise came and went in seconds. In its wake it left some boys crouching under their desks while others ran for the door, deaf to the instructions of the master. They streamed out on to the playing field on the south side of the library, screaming with an excitement that was underpinned by fear.

The library weather vane and its supporting tower first wobbled, dislodging fragments of mortar which pattered to the ground beneath the gable end, before crashing down on to the footpath along the northern side of the building with a dull and undramatic thud. The area around it was almost entirely devoid of people except for one lone figure striding head-down towards the library from the direction of the music school. The metal cockerel and masonry had landed at his feet and for one brief moment the school chaplain thought that judgement day had arrived earlier than expected and unannounced.

4.57 p.m. Esther Vine had a perfect vantage point of the day's events as she slowly impelled her wheelchair over the road bridge which crossed the railway line at the bottom of Bessborough Road. Just before the turning into College Road, she heard the swelling roar and swung her wheelchair to the right to face it as it thundered towards her from the direction of Harrow School playing fields.

Time seemed to slow as the huge jet aircraft crossed Lowlands Road and skimmed feet above Harrow-on-the-Hill railway station. Esther instinctively knew what had to happen next but was frozen with disbelief – aircraft simply don't crash on houses in Harrow.

Like some infernal son et lumière, two bright spotlights from either side of the aircraft's wings illuminated the slated rooftops as it passed over them and they trembled violently under the onslaught of noise. Individual tiles detached themselves and skittered down the roof slopes and Esther could clearly see the small, oval, lighted windows which ran along the length of the aircraft's fuselage. The high-pitched whine of its twin jet engines screamed above her head and its wings waggled slowly from side to side as though, hidden from view, a deadly battle for control was underway.

As it crossed College Road its left-hand wing dipped down and ran along the roof ridge of the terraced houses in Station Road. Tiles, chimney pots and bricks flew from its path like shavings from a wood plane.

Esther remained frozen as the events suddenly became frighteningly personal. St Ann's Road, her home and her daughter Rachel were directly in the path of the aircraft.

The sparring which took place between Gordon Whitemore and Charles Astbury had become almost a feature of BBC Radio's *World at Five*. As party chairman as well as Minister of Transport, Astbury was a smooth and polished advocate and a safe pair of hands either for explaining or defending almost any aspect of the Government's overall policy, as well as speaking to his own brief. The dual role gave him the public exposure he craved and believed he deserved and provided the building blocks he needed to construct a stairway to the ultimate goal of party leader and then Prime Minister.

Anchorman Whitemore's dour Scottish pragmatism exactly counteracted Astbury's polished, public-school confidence and the clashes between the two men had become almost legendary. It seemed that each inflated their stereotype as conflict developed, Astbury becoming more upper class, Whitemore's voice taking on a hard Glasgow edge that was normally entirely absent. In truth, their confrontations consisted mostly of battle cries and the clash of swords but rarely was a telling blow landed. No one was more irritated than Whitemore by this failure.

Astbury was responding to a question about lack of integration in the transport system – a question which he knew was coming and for which he had been well briefed. It was one which, he decided, needed to be answered with a smile in the voice, dismissive contempt that wordlessly challenged the intellectual capacity of the questioner.

Astbury started with a patronising chuckle before wearily humouring his way into the response. But Whitemore wasn't paying attention – and that affected Astbury's delivery because it was like talking to the back of someone's head. Whitemore stared at the monitor on the desk in front of him, nodding silently and holding his headphones tightly to his ears. Astbury's reply petered to a halt as Gordon Whitemore urgently signalled to him to cut so he could speak.

"I'm sorry to interrupt you, Minister, but we're getting reports of an air crash in West London. Details are few but it appears to be at either Harrow or Kenton." He was still clutching the headphones, attempting to turn snippets of garbled information being fed to him by the producer into a coherent commentary.

"There is talk of a fireball and a large loss of life. It seems the aircraft came down on a densely populated residential area. I'm now being told that it is in fact Harrow, just north of Harrow-on-the-Hill railway station..."

Astbury clearly needed to be brought up to speed with events and declined to make any comment, silently excusing himself, but before he had even reached the door of studio 5A he was posing questions to himself and rehearsing the answers – questions which he knew others would be queuing up to ask. With an event of this magnitude, he instinctively knew that his survival might well be on the line.

Had he altered, relaxed or interfered with safety regulations in such a way that his fingerprints were on them? Were there any warnings he had ignored? Did the recent air traffic control dispute have any relevance, in particular his refusal to give in to the demands of the controllers? What was the current state of play on the terrorist front? Were there any obvious traps as a result of recent privatisations and the inevitable cost-cutting and redundancies that followed?

As Astbury exited from the studio, one of his security men, his personal secretary and his Parliamentary Private Secretary were waiting for him. The PPS had a mobile phone held to his ear: "It's bad, Minister, very bad!"

Charles Astbury moved at speed towards the lift. "What do we know? He raised his voice and shouted the question again: "What do we know? Was it one of ours?"

The PPS replied that they knew absolutely nothing as yet. As they left the lift two more security men were waiting for them and Astbury had his emotions back under control. The retinue exited from Broadcasting House and divided between the ministerial limousine and a security car. Both immediately edged out into the rush-hour traffic of Portland Place.

"I'm obviously going to have to put in an appearance at the scene —"

"Sorry, Minister..." interjected the PPS, holding up his hand, "but I'm getting some more information. It's a charter flight carrying Britons – to Algeria it seems but there's some doubt as to whether that was the final destination..."

"Whose is it?" snapped Charles Astbury.

"Just a minute, Minister," replied his PPS, again trying to listen to the telephone and his minister at the same time. "It's a Varsity flight, apparently, Minister."

Astbury was silent. When he did speak it was with urgency. "Get me Sturgis."

"I'm afraid the Home Secretary's out of the country, sir. He's visiting US prisons, if you remember..."

"Hell. Better get me Bannerman then, he's the best junior minister. I want a cordon sanitaire thrown round that crash site."

"A what, sir?" replied the PPS.

"A cordon sanitaire, you fucking idiot!" The PPS looked as shocked as if Astbury had punched him in the face. He had never seen the cool, calm and suave man he willingly served so taut. In fact, he realised he had never before heard him swear.

"I want the whole area sealed off. Not just the crash site but

–" he paused momentarily – "for two hundred yards in every direction."

"That won't be easy, Minister, it's in the middle of a residential area."

"I don't give a shit where it is," Astbury shouted, "do it and do it now. And get me Bannerman. Oh, and keep one line free for incoming calls."

No sooner had he spoken than one of the phones rang. His private secretary answered and turned to look over her shoulder at Astbury in the seat behind.

"It's the Prime Minister's office, sir. There's likely to be an emergency Cabinet meeting this evening. They'll confirm the time later if it's on. I'll cancel dinner with your wife."

He nodded. "They'll want some answers." The cars were barely halfway down Upper Regent Street, still moving at a snail's pace. Astbury shouted to no one in particular: "Get a bloody police escort and have us blue-lighted through this lot – and tell them to get the traffic lights on green between here and Harrow." He paused, motionless, but the incessant fiddling of his fingers indicated that his thoughts were far from still.

"Get me Glennister, will you?" His secretary looked blankly at Astbury. "Andrew Glennister, chairman of Varsity Aviation. He's on the database." He knew because he had put him there.

7.00 p.m. In Mexborough, South Yorkshire, Bernard Tate ummed and ahhed about when he was going to have his regular two pints – early or late? He decided that as there was nothing on television that night he would go to the miners' welfare – or what had once been the miners' welfare – at about nine and then switched on the seven o'clock news.

Urgent mention of Harrow in the opening commentary immediately caught his attention. Although he hadn't seen him for several years, the last time he had heard from his brother he had still been living in Harrow. Time had disappeared so rapidly that it came as something of a shock to Bernard to realise that his brother had been living there for more than twenty years. The speed with which time passed once you had turned fifty was disturbing, Bernard thought.

The newscaster cut to the reporter on the spot, who stood against a backdrop of flames – great sheets of flames which seemed to engulf a whole town. He spoke with obvious shock directly to camera.

"... and it is impossible to gauge the scale of this tragedy. The aircraft's fuel tanks were fully laden and on impact were transformed into one massive curtain of burning droplets. It seems that an area as large as two football pitches has been virtually incinerated... So far we have absolutely no indication of how many casualties there might be."

Bernard remained transfixed and packed his pipe with tobacco methodically with an index finger while waiting for further details. He realised without any soul-searching that he felt like an outsider, an observer, rather than a person who might be intimately involved. "Edith," he shouted through to the kitchen.

"... debris from the two-hundred-and-fifty-seater aircraft is thought to have been flung as far as half a mile from the point of impact," the reporter continued, clearly struggling to remain objective and professional. The areas worst affected, however, are the streets directly behind me here, just a stone's throw from Harrow railway station. It's known that Greenhills Way Primary School has been completely destroyed but the number of casualties isn't yet known. It is believed to have been packed with parents and children for a dress rehearsal of the school's Christmas play..."

As the reporter spoke, ambulances and fire engines could be seen arriving across the road behind him in a cacophony of rasping sirens, the blue flashes of their emergency lights illuminating his face like the strobes at a disco.

Greenhills Way! Bernard remembered the school. It was directly opposite his brother's house. Moments passed before he took down the emergency telephone number for those seeking information; the realisation that he was a participant in this drama and not merely an observer taking a little time to register.

"Edith!" he shouted again.

Edith appeared from the kitchen, bread knife in her hand. "I'm getting your tea – I can't do two things at once."

"I think our Jack might be in a bit of trouble," he said, with no emotion in his voice. He pointed to the television. "Air crash on his street in Harrow!"

Bernard rang the emergency number but all he got was the engaged signal and despite trying several more times, the result was the same.

"Have we still got Jack's number?" he asked Edith, who clucked and tutted in irritation before producing an address book from the dresser. Bernard found his brother's entry, dialled the number and heard nothing but the constant monotone of an unobtainable signal.

7.05 p.m. In Jesmond, Kevin Whalley was also watching the news but by this time the reporter was no longer attempting to hide his emotion.

"As I stand here, burning people are staggering out of the inferno behind me. It is an appalling scene which has completely overwhelmed the emergency services. The first people to dial 999 were told there was a twenty-minute delay in ambulance services due to staff shortages. That delay has become an eternity as emergency vehicles from all over London are trapped in rush-hour traffic.

"As I speak, casualties are being laid out on pavements because there is nowhere else to put them. This dreadful tragedy is rapidly turning into a disaster as the official response is shown to be completely inadequate..."

Kevin reached his decision immediately. He would just have time to get the Metro to Newcastle station and catch the last train to London.

He found a large plastic measuring jug and watered his pot plants. He then went up to see his landlady on the floor above to tell her he was going away for a couple of days. Kevin knew his mother would agree to feed the cats – she always did and a telephone call confirmed it.

He decided on a wet shave and worked carefully on the fair stubble, which didn't really show anyway. A fine base coat of flesh-coloured foundation was applied to his newly shaved face before he went to the wardrobe and removed a ready-packed bag. The small, second wardrobe he unlocked contained just a few outfits. Kevin ran his hand along them and made a selection, removed a nun's habit and carefully folded it into his overnight bag.

It was only noon but Ailey Newman, in her office in the Empire State Building, was hungry. She tossed up in her mind whether she would drop down the seventy-two floors to the street below and have a special New York all-day breakfast or hang on until lunch and lose a few pounds. Before she could reach a decision, an e-mail message came up on her screen.

"Come here, Charlie," she screamed at the top of her voice. Charlie obliged and all six feet four inches of him gangled in from the next office.

"Jesus, Charlie, there's a big one in the UK by the look of it. Read this stuff." They scrutinised the screen together.

"What the hell do we know about Varsity Aviation? Is it just some little Brit Spitfire outfit? Come on, Charlie, info, please."

Charlie went next door and returned with an armful of directories and looked up Varsity Aviation.

"Yo, here it is. Are you ready for this – it's more complicated than Watergate. Varsity Aviation operates from the UK and is registered there for tax but it ain't a UK company." He moved to another directory. "But nor is it US-registered; wholly owned by Dolman International which is based in the Caymans." He was on to the third directory and began to do a little jig. "Parent company with a fifty-one per cent shareholding is... Barcroft Holdings, registered in good ol' friendly New Jersey – downtown Jersey City!"

"Bingo!" yelled Ailey. "Charlie, get me on this afternoon's Concorde flight to London."

CHAPTER TWO

Friday, December 7th, 1990, 5.05 p.m. The first hundred yards or so from the Bessborough Road railway bridge towards the inferno of the crash site seemed to take Esther Vine an eternity. She spun the wheels of her chair in a frenzy of panic and despair and was barely conscious of the friction burns on her hands and fingers as she drove herself forward, her breath rasping and gulping.

All thoughts of whether her house might be damaged or destroyed had gone as alarm rose in her. Rachel's well-being and safety was all that concerned her and those thoughts tumbled over each other in a battle to keep her hopes alive. She might be unhurt, she might have survived, the aircraft might have missed the house, she might have been spared, there might still be time to save her daughter – please, God, let her be safe.

As desperate anticipation consumed her, Esther continued to thrust the wheels of her chair forward, down College Road, across it and into Clarendon Road, weaving in and out of the stationary cars which littered the carriageways, screaming at shocked and motionless pedestrians who stood staring almost with their mouths open, "Get out of the way – get out of the way!"

The fireball was still growing, roaring and crackling as Esther neared St Ann's Road. She could hear windows exploding, showering glass like glittering confetti into the night air. Her wheelchair bumped over fallen masonry, tilting first one way and then the other, gradually slowing until all momentum was lost and the muscles in her arms ached as she tried to force the chair over bricks and tiles which littered the street. The slower her progress the louder her sobs and cries, her shouts and screams, as despair obliterated hope and sucked from her the little energy she still had.

Fresh explosions of flames and sparks sent smoking rubble arcing through the air to hit the street with a clatter, adding to the obstacles in her path. A piece of house brick glanced off the side of her face but Esther's focus was solely fixed on where she believed her house to be. She could not be sure as all the usual landmarks had either been erased or were masked in clouds of swirling smoke and eruptions of orange flame.

From somewhere, Esther found renewed strength and the chair lurched forward once more, down the road, swaying and bucking – driven only by the willpower and determination of a frail sixty-year-old woman.

She finally came to a juddering halt amidst rubble within sight of St Ann's Road. The name plate attached to the side of a house stood out clearly in the light of the fires. Esther, stooping forward with the effort, worked at the wheels in a fury of concentration, determined to get them moving again, determined to keep going, determined to be with her daughter.

Sounds of screaming mingled with the explosions of gas cylinders, aerosols, cleaning fluids and car petrol tanks. Esther trembled with exertion and sweat rolled down her now sooty face, making tracks parallel to those formed by her tears. One more push would do it! Just one more and she forced all her remaining energy into her arms and concentrated her thoughts. The wheelchair suddenly shot forward, the front rearing up under the force of Esther's willpower. It spun abruptly to the right and tilted backwards before falling on its side, tipping her into the road to fall impotent and helpless amongst the growing volume of smouldering detritus.

Tiles, pieces of burning wood and twisted fragments of motor car continued to clatter and thud around her and Esther sobbed with the frustration of failure. She had let her daughter down, deserted her, left her to God knows what fate. For the first time she could ever remember, Esther cursed her disability, shouting out the bitter words with a choking anger, "You stupid, useless old woman!"

*

5.05 p.m. When the shout went up, Trevor Eades was struggling with the pronunciation of the word *cerveza* in the fire station rest room. He was determined to speak Spanish at least falteringly by the time of his holiday in June. Had it not been for the fact that he was behind with his night-school homework, he would not have agreed to give up his rest day and stand in for Dusty Miller. He was relying on a long, quiet watch during which he would ignore the card school, the darts and television and get down to studying. With luck he could be up to date by the end of the watch.

He hit the mat at the bottom of the pole and scrambled aboard the appliance. Lights were up and the siren was sounding even before the big oak doors of the fire station swung open. Already the talk was of a big 'un.

When they joined the traffic jam in Bessborough Road and came to a halt, they could see the flames licking the skyline ahead of them and Trevor's stomach began to churn. It was the biggest he had ever seen.

The siren blasted its raucous dual tones as they buttoned up their uniforms and protective clothing and completed the finishing touches to their equipment, but the appliance could only inch forward. They all stared ahead, willing a gap to open up in the motionless traffic, signalling to the motorists to drive up on to the pavements to give them passage – but none obliged.

5.06 p.m. The time to walk briskly from Tom Harrison's office to College Road would, under normal circumstances, take five or perhaps six minutes. On this day, despite running as rapidly as he could, it seemed to take forever. Tom sprinted without pausing, throwing his body from side to side as he swerved and swayed round incredulous people who stood staring at the expanding firestorm on the far side of the railway tracks.

He had never run so fast despite the business suit and tie, but the long strides felt as though they were in slow motion, like exercises performed in treacle or the desperate, dragging sensation of a dream when escape is denied.

At last he rounded the corner into College Road and the scale of the devastation confronted him with such force that his pace slowed involuntarily to little more than a jog. Without realising he had done so, he came to a halt and stared around him. The first few rows of houses facing the railway station remained standing but beyond them was an inferno and through the flames it was impossible to determine which buildings had been demolished and which remained standing. It was, in fact, academic as they all burned with the same roaring intensity. Already he could feel the heat on his face and hands.

A sudden explosion spurred him back into action and he ran into Clarendon Road, overtaking a woman in a wheelchair who was, bizarrely, heading towards the fire and not away from it. She came to a halt amongst the rubble and Tom continued past her without a word, feeling his face beginning to tingle in the radiated heat.

He had no clear purpose and having reached his destination suddenly felt impotent. The Pavlovian reaction of wanting to help was suddenly dwarfed by the enormity of the situation. He could not put out the fires, he could not clear the rubble, he could not enter the inferno and save anyone. In fact he was nothing more than an observer like all the other useless observers, just a little closer to the devastation. As another explosion produced a spattering of rubble around him, Tom realised just how ineffectual and ill-prepared he was.

A movement across the road in Greenhills Way caught his eye and Tom was transfixed by it. A figure exited from a burning house and walked across the road towards him at a pace that was rigid, measured and slow. Its arms were held out horizontally, leading the way like someone sleepwalking and it was dressed entirely in black, the clothes old and tattered with strips of material hanging down from the sleeves.

There was a strange air of unreality about the scene and as he watched it, the heat and noise and smoke all seemed to subside. There was nothing else in his immediate world but the silent, remorseless progress of the creature in front of him. Tom remained motionless, watching, uncomprehending.

Suddenly, he broke the trance and stepped forward to meet

the figure, from which he could now see wisps of smoke issuing. As he did so, the screaming from all around him, echoing in the rooms of burning houses, and the explosions and sounds of a greedily consuming fire, again crowded in on him, buffeting him with sensations. But the form in front of him remained silent and its methodical, ghost-like progress towards him continued unrelentingly.

Even before he reached the apparition, a feeling of dread overtook Tom. He ran forward but stopped in front of it, overwhelmed by his inadequacy.

He could clearly see that the strips hanging down from its arms were not material after all but skin. Other strips of burnt skin hung down from the face – the forehead, cheeks and chin. The raw flesh beneath was blackened. What few clothes it was wearing had been charred and the hair was a smoking mass, strands shrivelled and fused together in globules. The build and figure was unmistakably that of a woman.

Tom stared in disbelief, frozen into immobility because he simply did not know what to do. But even as he mentally grappled for the right response, a gust of wind fanned the charred hair and clothing into life, little orange flames suddenly appearing on the woman's breast and head.

Tom removed his jacket and as gently as possible covered the upper part of her flickering body to smother the flames. The acrid stench of burning human hair filled his nostrils. He knew his action was nothing more than a gesture and it was obvious that the woman could not possibly survive. He talked gently to her and his words broke the trance as she fell silently to her knees in front of him before rolling on to her side in the road. Tom could see tears on her blackened face.

As he impotently watched her dying, a piece of roof slate hurtled out of the dark, hitting her on the forehead and causing the black skin to separate into a scarlet gash. Tom had probably never felt such anger in his life. Stung by this final indignity, he scooped her into his arms and walked rapidly away from the fire in the direction of the railway station. He was surprised by how light she was.

He knew he was not going to save her but he wanted her

not to feel alone and it felt like the most important act of trust and compassion he had ever performed in his life. He was later to discover that this scorched and charred thing, almost unrecognisable as a human being, was in fact a girl of just sixteen.

6.30 p.m. David Denton coughed himself into consciousness. When he inhaled, a painful burning sensation choked his lungs so he tried easing a thin trail of air up his nostrils but it had the same effect and he coughed in great whooping bouts. As he desperately sucked in air at the end of each spasm, the searing pain again stabbed his lungs and denied him the oxygen he so urgently needed. With the pain and air starvation came a dreadful feeling of suffocation and claustrophobia. He flung his head from side to side in a frantic search for clean air but there was no escape from the cloying smoke.

He realised his eyes were closed and opened them a little. The feeling was exactly that of standing downwind of a bonfire when the wind suddenly alters direction and wafts acrid and stinging smoke into your face. He couldn't believe how painful it was and clenched his eyes shut again, screwing the lids tightly together to squeeze out the hurt but it remained for many seconds after.

He could remember bending over a drawing board with Billy McCann, trying to lose a few lines of copy from the brochure. He recalled suddenly looking up and it was almost surreal how the facing wall imploded, bellying out into the room in a parabola of construction blocks, fragmented plaster and shattered battens. Oddly, he couldn't remember any noise.

He tried to move and couldn't. Pressing on his chest was something wooden. He guessed it to be the drawing board but there was something extremely heavy on top of it. He could see nothing in the darkness and was unable to reach round the board to remove whatever it was that was slowly killing him. His chest was carrying too much weight and was responsible for reducing his air intake to a trickle. When he tried to move his legs they refused to budge, remaining utterly motionless. The only movement left to him was in his hands, which were raised up to his chin as if in prayer. David was suddenly aware that his whole body burned.

With a grinding crash, the floor moved beneath him, dropping several inches, jolting the remaining breath from him. A pattering of falling masonry filled the tiny space he inhabited. He became aware of an icy draught which tingled his left ear and turning his head to the side, drew a breath of cold winter air, which was smoke-free, fresh and wonderful. He sucked at it greedily and coughed to clear his lungs of smoke. Clean air flowed in to replace it. David eased open an eye and it was no longer painful; he could see lights shining through a jagged gap which had opened up in the masonry – orange street lights and blue flashes, a moving portrait of hope.

A bizarre and distant memory of childhood suddenly leapt from the filing cabinets of his mind – of the first day he swam a width of the swimming pool underwater. As he reached the far side and began to push upwards to the air, someone's hand pressed on top of his head and held him under just as he was about to surface. His lungs were at bursting point and a desperate panic overwhelmed him. When the hand was removed and his mouth rose above the water, the relief was overpowering just as now.

The jarring movement of the floor had eased the weight which had been pressing the breath from him and with a supreme effort David was able to push the drawing board to one side. Something heavy hit his face with a dull thud and a soft and yielding burden remained on top of him. Even without clear light he instinctively knew what it was and tried to control the revulsion which began to well inside him. He pushed Billy McCann's head to one side and knew by the way it lolled back that his neck was broken. In fact his head was barely attached to his body. David knew that the wetness on his hands and face was Billy's blood.

With a final exhausting, teeth-gritting effort he pushed the body from him then turned back to the gaping hole in the wall, sucking desperately at the clean air. He liked Billy and even in these circumstances there was a terrible sadness and sense of loss. But even more unbearable was the realisation that this was not just part of some scary little mishap. No one was suddenly going to walk in and make all the terror disappear. David was aware that his life was quickly ebbing from him.

When he tried to change his position his legs again refused to move and as he explored them with his hands he knew beyond doubt that the beam which lay across them had smashed the bones. As if the act of acknowledging the injuries had triggered his sensations, pain flooded up from his legs in waves, each one stronger than the one before.

6.55 p.m. Vicky Denton continued working, waiting for David's key in the door to signal it was time to stop. Six o'clock came and went and as the time moved towards 7.00 p.m. she began to feel irritated.

As she switched the television on for the seven o'clock news, the phone rang. She expected it to be David with an explanation or an excuse but it was Emma.

"Thank God, you're all right, Mum. I've just heard."

"Heard what, darling?"

Mount Park Road and its suburban tranquillity was too far away from either Northolt Road or Sudbury Hill, the two major thoroughfares, for the noise of the emergency sirens to have reached Vicky. A wailing, flashing, desperate fight for life had been taking place just out of earshot and without her knowledge.

Between sobs, Emma, in a few frightened words, outlined the scale of the tragedy. As she spoke, Vicky could see the muted television pictures in front of her.

"Dad okay?" Emma asked.

The words struck a chill into Vicky and she was incapable of answering. Pieces of information clicked into place one after another like the relentless progress of a digital clock: brochure design job – McCann Products – 4.30 p.m. – Station Road – late – no word. The fear concentrated in her stomach and chest making it almost impossible to speak or even breathe.

She tried not to communicate her panic to Emma and hung up with some final words about being sure that Dad was okay, to stay at her friend's and she would ring her later.

Vicky scrambled to find the telephone directory and McCann Products' number, dialled it and got the unobtainable tone. She tried again just in case she had misdialled but it produced the same result, a persistent bleep... bleep – bleep... bleep. She wanted to scream.

After hanging up she stood inert in her pleasant living room, which had not been designed with such a scene of despair in mind. Vicky was aware of repeating one word over and over. "No, no, no, no..."

The emergency telephone number flashed on to the television screen and she snatched at the phone and dialled it. Her reward was an engaged signal. She hit the last number redial with a similar result. And again – and again – and again.

"Answer me!" she screamed unheard down the insistently busy line.

The idea came like an inspiration despite being mundane and obvious and she rapidly scanned the list of household emergency numbers next to the phone and dialled the police. The ringing tone sounded but there was no reply. After an eternity of waiting she redialled and got the engaged signal. Vicky screamed with frustration and anger.

"Think logically," she said out loud to herself. "Where might he have gone if he'd finished his meeting early?" She knew there was no reason why the meeting should have finished early and if it had, he would have come home. He would not have gone to a pub because David, in this respect at any rate, was entirely predictable.

Without calculating where she was going or what she was going to do when she got there, Vicky found herself reversing the car down the driveway with its rear wheels spinning. The glow from hundreds of burning houses on the far side of the playing fields provided the obvious beacon to follow.

6.57 p.m. Louise Watson was furious to be late arriving at the crash site. A Friday evening, after-work drink over in Wembley Park delayed the news from reaching her. What a great story to be late for! She could vaguely remember talk of the Harrow and Wealdstone train crash but that was before she was even born. Here was another Harrow disaster but there were two things different about it: it was, it seemed, much, much bigger and she was on the case. There would be others from the *Evening Chronicle* there and from the nationals but this was her home patch and she had the advantage of local knowledge.

She walked briskly towards the glow, having abandoned her car on the Watford Road near the Harrow School bathing pool. The camera bag was beginning to weigh heavily on her shoulder because, fortunately, she had stocked up with enough film to open a medium-sized photographic shop, ready for Monday's job.

On reaching the roundabout which was built over the railway lines where the Watford Road became Sheepcote Road, Louise was surprised to find her route blocked by police in navy boiler suits. They were strung across the roundabout, diverting all the crawling cars and curious pedestrians along Kenton Road. As a matter of course she held up her press card and carried on walking.

When the shout came – "Oi, you, where d'you think you're going?" – she responded with the word "Press," throwing it back over her shoulder.

"I'll bloody press you if you don't get your arse back here."

She didn't want delay or confrontation and turned back, her annoyance hidden behind a smile. "Evening Chronicle."

"No one's going through there. It's a bloody disaster area."

The facade cracked. "It's my job, that's what I do – I report on disasters!" She ignored the fact that so far in her career she had never been within shouting distance of a disaster but that wasn't the point.

"You'll do as you're fuckin' told, lady, or you'll be in the back of that van there! The whole area's been sealed off, all right?"

There were no numbers on his shoulder and her demand to know who he was and from which force was met with a final warning to fuck off or be lifted.

It was the first time Louise had ever had dealings with police not in uniform and was unclear about her next move. She looked at the thick neck and interlocking eyebrows and decided her options were limited. A lecture on press freedom or the necessary defence of democracy, she decided, was not going to bring enlightenment to the hard and unblinking eyes.

Fuming, she turned and walked back in the direction from which she had just come, but only as far as the entrance to the old College of Technology. With a quick glance over her shoulder to check if she was being watched, Louise ducked through the entrance gate and hurried across the grounds towards the railway embankment.

A search unearthed a hole in the chain-link fencing through which she squeezed and dropped down the embankment on to the railway track. The station was no more than two hundred yards to the left and after sleeper-hopping along the track and then carefully crossing the wide fan of railway lines, avoiding all the live rails and scanning left and right for approaching trains, she jumped up on to the platform of Harrow-on-the-Hill railway station, which had been cleared of passengers and closed to the public.

Heading up the stairs and towards the exit, Louise got no further than the booking hall. Its floor was covered with bodies, some burnt beyond recognition, others bleeding from impact wounds, and lines of living faced lines of dead with only feet between them. There was an overwhelming smell of burning.

Paramedics and what seemed to be ordinary members of the public moved around between the living, staunching wounds, wiping faces and talking quietly. It was difficult to be certain because of the grime but one of them looked very like the solicitor, Tom Harrison. Louise made a mental note to talk to him later. Whatever their capacity, official or unofficial, everyone's movements seemed stilted, unreal, almost undirected and no one had any interest in her. Victims and helpers alike all appeared to be utterly traumatised.

There seemed to be little in the way of medical supplies and equipment and the noise from the street on the far side of the entrance doors, which opened directly on to the station forecourt, was of sirens, shouts and revving engines and there was an all-pervasive sense of chaos. The clattering of a helicopter drowned out most other sounds and sent smoke and dust whirling around the ticket hall in pungent spirals.

Injured bodies were lifted on to stretchers and carried out through the doors but other bodies were immediately brought in to replace them – some living, some dead. Louise had seen dead people before and had witnessed the dreadful grief which nearly always accompanies them. She had seen mangled bodies cut from car wrecks, house fires which had destroyed whole families, but never before had she stepped unsuspectingly into such horror. She fought back nausea.

It was minutes before Louise remembered her reason for being there, reached for her camera and began to look at the scene through a viewfinder. Its miniaturised, two-dimensional imagery stripped away the pain and pathos and turned reality into unreality – making the unbearable bearable.

7.05 p.m. The first mile of Vicky's journey in search of David passed in a blur of screaming rage and frustration with her hand almost permanently pressed down hard on the horn. The whole world, it seemed, had decided to drive at a snail's pace, to stop at every crossing whether anyone wanted to cross or not and to wait for an almost empty road before pulling out into a line of traffic. As she overtook one car she knew for sure that the next would also be driven by someone with a greying, balding head, who had heart trouble and difficulty in finding top gear.

As she crossed the roundabout between Northolt Road and Lower Road, the car wheels rebounded from the kerb, squealing in a burst of blue tyre smoke. Even as she spun the steering wheel to correct the skid, she didn't really notice the danger – or care about it.

Ahead of her, as she started down Bessborough Road, was a forest of red tail lights and caught between them, a dozen or more flashing blue lights. The road was at a standstill and as she dropped the driver's window and leant out, she was met by a cacophony of sirens and car horns. Without hesitating, Vicky swung the car out of the line of traffic and headed up the oncoming carriageway. There were almost as many cars heading towards her, away from the disaster. Her headlights were on full beam and the horn barked a warning that was lost amidst all the other noise.

Seconds later her car was forced to a halt by an oncoming ambulance which had nowhere to go to avoid her. It screeched to a standstill directly in front of her car, its sirens wailing, and although Vicky could not hear the invective being hurled at her by the driver, she could recognise the gestures. She escaped the situation by spinning the car across the carriageway as a battered Ford Transit screeched towards her with all wheels locked. Vicky ignored it and headed down the nearest side street, where she left the car double-parked before running back to Bessborough Road and continuing towards the fire on foot.

After a few hundred yards her legs slowed from a run to a trot. She wanted them to keep moving but the muscles ached for lack of oxygen and her lungs hurt as they heaved with effort, grabbing at air. Spittle flew from her mouth and feeling it gathering on her chin, she dragged her hand across her face, trying to make her legs move faster, willing them to run.

Four hundred yards from the station, a solid mass of people blocked the pavement and Vicky tried to force her way through them, pushing and elbowing, battling to pass with the words "Excuse me," before abandoning them in favour of the simple demand "Move, move, move!". There was so little breath with which to push the words out that even Vicky could barely hear them.

She began to grab at people with her hands, dragging them backwards, pulling them off balance and forcing herself forward. Their faces were full of excitement as they pointed and gestured at the glow beyond the station, watching ambulances speeding from the scene. They stood and they stared and Vicky hated them for it.

7.10 p.m. As long as David kept his head turned towards the gap which had opened up in the wall of the building he could breathe, he could see, he could plan.

It was over a foot wide and through it he could see blue lights flashing in the world outside amongst the burning glow, a world he desperately wished he was part of.

The reason his body felt so uncomfortably hot suddenly became clear – he was literally being slowly roasted by the suspended concrete floor on which he was lying. He worked out that flames from the room below must be licking at it underneath, turning it into an enormous griddle and he was the steak. David realised that doing nothing was not an option.

By shuffling the upper part of his body towards the wall, trying to ignore the pain from his trapped legs, he could actually reach the gap. Having got there he had no idea what to do. He tried shouting but the futility of it immediately became obvious as his lungs heaved and rasped merely to issue a moan. He needed a light to flash through the gap, a flag to wave, something to draw the attention of those below that here was a living person in need of help. He could think of nothing to use and then he remembered the drawing board. It was within reach and he shuffled his body back towards it, feeling through the smoke with his right hand until he felt it, moving his hand this way and that trying to work out which side of the board was which – which side had the drawing on it.

He could feel its smoothness stretched taut by the big brass drawing pins, the drawing they had been working on, the drawing that represented two months' hard work and two months' income; the drawing that David now hooked his fingernails under and ripped from the board.

He transferred the paper to his other hand and moved his body back towards the gap in the wall. For a moment he lost track of time and place and realised he had lapsed into unconsciousness.

Ignoring the pain that clawed at him, David shuffled close to the gap and reached through it, pushing the paper ahead of his hand. With a huge effort, he forced his arm, his shoulder and part of his head through the gap and into the outside air and with the limited mobility he had in the restricted space, began to move his arm up and down, waving the paper like a big white flag of surrender. The sweat rolled from him, his back burned and the pain from his legs was almost unbearable. Death suddenly seemed quite a welcome option.

David continued to wave his arm up and down, backwards and forwards with increasing desperation until a sheet of flame singed his fingers and forced him to snatch his hand back.

There was very little of the drawing left as it had been ignited by the fire from the floor below.

He held on to the remaining fragment of paper as long as he could, as though this flaring piece of tracing paper was the only thing which could save his life, and his arm thrashed around in a frenzy of movement until his fingers began to burn and only then did he release the last remaining scrap. For several seconds he watched its charred and glowing remains spinning skywards in the updraught from the burning building. It occurred to him that he hadn't taken a copy.

A clatter against the wall just below him brought David back to reality – he must have drifted into the comfort of unconsciousness once more. A yellow fireman's helmet appeared on the other side of the gash in the wall.

"Are you all right, mate?"

David wanted to kiss the man, to shout and laugh and thank him but managed only a few laboured words. "No, my legs ... trapped ... I think they're broken." To David, the man looked about sixteen years old.

The fireman turned his head and talked to someone on the ladder below, passing down the information that he intended going into the building through the gap in the masonry. David could just make out the reply. "Be careful, Trev, the building's unstable!"

The fireman eased David back into the building, pushing him away from the opening and struggled through after him. The beam was heaved from David's legs and once more a wave of pain surged over him.

"Hang on, mate, we're going to get you out of here. Use your hands to help me as much as you can because I've gotta get you through that gap and you're no lightweight." He slipped a rope under David's armpits.

Forcing himself forward with his hands and with the fireman pushing, David managed to squeeze his head and shoulders through the gap, out of the smoke-filled office into the fresh air and sucked at it greedily. The second fireman grabbed him and eased him down on to the turntable ladder but the pain was finally too much.

The last thing David saw before he lost consciousness was the face of the young fireman following him through the gaping hole in the side of the building. As the man's top half emerged a low roar like distant thunder came from the building as it jolted and rocked, causing the ladder to sway erratically. With a sound of rending and grinding masonry, the gap in the wall closed as neatly as it had opened and the bulging but unseeing eyes of Trevor Eades stared down on David as he was slowly lowered to the ground.

7.45 p.m. The ministerial entourage arrived in the station forecourt by helicopter, with Charles Astbury looking sombre and haunted. The press was clamouring for information as the void created by an absence of hard news had been filled with rumour. They were all aware that a nation in shock was seeking explanations.

Even those journalists who had been around long enough to watch Astbury's career develop (from young firebrand of the Right to cabinet minister and chief spin doctor) had never seen the minister so vulnerable, shorn of his protective veneer, the hard carapace that shed criticism like water. A throwaway comment by one old hand from long ago – that if Astbury fell in a pit filled with shit he'd come out smelling of roses – had earned him the nickname Rosie.

He came out of the booking hall, his face white, but even when he stood in front of the battery of cameras and outstretched hands clutching pocket tape recorders, he failed to engage the usual gear. He seemed hesitant, unsure of himself and the words came out with difficulty.

The City-based journalists had long ago learnt that shouting questions at Astbury, hectoring him and interrupting, guaranteed they would be ignored. But now their discipline deserted them and they clamoured for answers, one question cutting across another, a crescendo of voices swelling ever louder as each reporter tried to be heard above the others. For a few moments Astbury stood before them seemingly transfixed but eventually he gave the nod to a favoured TV commentator who immediately moved closer so that Astbury could hear him.

"Is there any information about the cause of the crash, Minister?"

"Yes, there is," replied Astbury, barely audible, "but before I take your questions there are some things I would like to say." In sincere tones, he heaped praise on the rescue services, confiding to the viewers that at least one fireman had lost his life. As he dealt with these routine acknowledgements he appeared to find strength from somewhere and began to reach for the old mantle of authority – but it was still far from a snug fit.

He concluded by revealing that he had reason to believe the aircraft was in collision with a helicopter and although it was too early to be precise, it appeared that the helicopter was flying in the wrong airspace.

With an inclination of his head he invited another question from another known and sympathetic reporter. He clearly was in no state to throw himself on the mercy of the wolf pack. Before the question could be posed, a female voice cut angrily through the babble and Louise Watson's shouted words were as much a statement as a question.

"The emergency response has been a disaster and injured people are still lying in the streets. This is a direct result of Government cutbacks. Do you accept responsibility?"

Astbury looked confused until anger flashed across his face as he pretended he had not heard the question. He turned to a recognised daily paper reporter at the front of the crowd, inviting a question.

"Is there any suggestion of terrorism, Minister?"

"It's too early to be definite about anything but there are no indications so far. We will of course be holding a full inquiry and will be doing our very best to establish the full facts surrounding this appalling tragedy."

"Will that include looking at the failure of the emergency services?" Again Louise's voice cut through the clamour and again Astbury ignored her.

A middle-aged, male reporter at the front of the press crush questioned Astbury but there was no challenge in his words.

"Are you considering a public inquiry?"

Astbury was now back on track, the professional politician

dealing with questions of procedure rather than death and human misery, and he looked all the more comfortable for it. His lengthy response could be simply précised – considering all the options and not counting anything out or anything in. It was part of the politician's coping mechanism – the longer you talk, the fewer questions you have to answer.

Louise Watson continued trying to elicit a response from Astbury but she was now speaking out as much to expose his evasions in front of other reporters as to extract an answer. Eventually, she turned away in contempt and went in search of rescue workers, ambulance staff and all the others who were struggling to cope with a tragedy that overwhelmed them, psychologically as well as physically. If Astbury wouldn't face the issue then she would report directly from the mouths of those who were trying to cope against extraordinary odds.

A fire appliance growled past the station forecourt and squealed to a halt, its fire officer jumping out to look for instructions. It was a local crew and Louise ran over to them.

"Hallo, boys. Mind if I join you?" she asked as she climbed in through the open door. The few objections that were raised quickly petered out as she threw question after question at them about the difficulties of coping with an emergency of this magnitude. Suddenly, the fire fighters felt that someone was on their side, listening to them and that there was a chance of their grievances being aired.

7.50 p.m. David Denton was carried from the ladder to a safe distance from the fires where two firemen laid him gently on the pavement.

A battered white Transit van with peeling, stick-on lettering along its side – 'P & J Uphols ry' – appeared out of the smoke and pulled up alongside the still body. Paul Barony and Ivor Jones jumped out.

"Can you take him to a casualty clearing point?" The fire officer looked almost desperate, not wanting to leave David on the pavement but eager to get on with fighting fires.

"They're lined up five deep, they asked us not to bring any more. We'll take him straight to South Harrow hospital." They lifted David and placed him in the back of the van on furniture blankets. Another casualty was already inside the van – a man who held his hands over his eyes and moaned constantly.

Paul Barony switched on the radio as Ivor guided the van through the confusion of emergency vehicles, abandoned cars and people and crossed through the cordon of police before heading down Bessborough Road. The local FM station was giving a running commentary on the emergency and the commentator sounded angry.

"Please, please get off the roads. Whatever you're doing, wherever you're going, get off the roads. Kenton Road, Station Road, Pinner Road, Bessborough Road, they're all blocked and it's mostly sightseers. You are costing people their lives. Get off the road now! Go home, take your car with you – do not abandon it – and let the emergency vehicles get through."

As the Transit neared West Street, several cars in the snarled-up traffic on the opposite carriageway decided to do a U-turn. A small white car appeared beside the ambulance which had been forced to halt in front of them and Ivor slammed the brakes on as a cry of pain issued from one of the casualties in the rear.

The closer they got to South Harrow Hospital, the clearer the road became and Ivor was able to spur the protesting, rattling Transit into something resembling speed. He gingerly turned the wheel into the hospital entrance and scanned the array of signs for the emergency department. Failing to see one, he pulled up outside the main entrance and Paul ran through to reception, shouting as he went.

"Where's the emergency department?"

The receptionist looked worried. "It's gone, six months ago, we haven't got an emergency department; it's closed down."

"What am I supposed to do with the two geezers in the back of the van?"

"You'll have to go to Wembley Park General Hospital."

"This is a hospital, isn't it? And there're doctors here, aren't there?" he shouted, pointing to two passing people in white coats. "I'm a fucking upholsterer. These guys need seeing to now and not by me."

"I'm sorry but we're not equipped for emergencies; Wembley Park is."

"You bleedin' jobsworth," Paul shouted at him as he ran back to the van.

7.55 p.m. When Vicky finally reached the police cordon stretched across the junction of Bessborough and Lowlands Road, her insistence on being let through was loud. She was reluctantly allowed past by a young PC who did not seem to know quite how to handle her and passed her on to a harassed-looking inspector. He listened as her words came tumbling out, urgent and demanding, but it had little effect and he was adamant that she could not enter the site of the crash. Even in her desperation she could see that he was right and there was nothing she could do.

Vicky asked about the McCann building and the inspector checked with someone on his walkie-talkie. Vicky could not hear the reply but she could tell by the officer's face that the block was in the disaster area. His voice suddenly became quiet and intimate as he told Vicky that they had no information about the building's occupants. He rattled off a string of casualty reception points where survivors were being taken but admitted that it was not a complete list as the situation was changing almost by the minute.

Vicky turned away from the road block and could feel the energy draining from her. Wealdstone Civic Centre, Marlborough Hill School, Gayton High School, Headstone Lane Roman Catholic Church – David could be in any of them; he could already have been taken to one of several hospitals; he might be in any one of a dozen morgues or he might still be in amongst the flames.

She knew the most sensible thing to do was go home, to sit and wait for the phone to ring and for someone with a sad voice to tell her what had happened to her husband. But that could take hours, maybe even days, and she could not passively cede control to people she did not even know.

Vicky headed for the nearest reception point but fear no longer drove her forward and her pace had slowed to an unhurried walk. She no longer shouted and screamed at people who would not move; she no longer talked to herself and as she looked at the flames to her right and the plumes of sparks and smoke, her hope evaporated.

8.00 p.m. The fire appliance was directed to Greenhills Way School and when it arrived, Louise Watson kept out of the way of the fire fighters but remained close by. Another appliance was already playing water from three hosepipes on to the flames and that particular fire was now largely under control. Other fires raged all around them.

The school was made up of several buildings and the first one to be quenched of fire by the hoses was the assembly hall – a big Victorian structure with a high pointed roof. The charred roof beams still smoked and the road was awash with black water.

The fire fighters acted quickly but without panic as they moved into the interior of the building, knowing from experience there could be no survivors. Louise waited to be told she could also enter and after several minutes, one of the fire fighters re-emerged, his face blank, expressionless.

"I don't think you want to go in there," he said, without looking at her.

"Bad?"

He simply nodded.

Louise walked apprehensively to the main entrance of the building and was surprised to find that although the roof had collapsed, the rubble from it had been supported by the floor above the assembly hall. The hall itself was entirely charred and there was a stench like that of a doused barbecue but it was largely uncluttered by debris.

The only place where there was measurable rubble was around the entrance doors – mounds of it, like so many filled, black dustbin liners. The stone-flagged floor around them carried marks of burning in the shape of puddles, as though someone had poured paraffin under the doors and ignited it.

The dustbin liners gradually took on the form of blackened and burnt, crouching human forms – some big, some very little. Bones protruded through the taut and carbonised skin and lipless teeth were bared in open-mouthed grimaces. Louise realised that this was all that remained of the children's school play. Molten human fat was the cause of the burning puddles, not paraffin.

Little of what happened next was conscious. She left the building but had no idea in which direction she was walking, had no idea how far she had gone, where she was or who it was who shouted at her but it was the voice of a man that wrenched her out of her shocked state. "Will you please get out of here, this is a restricted area. If you don't go now I will call someone and have you removed."

She looked at the walkie-talkie the man clutched in one hand and guessed he meant what he said. In the background, a floodlight burst into life and she could clearly identify part of an aircraft. Surprisingly there were no fires in the immediate vicinity and Louise's thoughts seemed to be functioning on automatic as she unconsciously began analysing the situation. *Fuel tanks are in the wings, probably ripped off – that would cause the fires; fuselage is heavier – momentum probably allowed it to travel further, probably nothing flammable in it, so this is almost certainly part of the fuselage...* It would have been difficult to identify it as such but she accepted her conclusion.

The grey-haired man in the anorak turned towards the boiler-suited technician who had switched on the floodlight and signalled to him frantically, waving his notebook like a semaphore flag. "Turn it off, turn it off – I'll tell you when to switch on!" He turned back to Louise. "Immediately remove yourself from the vicinity or I'll have you arrested."

As he spoke, visions of terrified little children crouched in front of a locked door, waiting to die, engulfed Louise. She heard their cries of fear, sensed their panic and felt the overwhelming grief of their parents. Her voice screamed with a power she did not know she had and its vicious, rasping rage almost frightened her. She knew she wanted to kill the man.

"You fucking arsehole!"

She saw the shock on his face and heard her words echo around the streets of despair. She turned and left without saying another word. His reaction told her that there was something here she needed to know about but there was so much else that required reporting that she felt it was not worth the risk of being arrested.

10.30 p.m. Bernard Tate left the miners' welfare having exceeded his ration of two pints – in fact he had doubled it. He had talked to a couple of people about his brother but it had felt odd expressing concern for someone who was almost a total stranger to him. Bernard decided he would do nothing further until he heard officially what had happened to Jack.

11.30 p.m. As the *Flying Scotsman* neared King's Cross, Kevin Whalley got up from the dining car and returned to his seat in standard accommodation. He had decided to treat himself to dinner in a fit of rare extravagance but it had been wasted money. After the soup he had done little more than push the food around his plate as each time he went to eat, a pang of excitement screwed his stomach into a knot and he could not force the food down.

Through the darkness he could just discern the blurred name of Hitchin as the train swayed at full speed through the platform lights of the station. Kevin got up and went to the lavatory, taking his overnight bag with him.

Sister Mary of the Order of the Immaculate Conception returned to Kevin's seat carrying Kevin's bag.

4.06 a.m. The Concorde flight was uneventful but on time and Ailey Newman was relieved not to have spotted anyone she recognised on it – no other lawyers with similar intentions. She felt fine and as it was only 11.00 p.m. by her internal time clock she decided to get straight down to work, checked into the Heathrow Hilton, changed her clothes and arranged for a chauffeured car to take her directly to Harrow.

By the time she arrived, most of the crowds had dispersed but a police cordon still encircled the area. She told the driver to wait and tried to gain access to the crash site but charm did not work, neither did threat, and Ailey remained on the outside.

Sheer persistence eventually got her through but only as far as the control centre.

Tempers were short, people were tired, but by playing the legal card with all the New York confidence she could muster she eventually left the centre with a list of hospitals to which most of the injured had been taken.

Ailey knew it was going to be a long night and that she would have to deal with the greatest volume of collective grief perhaps even she had ever witnessed. This night there would be no talk of money. Resentment and pain would be harnessed and she would offer the injured and their relatives support; she would provide the bereaved with a focus; she would be an anchor for them to hang on to as they tried to understand their newly shattered lives. Eventually, in a day or two, she would talk money but by then the pages in her personal organiser would be bursting with names and addresses of angry people, everyone a potential litigant.

Ailey began her quest at the Wembley Park General Hospital.

4.30 a.m. Sister Mary was also seeking victims of the crash but it was the fatalities which demanded her attention. Almost by divine providence, it seemed, she found her way to the Headstone Lane Roman Catholic Church where the community room had been turned into a temporary morgue.

For several hours she moved between the dead, offering prayers, reciting Hail Marys and Our Fathers and discreetly masturbating beneath her habit. It was pure chance that a policeman noticed her unsisterly movements.

Sister Mary again became Kevin Whalley in an alleyway alongside the church where his wimple was removed and two policemen punched him to the ground. His shouts of "Leave me ... I can't help it..." failed to impress the men, who continued to kick him even as they recited the obligatory caution.

5.34 a.m. Vicky Denton's journey through the mansions of other people's misery ended at the Wembley Park General Hospital with the discovery of her own misery. A sombre mortuary technician showed her into a room full of covered corpses, each with a label attached round the ankle. They still wore their clothes and shoes and no one had had time to worry about cosmetic improvement.

Vicky had seen a lot of corpses that night, many appallingly disfigured, so when a technician pulled back the sheet from yet another, Vicky was relieved to see he had not been burned. Through the grime and smudges on his face she could see that it was David but instead of coming home with her he was slid back into his refrigerated cubbyhole.

CHAPTER THREE

Monday, December 10th, 1990, 7.10 a.m. Early starts had never been Tom Harrison's strong point but on this day, he had been sitting at his desk since shortly after 7.00 a.m. He had not slept properly since Friday.

Everything in his office looked reassuringly normal but somehow felt unreal. It seemed almost obscene that so much had happened, so many people's lives had been devastated and yet this slightly scruffy and unimpressive fragment of Harrow remained the same.

The offices had been downwind of the crash site and a thin film of oily soot had covered every surface. Mrs Benson, the cleaner, had been brought in on Sunday to wipe it away but Tom knew it would not be possible to remove his memories so easily. Despite the liberal application of polish and cleaning fluid, the smell of burning still hung in his nostrils, every breath reminding him of the disaster and in particular one charred, sixteen-year-old girl called Polly Bentham.

Over the weekend, in a kind of daze, Tom had gone back to the scene, discovered Polly's name from a surviving neighbour in Greenhills Way and reported to the police who had shown him the mortuary records.

Tom switched on the radio to hear the morning's news, pulled open a desk drawer and removed a bundle of files. It was more an attempt to return routine and normality to his life than any desire to get on with work.

Tom flicked through the files one by one. A public order offence – George 'Geordie' Wilson charged with gross indecency; *Somerville versus Quality Windows Ltd* – a contract dispute; Ronnie Mash – driving with excess alcohol; the ongoing saga of Millie Arthur and her roots and Sandra Lockett, supposedly shoplifting from Woolworths. He placed the files in order of urgency on his desk and wondered if he could find the enthusiasm to do anything with them. There was a similar selection of impending cases, slightly less urgent, in a drawer on the other side of the pedestal desk.

So pervasive had been the oily clouds of smoke from Flight 469 that Tom discovered smuts had found their way between every page in every one of the files, forming a thin film which smudged at the touch. As he rifled through the papers and the smell of burning intensified, again visions of Polly flashed across his mind.

Over the weekend, newspapers had produced enough copy and pictures to last a lifetime but the dailies had obviously felt cheated. The timing of the crash on a Friday evening, just hours before going to press, had not allowed them scope to do the story justice. Broadsheets were particularly curtailed because of their earlier copy deadlines but the Sundays, of course, had had a field day and now, with Monday's papers, the dailies had finally been able to indulge themselves with the greater part of every paper given over to personal tragedies, lucky escapes and acts of bravery.

One of the fatalities was Paul Thackstead, Tom's best friend until Paul's marriage to the tight-arsed, tight-lipped Vanessa and the demands of three small children had gradually prised them apart. Tom felt deeply saddened that an era of his life had ended; the time of youthful excesses, powerful camaraderie, confidence and enthusiasm. But such was the impact of the last few days that there was little capacity for the grief that Paul was entitled to. It was a shame, but mass slaughter, he realised, had the effect of diluting individual tragedies, which became little more than scenes in a far bigger tragedy.

The main editorial line was consistent in almost every paper – the failure of the emergency services and whether Government was or was not responsible for it.

Tom looked down unseeingly on the file *Henderson versus Chilled Chicken Emporium* and knew that the role of the emergency services was not the real story and the most efficient in the world would not have saved Polly Bentham. The question which worried him and constantly gnawed away at him was how something so terrible could ever have happened at all. There were no answers, he knew that. Shit happened.

Loose glass in the front door rattled as someone slammed it shut after them. He knew by the sounds of measured progress through the building that it was his father. Attracted by the sound of Tom's radio, Harry Harrison peered through the doorway.

"Morning. You're an early bird!"

It was 7.30 a.m. and for a moment Tom thought the same troubled sleep might have been responsible for bringing his father to work so early, and then he remembered that his father was always early. His routine was so regular that the great explorers could have circumnavigated the globe using Harry Harrison's bowel movements as a chronometer.

"Well, what a to-do!" Harry said, sitting on one of the client's chairs and crossing his legs.

"What a to-do," Tom repeated to himself. A tragedy of world status and it was a 'to-do'!

His father looked like a new car that had just been valeted. Everything about him was clean and shiny, uncreased and glowing – faultless. The wavy hair, greying at the temples and held in shape with a gel so firm you could set concrete with it; pink striped shirt, white collar and school tie, tied with a small, single knot (his father would sooner go naked than use a working-class double knot such as a Windsor); a neat and greying moustache trimmed daily; 'waistc't' with its chain and Albert fob; highly polished black Oxford shoes; and of course the Masonic signet ring on his little finger, its face set to the side as though impressing dollops of hot sealing wax was an everyday occurrence. There was no doubt he was a handsome man.

Tom's memories of his father were that he had always looked like this: a successful, self-important, self-satisfied, middle-aged man even when he was young. Whereas some men try to cling on to their twenties and thirties long after they have gone, in a desperate attempt to keep middle age at bay, his father had embraced it eagerly. He had grasped at its attitudes, stuffed himself full of its prejudices and lusted after its certainties as if together they constituted maturity.

Tom hadn't had the opportunity to speak to anyone about the things he had seen and done and heard – the powerful feelings which had overwhelmed him and the death that had surrounded him. His father had not asked about any of them and by carefully marshalling his conversation had failed to provide any opportunity for Tom to unburden himself. Tom was neither surprised nor angry because he knew his father was incapable of discussing anything as personal as feelings and to have gone down that road would have sent Harry bolting for safety.

"We'll get a lot of work out of this, Tom, I've no doubt," said Harry, examining his manicured nails. "It's an ill wind..."

Tom didn't respond. Eventually what little conversation there was between them trickled to a halt and Harry Harrison excused himself; having wasted a few minutes of his day in talking to Tom, he would have to accelerate his schedule to get back on track.

Tom tossed the Henderson file back into the drawer to wait its turn and pushed his chair back on to its rear legs. There had to be something more important to do.

8.00 a.m. Vicky Denton had been up since shortly after 6.00 a.m. but had been awake for much longer. It was a little over forty-eight hours since she had discovered David's body and so far she had not been able to shed a single tear. But Emma had not stopped crying. Vicky could handle her own pain but to watch her daughter's suffering was more than she could bear. She wanted to extract it, absorb it, add it to her own misery, freeing Emma to be a carefree teenager once again. Sleep was the only release and at the moment she was still lost in its oblivion. Neither of them, she knew, would be carefree again for a very long time.

Vicky became suddenly aware of her actions – that she had not stopped moving around since getting up. The plants had been watered, washing-up done, work surfaces wiped down, tea had been made and drunk, magazines and papers tidied, showering completed and her restlessness had taken her from living room to kitchen and back several times, long after there was anything left to do in either room. Only by constantly moving was it possible to prevent the great dark bird of despair from perching on her shoulder.

The paper arrived on the doormat with a plop and Vicky pounced on it.

The weekend had been spent attempting to trace David's last hours, with some success. She had found and met the two upholsterers who had used their battered Transit as an ambulance. She had worked out exactly how long it had taken before David had received medical attention and was certain that if treatment had been readily available, her husband would probably still be alive. As a consequence, she had scoured every column inch of every Saturday and Sunday newspaper looking for the background to policy decisions which had closed local emergency departments, curtailed ambulance services and shed health service staff. There had been no shortage of coverage.

She now had names of ministers responsible, dates, the limp words which had masked cost-cutting with talk of efficiency, numerous warnings from health staff which had now been translated into reality, and anything pertinent had been carefully clipped from the newspaper, dated and slotted into a wallet folder.

The evidence of failure which she had amassed was overwhelming but what was still extremely sketchy, however, was a reason for the crash. All that had been publicly revealed was that Varsity Flight 469 was a charter aircraft en route from Northolt airport to Nigeria, via Algeria, carrying a group of oil field workers. It had collided with a helicopter near Harrow before crashing whilst the helicopter had gyrated wildly as the pilot tried to fly it by the main rotor alone – having lost the stabilising effect of its tail rotor – and had subsequently made a heavy emergency landing on a school playing field. The pilot, Peter Thornton, was in intensive care and his passenger, a businessman called Eric Lloyd, was on life support.

Vicky began reading the newspaper whilst still in the hall, moving briskly towards the kitchen. She would go to the corner shop and buy the rest of the daily papers when she had finished reading this one, she decided.

Funeral arrangements had already been set in train but she found it impossible to contemplate cremation. The thought of consigning David's body to the flames so soon after it had escaped them revolted her but burial presented other problems. Local undertakers were unable to cope with the demand and there were insufficient sextons to dig graves, and on top of it all, police were not yet prepared to release his body. As a consequence, David's remains were languishing in a chilled storage drawer at a mortuary in Hounslow.

Vicky was determined that he would spend the last twenty-four hours before burial here in his own home but had no idea when that would be. Anger began to well up inside her yet again and she was aware that the void left by David's passing was slowly being filled by the need to avenge his death.

8.30 a.m. Andrew Glennister, with his customary purposeful movements, climbed out of an inconspicuous black cab and entered a four-storey Georgian building in St John Street, almost within sight of the scales of Justice atop the Central Criminal Court at the Old Bailey. He was shown into a small meeting room in this rather unpretentious outpost of the Ministry of Transport, where Charles Astbury was already waiting for him. The two men shook hands and the warmth of their greeting hinted at a long-term friendship. They began their discussion without the pleasantry of coffee and unaccompanied by officials.

9.00 a.m. Vicky Denton waited as patiently as she could in the reception area of Mappin, Jones and Harrison. Mr Harrison senior did have a client with him, she had been told, but it was possible he could see her briefly in a little while. Vicky remembered the ageing and sparrow-like little receptionist from her last dealings with the firm, two or three years ago, when she had been defending a claim for unfair dismissal after an AD had walked off the set in a huff, later maintaining she had been sacked. That time the case had been straightforward and she had won but on this occasion she wasn't quite sure what it was she was seeking.

She was conscious of crossing and uncrossing her legs as the ordeal of waiting began to gnaw at her patience. "Do you think his meeting will last much longer?" she asked, ostentatiously looking at her watch.

"It does seem to be going on a little, doesn't it?" replied Miss Rush, perched neatly behind her immaculately ordered desk. She stopped typing in response to the question, her hands fluttering from one pile of papers to another without actually touching them, serving no real purpose other than providing her with a focus so she didn't have to look at Vicky.

Her fingers returned to the keyboard of the electric typewriter and rattled out a smooth drum roll of noise. She sensed Vicky's mounting irritability and offered, "I believe Mr Harrison junior is free. If you're short of time you could possibly see him instead."

Anything rather than wait, Vicky took up the offer, was directed up the half-flight of stairs and along a corridor to the door of Tom Harrison's office.

He welcomed her into the rather tatty room with a smile and a reassurance which made her feel at ease but she cut across his civility and got straight to the point. She didn't so much outline her legal needs as pour out her anger.

"I can't believe the reaction of the Government, the aircraft owners – everyone. Why aren't they shouting and screaming for answers? It seems all they want to do is keep the lid on things, stiff bloody British upper lip and all that nonsense. Don't be emotional, don't overreact, take your time and all will be revealed. Well I don't believe them. It's like they're all standing together in a circle looking outwards, protecting their own backs, looking after number one. That seems to be their first priority. Okay, a few hundred people have been killed but we've got the trains and buses running on time again. Do you know what one stupid old fart of an MP actually said? 'This sort of thing was a nightly occurrence during the war and we just took it in our stride. There was no hysteria then, we just got on with our lives.' Can you believe it? 'We have to keep a sense of proportion,' he said."

Tom listened silently.

"My husband is dead and I'm scared that no one really gives a damn. Give it another week or two and his memory is going to be sacrificed to some trade agreement or other. You know the kind of thing – don't be horrible to the airline industry; it's doing its best to earn us money. Well I don't care about that, I want answers and I'm prepared to push as hard as I possibly can to get them. If it was terrorism then tell us, for Christ's sake. Does that sound like I'm being overemotional or irrational? Am I being unreasonable?"

"Not at all. I understand how you feel and I know I'd feel the same. The answers may be difficult to find and it isn't long since the crash so I think we have to be patient – for a little while at least. Today is the first working day since it happened." Tom spoke calming words which were carefully weighed so as not to inflame Vicky's passionate sense of injustice or trample over her vulnerability. He had had similar feelings and also wanted redress, some admission of guilt or at least an apportioning of blame.

"I feel there must be something I can do to make things happen. I'm not very good at waiting for things to come to me, even at the best of times."

Tom realised why he immediately warmed towards Vicky Denton. With far greater anger and a great deal more zeal, she was articulating exactly what he felt. She wanted answers – so did he. A calamity had changed both their lives and rather than trying to push it away or 'move on', they both needed to acknowledge it, perhaps even to concentrate on it until they had filled themselves with enough understanding to allow the healing to begin. It would be painful, like picking at a scab which was not yet ready to peel away, but at least they would be trying to shape events, not being buried by them. Vicky had handed him a mission – the very thing he had been waiting for and he knew that *Henderson versus Chilled Chicken Emporium* was in danger of not getting the attention it deserved.

He instinctively liked the woman in front of him. She was certainly very attractive – small, petite, with dark brown eyes and shoulder-length black hair, taken back and brightened with the deep red of henna. Her skin was dark enough to reveal an ethnic influence of some kind but her features gave no clue as to what it might be – Indian, African, Middle Eastern. But it was her directness and determination that he really liked. He knew intuitively that she had great strength of character and a persistence which left him in no doubt that, one way or another, she would find answers. There was an extraordinary self-assurance about her which reached out through her grief. He had not come across anyone quite like her before and his admiration was tinged with a touch of apprehension. She was a strong woman and he wasn't quite sure who was in charge of the meeting.

Vicky, for her part, was impressed enough by Tom to want him to represent her. His empathy with her loss was, she felt, unusual in a man and as he explained his own experience of the disaster the reasons became obvious.

She saw him as a typical product of the privileged middle classes but with a huge stripe of humility running through him. She could not help being aware that he was also tall and good-looking behind his tinted, wire-framed glasses.

Tom verbally chopped the situation up into small digestible chunks, often omitting the direct article from the beginning of sentences. "Position is this..."; "Result is likely to be..." He dissected the situation confidently, setting out the pros and cons like they were two opposing football teams.

"You feel the Government's responsible for your husband's death but – legally speaking – it's complicated."

Vicky looked irritated. "Can't we sue them for neglect of duty or some such thing?"

"Not just like that. Causation is at the heart of it."

Her irritation turned to agitation. "You're not telling me there's nothing..."

"No, no – all possibilities depend on finding out exactly what happened. What's the cause? Who's the cause? Otherwise you're firing from the hip."

"So what can I do? Now, not tomorrow."

"Discover more about who owns the aircraft involved and start banging on their doors because you can bet they'll be running round in small circles. Next, keep an eye on the

Government's responses because they'll almost certainly set up some kind of inquiry."

Vicky felt reassured momentarily that this was someone who understood her anguish and the need to get things moving.

Tom floated the obvious possibility of negotiating no-fault compensation in the longer run but almost instantaneously saw that this was not Vicky's focus. She was refreshingly curt. "I don't care about the money, it's answers I want."

Tom could hear his own words in reply but could barely believe them.

"Look, we won't worry about money for now because this firm is not interested in making a profit out of what's happened. Like you, we want to get at the truth so let's see how it goes and we'll keep the costs to a minimum. I don't intend to charge for my time."

Tom knew that if his father could have heard those last few words, his hair would have sprung free from its glue, his starched collar would have pinged itself straight and he would have accepted expulsion from The Square as only right and just.

It was only after Vicky had departed with a warm handshake, that Tom realised he had forgotten to mention inquests.

1.05 p.m. Charles Astbury timed his statement on the Harrow disaster, as it had now become colloquially known, to make the best use of the media. It would dominate the lunchtime TV and radio news and as it was live it would be impossible for producers to edit his words and difficult for commentators to put a spin on them. That would come later, in the evening coverage, but for now the control was his.

His statement in the crowded press room of the Ministry was larded with concern for victims of the disaster and his face carried in its smooth and privileged roundness just the right amount of gravitas. His heart had been touched, his emotions troubled and his determination strengthened. He would personally ensure that all the facts surrounding the incident would be fully explored, no stone would be left unturned and there would be no shortage of resources.

He confirmed that Eric Lloyd, the helicopter owner, had now

died as a result of his injuries but the pilot, Peter Thornton, had survived and was out of danger. He had been interviewed just hours earlier and had confirmed that the helicopter had been flying above the ceiling set by West Drayton air traffic control. Charles Astbury said he had no wish to jump to conclusions but this did now appear to be the most likely cause of the crash rather than terrorism or mechanical failure. Unfortunately, the two flight recorders from Flight 469 had not yet been found and were presumed to have been destroyed by the extraordinarily high temperatures of the inferno. They may still, of course, be discovered in the hundreds of tonnes of rubbish, rubble and ash which were still being removed from the site.

"I am convinced that time is of the essence and have decided that the best course of action will be that which will produce the speediest results. As a consequence, I am pleased to announce the immediate establishment of an inquiry which will be conducted by a Special Air Accident Investigation Unit (SAAIU) – a unique entity which will be made up of personnel from the highly respected and independent Civil Aviation Authority and the Air Accident Investigation Bureau, which is under the auspices of my department. It will have the resources it needs to fully investigate the causes of the Harrow crash and draw on the expertise of specialists in the field. This unit will effectively represent the many different groups with a genuine interest in this appalling tragedy.

"The inquiry will have no limits on the areas it can explore – in fact nothing will be excluded from its remit. Although it will have the full support of the Ministry of Transport, it is important to stress that the SAAIU will be entirely independent and I understand it hopes to announce the inquiry members by tomorrow but certainly no later than Thursday. I think of all the options open to us this is the one most likely to provide the answers we are all seeking."

There was an audible hum amongst the journalists as they mumbled their dissatisfaction to each other. Several spoke at once. There was one burning question on all lips – was this another Lockerbie? Was this an attempt to bring the unresolved situation in the Middle East to the front door of one of the nations most responsible for its creation? A seasoned *Guardian* reporter put the question into words, but Astbury brushed it aside as though it was an irrelevance.

"I've explained about the helicopter and there is nothing more to say." Almost as an afterthought he added, "There are those who see a conspiracy in everything."

"What about a public inquiry, Minister?"

"That, of course, is a possibility but it is unlikely it would report for a year, perhaps even two, and that simply is not acceptable. I believe that what I have just outlined – what I would term a 'professional inquiry' because of the highly knowledgeable people who will sit on it – strikes just the right balance between the needs of the public and the needs of the aircraft industry, which has to have its legitimate concerns addressed. After all, future safety lies with them and the lessons they can learn from this unfortunate mishap!"

"When will this investigation report?"

"Obviously, an incident of this magnitude is not going to be an overnight job. We will provide all the means necessary for the earliest possible conclusion."

"How long?" echoed a chorus of press voices, including Louise Watson's. She was determined to extract some decent copy for the *Evening Chronicle* and wanted facts not reassurances.

"It could be some months but of course there will be an interim report which will almost certainly tackle the main areas of concern. You have my personal assurance it will be delivered as quickly as possible..."

"... But how can a SAAIU inquiry consider the failure of the emergency services? It is simply not within its remit. Has the Government chosen this course in order to hide the failure of its cost-cutting policies?" Louise did not even try to hide the contempt in her voice.

Astbury responded as if he thought the question had been complimentary. "My colleagues and I are convinced that a SAAIU inquiry is the only feasible option." He allowed himself a dismissive smile but not so dismissive that it would be seen as disrespectful of the dead. "I suspect that political gesturing will not provide us with the answers we seek. At the moment, facts about the causes, not the aftermath, are what we want and are determined to discover." He carefully avoided setting any timescale and virtually ignored Louise Watson's question.

A short and insignificant-looking journalist, squinting through thickly distorting spectacles, announced he was Anthony Berrens from Jetstream, one of the aviation industry's trade publications. The rest of the gathering momentarily silenced their clamouring as his credentials signified a position of special knowledge and he delivered his question to almost complete silence.

"The collision with the Bell Jet Ranger may have played a part in the crash but what was a P11 doing in a designated no-fly zone for fixed-wing aircraft?"

The near silence became total and Astbury's customary fluency deserted him. When he did speak, he fought back his natural instinct to attack and belittle the questioner.

"Any no-fly zone is only an exclusion area under normal circumstances and of course we don't know what the circumstances were – which is precisely why I've announced the setting up of an inquiry. Any speculation would pre-empt its investigation."

Berrens tried to follow up with a supplementary question about the course of Flight 469 but the rest of the press pack had already extended all the deference he was likely to get and pursued their own agendas. Astbury simply ignored him. Other questions were largely parried with references about not wanting to pre-empt the inquiry.

All in all, Astbury felt it was not a bad performance and on leaving the podium went directly to his office to watch the rest of the programme on TV.

Mike Smith, Tom Harrison's managing clerk, had months previously brought a small television set into his almost equally small office to watch the Italia '90 World Cup and had never taken it home again. It was there that Tom and he watched the broadcast.

"I don't know what a SAAIU inquiry is but a pound to a pinch of shit says it's not good. Am I right?" Mike asked Tom.

Tom shook his head in disbelief. "Let's put it like this – at an inquiry of this kind we've got no right to represent our clients, we've got no right even to submit statements; those conducting it will determine who they will examine as witnesses and who they won't and almost certainly their full findings will not be published. Apart from that it's about as genuine and trustworthy as a Bangkok Rolex."

"The Nelson approach: telescopes, blind eyes – that kind of thing?"

"Absolutely! Mike, I need to know exactly what its procedures and statutory provisions will be. Can you get on to it – like now?"

"So we're really into this one, then?"

"Looks like it!"

"Only natural really! Mappin, Jones and Harrison – that well-known international law consultancy. Which of our offices do you reckon we should handle it from, then – Paris, Rome or New York?"

"I think we'll keep it here at our London Head Office," replied Tom. "It's best handled by the senior vice president, don't you reckon?"

"Yeah, always supposing you can fit it in between a 'masturbating in a public place' and a 'nicking from Woollies'... Bit of a looker your Vicky, isn't she?"

"The enquiries, Mike!"

"Okay!" replied Mike without moving.

"Now," said Tom, giving him a shove.

Like Astbury's, Andrew Glennister's performance was also a polished affair. As president of the company which owned the aircraft, ultimate responsibility could be said to lie with him and questioning by the programme's presenter was robust.

Glennister's greatest asset was the sense of normality he could produce at will. His clothes were modern and well tailored; even his demeanour appeared honestly unpretentious. He had long ago learnt to modulate the American monotone which he had grown up with and deployed smiles like compliments. Off camera, his inexhaustible energy often found him conducting three conversations at once as he moved at speed between appointments – restless, animated, exhausting to watch. It had earned him the nickname Bionic Man but on camera he was the opposite – calm, relaxed, thoughtful and very reasonable.

According to Glennister, responsibility and even ownership of Varsity Aviation was a much more amorphous creature than at first appeared. Yes, he was president of the company but of course such a position was largely non-executive and although he played a part in determining policy he could not be held responsible for the day-to-day operations of a comparatively small organisation. Yes, he agreed, the much bigger and wealthier Dolman International did have a stake in Varsity, although the exact percentage he could not remember off hand, and yes, Dolman was wholly owned by Barcroft Holdings but complex ownerships were now commonplace in a deregulated capital market. Without such cross subsidies and financial support, combined with the sharing of modern management skills, a small company such as Varsity would have been taken over or gone into liquidation years ago.

The questioning moved on to responsibility for compensation, should Varsity be found in any way to be negligent. Glennister made it clear that as part of Barcroft's modern and far-sighted management policies, individual companies were granted as much freedom as possible, away from the leaden hand of centralised control.

The presenter summarised Glennister's reply in the form of a question. "So Varsity sinks or swims on its own?"

Glennister obviously didn't like the assertion that he was washing his hands of Varsity, even if it was true, and went on the offensive.

"Look, there's no question of Varsity being in the wrong. The cause of this accident is pretty clear for anyone to see. I'm at a loss to understand your line of questioning. However, let's be totally hypothetical for a minute and say that Varsity was in some way held to be culpable. It is a responsible company and capable of meeting all its own commitments. End of story!"

"Through insurance, presumably – if it came to that?"

"Certainly," responded Glennister.

"Does Varsity have coverage beyond its Warsaw Convention liabilities?"

"That's irrelevant," snapped Glennister, as his composure momentarily slipped.

"With respect, Mr Glennister, I don't think it is. You have made it clear that Varsity is on its own in this and I have to assume that under international law you are able to cast it adrift. However, should there be any large claims against Varsity it would appear not to have the capital to meet them. Under the Warsaw Convention and its assured compensation, only the passengers who bought tickets on the aircraft would be covered, and then for –" the presenter looked down at a chart in front of him – "a maximum of thirty-five thousand pounds each. The hundreds of other dead and injured victims would have no chance of pursuing a claim against you. Does that sound right?"

Glennister was back in control and delivered one of his honest smiles.

"This whole problem is hypothetical. There is no question of Varsity being at fault. All I've done is to answer your questions and explain the legal situation behind a complex ownership structure. What would happen in the unlikely event of something untoward arising is another situation entirely. It almost certainly would be dealt with sympathetically and generously. We, as an international organisation, are aware of the need to foster good relationships worldwide and that we would do. After all, it's our reputation which is at stake."

"And what if 'fostering good relations' required a pay-out of millions, possibly hundreds of millions of pounds?"

Again Glennister smiled at the presenter and now, he was totally in control. "Jim, if anything dreadful like that ever happens, invite me back on the programme, will you? I'll give you exactly the same answers then as I'm giving you now."

Charles Astbury leant forward and switched off the television set. "Good man; not bad. Not bad at all!"

*

1.25 p.m. Vicky Denton switched off her set and swore. "You slimeball!" She had no idea how the inquiry would be conducted but felt intuitively that it would probably end as a cover-up. The relentless pacing began again, from kitchen to living room and back as she fumed, stamped and conducted silent, bad-tempered conversations with herself.

"Mum... pleeease..." implored Emma, from the corner of a sofa in the living room where she was slumped, damp and crumpled tissues in her hand. She was still not dressed and her eyes were swollen from crying.

"I'm sorry, darling..." She sat beside Emma, putting an arm round her. They remained in silence, holding each other.

"I want to die," whispered Emma in a sad little voice.

Vicky talked softly to her, stroking her hair as she did so. She could do no more than offer love and a string of clichés about her daddy wanting her to go on living, about time healing, being thankful for the years they had together, keeping him alive by always remembering him and even though she knew they were all trite, they were none the less comforting for that. But all the time, anger was chewing away at her.

3.00 p.m. Vicky gently disengaged herself from Emma's hold. They had even managed a little laugh together and a kind of calm had replaced Emma's raw pain, temporarily at any rate. Her eyes were now dry but throughout this quiet period, Vicky could not disengage her thoughts from Flight 469.

She went to the phone in the kitchen and called Tom Harrison to ask if he knew the implications of the inquiry announced by Astbury.

The SAAIU would, Tom explained, confine itself strictly to the reasons for the mid-air collision. It would consider anything which might have played a part – air traffic control, aircraft maintenance, pilot competence, the adherence to safety regulations, weather conditions and so on, but it would probably answer few of their questions about Varsity Aviation.

What it could not do was consider anything which happened

on the ground. The whole controversy surrounding capability of medical and emergency services would be completely outside its remit. Some of the most important answers they sought would be ignored and there would be no critical examination of Government policies.

His guess was that it would be held in private with no personal testimonies and no cross-examination – simply statements on paper. None of the witnesses would be aware of what the other witnesses had said and although Astbury had committed himself to an early interim report, it would almost certainly be little more than a short summary of events. Interestingly, he had given no assurances about the final report and going by similar inquiries in the past, it would almost certainly never be published in full.

Tom's grasp of the detail confirmed Vicky's confidence in him but it did nothing to dampen her annoyance. It was exactly what she had suspected and she resumed her pacing but was interrupted by the phone.

"I was so sorry to hear the news, Vicky. My heart goes out to you and while I know there's nothing I can say to help, if you need me, perhaps later, I'm here." It was an ex-work colleague who had also become a friend.

"Jill. Nice to hear from you. I thought you were in Tokyo or Takoradi or somewhere like that."

"Yes, I was – Tokyo. I got back a few days ago. Are you coping?"

"It's bloody awful… I rang everyone I could think of over the weekend to let them know and, oddly enough, I actually found it helped a bit."

"Can I do anything, anything at all?"

"If I think of anything, I'll ring you. I'm just so fucked off with the mealy-mouth bastards who are supposed to be in charge of this thing. Getting anything out of them is like getting blood from a stone and it makes me want to scream. It just stinks of cover-up."

"Can't you front them out in some way? Embarrass them, force them to talk?"

"How?"

"Come on, Vick, you're in the media, for Christ's sake. Find a good journalist; pour your heart out to them." Jill paused for thought. "Of course! Do you know Louise Watson, on the *Evening Chronicle*? She's pretty trustworthy. Done some good stuff – hard political exposés, that kind of thing."

When the call was over Vicky began her pacing again but not for long. She picked up the phone and called the *Evening Chronicle*, asking to be put through to Louise Watson.

"I've got to go out for a little while, but I promise I won't be long." The way in which Vicky delivered her words to Emma implied important business that could not be delayed. There was an unspoken assumption that it had something to do with 'arrangements'. In fact Vicky drove straight to the offices of the Evening Chronicle. She guessed she wasn't the only person who felt marginalised and ignored by the official processes and thought there must be others who, like her, were desperate not just for the truth but for – consideration. That was the missing element, she decided – consideration.

She didn't want the agenda dictated by a Government minister with his own interests to defend. She was one of the players in this desperate drama and had no intention of being a recipient of charity – because that's what it felt like, waiting for crumbs of information to be brushed from someone else's table. "This is suitable, this isn't,"; "They can have this but we won't tell them that!" She knew that this is how it would be. And as the pain of raw wounds and equally raw memories began to diminish so the flow of information would trickle ever more slowly. Within months, the Harrow disaster would become just another political issue and would be handled as such – played for advantage, with reputations, careers and money predominating. The present fulsome condolences and promises of exhaustive inquiry would be smothered beneath a blanket of self-interest.

She finally realised that this was what she was fighting against as she pulled up outside the *Chronicle*'s offices and hunted for a parking space.

6.10 p.m. The Late final edition of the *Evening Chronicle* plopped through the door. There was no ego involved in Vicky's pleasure at seeing herself on the front page and her only concern was to check that she had been fairly reported. The headline was clear enough. ***"Tell us the truth," says disaster widow.*** *TV director, Vicky Denton, whose husband, David, died in the Harrow disaster, has issued a challenge to the Government and Varsity Aviation. "Come clean over what really happened." She accuses them of 'drip-feeding' survivors and bereaved relatives with snippets of almost useless information, and claims they are more concerned to protect themselves than to discover what really happened to Flight 469. Vicky has issued a call to all people affected by the crash to speak out. "Unless we shout, make a noise and demand information, the process of fobbing us off will continue – in fact it will get worse..."*

Before she could finish reading the report, the telephone rang and it continued for the rest of the evening.

Just as Tom Harrison had provided the catalyst which allowed her to express her confusion and resentment, so she now played a similar role for other bereaved people. One after another, relatives of the dead, survivors and even rescue workers poured out their feelings to Vicky. Her impassioned words in the *Chronicle* had struck a chord.

From someone whistling in the dark to keep her spirits high, Vicky suddenly found herself at the head of a large band of very diverse people, many of whom seemed to feel even more lost and bewildered than she. One was a woman called Esther Vine, whose daughter, Rachel, had died in the immediate impact of Flight 469.

In a lull between calls, the doorbell shrilled. Emma's Walkman ensured she didn't hear it and Vicky opened the door to a smartly dressed, briefcase-carrying woman in her thirties whose bobbed hair looked like a walking advert for Megahold Lacquer.

"Mrs Denton?" The accent was American. "My name is Ailey Newman, I'm an attorney. I know there's never going to be a good time to talk about this but have you got a minute? It concerns the death of your husband!" The nasal twang was definitely New York.

"In what way?" asked Vicky, without moving from the

doorway. Ailey offered her a card.

"I'm a senior partner with the New York law firm of Morton Gerrity and I think we can help you. Can I come in?" The phone rang, forcing Vicky's hand and she offered an unspoken invitation as she went to answer the ringing.

Vicky watched Ailey Newman while she took the call, which was from another survivor. She felt hostile towards Ms Newman and put it down to the way the woman had walked into her living room as if she had a right to be there. When Ailey Newman had spoken there had been no lowering of her tone, no artificial sadness in her voice – it was direct and matter of fact as though she was selling insurance but whatever was on offer, she was very confident of her product.

The moment the phone was replaced, Ailey spurned any niceties or small talk and got straight to the bottom line. "We have one of the biggest litigation practices in New York and our speciality is representing people like you, victims of man-made disasters of this kind..."

"I don't have any money...!"

"I don't want your money. In a way I'm offering you our money!" Her directness forced Vicky to listen.

"Ever heard the expression 'contingency suing'?" She didn't wait for a reply. "You guys don't really have it over here but in the States it's common. The airplane that killed your husband was owned by a US company. Sure, they'll try and pretend it's all down to their UK subsidiary but we've checked 'em out and we're pretty sure that won't stand up. As for the crash, we know from experience there's usually some fault that we can get them on." Vicky listened in silence.

"We'd like to act for you against Barcroft Holdings in the US. We can do it for nothing and you'll get a US-sized settlement if we're successful. I know it won't bring your husband back but..." She looked towards Emma, who was still playing music and oblivious to the two women. "Your daughter?" Vicky nodded. "It will sure make a difference to her future."

"And you take your cut out of any compensation we get?"

"That's the way it works."

It was only when Ailey spoke about having the resources to

"peek at the crap under every embarrassing Barcroft stone anywhere in the world," that Vicky began to show interest.

There was nothing incompatible with Vicky having already instructed a UK lawyer, Ailey assured her and Vicky gave her Tom Harrison's details.

As she watched the US lawyer walk briskly down the front path in the glare of the security light, she knew she did not like her. She was also convinced that Ailey Newman would make a much better friend than an enemy.

CHAPTER FOUR

Tuesday, December 11th, 1990, 8.33 a.m. Tom had managed to sleep the previous night – not well, not until late, but at least it had been a few solid hours.

The best way to deal with something as potentially big as Vicky's case, he had decided, was not to allow it to overwhelm him. Break it down into sizeable pieces and then tackle them one at a time as if each was a case in its own right. Vicky had called him ten minutes earlier and he had provisionally agreed to act for the people who had telephoned her – if they wanted him to – and she was to arrange a meeting so he could talk to them directly.

He checked the time. *Attainable goals*, he thought, as he sifted through Vicky's pile of newspaper cuttings, casting an occasional eye out of the window to check if the cafe over the road had opened – coffee and a Danish could only help the thought processes.

As the cafe's CLOSED sign reversed on its chain and transformed into OPEN, his phone rang. Miss Rush had not yet arrived and his line was connected directly to the switchboard.

"Mr Harrison, please. Tom Harrison!"

The voice sounded as though it belonged to a girl of fourteen but was, in fact, a researcher for the local radio station. "I gather you're acting for local people – victims of the disaster," she said, with a voice that sounded bored, as though it had only half turned up for work.

"Well, yes, it looks that way." He wondered how the hell she had got hold of it so quickly. He felt vulnerable as he did not yet know any of the people or what they wanted him to do for them.

"For what reason? I mean, is there something you know that hasn't been made public yet – negligence, incompetence, criminal deception, something like that?" For a fourteen-year-old she was extremely forthright.

"At this stage we're simply seeking information," he replied, trying to marshal his thoughts as he spoke. "People aren't at all happy about the lack of information."

"So you're just asking for information, nothing else?"

"No, I didn't say that." Entirely unfamiliar with this kind of media pressure, Tom was not sure how much he could, or should say. It seemed safe and rather obvious to mention compensation whilst emphasising the need for transparency and information.

"My clients are extremely unhappy about the lack of a public judicial inquiry and would like the minister to reconsider his decision to defer this option."

"Does it have anything to do with the eyewitness report that said flames were seen coming from an aircraft that could have been Flight 469 before it hit the helicopter?"

"It's too early to go into detail," said Tom, "but I wonder if that's the same report that I've got. What's your source?" he lied, fishing unashamedly, this being the first he had heard of it.

"It's just something we've heard. So you are suing on behalf of Harrow people?"

Once again he retorted, "I haven't said that!" Warming to his new role, Tom added, "We want accountability and to get that there is an urgent need to know the facts."

"In that case, we'd really like you to come on the *Robby Robertson Show* this afternoon and talk about it. About three o'clock? Can you make it?"

Oh God, he thought, *this is the starting gun.* "Of course, I'd be delighted." Another lie.

As he hung up he knew he would have to be extremely precise in his choice of words because the powers that be would be listening and analysing every one of them. Any ill-judged language could jeopardise all kinds of actions further down the line. He would conduct the whole interview with that in mind but he wanted no one to be left in any doubt about his determination. He knew, however, that once he had gone public there was every likelihood the whole thing would develop a life of its own.

The phone rang again. "Hi, this is Maggie Cribbins of *Newsday*. I understand you're representing survivors of the Harrow disaster..."

She was followed by national radio news, regional and national television news and foreign correspondents from Europe, the US and even Japan. Eventually, a breathless Miss Rush, unable to get through on the phone, arrived to inform him that "some newspaper gentlemen" wanted to speak to him. He instructed her to keep them in reception.

Before he had even reached the door, the phone rang again but this time it was an outraged Mrs Norbert who had spent £2,000 on having mock stone cladding stuck to the outside of her end-of-terrace house. Not only had it lost its power of adhesion but the pieces which were falling to the ground were taking chunks of original brickwork and mortar with them. Nothing would stop her from suing, she declared, and wanted Tom to represent her. He really could have done without this.

"Save your money, Mrs Norbert. The company will either be untraceable, have ceased trading or will do so the moment I contact them. They will simply shut up shop and open again the next day with a new name." She was not to be dissuaded and Tom made an appointment but what he really wanted to say was, *I would sooner have cow shit spread over my house than that stuff; why did you waste your money?*

When he eventually arrived in reception he walked into a scramble of shouted questions and hand-held tape recorders and for one moment was lost for words. Miss Rush tried to ignore the pandemonium, to which she was completely unaccustomed and unprepared, by continuing to hammer at her electric keyboard as though her life depended upon it and left the telephone switchboard to its constant ringing. The shouts of journalists grew louder and noise levels climbed.

"Please be quiet!" Tom shouted but with little discernible effect.

"Shut up, will you?" This time he yelled at the top of his voice and there was a response, the noise fractionally subsiding. "Right, I'll go round you one at a time and you've each got two questions, okay? Between you, that should cover everything worth asking."

Immediately, someone tried to jump the queue, shouting a question at him. Tom acted decisively. "That wasn't the agreement! I'm not going to have this turned into a pantomime and unless there's some kind of order I won't answer any questions from anyone, so it's up to you." He waited long enough for them to realise he meant what he said and then spoke again. "Right, I'll start with you," he pointed at a female journalist entirely at random. What do you want to know?" It seemed to work and he went round the reporters one by one.

Midway through the impromptu press conference he quietly asked Miss Rush if she would mind getting him some breakfast. She didn't 'do messages' but on this occasion she either took pity on Tom or was delighted to escape the ravening horde and went in search of coffee and pastry. Relishing her importance, she weaved through the reporters with her mouth and, seemingly, her nostrils clamped shut, as though all journalists had pneumonic plague and one whiff would finish her off.

The press pack finally departed and despite their aggression and rudeness had performed a useful function – they had concentrated Tom's mind wonderfully and he was finally beginning to chart a path through the first obstacles of a littered landscape. And with so many people looking to him for answers, he even began to feel partially in control. He reached for the phone and called Terry Lewis.

"Tom, how lovely to hear from you, my boy; hope you're well. Tragic happening, tragic. Brought you a bit of business, I see. Anything I can do for you?" In four short sentences, Terry Lewis had managed to cover all the pleasantries, had dispensed with an inconvenient tragedy, showed he was abreast of the news and had got to the bottom line without sounding rude. It was an accomplished part of his sales performance, polished over many years as the local MP.

Now in advanced middle age, he still had a reputation as a Mr Fixit but he also had another tag – as a womaniser. Tom could just imagine his chat-up lines: "Grace, how lovely to see you! Grace by name, grace by nature. And your business is prospering so well too. Of course I was a great admirer of your late husband, God rest him. And as he's gone, sex isn't entirely out of the question, I presume?"

Tom's knowledge of Terry went back years, largely through his friendship with Tom's father. They were both local establishment figures – members of the Constitutional Club, Rotarians, Conservative Party members and Masons, and no doubt other more dubious gentlemen's organisations that Tom knew nothing about.

To Tom, Terry Lewis had all the sincerity of a second-hand car salesman, which wasn't surprising considering that's how he'd made his money. Now he had a Japanese car dealership, an equipment hire company and numerous other commercial interests as well as being an uncritical and reliable Tory backbencher. He would never set foot on the ministerial ladder but was apparently well appreciated for keeping ministers informed of any backbench machinations, rebellions or potential embarrassments. Everyone, including Terry, assumed his loyalty would eventually be rewarded with a knighthood.

"How's the old man? Still keeping you on the straight and narrow?"

For the first time in all his dealings with Terry, Tom felt he was not just 'Harry's son'. He wanted something from Lewis and knew he could make demands on the man because of the power he held over him. That power was an angry electorate of which Tom represented a particularly vulnerable but vocal proportion. The mood amongst the people of Harrow – not just the ones Tom represented but all of them – was one of disbelief turning rapidly to anger.

"I need to see you," said Tom, ignoring Lewis's questions.

"Of course, old boy, ring my secretary and tell her to make space in the diary. She'll be able to find something for next week, I'm sure."

"It won't keep until next week, Terry, I need to see you today. People are expecting some action from you and we need to discuss it."

"Of course, old boy, I understand exactly. What about Friday?"

"I suppose it could wait," replied Tom, with heavy emphasis on the 'could'. "I'm sure *Newsday* will understand how full your diary is when they interview me tonight."

The laugh which came down the line sounded slightly strangulated, as though forced through clenched teeth. "You're a boy. If it's urgent, of course I can see you, Tom. My showrooms, about three thirty?"

"Here, at one thirty," replied Tom.

11.30 a.m. The morning had been almost overwhelming, not least because it had been so unexpected. From a suburban practice where excitement revolved round new brands of instant coffee, the world had gone mad. The phone rang again – Miss Newman was waiting to see him. The name meant nothing and he could hear the irritation from the other end of the line as Miss Rush began to question the woman. It was the American accent which jogged his memory.

"Ailey Newman," she said with no smile as he greeted her at the door to his office. She walked in, sat down and snapped open her briefcase without even glancing at the surroundings. Greetings were pushed out of the way with an economy of words and Ailey got down to business. She outlined her background in contingency suing and was convinced that the Harrow disaster represented plums waiting to be picked.

"We are talking a king-size action here, Tom. I mean mega bucks. No offence, but to be honest, I doubt if your practice has got the resources to handle it alone." Tom tried to view his offices through the eyes of an international lawyer with a suite on the 72nd floor of the Empire State Building. The threadbare carpet, which he'd been meaning to do something about for months, seemed to perform a dance, shout and wave and call out *Look at me, over here!*

"There are two ways of going about this," Ailey continued. "You can sue Varsity here in the UK and if you win they'll file for receivership. Your clients will get zilch. Even if they're bailed out by Dolman International or Barcroft Holdings – which is about as likely as turkeys voting for Thanksgiving – the awards made by your courts are a joke compared to ours. When we win it hurts them."

"Of course, money would be welcome but my clients want answers, not just a pay-out, or more likely, a pay-off. We have to get the right questions asked of the right people before we know who to hammer."

"Believe me, the bigger the payola the fewer questions they'll want answered."

He didn't want to admit it but Tom thought she could be right. He simply wasn't used to such bluntness. It was so – well, so American! Anyway, who was he to decide other people's morality or motivation and if there was money available, he owed it to his clients to at least give them a shot at it.

"The other way, of course," continued Ailey, "is to go straight for the jugular and file an action against Barcroft in the US – and that's what I'm saying we should do. Of course, we'll need an agent in the UK and we'd like you to be our man."

"And you want my clients?" Tom hadn't meant it to sound quite so accusatory.

Ailey produced several computer printout pages from her briefcase and waved them at him. "I've got my own clients, buddy!" The tone was unmistakably *Up yours!*

He felt it wise to be a little conciliatory. "Sorry, that wasn't meant the way it sounded. But you would like us to pool clients, obviously."

"The bottom line is this, Tom. We've both got clients, I've got the money, you've got local credibility. The more clients we represent jointly, the more we make. Now, I can afford to chase Barcroft and any other mothers who want to keep their actions from public view – I can afford to chase them all over the globe if that's necessary to get a result. Lots of little actions against them with lots of bleeding hearts and outraged righteousness, but no resources and they'll walk. One big action with big resources and we'll get 'em, I'm sure of it – I know it!" For the first time she cast her eyes around his office. "It would put your practice in the major league."

The threadbare carpet again leapt up and waved. He'd

inherited everything from the previous occupant, who had dropped dead from a heart attack on the very carpet in question. The only impression Tom had made was the large and incongruous abstract painting hanging behind the desk. It was the only bit of Tom's personality on show and yet somehow it gave him consolation.

Tom guessed she saw him as a hick lawyer who could be manipulated and would undoubtedly expect him to organise the administration, provide knowledge of the English legal system and display his credibility as the local man on the ground. Of course, she would need all those things but primarily she wanted his clients – the clients he hadn't even signed up yet.

He also knew he was being patronised by someone who was used to large-scale success and was wielding money like a blunt instrument. He would love the resources she was dangling in front of him and there was a lot of sense in what she was saying. He might eventually even go along with her but in reality it would be his clients who decided, not Ailey Newman. Again, a little flash of awareness illuminated his thinking, reminding him of his newly acquired power. He realised he could, if he wanted, exert considerable influence and sway the decision, and he found the thought of that responsibility quite daunting.

"I'm not in any position to agree or disagree," he said with no emotion in his voice, giving Ailey no indication of the responsibility he felt. "We haven't even initiated an action here in the UK yet."

"Exactly!" enthused Ailey. "That gives us a great opportunity to co-ordinate our strategy. We can go for them together. It's the only way to do it!"

"I know that at least one client won't wear it and will want to keep an action going here in Britain. It's much more important to her than money."

"Jesus, you know how the system works. If we get a result in the States it will only be on the basis that all claims and actions are dropped – worldwide. If Barcroft are going to feel for their billfold it will be to buy off everyone, your lady included. So, rather than wait for that to happen she might as well join us now. It's crazy otherwise."

The more Ailey pushed him, the more Tom felt himself reacting against her. Had Ailey been offering him eternal youth and a fortnight in the Seychelles with Kim Basinger, Tom felt he still might refuse her.

"I'm here to represent my clients' wishes, not railroad them." Tom realised that he actually meant what he was saying.

"Look, for the time being it's cool. You've gotta keep 'em sweet, I realise that," she replied, smiling for the first time, with a mouth that seemed to have twice its proper share of extremely white teeth. "But you've got to know and I've got to know that at the end of the day they're with us if we're going to get the best result." Her voice was just a little too sharp, her speech a bit too fast and staccato to be comfortable and every phrase was delivered with just a little too much intensity. It felt like a violin being played on all the high notes.

"These are early days, Ms Newman..."

"Ailey, for Christ's sake, the name's Ailey..."

"You don't need a decision this minute. Let's keep in touch and see how things work out. Okay?"

Ailey got up to go and replaced her client list in her briefcase with a flourish. "That's our bread and butter, Tom, but I'm going after the caviar! I'll see myself out."

He tried not to laugh because she hadn't intended it to be funny.

As she was halfway through the door she stopped and looked back at him. "What do lawyers do in the evening in downtown Harrow, Tom? Do they ever go for a drink?"

"They do sometimes."

"Do they this evening?"

Tom shook his head. "Afraid not. But they might some other time." Options were always worth keeping open, he thought and, despite the voice that could cut glass, and the sensitivity bypass, she was extremely good looking.

"I'm gonna take a rain check on that, you hear? Take care now!" Her whole delivery sounded like a cross between New York brutal and a good ol' boy sucking on his corncob.

As soon as the door had closed and he could hear Ailey's footsteps descending the stairs, Tom clicked through to Mike Smith, who'd been trying to speak with him all morning.

"Yep?" replied the clerk with a mouthful of sandwich.

"You wanted me, Mike?"

"I certainly did. Could you grant me an audience now, Your Highness?"

"With pleasure; I'm always at the disposal of my peasants."

Mike swung into Tom's office, dragging a cloud of expensive aftershave behind him.

"I know it's a right pain but can I mention that very boring word called work, you know – paid work?" Tom gave him a half-smile.

It had been a battle to employ Mike as managing clerk, a decision his father had fought long and hard. Mike wasn't the 'right sort' – his strong cockney accent jangled alongside the rounded English of everyone else, like a whoopee cushion at a royal investiture. He was a bundle of contradictions, was Mike. His dress sense was immaculate and stylish and he verged on being an appalling clothes snob. That was, however, the only snobbish thing about him.

His job consisted of helping with conveyancing, researching, controlling and administering the entire workload as well as acting as a dogsbody – mostly cheerfully. But he never missed an opportunity to watch, listen and ask questions and had enrolled for a part-time law degree because one day, he maintained, he was going to qualify as a solicitor and specialise in criminal law. He was going to be one of the best. Tom didn't doubt it.

When Tom first met him, Mike had been filling in as a bookie's runner – for Jolly Joe Hymers, mostly at White City, Wimbledon and Hackney dog tracks. When a punter placed a large bet, in order to spread the risk, Joe would lay some of it off with other bookies and that was Mike's job. The skill was to get at least the same odds as those Joe had given when he took the bet and that's all he expected. If, on the other hand, Mike could place the money at better odds than those Joe was offering, there was a bonus to be won and that went straight into Mike's pocket. There was no secret about it, nothing underhand, it was just what bookie's runners did – it was how they made their money.

Mike first met Tom when he was a witness at Jolly Joe's trial when it transpired that he was anything but jolly. A runner called Stan the Man had committed the cardinal sin of not laying off one of Joe's bets but deciding to carry the risk himself. When the rank outsider raced home twenty lengths clear of the other five dogs, Stan was left carrying the can and was unable to pay Joe what he was owed. He was into him for nearly two grand.

A serious 'smacking' was the expected retribution for such a misdemeanour but when both Stan and his wife were run down by one of Joe's men and seriously injured, Mike felt the injustice needed to be rectified. He gave evidence against Joe, at no small risk to himself. By the time the trial was over and the conviction won, Tom had grown to trust and like Mike. When Mike tentatively asked him for a job, Tom did the only thing he could decently do – he stalled for time.

"Come back and talk to me when you've got three A levels."

A year later Mike turned up at the offices with three A levels – not the best passes in the world, but passes. Tom was so impressed that he felt obliged to offer him a job. That was some time ago and then, as now, Mike usually looked as though he had just stepped out of the fashion section of *GQ* Magazine.

"On the Jackson completion – the little access lane ain't part of the property and the owner's unknown. No trace anywhere. What do I do about it?" asked Mike.

"Leave it there and I'll have a look at it later. It'll need some kind of indemnity. Next!"

"Brady's been caught with his fingers in someone's till again and they're holding him down at Bridge Street nick. He won't accept no one but you. The cops just want him out of there before he stinks the place out."

"Get down there, tell Brady it's you or no one and get him out. If he complains, leave him where he is. Next."

"It's those chilled chickens, they're coming home to roost. Henderson reckons you'd promised him the draft affidavits by yesterday."

Tom put his face in his hand. "Oh damn, I did. Doesn't he know we've had a few problems here? Make our apologies..."

"Our apologies? Just a minute, Your Majesty, I had nothing to do with this."

"Okay, all my fault. Be honest with him; tell him it'll be about a week – at least a week. Anything else?"

"No, that's it for now." Mike got up to leave. "Fancy a game tonight?" he said, stretching and clicking his fingers. "I feel in devastating form."

"Not a chance," Tom replied.

In the eighteen months he had been there, Mike had introduced Tom to two things – snooker, at which he found he was surprisingly good, and dog racing, at which he was terrible. He could never pick winners but loved the spectacle of it all: the bright green of the grass, the floodlights, the yelping and baying of the dogs as the hare started its electronic whirring, the extraordinary characters to be found at every dog track and the uncertainty of it all mixed with elation on the rare occasions he picked a winner. It was a combination of sleaze and excitement and despite Mike having given him chapter and verse on the extraordinarily crooked nature of dog racing, Tom still loved it. It felt naughty and rebellious – like having a girl's name tattooed on his knuckles.

1.30 p.m. Punctual to the minute, Terry Lewis was shown in. He enclosed Tom's hand in both his own, slapped him on the back, punched him playfully and laughed a lot. It was like being greeted by Barnum and Bailey.

Tom had never been able to understand the relationship between his father and Terry Lewis as they were complete opposites. Terry tried to be the gentleman but everything about him was just slightly overdone, verging on the flamboyant, from the voice to the tie, the gold jewellery to his weight. His mellowed but still audible Birmingham accent shouted state school but despite his bluff bonhomie he was no fool and Tom knew you didn't deal with Terry Lewis empty-handed.

"In the news then, I see! Going to beat us with a big stick are you, Tom?"

"Maybe," said Tom seriously. "You and a few others." The jollity gradually disappeared from Terry's face.

"No government could plan properly for a disaster like this, Tom; it's just not financially feasible. You'd have people, equipment and beds tied up all over the country just on the chance that a plane was going to drop out of the sky. Because someone has died it doesn't automatically follow that someone else is at fault, now, does it?"

"I don't want a political debate with you, Terry, but your well-heeled pals in parliament have screwed every public service there is and you've gone along with it – all the way. People have died because of it – lots of them. Anyway, that isn't why I wanted to see you." Tom found it difficult not to show his irritation; in fact he didn't even try to hide it.

Without mentioning the US involvement, he outlined developments surrounding the Harrow disaster. Terry's face was set in concentration, his head nodding from time to time in agreement. "Excellent, excellent. If there's anything I can do, just let me know."

"There is," replied Tom. "I want you to raise certain questions in the House..."

"Tom... everything possible is being done. No one's hiding anything, I can promise you. If there's anything to discover the inquiry will find it, take my word."

Tom ignored him. "I want you to put down questions to the Minister of Transport, Charles Astbury. I want you to ask him, first, why was Flight 469 in a no-fly zone; second, why was it flying from Northolt airport; third, what was its flight plan; and fourth, what confirmation is there of reports that flames were seen coming from it before it collided with the helicopter."

"The inquiry will answer all those questions, Tom."

"I want them now, not in twelve months or two years' time."

"Think about it carefully, lad, you don't want to start a hare running that goes nowhere. It will only ... how shall I put it? ... well, make you look a bit silly, a bit – amateurish."

Tom felt the insult slide in like a very sharp knife and a flicker of doubt flashed across his mind, but it was gone just as quickly as he paused and looked penetratingly at the man in front of him. This was all part of Lewis's armoury and the only way to deal with it was to hit back. "And it won't do your prospects much good if you're forced into representing your constituents for once in your life and embarrassing your paymasters, will it?"

"That was uncalled for." Terry Lewis was furious and Tom suspected it was his first genuine reaction of the day. Terry pushed himself out of his chair. "I'm not going to be insulted like this, particularly by someone who's still wet behind the ears and probably wouldn't even have a job if it wasn't for his father."

The gloves are off, Tom thought to himself and was delighted that he had hit home so successfully. "I've got three radio and two television interviews later today, Terry. How's it going to sound when I say that the local MP refuses to ask any questions in the House about a disaster from which he's doing rather nicely? Every piece of your overpriced plant has been hired for clearance work, hasn't it? I checked earlier – and don't bother accusing me of blackmail because I'm well aware of it."

"You long streak of piss..."

"Can I take that as a yes?"

6.10 p.m. The day had been long, it had been wearisome and it wasn't yet over. Tom walked slowly across the now silent and deserted reception on his way back from another interview, checking at Miss Rush's desk to see if he had any messages. As he started to ascend the half-flight of stairs his father's door opened.

"Tom, have you got a minute?"

It seemed the only time conversations between the two of them flowed easily was when Tom made an effort to jolly things along but he was in no mood for that and went into the office unwillingly. As a consequence their 'little chat' was faltering and uneasy to begin with and gradually deteriorated further as it progressed. Tom didn't even bother to sit down.

"Terry was very disappointed with you, Tom."

"No, he wasn't, he was furious."

"You didn't have to threaten him."

"Yes, I did."

"You have to know how to handle him. Really, he's got a heart of gold."

"Yes, sure, and a bank balance to match."

"Tom, don't you think you're getting a bit ... well ... out of your depth with all this? This isn't the kind of work we want, is it? It's not really us."

Tom moved wearily towards the door. "It may not be your choice, Dad, but it's exactly what I want. So much so, that I'm doing it for nothing."

Harry Harrison's voice took on an edge that almost crackled. "What did you say?"

"I'm not charging for my time and I've undertaken that the firm won't make a profit out of it. It's a costs-only case."

His father got up and moved from round his desk. "How dare you take such a decision without consulting me? You might be a partner but if you want me to spell it out for you – you're a junior partner..."

"... as you never tire of reminding me."

"You didn't have the authority to make a decision of that nature. We're possibly talking about a great deal of money here."

"Yes, and we're also talking about a great deal of local credibility, amongst other things. I've done exactly what was necessary." Tom kept his voice emotionless but he could see by his rapidly rising colour and raised voice that his father was becoming progressively angrier but, as always, he struggled not to let it show.

"You had better get some damned well-paying clients to compensate, that's all I can say..."

"Actually, I wouldn't have mentioned it but if you want a little breakdown of fees, I've earned this practice twice as much as you have over the last couple of years but yes, I take your point, and I will make sure our – my – profitability is maintained. Okay?" The question was rhetorical.

"I mean it, Tom!"

"I'm sure you do."

Tom left his father's office and continued his trek back to his own and without removing his coat, picked up the phone. "Hi, Vicky, how are you? A lot's happened. I've got a couple of hours before the next interview, can you face a drink?"

Tom felt a momentary tingle of excitement when she replied "Yes!"

CHAPTER FIVE

Thursday, December 13th, 1990, 8.00 p.m. The rain perfectly complemented Tom's mood as he nosed the car into another tree-lined suburban avenue – which looked exactly like several others he had already driven down. The wipers failed to clear the screen properly and he squinted ahead through wet reflections of orange street lights and wished he hadn't bought tinted spectacles – a vanity which affected his night vision.

The closer they got to the meeting, the less conversation there was between him and Vicky and apprehension began to claw away at him. When he missed the street turning Tom felt a sudden burst of irritation and knew it was fuelled by nerves.

The house was unprepossessing but large – a Victorian semidetached mansion which had seen better days. Conifers, laurels and rhododendrons crowded in on the short tarmac drive and held the street lights at bay. A middle-aged, quiet and still-faced woman answered the door and Vicky introduced Tom to Marion Livsedge on the doorstep. She had lost her nineteen-year-old son, Martin.

With few words she ushered them through the hallway, into the living room and out the other side into an expansive extension which she referred to as the games room. In the recent past, she would probably have shown visitors into the room with pride but not now. It was just another room.

A quick mental headcount showed there to be upwards of twenty people present, sitting on a variety of wicker sofas and chairs, dining chairs and even a beanbag had been utilised. Tom could identify some of those who were couples by the way they clutched each other's hands.

The room was filled with incongruities. A bar with a deep-buttoned, upholstered front occupied one corner and although its glass-fronted cupboard of glasses and bottles was invitingly illuminated, no drinks had been poured. A table tennis table had been dismantled and stacked against one wall and on an occasional table stood a collection of boxed games. On one wall was a dartboard, recessed into a tyre to protect the masonry from misaimed darts – inadequately, judging by the numerous pock-marks in the plaster. Everything seemed out of keeping with the purpose of the meeting – a room for pleasure and relaxation pressed into service for anguish and despair.

Marion Livsedge made a special point of showing him a large coloured photograph of Martin, which was hanging on the wall near the bar. There was also a man in the picture with him who Tom took to be the boy's father. It was one of those silly pictures where they were both playing to the camera, arms outstretched, laughing with open mouths, one wearing a fez, the other a turban. She offered no explanation for the headgear but it seemed important to her that Tom should see her son. She smiled proudly and Tom could see the glint of tears in her eyes.

He could feel the son's presence and imagined the scoldings that were issued when Martin's mis-aimed darts chipped pieces of plaster from the wall; the parents' protestations that they were terrible at drawing when he pestered them to play *Pictionary*; the raiding of the bar when his mates came back with him late at night.

The greatest of the incongruities was the dining table, set with an unambitious buffet and pushed out of the way against a side wall. Bridge rolls and triangular sandwiches, crisps and peanuts, quartered tomatoes and sliced cucumber, cups and saucers and paper plates. It could have been a cards night or a meeting of the gardeners' club but for the expressions of those present. Each was the same – unsmiling and drawn, with apprehension burnt into their eyes. And all of them focused on Tom.

Once the introductions were completed they were directed to the buffet and Tom knew he had no hope of remembering the string of names which had been given him. The atmosphere was almost unbearable – twenty or so people munching on little sandwiches and making laboured small talk when he knew they were dying inside.

The process of taking refreshments seemed to last an eternity but eventually a man cleared his voice. It was the one in the picture alongside Martin – his father. "Could I have your attention, please, ladies and gentlemen?" Mr Livsedge began tentatively.

The muffled voices faded away almost instantly and cups and plates were deposited on the table. Tom sensed it was a relief to everyone that they were finally getting to the real purpose of the meeting.

"I just wanted to thank everyone for coming along this evening, particularly as it's so wet, and particularly I wanted to thank Mr Tom Harrison for giving up his time." He spoke like he was addressing the bowls club annual general meeting. "I think you all know that Mr Harrison is a solicitor and is representing Mrs Vicky Denton. I know most of us were touched by Mrs Denton's words in the *Evening Chronicle* and it seemed sensible for us to all meet and explore the possibilities.

"So, I'm going to ask Mr Harrison to outline his intentions and then I think we should consider whether it's something we want to be involved with or not. Mr Harrison." There was a flutter of applause as Tom took the floor.

He stood in front of the expectant faces and his heart sank. It was like stepping into a huge vacuum and, momentarily, he wondered if he had the ability to fill it. He had not planned in detail what he intended to say but the words seemed to form themselves.

"I can only guess how you're feeling because I didn't lose anyone in the disaster and whatever I say will always be coloured by that fact. Despite that, I do feel a part of this awful tragedy. I know that nothing I do will alter what's happened, it won't bring anyone back, it won't deaden your pain and in the end it may not even increase your understanding by that—"

"But it might increase your bank balance by quite a bit..."

The interruption was spoken bitterly, spat out by a short, stocky man in his thirties who coloured as he spoke. It so surprised Tom that he momentarily struggled for a response.

Eventually the words for his reply began to slot themselves into some kind of order.

"Yes ... I can understand, I think, why you might feel like that but in fact I'm not charging for my time."

"No hidden fees, no backhanders?"

"No."

Although the accusation was heavy with disbelief and stung him, there was no outrage in Tom's reply; it was simply a statement of fact.

"What reason is there to get the law involved in this? I can't see any sense in it at all. It was an accident and nothing you do can alter that." A middle-aged woman fought back tears as she spoke.

"Why not let Mr Harrison outline the situation and then ask questions." Vicky intervened and other voices quietly supported her. It wasn't the start Tom had expected.

"Mrs Denton has asked me to act for her and the reasons are simple. Her husband died unnecessarily as a result of a combination of circumstances. He died because a plane crashed on him but also because he didn't receive prompt treatment; had he done so he would probably have lived.

"I'm sorry, I can't remember your name," Tom said, looking apologetically towards the woman who had spoken, "but you said it was an accident. That implies it was unavoidable, a combination of unforeseen circumstances that no one could do anything about. I'm not sure that's true. There are literally thousands of things which could have had an influence.

"Decisions are taken every day which affect our lives, decisions that we're not even aware of. Because it's losing money, perhaps aligned with bad management, a components company might decide to use cheaper materials, which results in a faulty screw which severs and causes an engine failure. Lots of similar screws might be in use all over the world. That's just a hypothetical example but this kind of discovery is important to saving life.

"In the case of Flight 469, I think it's essential to start asking questions of the aircraft's owners. It might not be their fault, it might be nobody's fault, but if we start asking questions it will begin a process which could eventually go right down the line to anyone or any company that has ever had anything to do with that aircraft. And if we find anything wrong, there could be several outcomes – we prevent it happening again, we apportion responsibility and, if it's what you want, we can insist on compensation."

"And you'd get your money out of that?" It was the same man again.

"No, not that either," Tom replied without any trace of having been offended, "but I suppose it is a possibility."

"Why are you talking about money all the time? My little girl was burnt to death and I wasn't with her because I'd gone to buy Christmas presents. That was more important than being with her, and she died." She began to choke over her sobs. "I let her die alone in that hall ... I wasn't there to help her ... so frightened, and I wasn't there..." The man with her tried to offer comfort, speaking softly and touching her gently.

It was ten minutes or more before the group asked Tom to continue. The stocky man who had spoken earlier was not going to allow his scepticism to be brushed away too easily and again worried away at Tom the moment he prepared to speak.

"If your motivation isn't money then what is it?"

Suddenly, Tom found his reasoned, measured words had deserted him and the passion which he had tried hard to keep under control burst through. It was almost with relief that he allowed people to see how he really felt.

"I've lived in Harrow all my life and a lot of my acquaintances, their children, even my best friend died in that holocaust. I went to help and I saw things I never, ever want to see again – dreadful, awful things that made me cry, that took away my sleep and haunt me almost every minute of every day. I feel totally sickened by what happened and I want to play a part in unravelling the mystery that surrounds it. You are doing it for your children, your relatives; I am doing it for a sixteen-year-old girl. Her memory will live with me to the day I die. Although I had never met her before, I am all she has because her entire family died with her. She changed my life forever and I can't really say more than that."

As he finished speaking, Tom saw the body language of the aggressive man visibly alter and watched the hostility drain from his face. Although he did not seek her out, he also noticed Vicky's eyes holding him fixedly in a look which was both warm and admiring. He paused only momentarily before seeking refuge in solicitor speak.

"As I said, Mrs Denton has asked me to represent her. Once we know more we can consider a civil action against those to blame, for example Varsity. Whatever you might have read about this action or seen on TV, that we are doing it solely for compensation, isn't true. That is simply a way of approaching the process of enquiry."

"What reasons have you got for thinking Varsity might somehow be at fault," asked another parent.

"Nothing specific but there are inconsistencies. We don't know the true nature of the flight, such as why it was using Northolt, which is not the usual base for Varsity's charter work. Flight 469 collided with the helicopter in a sector of airspace where it shouldn't have been so the blame can't simply be dumped on to the helicopter pilot. For what they're worth, there are unconfirmed reports that Flight 469 was in trouble before the collision. On top of all this, the general attitude from Government and others directly involved is not one of searching after truth."

"Could it have been terrorists?" The man could not have been more than twenty-five years old.

"I honestly don't know. The minister three days ago was unduly hasty in dismissing that. Essentially we know nothing. And yes, of course, that is a possibility. If it was terrorists then we would want to know, just as an example, how they got the bomb on to the plane. It wouldn't be sufficient for the Government or Varsity simply to pile the blame on terrorists and forget their own security obligations."

"Surely there must be a recording of the conversations between the aircraft and air traffic control? That would give some of the answers, I'd have thought." The question was asked by an extremely smart woman, probably in her forties, who obviously knew her subject. Ironically, she looked like a senior flight attendant.

"Well, you'd have thought so, wouldn't you? In fact, you've hit on exactly the kind of thing that's worrying us. You may have seen that same question raised by some media and the only answers provided so far are confusing and contradictory. They've talked of technical difficulties with the recording equipment, they've said that they 'believe' contact was lost before the emergency and, thirdly, that the recording might have been mislaid. It all amounts to the same thing – no recording. We want to know why. If the Government is trying to hide something, they will play up the natural confusion which always seems to surround a tragedy of this magnitude – but they are running out of time for that to hold any credence. We now want definite answers which we can pursue."

"So what do you want from us?" The question was from another, older man but it again had the unmistakable edge of aggression honed into it. The constant doubt was beginning to rattle Tom.

"You jointly requested this meeting and I am simply trying to outline the choices. I will be acting for Mrs Denton but the more people I speak for, the more seriously the case will be taken. It's the old story of unity being strength. And to be honest, we'll need both – unity and strength because this whole thing could be a long and difficult process and there may not even be very much at the end of it. On the other hand, we might actually find out what really went wrong and make sure it doesn't happen again."

The same man came back at him again. "And how long is this all likely to take?"

"To be honest, any resolution could take years but I'd hope to make discoveries along the road."

"Won't there be an inquest?" asked the same man.

"Yes, there will. There has to be, by law, in all matters relating to suspicious deaths," he declared, whilst inwardly cursing his inability to remember the most elementary matters. The thing is, he'd never done an inquest and imagined it was a routine, perfunctory hearing overseen by an ageing medico-legal who had failed to make the grade. "An inquest is very limited in scope, mainly looking at the immediate cause of death and –" this led to another point he'd overlooked – "anyway before we get to an inquest the authorities will have to consider any criminal liability, you know, of pilots and controllers and so on because that has to be dealt with first. It could all get bogged down. I'm afraid I don't know when the inquest will be but I'll try and find something out by next week. And that brings me on to what I think is an important first step..."

With his last words, Tom told the group that a public meeting had been arranged for the following Tuesday to which all relatives and survivors were welcome. He hoped that from it a collective decision would emerge on the best way to proceed.

The meeting broke up into informality again and more tea was poured. Tom could pick up snatches of hushed conversation from different groups which had formed. Some were still expressing doubts about lawyers, other seemed too distressed, too much in shock to make any decision but almost a half of those present eventually made their way to Tom and asked for his card.

The evening quickly descended into stilted small talk and Tom excused himself and left with Vicky. In the car on the way back to her house, Tom suggested a drink. He wanted to surround himself with some semblance of normality after so much collective grief. The rattle and clatter of glasses and bottles, vacuous conversations and the sound of untroubled people enjoying themselves all seemed very inviting at that minute.

Vicky, on the other hand, seemed a little bit edgy and preoccupied. "What's all this about an inquest? You never mentioned that when I first came to see you."

"Bit of an oversight, I'm afraid," Tom admitted. "Mostly, they're ineffective and a waste of time on the bigger questions. How did he die? He went over a cliff! But whether he fell or was pushed isn't asked. See what I mean?"

"Glass or share a bottle?" he asked as they found a table.

"What the hell, make it a bottle!"

"Dry white?"

"Fine." She watched Tom as he went to the bar to order and spoke to a group of three people who were standing drinking.

He obviously knew them well and despite the gravity of the situation, Vicky couldn't help making her usual character judgements. One man looked like he might be a salesman and was loud and insensitive and Tom was obviously not that close to him. The second man was stylishly dishevelled and she put him down as a writer – perhaps an artist or maybe a designer. He put his arm round Tom's shoulder and his expression signalled it was a gesture of genuine concern. Tom acknowledged it by putting an arm round the man's waist. It lasted only briefly but for both men it was an unselfconscious expression of friendship and Vicky found it warming. The third person, a woman, was younger than Tom and in her twenties – blonde, attractive and a touch overly eager in competing for Tom's attention. Vicky thought she might have been a nurse but she was certain that Tom and she had once had an affair, probably short-lived. The woman still wanted him but Vicky could see that Tom had no residual sexual interest in her.

He returned with a bottle, misted with condensation, and two glasses. "Sorry, I only live round the corner; it's my local wine bar. Jacob's Creek okay?"

"Fine." Actually, Vicky disliked the over-oaked, cloying Australian Chardonnays but it didn't seem important at that moment. "What happens next?"

"We talk about something other than Flight 469, if that's okay?"

"I'll try but I can't guarantee it."

"How's Emma?" enquired Tom.

"She's gone to her aunt's –David's sister – down in Brighton for a few days. She's got two girls around Emma's age and I think it'll be good for them to be together. Anyway, she was keen to go and that's probably the most important thing – that she starts to take control. Like your wine, do you?" Tom's glass was almost empty.

He smiled at her, his fingers round the stem. "I hope you don't mind this," he gestured to the wine bar with a sweep of his arm. "I know you're suffering just like all the others there tonight but I just needed to escape the magnitude of it for a while. Is that selfish of me? Does it make me insensitive and unfeeling?"

"Not a bit. I understand exactly how you feel and I wanted a drink as much as you did and for the same reasons. It seems I can handle my own grief but not other people's. So what does that make me?" The smile was welcome and there was also a softness in her almost jet-black eyes which he hadn't seen before. "You're an interesting man, Tom Harrison."

"Oh really?" He smiled, unsure of what else to say and refilled both glasses.

"You're full of contradictions. Public school, was it?"

"Does it show? It was only a minor one, if that's any mitigation."

Vicky looked at him appraisingly. "Did you like it?"

"Hated it! I've never looked back on my school days with any warmth at all. Couldn't wait to leave."

"Why?"

"I don't know really, I just felt sort of semidetached. The petty discipline, myopic masters whose entire view of life was contained within the walls of a not particularly successful school. It all seemed so inconsequential. I think my final report summed up my attitude perfectly. 'Harrison has whiled away his time at school with a cheerful indifference and maybe one day he might learn to take life seriously. His exam results were as big a surprise to him as they were to everyone else.' I got my A levels, you see! No one thought I would."

"And you've always worked for your father?"

"Yes, well, after university and bumming around for a couple of years. Theoretically I work 'with' him now and not 'for' him and this is beginning to feel like the psychiatrist's chair."

"Don't let it worry you; I think I'm a frustrated journalist. You seem very different to him. Do you get on?"

"I suppose the honest answer is – no, not really. I'm quite fond of him, I suppose. Funny, I was thinking about this the other day. He huffs and he puffs and he blusters but somehow there's no substance there. The practice is his substance and if you took that away I don't think there'd be anything left. It's a bit like a rerun of school – great concern over things which are largely inconsequential. And that's the real difficulty – we have very different ideas about the kind of legal work we should be doing. I'm mainly interested in litigation or a case like yours that has some real meaning, which has genuine importance. If I succeeded in forcing things in my direction, then we would be doing headline cases and, essentially, he'd be left with the mundane stuff – the junior role and no way of making sense of his life."

"You haven't mentioned your mother."

"She died when I was twenty."

"What, ten, twelve years ago?"

"Eleven."

"Bad time to lose a parent."

"Yes, I suppose so. And she was such a great character – a woman out of her time and probably out of her place. So what about you?"

Vicky ignored him. "Is that why you're still working with your father – family loyalty?" Tom was immediately conscious that Vicky had purposely avoided answering him and that her question was contrived. He'd seen it too many times on the witness stand to mistake it but he let it go.

"Good question." Tom paused, considering the answer. "I think I used to prefer being a big fish in a small pond but the time for change is coming. It's time to move on."

"Fresh challenges?"

"Exactly!"

"You ever been married?"

"Hey, hey, hey – what is this? *Question Time?* What about you, Vicky Denton? What inner truths are you prepared to reveal?"

"Believe me, my background is boring. Nothing worth relating."

Again Tom detected a determined avoidance. Under other circumstances he would have chivvied away until he got a response, whatever it was. But he wasn't sure if her silence was related to the death of David; that thoughts of her past, of a period before the disaster, simply inflamed the wounds, but he couldn't let it pass entirely.

"There's a flat vowel or two – hardly noticeable but they're there. From the north?"

"Manchester. State school, drama school, aspiring actress turned drama director. One husband, one child." She rattled through it as quickly as she could and her tone brooked no more questions. "And now one widow," she added, her mood visibly changing.

"Sorry, Vicky, shall I take you home?" Tom asked quietly.

"Not before we've finished that wine," she replied and reached for the bottle.

CHAPTER SIX

Friday, December 14th, 1990, 9.30 a.m. There was a rattle on Tom's door and Mike Smith poked his head round. "You wanted me, squire?"

"Just arrived? What's this, half day?"

"Oh, very droll. Matter of fact, I was trying to stop your chickens from getting stuffed, so to speak. Mr Henderson, remember him?" Mike waved some papers at him. "Little things called some draft affidavits – remember them?"

"You haven't finished them, have you?" Mike smiled smugly. "You have! What a champ; you're forgiven." Tom grabbed the papers and looked at them cursorily. "Inquests, Mike, what do we know about inquests?"

"I know what I know and it ain't a lot."

"See what we've got in the library?"

"Oh, the library. Is that the same room where Dasher keeps the coffee, you know, next to the khazi, just before the bike store?"

Tom grinned. "Got it in one! Anything on inquests will do nicely."

Mike deposited the draft affidavits and Tom read through them. It was all good, strong stuff. Having advised Henderson to bypass an industrial tribunal and go straight for a High Court hearing, the case needed to be strong. On the basis of the affidavits Mike had obtained, it would never go to trial. He was certain the Chilled Chicken Emporium would offer to settle – the only question remaining was for how much. It would have to be big, he decided. Tom made some corrections and comments on the papers.

Mike reappeared clutching a leather-bound volume. "Aren't you the lucky one. Hot off the press, this is – '*Jervis On Coroners, 7th edition; The function and purpose of inquests in England and Wales – 1955*'. I've already looked at the last page – it was the coroner what did it."

Tom took the volume from him. "Mike, why do you always have to be so bloody cheerful? Take these and rewrite them. I've marked the sections that I think should be excluded and the order each one should go in." He handed him the affidavits.

"I thought you might also like to take a gander at this." Mike produced four pages of duplicated paper simply headed 'Inquests'. "You know I borrow all the legal practice coursework stuff from Tony Waisey over at Mathers? Well, he gave me this a few weeks ago and that's it – the total sum of a solicitor's training in inquest work! No wonder you're sitting there scratching your barnet. But look, look at this." Mike was pointing at a highlighted paragraph. "Interesting, isn't it? *Inquests may not be used in order to obtain information specifically for use in a civil action.*"

Tom looked at Mike with the face of an innocent. "As if!"

Tuesday, December 18th, 1990, 7.30 p.m. "... and I will continue to represent all of you to the very best of my ability in this dreadful period of pain and suffering, just as I have in better times. I know there are many issues that remain unidentified and believe me, I am doing everything within my power to get those clarified. I wanted you to know that."

Tom watched Terry Lewis as he performed smoothly and effortlessly, doing what he did best – charming a crowd. Tom wondered how many of those listening could sense the teeth-grinding insincerity and, judging by the response, quite a few. The council chamber of the town hall was virtually full and people hung over the railings of the public gallery, trying hard to hear the speakers below. In Terry Lewis's case it was unnecessary as his flat Brummie vowels were pumped out with force and bounced around the glass dome like verbal ping-pong balls.

For the second time in only days, Tom felt the unmistakable flutter of anguish, beginning in his stomach and then quickly working its way through his entire body, revealing itself, as always, in constant yawning. What, to an outsider, looked like complete indifference and boredom was an indication of high tension.

Ideally, he would have liked to be alone somewhere quiet but having made the decision to speak last, he needed to listen to what others said. As usual, he had no idea what he was going to say and concentrated on the other speeches in the hope that they would provide a key to his own thoughts. He envied little about Lewis other than the ease with which he played a crowd but unfortunately for him, on this occasion, things weren't going entirely his way.

"... but this evening belongs to you, not me. Over the years we've heard talk of solidarity, people power, community action and you are all those things brought together under one roof. As survivors and relatives of the deceased and injured of Harrow, you have decided spontaneously that you need a voice in order to see that truth and justice are not forgotten. I respect that voice, I admire it but above all I will obey it. Thank you."

As Terry was about to step down, satisfaction oozing from every pore, his face glowing despite the lack of heating, a loud voice echoed around the chamber.

"Are you going to support the call for a public inquiry?"

Terry Lewis paused but didn't reply.

"Did you hear me, Lewis, we want a public inquiry."

Lewis left the podium pretending he had not heard but it angered sections of the crowd.

"Bloody traitor. What've you got to hide?"

Lewis kept moving and by the time he reached Tom, the satisfaction had disappeared from his face.

"Sorry about our little misunderstanding the other day," he said as he pumped Tom's arm. "I know how fraught it can get when a lot of damaged people are demanding things from you – like now." He inclined his head towards the crowded hall.

Tom nodded and said nothing, knowing that as one of the principal players in this drama, Terry would want to be seen as being on good terms with him. Tom was a necessary token which needed to be displayed, as important as a poppy on

Armistice Day or sipping a drink with a black man during an election campaign. Terry Lewis would not want to be isolated and he also did not want to be dragged into a battle of recriminations over Government policy and the lack of a public inquiry, so he judged it time to leave, in case other speakers took it into their heads to attack him.

Vicky and Tom had agreed that the press should be admitted as publicity was one of the few weapons they had. However, both were surprised by the numbers that had turned up. Louise Watson was busy as always, going from person to person, working on the background to the story as well as the story itself.

It was difficult to estimate how many survivors and relatives were there but certainly more than a hundred. Tom recognised some of the faces from the meeting at the Livsedges' the previous week. A group of people in their twenties and thirties sat together and he guessed they were parents of the children who died at Greenhills Way School. All still appeared to be in shock.

Just in front of them were two teenagers whose story had already been told in the press and Tom recognised them from their pictures – Tracey and Dean Yardley. They had lost their parents and an older brother and sister. Their grandparents lived in the house next door and they too had died. He could not begin to imagine what life must feel like to them.

A dignified-looking elderly man sitting alone he knew to be Maurice Wreford. He and his family had been having a tea party, a birthday celebration for one of his grandchildren, when the ice cream ran out and Maurice had gone to the corner shop to buy more. In the few minutes it took to walk there, almost his entire family had died – eight people from three generations.

In the seat next to Maurice was Troy Dawson whose wife had been killed. She had been trapped for several hours and was thought to be another of those whose life could have been saved had it not been for the failure of the emergency services.

All around the hall were faces which looked familiar but he could not be sure if they were ex-clients or if they had been the subjects of recent news stories.

Esther Vine had taken a seat close to Tom but so far had spoken little. She had already made it clear that her principal desire was to bury her daughter, Rachel, to mourn her and hope that the pain would eventually begin to fade, freeing her to think of other things – at least some of the time. He smiled at Esther and she shook her head sadly.

"I'm not so sure about all this, Mr Lawyer. Maybe it's better we forget about questions and just remember our loved ones. Already people are getting ready to tap dance on their graves and they're not even buried."

Esther's words reminded Tom of the delicate eggshells he would need to step between when he spoke and that reminder caused his stomach to contract.

"Why not hear people out, just for this evening," Tom replied, "then see what you think."

Esther smiled and shrugged her shoulders non-committally.

Vicky's attitude was the opposite for she sought answers and possibly blood. Someone, perhaps many people, were responsible for David's death and she wanted every name, details of every culpable act and she wanted to dictate their fate. As Tom watched her, she took to the podium with a resolute face.

Her words were impassioned as she called for the meeting to unite round an agenda of demands. It was an entirely political speech and it was as well that Terry Lewis had left.

"So, Mr Lewis will obey our voice, will he? Just like he did when we told him not to close down hospitals or privatise the ambulance service or reduce the number of fire stations..." Despite this being Tory heartland, with many of those in the hall having voted for the policies which Vicky was publicly shredding, not one voice was raised in dissent.

Tom admired her oratory. She delivered her words not persuasively but as a challenge – this is what I believe, this is unarguably the truth and you have to agree with me.

"In the last few years, this country of ours has changed. Once there used to be lots of gods but now there's only one and that's the god of money. I don't know what led to the dreadful disaster here on our doorstep but inside me, my instincts tell me that money was at the bottom of it." Again there was no dissent from the crowded hall.

"What we have to decide tonight is our ultimate goal – why

we have come here, what motivates us and what outcome we're looking for. I can only speak for myself but it isn't compensation. My husband is dead and I want to know why."

Ailey Newman had sidled up to Tom without him noticing: "Quite a lady, eh...?"

Tom found himself agreeing enthusiastically.

"... I don't want to be fobbed off with excuses. Firstly I owe it to myself to discover the truth – not the government's truth nor Varsity Aviation's truth nor even Mr Lewis's truth but the real truth. And I want it for two reasons. So I can understand how and why my husband died. I knew everything else about our life together; surely to God I owe it to him to discover all I can about his death. But I also want to stop something similar happening to other husbands and wives, other men, women and children in other towns.

"There seem to be three options facing us. We can pursue every opportunity open to us to uncover the facts behind the disaster and that means keeping control of the fight here in Britain. Most of you have already been approached by an American lawyer who wants you to sue in the States. If you take that route you will have little or no control over the outcome other than to take the money and run. The third option is do nothing and accept what's happened.

"Those are the choices facing us. If you seek compensation in America it will be at the expense of discovering what really happened, make no mistake about it. Any money that's offered will be to buy your silence and it will be a trade-off – your dead relatives for cash."

Vicky stepped down to thunderous applause.

"She's a natural," said Ailey above the noise. "They would love her back home. Congressmen can't resist passion. It's because they haven't got any of their own." Ailey leant close to Tom so she could be heard – perhaps too close. She placed a hand on his arm and he could feel the warmth of her expensively perfumed body which was so intimate it felt out of context. "Have you thought any more about my offer?"

"I'm still thinking about it." Tom fought back the desire to say – *Just leave me alone!* He excused himself and headed for the lavatories, found an empty cubicle, locked himself in and sat on the unraised seat with his head in his hands, trying to control his nerves.

Why did he feel like this? He wasn't expecting anything sensational to come out of the meeting – at best some determination of the path people wanted to follow. It would certainly start to throw up the main players – the natural leaders, the political manipulators and the inevitable committee joiners who would seek any forum just to hear their own voices – but he could cope with them. Of course he wanted more clients – as many as possible – and to get them he had only to say the right words. So what were the right words?

He arrived back in the chamber to see Bernard Tate stepping towards the podium, his crinkly white hair carefully combed up from just above his left ear and distributed across his bald head like the little, incoming ripples of a high tide. His wife, Edith, stretched out her arm to brush some dandruff from his shoulders as a parting gesture. An unlit pipe had been clutched in his hand all evening and now, as he spoke, he used it to stab at the air to emphasise specific points.

Bernard warmly supported Vicky – he couldn't have done anything else, for after a lifetime as a trade union negotiator he had been saying similar things about government policy for years. But his words seemed to pour a soporific balm over the occupants of the hall, extinguishing the fires of passion which Vicky had so effectively stoked.

Bernard hedged his sentiments with such utterly reasonable phrases as "on the whole", "by and large" and "keeping our options open". His very reasonableness trod an indistinct line between ineffectiveness and manipulation but his strong South Yorkshire accent proved difficult for some of the mostly southern audience to understand.

"Now, he would make a great congressman," confided Ailey with a chuckle.

Tom was trying to get the measure of Bernard but it wasn't until his last line or two that his position became clear. For the first time, Bernard showed a glimmer of passion as he stabbed at the air with his metal-stemmed pipe, reminding the hall that they were making decisions not just for now but for the future.

"One thing I know – we'll not change the world but we've got a right good chance of making our mark. Our loved ones are dead but we can turn their passing into something concrete, something we can remember them by. Believe me, I've spent my life negotiating and if you go to't table with fine words, passion and nothing else but empty threats, you get nowhere. You go armed with ammunition and you've got a good chance of succeeding.

"I don't want to be scratching around for a bob here and a bob there to pay for't next bit of photocopying or some rip-off investigator who doesn't know what he's doing. I want to get them who're responsible for killing our Jack. The only thing they understand is money – that's what hurts 'em. I'm all for hitting 'em with as big a stick as possible and that means having a go in America as far as I'm concerned. And before you accuse me of being mercenary, let me tell you here and now, I'm not..."

Vicky had joined Ailey alongside Tom and raised an eyebrow in response to Bernard's words.

"... I just know what works and what doesn't and I want to win this one. Thank you."

The applause was measured and short-lived but Bernard Tate had defused the charge to the barricades of truth and justice, thought Tom. Instead he'd prepared the ground for negotiation and compromise.

Tom was beginning to clarify his thoughts when Esther Vine beckoned to him from her wheelchair. He knew he would have to speak shortly and really did not want to be interrupted but felt obliged to listen to her.

"Am I a stupid woman or are people talking in riddles? Why does that woman talk about truth and that man talk about money? Are we deciding whether our loved ones have a value? I don't understand."

Esther, Tom guessed, was far from stupid and understood perfectly but he answered anyway. As he had suspected, two different agendas were developing and having to crystallise them for Esther's sake, helped him as much as it did her.

"Legal actions are often as much about compromise as they

are about law. If we sue in the States and Barcroft Holdings are at fault, and they think we've got a case, they'll want to settle. But they'll only do that if we drop all other actions against them everywhere in the world. They won't admit any guilt, no one will find out what really went wrong and a curtain will be dropped on the whole issue. It will be business as usual for them, albeit with a slightly smaller bank balance. So, it's a bit of an either or situation – either we keep the case here in Britain and try and find out what really happened and certainly get less compensation because our courts tend not to make massive pay-outs, or we go to the States, discover just enough truth to embarrass them and get a thumping big pay-out."

"Then, once they've paid, what do you do with that embarrassing information?" Esther, it seemed, had the ability to carve a situation into its component parts with the precision of a surgeon.

"You forget all about it," said Tom, "that's what you do, because you'll sign away the right ever to sue them again and nothing will ever come out in court. Is that what you want?"

More to the point, was that what he wanted? The solicitor in him was used to compromise as it was the basis on which he embarked on most civil actions, always advising his clients that if their case actually reached court no one was likely to win other than lawyers. But was that what he wanted in this instance?

"I'm a lawyer; I'm only supposed to have legal opinions. I'm here to represent your views, not mine."

"Yes and little green people have just landed in spaceships…! Tell me some truth now, Mr Lawyer." Esther held his look without blinking.

"All right. Tom Harrison the bloke wants to know why that aircraft crashed. If it was a genuine accident then maybe we'll learn something which will prevent it ever happening again. If someone was responsible then I'd also like to know that as well."

"To punish them?"

"To expose them – there's a difference. The whole world works on trust. The people who climbed into that aircraft trusted the airline. We trusted them to keep it in the air. Someone broke that trust."

"Okay and what about Tom Harrison the lawyer?"

"Like I said, he does as he's told."

For the first time, the flicker of a smile flashed across Esther's eyes. "And you're doing all this searching for truth for nothing, I hear."

"That's right."

"I'll tell you something, Mr Harrison the lawyer. If I don't pay you I've got no right to tell you what to do. I like to tell lawyers what to do otherwise they poop on you. If necessary I will pay for my own lawyer for my Rachel but what I really want, Mr Harrison, is to give my lovely daughter a proper burial and then cherish her memory. Nothing else has any meaning."

"... it doesn't take long for the vultures to arrive and start scrabbling for their pickings." The aggressive tones were unmistakable – it was the short, stocky man who had challenged Tom at the previous meeting. "... Personally I don't want any of these bloody parasites anywhere near my daughter's memory. To hell with lawyers, that's what I say, because they're interested in one thing only – what they can make out of you. They might say they'll do it for nothing but you've all heard of a sprat to catch a mackerel. I say we should handle this ourselves."

Obviously, Tom's speech which had mollified the man just five days previously had subsequently been consigned to the rhetorical dustbin. He knew he would have to get used to extreme mood swings with people so damaged, and allowed the objection to wash over him.

The man left the podium and there seemed to be little support for his views. Tom gauged that someone now needed to take charge and prayed that his mind would clear when he actually stood up. As he took to the podium he noticed that Ailey had moved alongside Bernard, taking his arm, talking into his ear.

As soon as Tom began to speak, passion again claimed him and a string of deeply felt sentiments queued up, waiting to be spoken. He felt it important to repeat his own experiences and why they had prompted him to work *pro bono*. He wasn't looking for approval, it was simply that he could never speak of the disaster without talking about Polly Bentham – and each time he did so he felt that same despair welling up inside him and without any conscious help it morphed into anger. He had no idea how he sounded to his audience but Vicky was in no doubt – his voice was strong, clear and wielded conviction and sincerity like a cleaver.

"If you have any doubts about my integrity then I suggest you find some other way of pursuing your cause and have nothing to do with me. I've got no desire to persuade anyone to do something they're not happy with. I do, however, feel almost as much a part of this tragedy as you do and if you want me to represent you, you'll get my very best shot. If you make that decision, I want your full support and confidence. I want your wholehearted commitment, not a begrudging, resentful, reluctant, half-hearted endorsement because I can't work any other way. I feel passionate about what I'm doing and I need you to feel the same.

"Okay, let's talk money because that's what's bothering many of you. You have to be clear that money will be an element – not to pay me but for the numerous costs which are always involved and they could be considerable. Unless you're on benefits or extremely low pay and you're almost devoid of assets you will not be eligible for legal aid for a civil action. The rules for eligibility are constantly being changed and each change makes it more difficult to qualify and usually excludes millions more people. And so far as inquests are concerned, there's no legal aid other than in exceptional circumstances, which might apply here. It's called an *ex gratia* payment from the Lord Chancellor's department. A hand-out not a right.

"It would help if you could make a decision fairly soon because the aviation inquiry could be established any day now and we have to keep on pushing for a public judicial inquiry. And –" as he had just discovered and remembered in time – "the inquests into the deaths will be opened within a matter of weeks and I need to prepare for it."

"What does that involve?" came a shouted question from the hall.

"The scope of an inquest is very limited. All it sets out to establish is who died, when they died, how and what the cause was. It's pretty much a formality but having said that, the main people involved will probably be represented by lawyers. Whether you use me or not is entirely up to you but I think you should be there. So you need to start considering fundraising strategies."

"So how much are we going to have to find?" came another call.

"How long is a piece of string? I just don't know. There will be travel and administrative costs, experts, researchers, perhaps barristers – it could be considerable."

From the podium Tom had a better view of the hall and could see a group of people sitting apart from the rest. They were obviously together, said little either to each other or to anyone else and, as far as he could recall, had played no part in the meeting.

Tom judged he had said almost enough and decided to bring his short contribution to a close. As he wound up he was again surprised by the depth of his feeling. "Most people allow life to roll over them and apart from a vote once every five years, they play almost no part in determining its politics or direction. Other, faceless people make most of the decisions and it isn't altruism which motivates them, its self-interest. They are rarely called to account and rely on apathy and indifference to protect them.

"Well, none of us here is apathetic or indifferent. We are hurt and angry and confused. Already the faceless ones are taking advantage of that so let's stop them, let's call them to account, let's force the truth out of them. For the second time in its history the name Harrow has become synonymous with disaster. By joining together we can inject some hope into our lives and I will happily represent anyone who feels similarly." The applause was long and strong and Tom felt tears welling up in his eyes.

As soon as the speeches were over the Harrow Support Group was formed and Tom was surrounded by people asking him to represent them. He watched his visiting cards rapidly depleting and when they had gone, had the embarrassment of scribbling his phone number on scraps of paper. It irked him to see Ailey with a briefcase full of literature about her company and endless cards. He half expected her to produce a table, chairs and drinks tray from it like some transatlantic Mary Poppins.

"Well done, Mr Harrison junior. That's quite a commitment." Vicky's smile was warm and Tom liked it.

"Great solicitor, shame about the stationery!"

CHAPTER SEVEN

Wednesday, December 19th, 1990, 8.45 a.m. The door opened without a knock and Tom's father charged into the office, slapping a bundle of newspapers down on the desk.

"This is just what we need. I presume you haven't read them yet?"

Tom picked up the top one, a tabloid, and on page three was a report of the previous evening's meeting. The headline was explicit: *'Vulture' Solicitor Angers Harrow Survivor.* With it was a picture of Mike stepping out into the street from the front door of the office dressed in his snappiest attire. You could almost see the swing of the shoulders and his hand flicking through his hair. To anyone who did not know him it screamed 'Jack the Lad'. The caption simply read, *One of the Harrow solicitors who is claiming to represent survivors 'free of charge'.*

"How could you have got us into this?" His father's voice was shaking.

"Into what?"

"This…!" Harry Harrison's finger poked at the page like he was squashing ants. "And why am I always right? I said we shouldn't employ him and I said you shouldn't have offered to work for nothing. You ignored me and that's what it's got us!"

"Just hold your horses a minute. You're having a thrombie over nothing. Some snivelling, unprincipled hack decides to have a go and suddenly he's right, we're wrong. Is that what you're saying?"

"I'm saying the practice can do without this, that's what I'm saying."

"Save your anger for the bloke who wrote this, father dearest.

Firstly, Mike is the greatest asset this office has had in years. Secondly, the reporting is totally misrepresentative of the meeting. Look at the picture. It was taken in daylight, which means it must have been shot before the meeting. They'd already decided to set us up. What you should be asking is why."

His father ignored the reasoning although his decibel level had started to reduce. "And is this true?"

He pointed to a paragraph which read, *The smooth reassurances of solicitor Tom Harrison persuaded dozens of shocked relatives to give him their trust. We only hope they won't be disappointed.*

"Absolutely – I hope they won't be disappointed," Tom said with transparent conviction.

"Not that – this; the piece about dozens of people giving you their trust. By that I presume it means you'll be representing them?"

"Yes, hopefully."

"How many?"

"I'd put it at about thirty but we'll know for sure when I receive their instructions."

"Thirty? Thirty? This has got out of hand, Tom." Harry Harrison's mood had perceptively changed. It was less angry and more dogged as he pulled one of the client's chairs close to the desk and sat down.

"In a way I'm glad this has happened because it's brought this ludicrous situation to a head. If you are determined to spend a great deal of your time without earning anything for this practice then we will have to rethink the type of work you undertake. You've avoided the commercial side for long enough. There's some new business come in and I want you to handle it." He held up his hand. "And I'm not going to listen to any argument."

"Okay, okay, fair enough, Dad. I'm not arguing. It's well paid, is it?"

"Extremely well paid."

"Like to give me a clue what it is?"

"It's commercial contract work – quite complex and a lot of it."

"Oh, of course, it had to be." Tom threw both hands up. "It's all right, I'm not disagreeing."

His father's mood had returned to near normal and he carefully replaced the chair from where he'd taken it. "It's important, Tom, and a new client at that so you must do your best."

"Who is it?"

"It's a catering services company."

Tom detected evasion. "Catering for what?"

His father had reached the door before answering. "Aircraft. Their main operation is at Heathrow."

Tom's shout was heard throughout the office, "I don't believe it!"

Despite the irony of the situation, Tom knew he would have to accept it. He flicked through the rest of the papers and another story in another of the tabloids leapt out at him. *Sex in the Afternoon Saved Billy's Life. Sex-mad Billy Dawson cheated on his wife and it saved his life. When he should have been at home on sick leave, sex-cheat Billy was visiting his girlfriend. His afternoon bed romp went on longer than planned and saved the sex-starved shop salesman's skin. Julie Sampson, the voluptuous 28-year-old blonde single mum, said, "He just couldn't get enough that afternoon..."* And so it went on. Tom threw the paper aside in disgust.

All the papers had their 'exclusive' stories. One was headed, *Soldier's Farewell. Life was too dangerous for Bombardier Jimmy Carswell, his mother claimed after her boy had done two terms of duty in Northern Ireland. So she persuaded him to resign from the army and just one month later he found a job as a roustabout for an oil company in Nigeria. It was to prove much more dangerous than the terrorists' bullets and Jimmy died before his plane had even left British airspace. Speaking from her home in Hackney, distraught Mrs Carswell said...*

Tom looked for Louise Watson's piece in the *Harrow Chronicle*. It was on the front page and was a sympathetic and accurate report of the evening's events.

Throughout the day phone calls came in from people who had been at the meeting, asking Tom to represent them. His reference to the forthcoming inquest was the most tangible event on the horizon, it seemed, and most were anticipating that as the first step in their campaign. Tom had gone through Jervis and while he now understood the structure and functions of a coroner's inquest he had no idea how it worked in practice. In fact, he only found out about the lack of legal aid as a result of a newspaper report in the file of cuttings which Vicky had given him.

He had never attended an inquest and had never represented anyone involved in one. The simple, everyday routine of what actually happened, how it opened and who said what to whom was nowhere within Jervis's covers. Quite simply, he did not have a clue.

Tom judged that sufficient time had elapsed for him to be able to speak to his father without pouring petrol on his ignited passions but before he did so he made a call to his prospective new aircraft catering clients, Wings of Sonning. He was professional and charming and feigned an interest he didn't feel. A first appointment was fixed at their Sonning administrative base and having done that, he went to see his father because he now had what he wanted – a conversation opener.

Having updated Harry, who visibly warmed to Tom's apparent eagerness, Tom led into it as nonchalantly as he could.

"Ever done an inquest, Dad?" He'd expected a quick run-down on the procedures but his father was as ignorant as he was.

"Can't say I've ever given it much thought. It's one of those things you expect to happen one day but it never does. Funnily enough, I fancy being a coroner, you know, when I've had enough of this place. A steady little retirement number, I thought!"

"But you don't know how it works?" Tom was surprised by his father's lack of knowledge because he thought it was exactly the kind of routine thing he would know.

"Not really, no."

"So you've no idea of the nitty-gritty – of what happens?" Tom was incredulous.

"The inquest is to determine cause of death so I presume anything which helps that would be permissible. But don't worry about it, old George will probably handle it and he'll guide you through it. All you have to do is rely on him."

Old George was George Fraser, retired solicitor, another of his father's local cronies and a regular golf partner. It was beginning to feel like the father/son relationship of years ago when Tom was reliant on his father's greater experience and he didn't like it, so left.

Back in his own office he looked at the phone. Could he just call George or should he treat him like a judge, in which case he wouldn't dream of speaking to him direct? He risked it and the voice that answered was grave and rough with a strong Scots accent. "Coroner's officer." It certainly wasn't Old George.

The "Oh yes?" which followed Tom's explanation of who he was and what he wanted seemed heavily laced with scepticism. But the man, Mack Caffrey, said it was fine for Tom to call round that morning.

"I'm always willing to give any new laddie a wee bit of a hand." It was a put-down if ever he'd heard one – a mild one but a put-down nevertheless.

3.30 p.m. The old Edwardian fire station had at some time long past been converted into local government offices and a coroner's court. Its facade remained unaltered – a massive terracotta monument to public architecture built round a grand arch through which horse-drawn fire engines would once have clattered, smoke billowing from a shiny copper boiler as it converted water into steam to drive the pumps. Arrows pointed along the side of the building to an unimpressive entrance tucked round the corner, immediately inside which was the coroner's office. An opaque glass screen with an inset leaded design divided the waiting area and its solitary oak bench from the office proper. A typewritten notice was pinned to the window. *Please ring once for attention and wait. You will be dealt with as quickly as possible.* Underneath in biro were written the words, *DEAD FUNNY.*

Tom rang. He could hear people chatting behind the partition and their conversation never faltered. Judging by the laughter it was quite an amusing story that was being told. He waited but the story continued and the sliding panel remained closed.

He rang again with no result and finally placed his thumb on the bell push and left it there. It took about twenty seconds for the screen to fly back and a livid, scowling face to stare at him through the opening, the features broad and craggy, sideboards greying and bushy and the nose glowing with the first fruits of grog blossom.

The man spoke quietly and slowly with a menace that could have melted steel, "Can't you read, laddie?" It was Mack Caffrey.

"Button got stuck," said Tom, smiling disarmingly into the bloodshot eyes of what he felt sure was a putative serial killer. "I'm Tom Harrison."

The face returned the smile but it was as false as it was mesmerising. "You must be yon solicitor laddie. Well, well, well – sorry to keep you waiting! Stay there."

The screen slammed shut and a few seconds later Mack's stocky frame appeared through a door marked *Private*. Whilst the face looked like an unmade bed, the rest of him was smart – pressed sports jacket and flannels, highly polished shoes and crisp white shirt with a regimental tie bearing a crest. He could not have been anything but an ex-copper or ex-military.

"Now what can I do for you, laddie?" It seemed the meeting was to take place in the waiting area.

Tom decided to appeal to the man's ego. "I was hoping you could help me. I understand your knowledge of inquests is second to none."

"Is that a fact?"

"I just have a few questions about the processes – that sort of thing. I'm representing some clients and if I know exactly how it works it may make life easier for all of us. Does that make sense?"

"Perfectly." He purred, moving alongside Tom, one hand pressed gently into the small of Tom's back, impelling him towards the street door. "Are you a teetotaller, Mr Harrison?"

"No."

"Fine, fine," crooned the voice, heavy with the stale smell of something alcoholic. They stepped out into the street and immediately next door was the White Hart. "My personal office," smiled Mack's mouth while his eyes remained as dead as a herring's on a slab. He moved through the saloon bar with its labyrinth of mock Tudor beams and reproduction brassware into a snug at the rear and Tom realised the help he was requesting had a price on it.

He bought Mack a pint of bitter with a Scotch chaser and even though he didn't fancy it at this time of day, he was annoyed to find he had ordered a pint for himself. It was a macho attempt at saving face in front of the man. He knew without doubt that had he ordered the lemonade he fancied, Caffrey would have viewed him with utter contempt.

Tom started the conversation by saying he had intended to speak to the coroner directly, which was why he'd rung. The chill in Mack's voice left Tom in no doubt about what was expected of him.

"You deal with me, mister, and no one else. You understand me?"

The smile reappeared and the voice warmed to freezing point. "You can't be chasing the coroner, now, he's a very busy man."

Yes, thought Tom, *working hard on getting his handicap down.* He now regretted the 'innocent abroad' approach he'd made to Caffrey because the man had obviously interpreted it as stupidity, which would have to be corrected at some point.

They sipped their drinks amid small talk about the tribulations of being a coroner's officer. Tom steered the conversation round to the inevitable inquest into Flight 469.

"How many people are you representing?" Caffrey delivered the question like Tom was a homicide suspect.

"It was thirty-five this morning but people are ringing up all the time. I've no idea what the final figure will be."

"Have you ever done anything as big as this before?"

"No, have you?" It was meant to put Caffrey in his place and Caffrey registered it as such with a tight little smile.

"I'm having to deal with all 523 deceased from that crash, mister. That's 523 post-mortems, 523 statements, 523 families to liaise with." He threw the small whisky down in one and clenched his teeth with an "Aaaah".

"Post-mortems on every victim?" Tom was incredulous. But

it was obvious and wondered why he hadn't thought of it.

"Aye, laddie, of course. Have to establish cause of death. Some might have died of natural causes or some toerag might have used the confusion to bump off their old lady."

That had to be a copper's mind at work, thought Tom. But statements – shit, he hadn't even considered that yet.

"Will you just be leaving it to the police?" enquired Caffrey. "Of course you can take your own statements but there doesn't seem a lot of sense in that, does there?"

"I always make a point of taking my own statements," Tom replied with authority. "Have the police started interviewing yet?" He hoped the reply would be 'no'.

"Oh aye. Have they not interviewed your people yet?"

"No." Again Tom tried to sound authoritative but in fact, had no idea as to whether they had or had not.

"And the air accident investigators, have they not taken theirs yet either?" There was an exaggerated incredulity in Caffrey's question because he guessed, correctly, that Tom had not given it even a thought.

"We're expecting them to start any day now," Tom replied dismissively, trying to make it sound of little consequence.

Although resenting Caffrey's smugness, Tom nevertheless bought him another pint and the chaser to go with it. It was beginning to feel like talking to a premium telephone number where the recorded message dispenses information as slowly as possible in order to drag out the conversation and notch up a huge bill. But eventually, with probing, Mack Caffrey begrudgingly imparted information about how the inquest would actually function.

"When will it happen and how long has been set aside for it?" Tom asked as his final question, wanting desperately to escape from Caffrey's depressing company.

Caffrey slowly shook his head from side to side. "Tsch, tsch, tsch. There's an awful lot of witnesses, laddie." That was the best he had to offer.

Tom left Caffrey in the pub and headed straight back to his office. It was 5.30 p.m. and Mike Smith was leaving the building as he was entering.

"About turn," Tom said, grabbing Mike by the arm and spinning him round. The heavy clouds of newly applied aftershave indicated that Mike was probably on quite a hot promise that evening.

"On ya bike, guvnor," he protested but still allowed himself to be propelled across reception and up the stairs. "Come on, Tom, I've just won the equivalent of the lottery – I'm going to collect my prize."

"Later!"

"How much later?"

"Dunno." They entered Tom's office. "It's my fault, I should have thought of it before but the police and the SAAIU people are both going to be contacting our clients to take statements. They're also going to be told by Jack the Ripper that their loved ones have to be chopped up by the pathologist to establish cause of death. Some of them may already have been contacted but I hope not. 'A', we've got to tell them that they're going to be interviewed twice and that I want to be there when it happens. 'B', we've got to arrange to take our own statements. 'C', we have to prepare them for the autopsies and 'D' – and this is the worst bit of all – we've got to get their permission to cut their loved ones up a second time because we're going to do our own post-mortems."

The realisation that if there were to be post-mortems, he would want his own came to him the instant Caffrey mentioned the word. He had had a few experiences of blinkered pathologists looking only for those revelations that supported the police scenario and there had been no way of checking their findings as the bodies had always been disposed of afterwards. Tom was determined it would not be repeated on this occasion no matter how remote the chances were of discovering anything relevant.

"Now just a mo, I'm not going to chop anyone up – that's one reason why I got out of the racing game."

"Funny. Prepare them for what's going to happen but also fix a meeting. When?" He quickly looked in his diary. "Day after tomorrow – Friday, seven thirty. Check to see if that room over the Crown's available."

"Tom, I'm on my way out … oh fuck it!" Mike picked up the

phone. "Are you sure about this – that's just four days before Christmas. It seems a bit hard."

"I don't think our people are going to be doing much celebrating and we've got to get this moving before the police approach them. And there's always the chance they might go away to relatives for the holidays and stay there for weeks." Mike picked up the phone. "Thanks, Mike. Lots of tact, loads of sympathy and plenty of understanding, okay? There's only thirty-five calls to make."

"Actually, there's thirty-nine. Four more joined up this afternoon. Tom, why do you want your own pathologist?"

"Expert witness, isn't he? And when have we ever relied on the other side's experts?"

"Very true." Mike was about to reach for the phone. "Tom, how do you go about finding a pathologist?"

"Dunno. *Yellow Pages*, I suppose." He said it with a straight face.

It must have been approaching 9.30 p.m. when Tom heard the street door open. Mike had finally gone on his date about fifteen minutes earlier and Tom assumed he had probably forgotten something. He was surprised when his father's head appeared round the door – at the same time as one of his clients answered the ringing phone. Tom held his hand up to say, *I'll be with you in a minute*, and spoke to the client. As he did so he could see the benign expression on his father's face change to one of annoyance.

When the call ended and Tom had replaced the receiver, Harry Harrison immediately launched into a monologue.

"I saw the lights on. I really thought you were responding to our little talk and were getting to grips with your responsibilities but instead..."

"Stop there." Tom abruptly cut across him. "Stop right there," he said as he got up from behind his desk, walking round it to confront his father. "As far as this goes I'm not your son I'm your business partner. We've agreed a course of action and that's the end of it. How I apportion my time is my affair. Do you understand? If you want to talk about it then you make an appointment to see me. Now please leave me alone to get on with some extremely important work because, unlike you, I don't enjoy being here at this time of night."

Harry Harrison left without saying a word but Tom could have sworn he heard the old bastard chuckle as he went down the stairs.

Newspapers were still full of speculation about how Flight 469 had met its end. They were all fairly predictable and ran the gamut of a bomb, terrorist missile, mechanical failure, pilot error and collision. Different papers seemed to be pushing their own theory and speculation was dressed up as evidence. While the aircraft itself was being reconstructed in the old airship hanger at Cardington airfield, journalists were publishing double-page spreads filled with graphics, setting out different scenarios.

What Tom found most disturbing was the way in which the airline industry's claims of total security, which had been used to reassure passengers for years, were stripped apart and shown to be a complete deception. There were constant references to Lockerbie and the Maltese/Frankfurt/Heathrow connections. It was, it appeared, simplicity itself to get a bomb on board an aircraft – any aircraft. Baggage-screening methods were exposed as being primitive and not very effective. Plastic explosives were almost impossible to detect by X-rays, particularly if the explosives were rolled out thinly and used to line a suitcase. He found it ironic that the best method for detection was a modification of the life-saving CAT medical scanner but there were only two of these in use anywhere in the world.

There was also speculation that a ground-launched, anti-aircraft missile such as a Stinger had been used. It seemed that several had been misplaced after the Gulf War and had never been accounted for. Of course, the IRA or INLA held prime place as possible culprits but the aircraft's destination of Nigeria raised the spectre of Arab fundamentalism. A further trail was opened up with the Nigerian connection. As the passengers were all oil industry workers *en route* to Nigeria, one journalist even developed a theory that, motivated by fear of commercial rivalry, an Arab oil-producing state might be the culprit. Of course, there was almost nothing to support any of these theories.

So fast had been Tom's learning curve that he could not believe his naivety in expecting Terry Lewis's parliamentary questions to produce results – and of course they did not. Most papers did not even bother to report them nor the answers which Astbury provided. It was all so much bullshit with all substantive issues being dismissed with the assurance that they would be explored at the inquiry. The only comment of interest was the report of the aircraft being on fire before the collision.

Astbury did tackle that question directly and said there was no evidence to support the speculation. Certainly Tom could find no confirmation of the rumours and he had even rung the radio researcher who had raised the allegation but she could add nothing new. Apparently, two listeners had rung in with reports of having seen flames issuing from the aircraft but neither had left a contact number.

If, when the world's largest Airfix kit was eventually reassembled, it might be that something vital would be discovered. If so, Tom suspected it would probably turn out to be mechanical failure which led to the aircraft losing height and a subsequent collision with Eric Lloyd's helicopter. The big question was – what failure and why? That was what he had to try and establish. Simple really!

The one person he had not spoken to the previous evening was Vicky and he wasn't looking forward to it as he was pretty certain what her reaction would be to the request for an autopsy. In the end he faced his fears and rang; her reaction was calm but firm.

"I want to see him – his body, that is – before he's touched. I had only one quick glance on the night of the disaster – so quick I can barely remember it."

"I'll arrange it." Tom's response was immediate and after he had hung up he called Mack Caffrey, who wasn't there. He buzzed Mike who eventually appeared, looking far from his normal dapper self. In fact he looked dreadful but smug.

Mike read the look on Tom's face. "No comments, okay?" But he couldn't hide the little smile at the corner of his mouth.

"I'm taking statements for most of today so could you contact the Law Society and get them to fax through a list of pathologists, choose one you think might be okay and fix a meeting so I can check them out."

"How the hell do I choose a pathologist? They ain't gonna have recommendations from their clients, are they?"

"Mike, use your ingenuity, your natural intelligence – and a pin. Get someone who's based nearby, that'll cut down the number for a start and reduce travel costs if we choose one of them. Why not ring your mates at Mathers and see if they ever use anyone and if so whether they're any good. You could also try Hawkes and Shelley and any of the other local firms. Some of them must have dealt with pathologists. Oh, and make sure they're well qualified, okay?"

"Yeah. Here, Tom, I don't really like to ask but should I try and do a deal with them? You know – a cheaper price for a job lot?"

"Mike!!" Tom dropped his pen on the desk with a clatter.

"Well, I had to ask!"

"'Economies of scale', not a 'job lot'. Yes, try it."

Friday, December 21st, 1990, 7.30 p.m. The number of people wanting Tom to represent them had risen to forty and most were present in the Crown meeting room. His decision to have post-mortems carried out was the right one, he had no doubt, as many relatives simply had no idea what their loved ones had died of. In many cases it could have been trauma, asphyxia, burning, loss of blood or a combination of all of them. It was important to know exactly which if there was to be a civil action.

He was also amazed to find that many of them had not seen the bodies. In most cases just one person had carried out the identification but other family members had subsequently been denied access. Des Niven, a burly, bald Jamaican, was in tears as he pleaded with Tom to make it possible. Hetty Mackay, a Trinidadian, was equally distressed.

"It's our custom, Mr Harrison, to wash our deceased and dress them; we make them look right to face their Lord. We care for our own; we don't leave it to some undertaker who's never seen them before in their life. It's our duty. We're not afraid of the dead."

Tom promised he would do his best but the problem was he had not been able to raise Caffrey and no one seemed to be sure where all the bodies were. They were distributed between mortuaries and undertakers in a fifteen-mile radius and some had been moved around as spaces became available in mortuaries closer to home. Permission had not been granted for any of them to be released for burial, even if they could be traced.

Mike had had problems finding a pathologist who was prepared to undertake the work as it seemed they were all too busy to cope with forty post-mortems. Tom hadn't seen Mike since much earlier in the day and had been expecting him back for the last two or three hours. Without some definite information he risked looking inefficient if not incompetent but as he was about to explain the situation to the group, Mike appeared through the door. Tom excused himself and went over to join him.

"Any luck?"

"Yeah, at last, but what a great list that was – half of them had turned their toes up. Anyway, it's a pathologistess and she makes the iron lady look like a powder puff, but she'll do it.

"Is she any good?"

"Let's put it this way. She's got so many letters after her name she sounds like a Welsh railway station."

"And the cost?"

"Well, she can't do them all herself and she's going to engage in a bit of subcontracting so it's going to take time but she reckons about three-hundred nicker a shot. Sound about right?" It did.

"Have you fixed a meeting for me to see her before I confirm it?"

"Yeah, the earliest I could, January the sixteenth."

"I suppose that will have to do – I'm away until the week before anyway. Ridiculous, isn't it? I feel guilty because I'm taking a holiday." It was a rhetorical question and Tom rejoined the group and called for their attention. He repeated the reasons why a post-mortem was necessary but when it came to outlining the costs it felt crass and insensitive but there wasn't any alternative. He suggested it was now time to start fundraising as this was not going to be the only expenditure.

When the evening came to an end only three families had taken the decision not to have a second post-mortem performed on their dead relatives. For the remainder, the decision was a painful one but they saw why it was necessary. Tom made his way over to Vicky and they walked to their cars in near silence. Seeing David had obviously become of major importance to her and Tom sensed she was suppressing her emotions and he could hear the tension in her voice.

"I went over to Hounslow earlier today and like you said, bodies have been moved – his was one of them and no one knows where it is now. It feels just like it did on the first night when I was running from one mortuary to another trying to find him. The big difference is I had hope then but now I've got none."

Tom pulled his overcoat collar up and round his throat. It was freezing. Vicky's coat was open but she seemed oblivious to the cold, looking ahead as she spoke, not even glancing at him.

"Can you help me – tomorrow – to try and find where he is; get me in to see him?

"It's the last Saturday before Christmas tomorrow, Vicky. I'm not going to be able to get anything out of anybody. What about Emma? Does she want to see him?"

"No, she really doesn't want to do that."

They walked in silence for a while and Tom could feel her mood deepening.

"There must be some people working tomorrow, for Christ's sake!" She almost shouted the words and although Tom knew it was illogical, he dreaded saying what he had to say next. He reminded himself forcibly that Vicky was just a client and she must understand he had a life to lead.

"I'm afraid I can't do it tomorrow in any case, Vicky, I'm going away."

"Oh yes, where to?" It was said as a challenge and not out of interest.

"Florence. It's been booked for a long time." He knew he

should stop there but Vicky's brooding silence forced him to continue talking and he felt the words jumbling together in their rush to be spoken. "It's an art holiday – paintings and sculptures by day, wine and pasta by night. I hate Christmas and just wanted to be away from all the hype and commercialism. I'm going with a friend."

"The man in the wine bar." It was a resentful statement not a question.

"Yes, Rob! How the hell did you know?" Tom sounded incredulous but Vicky wasn't listening. "How can they lose a dead body?"

"It won't be lost, it's just that everything's in chaos." Tom tried to answer as gently as he could but it had the effect of a spark in a petrol tank.

"Oh no, they've not lost it, just fucking mislaid it!" There was nothing vulnerable about her anger. It was hard and bitter and it almost frightened him. "Some wanking pen pusher treats my husband like a piece of shit and I'm supposed to sit back like the little woman and take it all. There, there, don't get upset, don't be hysterical, control yourself, we're doing all we can. Bollocks! I fucking hate jobsworths. I want to punch them in the face and see fear in their lifeless fucking eyes, anything to show me they can feel. They're a waste of fucking space. It should have been them who died, not David."

Vicky's voice had lost all its rounded, middle-class tone. It was pure Manchester. But what really disturbed Tom was the thought that she was probably capable of doing precisely what she threatened. He walked alongside her, barely daring to breath. What should he do? His instincts told him to keep quiet but he felt he should offer support, an arm round her, a calming word or two.

"Your school never equipped you to deal with women, did it?" The Manchester vowels had disappeared but the anger hadn't. "And it sure as fuck never prepared you for someone like me!" The words were almost spat out, as cold as the clouds of condensed breath in which they were wrapped.

They walked a few more paces in silence while he grasped at half-formed words in different recesses of his mind, desperate to respond. Vicky suddenly spun round and clutched him with both hands, her head barely coming up to his chin.

"I'm sorry, Tom, I'm really sorry. You've done nothing wrong, in fact you've done everything right. Please forgive me. Please help me to find him." Her body was close to his and he could feel her tension but there were no tears.

Tom was horrified by his first instinct, which was to lean down and kiss her, but he dismissed it as quickly as it came to him and could hardly believe that he had almost given in to the impulse.

"Of course I will, just as soon as I get back. I promise you, we'll find him." He almost apologised for going away but stopped himself. She tightened her hold on him and he could feel his apprehension rapidly turning into something much more worrying.

Wednesday, January 2nd, 1991, 8.45 a.m. Mike was already in the office when Tom arrived back from his Christmas holidays.

"Had a good time then?"

"Wonderful – great sculpture, superb food, excellent wines, magnificent paintings..."

Mike pointed to the abstract above Tom's desk. "Didn't you find anything to replace that bloody thing – you know, a nice female nude or that bridge across the river, the one with the shops on it that Hitler was going to blow up?"

"That is a signed, limited-edition David Tremlett ... a very fine print."

"... I know, I know, you've told me before – *Chickens on the Road to Mombasa*. Only I can't see if the poor buggers made it to the other side... Anyway, one bit of bad news for you. While you were away I was doing a bit of chatting around and about, trying to glean a bit more on inquests and it seems you've got yourself into a bit of mire, me old son."

"What, again? And what is it this time?"

"Well, you know you made a statement about Polly whatsername? That could screw you for representing anyone else – you can't be a witness and a brief at the same inquest, it seems."

Tom looked heavenwards. "Shit, shit, shit!" He paused and

fiddled with a pencil on his desk before speaking. "The only way it will come out is if I'm called to give evidence. With hundreds of victims, Mike, what are the chances of that, do you reckon? My estimation is that it's small to non-existent. They'll almost certainly read my statement as it's not particularly controversial, just bloody sad."

"So you'll risk it?" Mike asked.

Tom thought for a while. "Yes, I reckon so as my credibility won't be on the line..."

"Okay then, be it on your own head, mate. So what's on the agenda?"

Tom had thought of almost nothing else for the last couple of days. "Caffrey, he's top of my agenda. You got stuff to keep you busy?"

"And the rest!"

Tom could hardly believe his luck when at 9.00 a.m. sharp Mack Caffrey answered his call to the coroner's office.

"MacCaffrey." He said it as one word.

Tom gave him as much detail as he had of David's disappearance and asked for any information he might have, making every effort to keep any hint of antagonism out of his voice but it was with difficulty.

"Lost the chappie, have you?"

"No, Mr Caffrey, you've lost him – or at least someone has and what I'd like you to do, with urgency, if you don't mind, is find him again. His wife will be with me at 9.45 and naturally she's very upset so I'd like to know the exact situation by then." He was half tempted to add – *and if you don't, I'll set her loose on you.*

"I've got 523 bodies to keep track of, mister."

"I know, Mack, but she's very distressed." Tom softened his tone and came as close to grovelling as he was ever likely to. "I know you're busy but I'd really appreciate it if you would do what you can. The woman is distraught." Before he even realised he was going to say it, Tom added, "Find him and I owe you a big drink next time I see you."

"Leave it with me, laddie."

Thirty minutes later Caffrey was back on the phone, the purr of self-satisfaction clearly audible down the line.

"I have your chappie, Mr David Alan Denton, and he's here at Harrow mortuary."

"Thanks, Mack."

"Aye well. If there's nothing' else..."

"Whoa, whoa, just a minute," Tom shouted down the line as Caffrey was about to put the receiver down. "We'd like to arrange to see him."

There was silence from the other end.

"Hallo, Mack, can you hear me?"

"Aye, laddie, I can hear you but I don't like what you're saying."

"Why, what's the problem?"

"I'll tell you what's the problem, mister. I've got to check with the police to see if it's okay with them; I've got to check with the pathologist to see where he's at; I've got to check with the mortuary and I've got to be there when you see him. Do ye understand what I'm saying?"

"Yes, I do, but I'm afraid it really is necessary." Tom swallowed his pride and stroked, massaged and caressed Caffrey, assuring him that the sooner he got this one out of the way, the sooner Tom would be able to get off his back and finally it was agreed, albeit with great reluctance.

When Vicky was shown into his office it was with almost complete nonchalance that Tom said, "It's fine, all arranged for three o'clock today." Inside he was turning cartwheels.

Later that day, as Tom was about to leave the building, he passed Mike at reception talking to Miss Rush and said, as matter of factly as he could, that he was going to the mortuary and probably wouldn't be back until about five.

"The mortuary? Has he ever been to a mortuary before, Dasher?"

"Not as far as I'm aware," replied Miss Rush, "and don't call me Dasher." But she couldn't hide the pleasure that someone had devised a nickname especially for her, someone for whom she had a huge soft spot.

Caffrey and the mortuary attendant were in the office smoking when Vicky and Tom opened the door and the stench of acrid, stale smoke engulfed them. The moment Caffrey set eyes on Vicky his face took on what he would probably have described as a warm look of care and concern. In fact it was deeply lecherous and stopped just short of drooling.

"Aye, Mrs Denton, I presume." Vicky nodded. "My sincere condolences on the tragic loss of your husband..."

Vicky wafted the cigarette smoke away with her hand. "Yeah, sure. Can I see his body, please?"

"I know this can be very – upsetting..."

"I don't want words, Mr Caffrey, I just want to see my husband, all right?"

"Aye, as you wish, Mrs Denton." Caffrey hated being dismissed so peremptorily and snapped at the mortuary attendant. "What number is he, man?"

The attendant stubbed his cigarette out deliberately and got up with studied sloth. As he led them through into the mortuary he said to Mack Caffrey in a raised voice, which was meant to be heard by everyone, "I warned you, Mack, it ain't a pretty sight."

The cavernous white tile and stainless steel room echoed as they walked the length of it, the attendant checking numbers on what looked like large filing cabinet drawers. Having found the right one, he waited for the other three to catch up and then pulled the drawer open with a sudden and energetic tug. With a swish of metal runners the drawer reached the end of its travel and stopped with a jolt and as it did so, something perched on top of the body was dislodged and fell to the floor with a clatter like that of a frozen chicken being dropped. It skittered across the tiles until it hit the wall, rebounded and came slithering back towards them, coming to a halt in front of Vicky. It was unmistakably a frozen leg.

Vicky stared at the leg but did not immediately react. It was only when she raised her eyes to the frozen body in the drawer that Tom could see the horror in her face. He stepped forward, put his arm round her and quietly said, "Come and sit down."

There was no resistance as he moved her towards the office. He looked back at Caffrey and the attendant and snapped out, "Wait there, both of you!" It was an order.

Vicky sat at the desk in the smoke-ridden atmosphere of the

office. "I'm all right, honest. Just leave me alone for a minute."

Tom strode back into the mortuary and again looked silently on what had once been David Denton. One leg was missing from where it had been crushed, just above the knee and there was now no mystery where it had gone. A crude and jagged incision began just above the pubic bone, ran the length of his torso and terminated just below the chin. It had been sewn back together with a few crude stitches but between the stitches the cut gaped open, the freezing process having mellowed the bright red of blood and tissue to a dull brown. The top of his head had been sliced off about an inch above the brow. At the back of his head top and bottom sections of the skull met as though hinged but at the front, they were wide apart revealing the congealed interior. Tom imagined the two parts would snap together like scallop shells if he put his finger between them.

In one continuous movement, he turned away from the corpse, lowered his head and vomited on to the white-tiled floor. It splashed over his shoes and trouser bottoms and he could see from his watering eyes that it had also splattered Caffrey's shoes.

"Jesus fuck..." Caffrey yelled as he stamped his feet on the floor.

Tom searched for a tissue with which to wipe his mouth and eyes and not finding one, used the back of his hand.

"Who did this?" His voice was brittle with anger.

"It's the post-mortem, isn't it," replied the mortuary attendant but there was guilt in his voice and his eyes avoided Tom's.

"A pathologist did this? I can't believe it! Who was he? What was his name?"

Mack Caffrey's voice began to ooze like gravelly honey. "The Home Office doesn't have that many pathologists, Tom, and there's an awful lot of people to examine. Everyone's under pressure, terrible pressure, and sometimes you have to take short cuts. This isna murder, it's no more than a formality..."

With this closing of ranks a sudden realisation came to Tom. "He did it, didn't he?" Tom cut in, inclining his head towards the attendant. "A bloody mortuary attendant has been playing pathologist – with a spade by the look of it. I don't believe it."

"Aye well, needs must... He just did the incisions."

"Jesus Christ, it's like Sweeney Todd's kitchen. Why didn't you tell me that this excuse for an autopsy had been done?" Caffrey merely shrugged.

"I'll be talking to you later." Tom turned and walked towards the office. "And put that poor bastard's leg back where it belongs."

Vicky was sitting where he had left her but was leaning back in the chair staring at the ceiling.

"I'm okay," she said, looking at him. "Really I am. I'll survive."

"Shall we go?"

"Please."

They drove in silence until it was broken by Vicky asking for details and Tom explained what had happened. They again lapsed into silence.

"What does the word 'shrapnel' mean to you?" Vicky asked.

"Bits of an exploded bomb or shell, I suppose. Something like that," Tom replied. "Why?"

"There was a pile of autopsy notes in that office and I had a look through them. I was looking for David's but it wasn't there but there was one which said something like, 'Series of entry wounds – small, irregular perforations'. Then it had the word 'shrapnel' with a question mark after it."

"Good God! Did you see whose notes they were? Presumably one of the passengers?"

"No, it wasn't a passenger, it was someone on the ground – called Baker, lived in Station Road." She reached over and pressed a button on the central console and the passenger window purred open. "Tom, can you smell sick?"

CHAPTER EIGHT

Friday, January 4th, 1991, 10.00 a.m. If anything, Tom's anger had increased over the past couple of nights. He had been trying to raise Caffrey since before nine but without success. He was also irritated to find that Baker, whoever he was, was not one of his clients but he had no time to take it any further as his new commercial work looked set to take up most of the day. His first meeting with Wings of Sonning was on Monday and he needed to prepare for it. They would expect some serious attention.

On top of all this he was also being approached by people who had been injured in the crash and by those whose property had been damaged. The ways things were going it might be necessary to find another assistant or refer the work to other local firms, which might overcome unspoken parochial jealousies. As he was about to press the redial button the phone rang.

"Hey, Tom, how ya doing?" It was the nasal twang of Ailey Newman and he was not in the mood for her but forced himself to be polite.

When she asked if he fancied going to a party with her the following Saturday at Lincoln's Inn he automatically began to grope for excuses but hesitated as a thought occurred to him.

"Ailey, have you got a client with a deceased called Baker?"

"Might have," she replied.

"Come on, Ailey, I'm not poaching or anything – it'll just save me a lot of work if I know they've already got a lawyer!"

"Okay, they're mine."

"Thanks," Tom replied. "Hey, I've just checked and it's fine for Saturday. Give me a ring nearer the time."

Mike came in with an update. The Chilled Chicken

Emporium had not yet responded to their case and Tom guessed they would probably drag it out until the last minute – and that was a long way off. However, he needed to talk to Henderson and would probably have to go through the process of briefing counsel.

A date had been fixed for a county court hearing of the case against Charlie Hanson and his company, Giftique. Charlie had set up in competition with his previous employer after being dismissed and his contract of employment forbade him from conducting business within a fifty-mile radius of their premises, and his warehouse was, in fact, exactly fifty-three miles away. So the whole case revolved round whether sending goods by mail order into the fifty-mile zone constituted a breach of contract. Boring but important – to Charlie at any rate.

Tom wanted to see Caffrey but knew the man would avoid him so he figured the best chance was at lunchtime. He gave up on phoning and went directly to the snug of the White Hart; he thought it was a pretty safe bet –and he was right.

Without Tom to buy him the whisky, Caffrey had restricted himself to a pint and sat in one corner of the small room with a glutinous-looking meat pie and a dollop of brown sauce in front of him. There was a flicker of apprehension in his eyes when he saw Tom but Caffrey was too old a hand to be phased.

"Tom." The stubby yellow teeth made a fleeting appearance. "Awful shame about Wednesday; aye, an awful shame."

"I'd have called it a disgrace. Why didn't you warn her he'd already been cut up?"

"Tell you the truth, laddie, I didna know. I should have checked but you were in such an awfa rush..."

"Well, it's done now. Forty-two clients have now asked me to represent them and thirty-nine of them have authorised post-mortems.

"As you've seen, it's all under way, laddie."

"No, you don't understand. We want to conduct our own."

The silence was electric. Caffrey took a bite out of his pie, wiped his mouth with the back of his hand and took a long swig from his beer. His eyes never left Tom's but Tom held his stare.

Caffrey spoke quietly. "Why do you want another round of post-mortems?"

"I think that's my clients' business."

"Oh, is it now? But it's my business as to whether I let you. Two post-mortems, that's a waste of everyone's time."

"You can make life difficult, I've no doubt, but you can't prevent it. And while we're on the subject, I want copies of all the Home Office pathology reports which relate to my clients. Here's a list of them." He placed an envelope in front of Caffrey. "I'll update you with any new ones as they come in."

"Kiss my arse, mister!" He took another swig.

"A temptation I reckon I can resist, Caffrey. Just do your job."

"Listen, mister, some smart-arse, wet-behind-the-ears lawyer isna gonna turn this pantomime into a farce. Have you got that?"

Tom turned and left but not before he caught Caffrey's final words.

"Jesus, the man thinks he's Perry Mason!"

Monday, January 7th, 1991, 3.30 p.m. Andrew Glennister moved quickly from his Mercedes into the nondescript office of St John's Street and made his way to the room where Charles Astbury was waiting for him. Astbury was able to tempt him with a small, single malt whisky as neither of them had any pressing appointments for the rest of the day.

"What's new, Charles? Anything from Cardington?"

"Yes. They've found the flight recorders." Astbury's face had lost its usual rounded, privileged look and there were dark rings under his eyes and a greyish tinge to his skin.

Glennister sat forward. "Do they show anything? When are you going to announce it?"

"Hold on, Andrew, we have to be extremely circumspect about everything we do. We'll announce it in due course but there's not a lot of point in making a song and dance about it as they're both damaged beyond salvation. We've got all kinds of experts crawling all over them trying to piece them back together and extract information but I'm assured it's a fruitless exercise. But we'll wait until we know for sure."

Glennister took a large sip of whisky. "Anything else of interest?"

"Whose interest, Andrew?" Astbury's voice was cold as he gave a little mirthless chuckle. "I don't think there's much to interest you."

"Have you read the newspaper reports – the formation of this group, the Harrow Support Group? Who's the guy who's heading it up?" Do you know anything about him?" Glennister asked.

"I've got enough on my plate without concerning myself with some nonentity of a high street lawyer. He's a conveyancer, a contracts man and champion of the Valium-dosed, middle-aged, middle-class lady shoplifters. No doubt there'll be lots of bluff and bluster and he'll rattle a few threats in your direction, you'll pay him a few quid and I suspect that'll be the end of it."

"All the same, Charles, he's representing a lot of people and it could be very, very expensive. We need to know what he's got – he needs watching."

"And watched he is. Pour me a big one, please, Andrew. Christ, I need it! You've got insurance to cover you while my arse is hanging in the wind!"

Tuesday, January 15th, 1991, 2.00 p.m. Tom felt reasonably pleased with himself. He had spent time on the Wings of Sonning contracts and felt on top of things and was largely up to date on the litigation work. He was consciously pushing more and more work on to Mike, much of it work that would normally have been handled by someone on a training contract or even a legal executive but Mike was coping with it well. He buzzed for him.

The door swung open as Mike made his way in. "Yo!"

"The firm's library that you hold in such contempt – see what it's got on pathology, will you, Mike?"

"Now?"

"Now!"

"Decided to chop them up yourself, guv?" Mike saw the incredulous look on Tom's face and wished he had never spoken. "Sorry, Tom, out of order."

"I've got to hold a halfway intelligent conversation with someone tomorrow in the scientific equivalent of Mandarin Chinese. I want at least to look as if I know what I'm talking about." Tom's monotone delivery and the fact that he made no reference to Mike's tasteless remark was all the admonishment that was needed.

Mike went to check what publications they had but it was some time before he returned. When he did he was shaking his head.

"Nothing there?" Tom asked.

"No, not really, but there are a couple of real corkers. Listen to this – it's the scientific opinion of rape, and I quote, '*The allegation that there was no consent must be examined with great care, for a girl frequently concocts such a story after her arrival home, and when she is faced with giving some explanation to her mother to account for injury, blood stains on her clothing or a subsequent pregnancy.*' Can you believe that?"

"You're not serious?" Tom asked incredulously.

"Kosher! On me mother's life. *Forensic Medicine*, Simpson, 6th edition."

"When was it published? 1890?"

"No, 1969." Mike delivered the date syllable by syllable. "And it's still in use!" He offered the book to Tom with his finger on the frontispiece. "Look, there, 1969. But there's more – and if you're gay, Tom, then let me apologise up front. '*Recent years have seen a disquieting increase in homosexuality. "Homo" and "queer" have become almost playful epithets and the psychiatrist has done little but excuse or condone such practices. They are rotting the fabric of the Arts as well as the more solid principles of family life and the law properly regards such unnatural practices with a stern eye.*' Can you believe it? The law was changed in 1967 to make practising homosexuality legal but Mr Simpson's not having any of it. Off with their testicles, I say!"

"I'm not sure what this has got to do with an air crash. Is there anything in there that's useful?"

"I doubt it – all horrible pictures of people who've been strangled or had their brains blown out. Dear me, just look at that for a suicide."

Mike held up a picture of a man who had cut his own throat so completely that only the spine attached his head to his body.

The colour drained from Mike's face as he suddenly remembered what Tom had recently been through. "Jesus, sorry, Tom."

"It's okay."

"You're not going to puke, are you?"

"How did you hear about that?"

"Don't worry, there's only me and a half-million *Guardian* readers know about it."

"What?" Tom yelled.

"Only joking. Actually, it's a long story." Mike thought it better not to show him the diary piece which identified Tom by everything but name.

"Hang on a minute – is there anything there on entry and exit wounds?" He took the book and skimmed through it, wincing at some of the pictures, but found what he was looking for. "Here we are, bullet wounds, stabbings, blunt instruments. That bit at least might be useful."

Mike produced another, slim little book, not much more than a booklet. "Now, if you just want a bit of basic info on the body and the right words to use, then I reckon this is the one – Faber's *Anatomical Atlas*. Do you know where your *extensor carpi radialis longus* is?"

"No, but knowing you I'd guess it's somewhere below my waist and above my knee."

"Wrong – muscle in your arm. You realise you can make yourself look a bit of a pillock if you learn a few technical phrases parrot-fashion but can't answer any questions about them. Like a foreign language – 'My postillion has been struck by lightning!' 'Oh, really, sir, would that be the 1975, side-valve, crank-operated postillion or the '83 double-reciprocating, bevelled-flange postillion with optional centrifuge?'"

"A postillion is a person, Mike!" But Tom knew he was right.

On his way home that evening Tom called in to Sainsbury's for some bread and frozen dinners and close to the checkout was a carousel of books and on special offer was the *Sainsbury Book of First Aid*. There was no reason for it but he felt embarrassed as he slipped a copy surreptitiously into his basket, pushing it beneath a packet of noodles. He couldn't believe that Ailey Newman was ever reduced to such things.

Wednesday, January 16th, 1991, 3.30 p.m. Christine Olins did not seem overjoyed that she was being offered a pathology contract worth some ten thousand pounds, in fact she appeared irritated by the workload it represented. She was not a warm person but despite her forthright manner, she exuded competence and efficiency.

Sensible suit, pearl necklace, low-heeled shoes and functional bobbed hair, showing the first streaks of grey, all seemed somehow right, thought Tom – the identikit of what you would expect a forty-something female pathologist to look like. She produced similar feelings to a doctor with greying temples and warm hands – she was confidence-inspiring.

"Why do you want second post-mortems?" Tom hadn't expected the question, assuming she would automatically understand. He told her as much and added his concern about Home Office standards.

"I'm extremely disturbed by the state of at least one of the bodies – and probably several others. The PM wasn't carried out by a pathologist but by the mortuary attendant."

"It's not unusual where there are multiple deaths and you're not really expecting to find anything very revealing." The bubble of confidence which enveloped Ms Olins had just been punctured.

Tom ignored it and continued. "I'm also having problems with the coroner's officer, who's refusing to allow me to see the other path reports – and he promises to be as difficult as possible in allowing access for you to do your stuff."

"You must have done something to upset him. It's highly unusual to refuse to pass on pathology reports where there is a genuine interest. Anyway, he doesn't have the power to prevent me from doing my job and I have every right to ask for copies of the first path reports on all the victims you've authorised me to examine."

"What about the ones who aren't my clients?"

"No, you won't necessarily be allowed access to those unless

I'm being asked to make a judgement, in which case I could ask for the notes on anyone who might assist that judgement. Why do you ask?"

Tom explained about the Baker report and the use of the word 'shrapnel'.

Christine Olins's eyebrows did not even twitch in interest. "Doesn't mean much. It was someone on the ground, you say? An exploding Calor gas cylinder or something like it could easily produce shrapnel-type wounds. Home Office pathologists probably do a fair bit of army work and it's exactly the type of description they'd use. I doubt there was anything untoward."

Tom was annoyed. It seemed that if he raised anything of interest, Christine Olins's first reaction was to diminish it, to explain it away. It wasn't the spirit of enquiry he had hoped for and the irritation showed in his voice. "Well, I'd still like to see the Baker notes."

"It won't be easy. Perhaps if any of your other bodies have something in common with Baker, for instance they lived in the same street, we could then look for common causation and I could legitimately ask to see the notes. That's one possibility. Do you have any clients in that street?"

"To be honest, I don't know – just a minute." Tom fished a file out of a box and quickly looked through it. "Damn! No, not one."

"Not much I can do then," she said with no trace of concern.

"All I'm trying to do is find out as much as I can to help my clients and it's turning into a three-ring circus."

"Taking it all a bit personally, aren't you?"

"Yes, I am – that's probably because I am personally involved. Okay?"

"Well, we'll just have to do our best then, won't we? Did your clerk explain that I have a pretty heavy workload and I'll be doing them in batches? A colleague will have to do at least ten of them."

Tom nodded, feeling it was now probably immaterial who did the work as he had no great hopes of discovery. "When can you start?"

"I'm dependent upon the availability of the Home Office pathologist."

"He's got to be there?"

"Of course."

"Yes, of course." Tom was angry that he had revealed his complete lack of knowledge of the procedures involved and felt he now had the word 'amateur' stamped across his forehead. "Anyone else?"

"The police, naturally. So, by the time you've co-ordinated all those dates it probably won't leave a great deal of choice. It's going to take several weeks." Christine Olins got up, indicating it was time for her to leave.

Tom felt distinctly unhappy with the relentless, grindingly slow process which he knew he couldn't hurry. It was like a great glacier carving inexorably but almost imperceptibly through rock and he doubted he would ever get used to it.

"Ms Olins, I want you to be extremely circumspect about what you say in front of the police and the other pathologists, the mortuary assistants, coroner's officer or anyone else who's there when you perform your post-mortems, is that clear?" He ignored the slight cast of her eyes towards the ceiling. "I want you to pay particular attention to the types of injuries, their possible causes and anything which appears unusual."

Tom still had the word 'shrapnel' floating in his mind and its possible origins. No matter how remote his suspicions, he did not intend to abandon them yet. "With a civil action pending, I also want clear and unequivocal causes of death and a judgement from you on those victims whose injuries might not have resulted in immediate death – those who might have survived if they'd received prompt treatment. I'll put all this in writing to you, okay?"

After he had seen Christine Olins down to reception, Tom called in to Mike's office and pointed accusingly at him. "I'm going to give you a thrashing tonight."

Mike tried to cut the blue ball into the left centre pocket but it rattled in the jaws and remained on the table, perched a millimetre from the edge. Fortunately for him, the white had kicked on a speck of chalk dust and instead of running down the table to finish up in a perfect position to pot the only available red, near the bottom right pocket, it skewed behind the pink.

Tom peered down the table and decided that the pot was still on. "Not on your life," said Mike. Tom cued the white and it struck the red cleanly, sending it into the pocket with a satisfying 'plop'.

"Luck or what?" Mike emptied his beer glass.

"Luck never came into it," said Tom as he began to clear the table with a series of quick and fluent cue strokes. Mike could only stand and watch. "I hope you're as good at soliciting!"

"No gamesmanship, Mr Smith."

The last ball dropped into the pocket. "Pint?" enquired Mike.

"Please."

"You set 'em up while I get the drinks."

Tom racked the balls and when Mike returned with the drinks, he set them down, picked up his cue and broke. He made a hash of it and again Tom set about punishing him for his mistake.

"Do you know what this Harrow case reminds me of?" asked Mike. "It reminds me of when I was a nipper at my dad's warehouse. I set off a fire extinguisher thinking I'd just let a little bit of foam out of the nozzle to see what it was like and then stop it. No one would ever be the wiser. I pulled out the pin, pressed the handle and the bloody foam came out like Vesuvius. I tried stuffing my finger up the hole, wrapping my shirt round it; I even tried aiming it down the plughole in the sink, and the worst bit was, all the time I was trying to stop it I knew I was going to get one hell of a walloping."

"What are you trying to say, Mike?" Tom could go no further with his break and played an almost perfect safety shot against the baulk cushion.

Mike went to the table. "I reckon you've just set off the biggest bloody fire extinguisher since Noah's flood and I hope it doesn't finish up with us all getting a good hiding – metaphorically speaking, if you understand what I mean." He potted a red with a brilliant shot.

"We'll see."

"Don't take offence, Tom, but do you reckon you know what you're doing? We've never handled anything like this before."

"I haven't had those doubts since the first day. If there's anything to find, Mike, I'll find it, I'm absolutely determined. I know we banter about but we can only do that because we trust each other. There's something big here, all my instincts tell me so and I think it's going to get hairy at times. On this one, you're really going to have to trust me."

"Well, the clients seem to. Do you think they know you're making it all up as you go along?"

"I think one of them might!"

"Vicky?"

"Yep!"

Mike went quiet while he tried to pot a colour – the blue – but missed. "Why are you so set on the pathology, Tom?" They continued to swap places at the table.

"Because at the moment it's all we've got. Just think about it, there's an aircraft that was somewhere it shouldn't have been – that's all we know. All the physical evidence from that is in someone else's hands and the only things under our control are the bodies. It's probably a waste of time but if they hold any clues at all, we need to know."

"What about her ladyship, Chris the Impaler?"

"To be honest, I'm beginning to think that all pathologists..." he struggled for a simile.

"Piss in the same pot?" offered Mike.

"Exactly!"

"So where do you go from here?"

"Hang on a minute. When you want to distance yourself from something it's always 'you'; when you want to be part of it, it's 'we'. This is a 'we' situation. 'We' wait for the PMs and keep our fingers crossed." Tom took the frame and began to rack the reds.

"And if it's not a rude question, what the fuck are we looking for?"

Tom took an inordinate length of time to place the triangle in exactly the right position. "What are we looking for,

Sherlock?" repeated Mike.

Tom looked directly at him. "I haven't got a clue!"

"Well, I'm glad we cleared that one up. I thought for a minute you weren't in control."

They started the third frame.

"The way I see it, Mike, we're trying to hold together a bunch of clients with three different interests. There are the Esther Vines, who just want the whole thing to go away. Then there's the Bernard lot who want to take the money and run but the majority are probably behind Vicky, wanting to know what happened. That's certainly my motivation."

As he spoke, Tom was aware that he had never considered the whole case at any point – where it might go and what the various pitfalls might be – what the long-term implications were. Because the thought of it was so overwhelming he was engrossing himself in the minute-by-minute, hour-by-hour demands of simply coping with people's raw emotions and attempting to act as a weather vane for them, absorbing their grief and anger and running it to ground.

Tom continued to fiddle and faff around with the triangle and almost as though he could read his boss's thoughts, Mike stood silently by, taking a sip from his glass from time to time, allowing Tom the latitude to reach his own conclusions.

In Tom's mind, the similes piled one on top of the other. One moment he saw himself as a shepherd trying to marshal self-willed sheep with little success. The next he was a Don Quixote tilting at establishment windmills that were only in his mind. And then he was a builder faced with constructing an edifice that rivalled the Great Wall of China and not only had he not even laid the first brick, he was still waiting for planning permission.

An outburst of cheering from a nearby table brought Tom back to reality and he was surprised to find he had his drink in his hand as he had no recollection of setting up the table. He looked at Mike, who stood watching with an expression of benign tolerance. Tom realised that he would not have felt the freedom to clamber through his own thoughts so exclusively in anyone else's company.

"What do you reckon, Mike? Am I a prat? Am I going to let

everyone down? Should I back out and let them find a proper solicitor to represent them?" Tom placed an emphasis on the word *proper*, as though it was in quotation marks.

Mike potted a red before replying, placed his cue on the side of the table, placed his forefinger on his chin and pursed his lips in a pretence at thinking. "Now let me see ... well, there's some good news and some bad news. Let's start with the bad news. First, there's the little inconvenient factor that you know absolutely fuck all about any of this but we won't worry about that right now. More importantly, you're about to take on a multinational corporation who's probably got more lawyers on their books than Arsenal has supporters. Or it just might turn out to be a bunch of Arabs with a death wish and a penchant for blowing people up. Or, of course, it might be that the government has got its sticky little fingers in there somewhere with its own agenda entirely. And you never know it could be all of them but not to worry because we've got our Sainsbury's First Aid Book.

"Brown," he said, nominating the colour ball, picked up his cue and missed. "Bollocks." Having replaced the cue on the side of the table again Mike continued.

"I remember once, when I was a kid and interested in the Romans, seeing a drawing – an etching or something, of the arena. Two huge blokes were tying a teenage girl to four oxes – one for each arm and leg and all facing in different directions. They were then going to whack the oxes to make them pull and keep whacking them until the girl was torn apart. It was their idea of fun. I think you've just got yourself hitched up to four oxes, mate!" Mike smiled at him serenely.

Tom smiled unconvincingly. "And the good news? Don't tell me, we've got a rates rebate?"

"The good news, my son, is that I would back you to chart a path through all this crap better than anyone else I know. If I was one of these poor buggers who'd lost a loved one, I'd think myself very fortunate to have you in my corner..." Mike's voice left a question hanging.

Tom looked genuinely embarrassed by the sentiment and answered quietly, "Thanks, Mike, I appreciate that but there's a bit more, isn't there?"

"But we're just not equipped for it, Tom." Mike suddenly became very serious. "Let me tell you another little tale. Remember the Yorkshire Ripper case? The police investigation lasted years and they took over two thousand statements and thousands of other pieces of information and it was all bleedin' useless because they couldn't cross-reference anything and it became just an exercise in gathering bits of information that no one could access or do anything with—"

"But that was before computers," Tom interrupted.

"Oh, how bloody silly of me, Tom, no lessons for us there, then? Mate, we don't even have a little green Amstrad – nothing. I can't remember all the details but there were about nine points that would have helped them identify the killer – his appearance, his occupation, the fact that he was a regular in the Chapel Town hooker area, there was some marked money or something that the killer would probably have had, and so on and so on. Peter Sutcliffe scored on seven out of the nine points and it was all on record but no one clocked it. Jesus Christ, there was even a statement from a copper saying he thought that Sutcliffe could well be the killer and should be gone through with a fine toothcomb – but nothing happened because once it was filed it disappeared.

"Know how they got him in the end? Pure chance! A plod clocked him with a tart and did a PNC check on his registration plate and it came back as phoney. Took him in and he tried to stash a knife in the cistern. Pure bloody chance."

"Okay, Mike, you've made your point, we'll get a computer."

"No, mate, you still don't get it. Our office is a technology-free zone. It isn't just about getting a computer, we need a computer system. Everyone in the building should have a computer and they should all be linked together by a server so we can talk to each other electronically, access each other's information – heaven forbid, maybe even access the world wide web.

"We need laser printers, a scanner –" Mike saw the look of bemusement on Tom's face – "a bit like a photocopier that lets you put copies of original documents on to your computer. We should have mobile phones – they're getting better and smaller all the time. Jesus, Tom, you can't even programme your VCR.

And we haven't got a fax machine – do you want me to go on?"

Tom looked suddenly pleased. "Wrong, wrong, wrong! I got Miss Rush to order one two days ago..."

"Problem solved, then!" Mike delivered the words with exaggerated enthusiasm. "If you're to stand half a chance you're going to have to invest in all this – but more than that, you're going to have to change your thinking, Tom. You've got to get to grips with new technologies and see how it can change your working life. And while you're at it, we could do with a little video camera for recording crime scenes, that kind of thing. They're amazing quality now."

Tom thought for a moment. "You're right – I know you're right. Pull it all together, Mike, let me know the cost and I'll battle it out with Dad."

"He'll say no."

"I'll do it anyway."

"That's my man!"

Finally, they turned their attention back to the game of snooker and as Tom sighted along his cue Mike spoke again but this time his voice was low and much more intimate. "Vicky's a cracker, isn't she?" It was a rhetorical question. "And if I'm not mistaken, old son, you're showing a bit of ... how shall I put it...?" Mike paused. "Your interest isn't entirely professional, if you get my drift. Getting a bit fond, aren't you?"

Tom answered just a little too quickly and a little too aggressively. "Don't be stupid, Mike."

"Oh, I'm not so sure... Uncle Mike's got a fair bit of form in this department and his little peepers tell him different. All I'm saying is, Thomas, my boy, be very, very careful. One ping of knicker elastic and your career's down the plughole a bloody sight faster than my foam. Know what I mean?"

Thursday, January 17th, 1991, 9.15 a.m. Miss Rush hurried urgently upstairs with a formal, crisp white envelope embossed on the rear with a coat of arms signifying it had come from Her Majesty's Coroner.

"Must be George," said Tom, more to himself than Miss Rush. "Maybe he's got the hump over the post-mortem business or perhaps Dad has been sticking his oar in." He slit the envelope carefully with the knife he had been using on his toast and the hovering Miss Rush could see he was caught off guard by its contents and asked if there was anything more she could do.

"Thanks ... no ... just tell Mike the coroner is notifying all interested parties that he has deferred the opening of all inquests until March because of the magnitude of the task. Gives us a bit more time, I suppose."

Wednesday, February 13th, 1991 In terms of creating chaos, the timing was perfect. Another pile of boxes arrived at exactly the same moment as a large stationery delivery and the new photocopier. Miss Rush fluttered from one to the other, not quite sure what had happened to her world and terrified she would never master this new piece of machinery.

The boxes full of statements, background information and path reports joined the pile which had already accumulated in Tom's office and the only obvious advantage from this expanding volume of material was that it covered the threadbare patch in his carpet.

Harry Harrison appeared but only to shake his head and cluck just loud enough to be heard before disappearing. The previous four weeks had flown by but not enough time had elapsed to completely erase the embarrassment of Tom's date with Ailey Newman.

Lincoln's Inn had only been the meeting point and the whole party entourage had piled into cabs and driven up the Strand to the beautifully vaulted Georgian wine cellars belonging to Cunningham's of Piccadilly, hidden beneath Trafalgar Square. Cunningham's was introducing its new range of wines and the waiters moved deftly across the flagstoned floors carrying an endless supply of full glasses. What had begun with ostentatious sniffing and swirling, sipping and swishing around the palate, rapidly deteriorated into raucous laughter and voices raised loudly enough to be heard above the hubbub.

Ailey flitted from one group of guests to another – all shimmering silk, cleavage and perfume, marred only by a voice that could grate nutmegs. All the male guests appeared to be very successful commercial barristers and as Tom had little interest in either them or their work he spent the evening largely alone, hovering on the periphery of many different conversations, none of which enticed him to join in. He tasted a great deal of wine and knew he'd overdone it when he found his knees involuntarily buckling as he leant his head against the lavatory wall to urinate.

Towards the end of the evening he was eventually trapped by someone who had heard of his involvement with the Harrow disaster and was surrounded by a group of dinner-jacketed lawyers. They were in good spirits and it seemed every exchange had to end in a laugh. These were not the circumstances in which to discuss Harrow, Tom decided, but the men would not let the subject drop.

"A nice little earner, I would think," said one very pompous barrister who had the habit of emitting tiny globules of spittle from between his buck teeth. "You should be able to make your clients a pretty penny, I shouldn't wonder – not to mention yourself."

When Tom said, "My clients are more interested in why their relatives died than what they can make out of them," it sounded trite even to him.

"Very laudible," chortled the man.

Tom later swore to Ailey that what happened next was not intentional. His glass of red wine slipped from between his fingers and plummeted to the ground and unfortunately, it remained perfectly upright throughout the descent and when it hit the floor, wine shot upwards and outwards like a fountain, covering the white shirt fronts of everyone in the circle, including the buck-toothed barrister. There was absolute silence.

Tom inclined his head politely, said, "Gentlemen," turned and walked away. The tears of laughter in his eyes obscured the step three paces distant and the perfect exit ended when he tripped over it and fell flat on his face.

Ailey rescued him and they walked down to the Embankment. It was a cold but beautiful night and the skeletal fingers of the leafless trees in Savoy Gardens were etched in white by hoar frost, and the sounds of city traffic had diminished to a barely audible hum. It seemed natural for him to put his arm round her shoulders and when she laid her head against his cheek that also felt natural. When they stopped and she reached up and kissed him, he felt a surge of passion which had been absent for far too long.

"Tom?" Ailey inclined her head towards the Savoy Hotel. "They have some very, very big and very, very warm beds in there. What say we curl up in one?"

"Anything you say, Ms Newman." He returned her kiss and it was only then that he remembered his reason for accepting her invitation.

"I-have-a-favour-to-ask-Ailey." It came out as one long slur.

"Shoot!" She had a terrible knack of sounding like a B-movie actress.

"Would you show me the path report on your Baker client?"

"Why?"

"I'll be honest with you. There's something in it that really interests me."

"What?" Ailey disengaged herself and he could feel her warmth evaporating.

"It might show there was some kind of explosion after it crashed." The moment he had said it he could have kicked himself. He'd had no intention of letting her know he'd glimpsed the report and even less that he was pursuing any kind of explosion theory. It was the drink.

Ailey stood almost to attention. "Get one thing straight, you asshole. If there's any talk, any suggestion of explosions, I don't want to know about it, you understand. And even more important, I don't want Varsity to know about it. You got that? If some Mick or crazy Arab blew that plane out of the sky it's of no concern to me. I don't want to hear about anything that'll let Varsity off the hook. They're gonna pay and the fact that you came out with me just so you could see a report makes me really pissed. What were you going to do, Tom, screw me in exchange for it? Christ, you must rate yourself or even worse, you must reckon I'm so low I'm not even worth considering. Go fuck yourself!"

She turned and strode off towards the hotel leaving Tom swaying in the middle of the gardens and he wanted the ground to open up and swallow him. He could hear the tears in her voice and identified the personal rejection that lay behind her hurt but it was not until he had sobered up that the full import of what she had said sank in.

Over the following couple of weeks he'd phoned her several times because she was totally in the right and he felt ashamed and wanted her to know it. He had even despatched a large bunch of flowers but in return had received a formal letter asking him to confirm acceptance of her offer to be her firm's UK agent. He was still thinking about it.

Tom went down the stairs and sorted through the boxes until he found the one containing the final batch of pathology reports, picked it up and returned to his office, shouting "Later," over his shoulder in response to Miss Rush's panic about what was to go where.

Each time he looked through a report he found himself convinced that pathology was less a science and more a black art. Christine Olins was thorough, no question about that, and each report produced many lines of typescript but unfortunately, none of his books was much help in understanding them.

Faber's *Anatomical Atlas* at least enabled him to identify the bits of body referred to and Tom frequently found himself holding Faber in one hand while feeling himself with the other, trying to identify subcutaneous muscles and organs.

It was just such a day when Miss Rush quietly entered the room to see him bending forward, one hand holding the book, the other reaching back through his open thighs squeezing his buttocks. He was searching for his *gluteus medius* and *gluteus maximus* but whatever explanation he might have given her, he felt it unlikely she would have believed it. As a consequence he did not even try.

He found the whole process of trying to interpret the pathology reports rather depressing. When the pathologists' comments were reduced to their essence, they said very little. There were long descriptions of the state of the clothing and equally verbose explanations of the injuries and then they trolled through the external appearance of the body, internal appearance and, in the case of Ms Olins's reports, a detailed account of the procedures carried out by the previous pathologist, with all the bruising and discoloration which had developed as a result of that investigation.

When it came to the bottom line, there were but a few sentences of any real value and even those rarely carried a critique. He was angry to see that in many cases she had not even detailed a clear cause of death, the very thing he had asked for. In fact, there was little to choose between the original path reports and the ones she had prepared and when they were considered all together, they confirmed his worst fears – he still had very little to go on. There was a bit of useful information in a few cases, which helped to support the contention that, promptly treated, some people might have lived, but there was not a lot else.

Tom turned to the morning's mail and it seemed par for the course when the first letter he picked up was from Mack Caffrey giving a date in March for the inquest – Thursday 7th at 9.30 a.m. It sounded extremely familiar and Tom immediately checked with his diary – it was on the same day as the Giftique case, which was at 2.00 p.m. He was double-booked and there was no way he could do both.

He phoned Caffrey and the distinctive gravelly voice answered.

"Mr Caffrey, what would you say if I told you I wanted the inquest postponed?"

"I'd say 'on your bike', laddie!"

"It's a serious request."

"Aye and it's a serious answer. You've had all your path reports, is that right?"

"Got the last ones today – but there's lots of other stuff I'm waiting for." Tom was trying to keep the desperation out of his voice.

"Such as?"

"Well, you must remember. I wrote to you a couple of weeks ago asking for copies of the statements by Varsity Aviation, the police statements, eyewitness accounts, emergency services, Peter Thornton and all the rest. I haven't received a single one – not one! The inquest is three weeks away and even if I get all this stuff tomorrow it's got to be read and considered. I can't possibly do it in the time. It's got to be postponed."

The response was a dry and humourless chuckle. "You haven't quite got the hang of this, have you, laddie? We get the statements, you don't. That's how it works."

Tom couldn't believe what he was hearing. "What do you mean?"

"I mean you don't get them, you're not entitled to them."

"Don't talk crap, Caffrey."

Caffrey's response was another low chuckle. "Oh dear me, you're quite a comedian, laddie, so let me spell it out for you. You have no entitlement to see sweet bugger all. Aye, you can go direct to the different people involved and ask them if they don't mind giving you copies of their statements and maybe some of them will – but maybe some of them won't. But the Coroner's Office has no obligation to give you even the time of day, do you understand me? The statements are for the coroner's eyes alone and no one else's."

Tom was floundering. "But that's not how courts work. You can't prepare your case if you don't know what the other side is saying."

"That's how this court works. Now, just to save you a wee bit of time – I wouldn't bother asking the police nor Varsity because I don't reckon they'll be too sympathetic."

Tom knew instinctively that Caffrey was right and the realisation turned his anger into panic.

"Okay, let's try it another way! What witnesses does the coroner intend to call?"

"That's for me to know and you to wonder about..."

"You're not even going to tell me that?"

"No, laddie – you have no right to know. Now if that's all?"

Tom hung up and anger flooded back over him. He had an inquest in three weeks and was armed with virtually nothing. What kind of system was he dealing with? It wasn't only his ignorance; no one seemed to know much about them. Inquests appeared to operate in their own little world – a world he simply did not understand.

The phone rang – it was Ailey. She was the last person he wanted to speak to at this moment – Ms Confident Efficiency meets Mr Stupid. Chickens everywhere were fluttering home to roost, it seemed, but despite his reluctance Tom didn't hesitate to launch straight into his apology. It was as heartfelt and sincere as any apology he'd ever made.

"You owe me a drink, asshole!"

"Tonight?"

"Deal."

Tom felt slightly happier.

CHAPTER NINE

Wednesday, March 6th, 1991, 9.30 p.m. Tom flicked the remote at the CD player and increased its volume until sound filled the room, drowning out the distant drone of traffic. Ella Fitzgerald's magical tones swept over him…

"Every time we say goodbye, I die a little…
Every time we say goodbye, I wonder why a little…"

He lay prostrate on the sofa, his head on one of its overstuffed arms, feet on the other, reading glasses in one hand and a glass of white wine in the other. A file lay open on his chest and on the floor beside him were several others. He raised his head and drank from the glass.

"… who must be in the know?
Why they think so little of me, they allow you to go."

He metaphorically floated to the ceiling and looked down on himself. Thirty- years old, no wife, no children, no girlfriend – currently, at any rate – and a career that seemingly had made absolutely no impact on the world. A two-bedroom flat in a little block that someone had grandly called Manley Court – a block which estate agents described as 'compact and economic'; 'suitable for modern living'; 'ideal for the professional'. All euphemisms for small and boring as it sat almost unnoticed on the hill which was Harrow on the Hill.

To the left was a kitchen in which the washing-up hadn't been done for a day or two – but that wasn't unusual; to the right, a bedroom which the cleaning lady regarded with great suspicion. On that particular evening, in his current frame of mind, Tom felt far from successful. It was definitely time for a change.

> *"... but how strange the change, from major to minor,*
> *Every time we say goodbye..."*

He took another sip, a big one, and pressed the replay button. He wasn't a bad bloke – in fact he reckoned he was probably quite decent really. Bit short-tempered at times, sometimes drank a bit too much but pretty honest by and large. His greatest fear was that he should be seen as nice – just that, nothing else, nice! Mediocre, halfway competent, the kind of bloke old ladies liked. "He's so nice, dear!" Please, anything but that!

It was seldom that Tom felt like this and he knew the reason. He had done everything in his power to represent his clients in the support group to the best of his ability and so far had got nowhere. Was it his fault or was there simply nothing to discover? Either way, the inquest opened tomorrow and although it wasn't the most important event in the world, it would have been good to be able to toss something into the pool of discovery – something that would cause a few ripples and make Varsity sit up. He had wanted them to know they had a fight on their hands but as it was, it felt like Mike Tyson versus John-Boy Walton.

To make matters worse, his father was observing closely from a ringside seat with an irritating, *I told you so* look on his face. Tom had had to tell him about the double-booking of Giftique and the inquest and his explosion was short-lived but entirely predictable; the brittle peace which followed had produced three days of tight lips and monosyllables.

Tom had arranged an agent to stand in for him in the Giftique case and he still desperately hoped to be there but not knowing the running order of the inquest, he had to face the possibility that he might not. If he lost it because of his absence, the strains between Harry and himself could very possibly become intolerable. In fact, if he lost the case at all he would be accused of inadequate preparation, lack of interest or some such failure of duty and it might even be true.

Caffrey had, of course, been right and neither police nor Varsity had furnished him with copies of their statements, and solicitors representing Eric Lloyd's estate had openly laughed at him when he had asked for theirs. He did have those of the ambulance and fire services and they were useful in establishing the inadequacy of the resources with which they had tried to cope but despite that, Tom felt at a complete loss. The inquest was in the lap of the gods and the whole process felt totally antiquated.

He had seen Ailey a few times but their relationship had remained platonically professional with just a hint of possible naughtiness but he knew he felt no real passion for her – although perhaps a little lust. He had not dared broach the Baker pathologist report again and had found no other means of gaining access to it.

He took another sip and allowed Ella to move on to *Manhattan* and it was during the pause between tracks he heard the door buzzer and Vicky's voice on the entryphone. That was a first. In the couple of minutes it took her to climb the two flights of stairs, Tom had scooped up the dirty dishes and deposited them in the laundry basket, tidied papers, thrown shoes into the back of a cupboard and when he had finished, the flat looked exactly what it was – a bachelor flat that someone with no interest in it had tried to tidy in a hurry.

"Hi, this looks cosy," Vicky said, looking very pleased with herself.

"Take a seat, if you can find one that's not infectious. The good news is, the outbreak of bubonic plague in the left-hand corner of the kitchen was eliminated this morning and the pest control people say they only need one more visit."

"Lived in, I'd say." She collapsed on to the sofa.

"This is unexpected. Are you going to tell me?" Tom asked.

"I might." She picked up his glass and took a sip from it. "Jesus, Tom, you've got to stop buying Australian Chardonnay!" Despite that, she took a long drink from the glass and when finished she handed it back to him before smugly removing a piece of lined paper from her handbag. All that was written on it were the words *Edward Veezey, 27*

Station Road, now living with his sister Nellie Ford, followed by a Ruislip address.

"Yes?" he asked.

"His wife was a victim of the disaster, lived two doors away from the Bakers. He must be nearly ninety, doesn't have a penny but would like you to represent him – well at least his sister would. She's only eighty."

"How did you make contact?"

"She wrote to the support group asking if we had any men's clothes because the poor old fellow had only what he was standing up in at the time. It's obviously been awful for him. He went off for his usual weekly therapy at the day centre and couldn't understand why they wouldn't take him back home afterwards. He's only just accepted that his wife is dead. They were married for nearly seventy years."

"Of course, he doesn't realise what's involved if I represent him, does he? Post-mortem and all that stuff."

"I don't suppose so, not yet. I've said very little to them but it could mirror Baker's path report."

"Yes, I realise that. 'Excuse me, Mr Veezey, but could I arrange to slice up your beloved wife in order to get my hands on some papers that might or might not be of use to me?'" He dropped down on to the sofa next to Vicky. "God, Vicky, it's horrible, isn't it?"

Vicky topped up his glass and handed it to him. "Oh shut up! She's dead, for Christ's sake. Now, have you got anything that's more drinkable than this?"

Tom ended the evening in a lighter mood than he began it.

Thursday, March 7th, 1991, 8.30 a.m. When Tom arrived at the arranged rendezvous, under the arch of the old fire station, Vicky and Bernard were already waiting. Within minutes Ailey arrived, invited as an observer, but the atmosphere between her and Vicky reminded Tom of crisp, thin, early morning ice on the lawn, splintering underfoot no matter how gently you stepped on it. Esther had declined to attend and together the four of them walked round the side of the building and into the court entrance.

Opposite Caffrey's office was a broad flight of dimly lit stone stairs with a brass handrail which descended into the basement, turning back on itself from a half-landing. On the half-landing was a lavatory and as they passed it, the door swung open as someone exited and they were enveloped in the smell of hot bowels. Other, well-dressed people were also heading down into the gloom of the Coroner's Court.

"I've been down more inviting bloody mineshafts," Bernard offered to no one in particular.

The staircase ended in a small and inadequate waiting area which was crowded and all of them, not least Tom, were surprised by the number of people milling around. There was literally nowhere to stand and so they went straight through the single mahogany and stained-glass door which gave access to the court itself.

Tom had already reconnoitred it and knew that the bench on which he was supposed to sit was immediately on the right of the entrance. In fact the whole layout was unusual and very different to an ordinary court. The room was comparatively small, no more than about forty feet long and facing them as they entered, taking up the entire end wall, was the coroner's bench – elevated, commanding and designed to convey a sense of magisterial importance. Below it, on ground level, was an ordinary chair for the coroner's officer – Mack Caffrey.

Along the left-hand side wall were jurors' benches and above them, at high level, a line of frosted windows covered in pigeon shit. In the centre of the court was a rectangle of benches for relatives, to the right the witness bench and a lawyers' bench with its own lectern. The back of the court was taken up with two benches for the public and presumably press, for the rare occasions when they attended inquests. Scratched and carved messages ennobled the backs of them – 'Mickey '84', 'Danno rules', 'Tossers'. The last trace of varnish had long since disappeared from the parquet flooring, leaving a matt and splintering, tan-coloured surface.

At the time it was converted, there had obviously been some attempt to imbue the space with a sense of dignity, hence the abundance of solid mahogany. Its subterranean position, however, and lack of light, lack of maintenance and presumably lack of interest had long ago stripped it of anything resembling majesty. It was a dingy, dirty, gritty, grey cavern and cooing pigeons outside the dirty frosted glass were the only reminder of life outside. It was the perfect place to pronounce on death.

The court was full and near to chaotic. Tom had never seen so much legal representation under one roof. Not even in his wildest imaginings had he anticipated anything quite like this. Some faces were familiar, not from his having shared court rooms with them but because of their regular appearance in newspapers and on television. Every person or organisation with any interest in the inquest was represented.

The air was heavy with human and pharmaceutical smells as more and more people crammed into the court and once all the seats were taken they stood in whatever space was available. The usual attack of nerves appeared suddenly and dramatically and Tom was desperate to excuse himself, to be alone, so made his apologies and fought his way back to the lavatory on the half-landing. There was a queue even for the urinals and he abandoned the idea and rejoined the others, watching Ailey's reaction as she viewed the crowded court. She smiled, shook her head and uttered a theatrical "Wow!" He tried to see it through her eyes and understood exactly how she felt. A beadle with staff and tricorn hat would have complemented it perfectly, pronouncing the court in session and announcing a public hanging for stealing bread.

She leant forward and whispered in his ear, "Where's the wigs then? I want to see some wigs." Tom couldn't even respond, just wanting to be left alone with his nervous yawning. Ailey and Vicky found seats elsewhere but Bernard stuck close to Tom and they both had to remain standing in front of the witness benches.

"It's a right bloody bunfight, this," said Bernard, tugging at his sleeve. "You didn't warn us it was going to be like this. *No, I didn't*, thought Tom – *I wish someone had told me.* He tried to engross himself in his papers. Failing, he looked back towards the public benches and caught sight of Louise Watson in the melee and she smiled. Tom smiled back, pleased to see a familiar face. Her simple reassurance helped him control his nerves and now he just wanted the thing to get underway because he knew a lot of people were dependent upon him.

George Fraser, the Coroner, entered through a door at the back of his podium and Mack Caffrey came through the main door, pushing his way past people to get to his seat.

"Ladies and gentlemen ... ladies and gentlemen! I think we're ... er ... probably ... here. I mean all of us are here, those with an interest. Well I certainly hope we are." George managed to quieten the court despite his stumbling and stuttering. "Perhaps the representatives of the different interested parties could make themselves known." He read out the names of the different organisations. "And those representing relatives of the deceased?"

Tom gave his name and the number of people he represented – forty-two in all. A stern-looking barrister, a silk, he guessed, said he represented the two hundred and three airline passengers, and Tom was surprised they were all represented by the one lawyer and assumed it had been organised by the oil company which employed them.

George bumbled on. "I would like to formally open this inquest into the deaths of five hundred and twenty-three people at Harrow on December the seventh. As far as we know, a passenger aircraft belonging to Varsity Aviation crashed at approximately five p.m." The reason he had suddenly become so fluent was because he was reading from a prepared statement.

"However, it is quite obvious that these are not suitable premises for this inquest but in addition, there are investigations still proceeding. In light of both these considerations I am therefore adjourning this inquest until a date six months hence. I would like all the parties to consider whether it is their wish that, when we reconvene, there should be a jury summoned. I look forward to receiving your representations on this point in due course. Thank you."

He rose, with the intention of disappearing back through the door behind him, the door from whence he had come only minutes before.

"Is that it?" The voice was incredulous and a woman in the

centre of the court shouted again. "I'm asking you, is that it?"

For the first time George Fraser spoke with authority. "Madame, I have just announced that the inquest is adjourned." The colour was rushing upwards from his collar towards the top of his balding head.

"It's not good enough, I want some answers."

George was angered by the challenge. "Who are you?" It was really a rhetorical question and what he had wanted to say was, *Whoever you are, please shut up and go away!* She answered anyway.

"Sheila Manders. My son was seriously injured!"

"As I said, the inquest is adjourned but I have to tell you that even if it was still in session you would have no right to be heard as our purpose is to enquire into causes of death, not to investigate injury."

With that he exited through the door as quickly as was decent and Sheila Manders's voice followed him. "Bloody outrageous, pompous old sod!" Vicky immediately went over to her.

Caffrey had also risen and was heading for the exit but Tom managed to intercept him. "You knew it was going to be adjourned, didn't you?" He tried to keep the anger from his voice.

"Knew? Knew? There's nothing you can be certain of in this life, laddie." His rheumy old eyes came as close to a smile as they were ever likely to. "I'm sure you'll excuse me, I'm kinda busy, ye ken," and with that, pushed his way through the milling crowd and disappeared.

CHAPTER TEN

Friday, March 8th, 1991, 8.10 a.m. If it hadn't been for victory in the Giftique case, a contented client and a satisfied father, it would have been a day to stay in bed. As it was, there had been few occasions in his life when Tom had felt quite so ill at ease, so inadequate. He kept telling himself that he should have known how the inquest might turn out and that he should have prepared his clients for it. In reality, he guessed that most of the other lawyers had probably known all along that it was going to be adjourned, which only made him feel worse. Bernard had been fairly stoical about it. "Might have bloody known it," was about the most inflamed comment he had made.

The most irritating aspect for Tom was that he felt he had surrendered the initiative to Ailey; his greatest fear was, without progress in Britain, his clients would begin to defect to her, seeing the US action as their best option. The more clients he lost, the weaker would be his position and the less clout he would have to nail Varsity. He felt his credibility was seriously on the line.

Vicky had also said little but her anger was palpable. It had not been directed against him but against the system and one thing he had learnt about Vicky was that she was not a patient woman. Her parting words had been heavy with threat. "What now, wait another six months? And for what? We're playing by their rules and that's a big, big mistake." Vicky's most unsettling character trait was her unpredictability and she was quite right, he did not know how to handle her.

He had to dissipate his anger and rattled off what was meant to be a request to George Fraser for him to hold a full inquest when it was reconvened in six months' time – jury, representation of all parties involved, the whole works. He suspected that George's inclination would be to hold a paper hearing and simply read statements with no one else present before announcing his verdict. Tom was determined that would not happen if he could prevent it. He read through his third draft and despite tinkering with it again, it still sounded more like a demand than a request. He decided it was the best he was likely to produce, printed it out and had Miss Rush fax it through to the Coroner's Office.

Having done that, he wanted to forget about the inquest fiasco as quickly as possible as he knew it was vital to give everyone something else to think about – when one door closes another opens. It was therefore crucial to investigate the Edward Veezey connection to see if it held any possibilities. This had become a pressing issue now the aviation investigators were on the job.

Veezey's sister, Nellie Ford, was not on the phone so it would require a visit and as Vicky was the one who had made contact with them, her presence would hopefully reassure them – it might also give her something to concentrate on. Tom looked at the time and decided it was too early to ring Vicky – he would wait until after the weekend and let the dust settle.

Monday, March 11th, 1991, 8.11 a.m. Sheila Manders seemed completely relaxed when they spotted signs for the passenger terminals at Heathrow Airport. Vicky checked her mirror and saw that Wendy's Volvo was directly behind. Wendy had been extremely jittery but if anyone could keep her motivated it was Bridie Gallagher.

"Try the mobile, Sheila, see how they're doing."

Sheila pressed the bleeping buttons and Bridie answered immediately. "Jaisus, you made me jump outa me skin."

"Everything okay?" Sheila enquired.

"Oh sure. Wendy here thinks she's about to meet her Maker and I'm dying for the loo."

"You'll have to put them both on hold, Bridie. Good luck and see you soon," Sheila said as she ended the call.

Wendy and Bridie occupied opposite ends of life's spectrum. Wendy was thirty, middle-class and comfortable – largely insulated from life's coarser features. Bridie, on the other hand, was one of ten kids brought up in a three-bedroom Belfast back-to-back immediately after the war. She had lived in London since she was nineteen but despite this, her accent was that of someone who had arrived on the last boat. As Bridie could not drive, that role fell to Wendy.

Sheila was the only one of the four who had not lost anyone in the disaster but she nursed a discontent which matched theirs, having a fourteen-year-old son who would spend many more months in hospital.

"You all right?" Vicky asked her, without looking, her mouth dry and a pressing demand from her stomach, which indicated that its contents were beginning to dissolve.

"Absolutely fine," said Sheila, as cheerily as if she was going on holiday. "Actually, tell you the truth, I'm shitting myself."

"Me too," replied Vicky.

"If we're feeling like this, how's Wendy coping?"

"I don't like to think about it," said Vicky, taking a deep breath. "Well, here we go – good luck," she said, putting her hand out, finding Sheila's and squeezing it.

Welcome to Heathrow said the sign above the entrance to the tunnel and they headed into its artificial light in the inside lane of a dual line of traffic. Vicky watched her mirror intently as they approached the halfway point. "Come on, Wendy, come on, Wendy, you can do it." She watched and waited and then said with panic in her voice, "Oh God, she's chickened out, she's still behind me."

A screech of brakes echoed suddenly from the tunnel's walls, followed by the sound of rending metal and shattering glass and the distance between the two cars increased rapidly as the Volvo behind came to a halt. Vicky just had time to see Bridie leap out of the passenger door before her own car began to rise up the incline and she lost vision.

"I think she's made a balls of it. Try her on the phone, Sheila."

They came out of the tunnel and Vicky headed her car towards the terminals as Sheila frantically stabbed at buttons on an unfamiliar mobile she had borrowed. "Oh God, oh God, it's all going wrong."

"Just press redial," Vicky instructed as they reached the first roundabout and she swung the car round it, heading back towards the exit tunnel.

"It's no good, I've already pressed loads of numbers," Sheila moaned and continued pressing. "That's it, that's it, that's the right one. Oh my God, they're not answering. It's the tunnel, it's the bloody tunnel; we can't reach them."

They approached the parallel exit tunnel but before disappearing into it they could see that nothing was emerging from the entrance tunnel. "Yes!" they cheered in unison.

As she neared the midway point of the exit tunnel, still in the inside lane, with a long line of cars behind her, Vicky switched on the hazard lights and slowed to a stop. Sheila got out clutching a hammer and walked quickly towards the oncoming traffic in the outside lane with her hands held up, giving the drivers no option as she stepped out into the middle of the carriageway. A minibus screeched to a halt in front of her and the flow of traffic came to a standstill.

Vicky immediately swung her car across both lanes, blocking them and pulled the bonnet release; Sheila raised the bonnet and hit the distributor cap with the hammer until it shattered. Vicky twisted the steering wheel into the locked position, got out, walked up the carriageway until she found a storm-water grating and dropped the key down it. All went exactly as planned and the whole exercise was over in minutes. This was how they'd rehearsed it.

Wendy and Bridie were supposed to have followed suit but in their case all had not gone according to plan. As they followed Vicky's car into the tunnel, Wendy had become catatonic and Bridie had kept talking to her. "You're all right, Wendy, you're all right, just keep going, keep going. Okay, now start slowing down." Wendy said nothing, staring unblinkingly at the car in front, hugging its tail.

"Start slowing down now, slow down, gently does it. Come on, Wendy, it's time to stop, put your hazards on." Bridie raised her voice to a shout. "Put your foot on the bloody brake, Wendy!" The reaction was instant and Wendy slammed both feet down to the floorboards and the car stopped abruptly. The car behind rammed into the Volvo and the chain reaction went back fourteen cars in a cacophony of clattering metal and tinkling headlight glass. Bridie was thrown against the windscreen and dropped her hammer but still she leapt from the car and ran into the outside lane to stop the second line of traffic. A brand-new, gleaming red BMW attempted to swerve round her and what she heard next was a blood-curdling scream.

"You bastard!" It came from the open window of the Volvo as Wendy hit the accelerator, swung the steering wheel and in a cloud of smoke from spinning tyres, rammed the BMW against the wall of the tunnel with a grinding crash. Leaping out, she again screamed, "You bastard!" and, clutching Bridie's hammer began hitting the BMW.

She started at the front of the roof and worked towards the back, leaving puckered dents as she went, each one punctuated by a loud, metallic clang. As she started shattering the rear windscreen, Bridie grabbed her arm, reclaimed the hammer and held on to her. She could see three terrified Japanese businessmen inside the car, immobile as statues, their mouths wide open. "You did it, Wendy, you bloody well, sure as hell, did it!" They held each other and danced in circles in the part of the tunnel which was now completely devoid of traffic.

Whether they smashed the distributor or not was completely immaterial as the Volvo wasn't going anywhere and the twin tunnels of Heathrow Airport were at a complete standstill in both directions. Stage one was accomplished and the four women set about stage two.

Bridie and Wendy ran to the airport end of the tunnel clutching their home-made banner with the intention of suspending it from the top of the tunnel where it would make the greatest visual impact but they could not get up to it. Instead, they ran in and out of the snarled-up cars trailing the banner between them. *523 HARROW DEAD DEMAND A PUBLIC INQUIRY,* eventually draping it over an advertising hoarding in full view of the stationary traffic.

Vicky and Sheila tried to take their banner to the north end of the tunnel but a small group of furious car drivers refused to allow them past. One short, fat man was out of control and shaking with anger as he first hurled abuse at the women and then began pushing them, determined they would not leave the scene. As Vicky grabbed the hammer from Sheila, with every intention of using it, a series of sharp, amplified commands filled the tunnel.

"Armed police! Down on the ground – NOW. Get down on the ground, on your stomachs, arms out in front of you!"

Against the bright light streaming in through the tunnel entrance, Vicky could just make out the shapes of people pressed tightly against the walls on either side. They were unmistakably carrying firearms which were pointing directly at her. "Do as they say, Sheila," she said quietly.

"Like I'm going to ignore them, Vick? On your knees, gal!" They both sank to their knees and stretched out on the ground, arms out, palms down.

Vicky watched the figures as they moved towards them in short bursts, one covering the other until suddenly, they were directly above her – men in black uniforms with guns aimed at her head. She could not make out their faces against the backlighting from the sunlight at the end of the tunnel but could almost smell the testosterone.

One of them barked an instruction. "Hands behind your backs!" and both women obeyed, feeling and hearing the handcuffs ratcheting into place. They hurt. They were dragged to their feet and forced at the double towards the tunnel entrance, a man on either side, impelling them by their upper arms.

Waiting for them outside the tunnel entrance was a security van with one of its rear doors open and it was no accident that they were slammed into the closed door with force, dragged to their feet again and thrown into the back of the van, followed by their banners. Only when the door slammed behind them did the pain begin to bite.

The women had prepared a joint statement which said, "*We are members of the Harrow Support Group and have carried out these actions to bring attention to the Government's dereliction of duty regarding the crash of Varsity Aviation's Flight 469 and the subsequent death of 523 people. It is essential that a public inquiry is established immediately to investigate the real reasons behind this catastrophe and the Government's subsequent handling of it. We urge all those who share our concerns to register their protest with their MPs. We regret any inconvenience our actions might have caused.*" They had also each written Tom's contact numbers on their wrists in indelible ink.

It had been agreed that if they had the opportunity they would distribute this statement to the press and if they were arrested these were the only words they would say apart from giving their names and addresses. They were asked no questions and were given no opportunity to say anything whilst in the van and when they were bundled out, Wendy, the one they had been most worried about, kept repeating one word – "Bastards, bastards, bastards…"

"Wendy, don't say anything," Bridie reminded her.

"Shut your mouth, you," screamed an armed man as the women were rushed into a building between a double phalanx of outward-facing armed police, their eyes hunting for targets like predators.

The four were searched and locked into individual holding rooms and the initial questioning began immediately. Vicky did her best to control her anger but it infected every movement she made, turning her examination into an exercise in dumb contempt. She repeated the agreed statement a couple of times and to every question after that simply replied, "I've explained the reasons behind our actions and I have no further comment to make." Each time she demanded the right to call her lawyer and although no one refused, equally she was provided with no opportunity to do so.

After the initial questioning, it was a long, long time before anyone came to interrogate Bridie. When they did, it was a pair of seasoned professionals, accompanied by a woman police officer and the older of the two men spoke first. She had seen the same emotionless eyes many times during her life, usually following dawn raids on her house.

"Are your brothers involved in this?" Despite her intention to remain silent, she immediately responded.

"Don't talk shite!"

"So Gerry and Connor left it to you, did they?"

The warning signals began to flash anew and Bridie repeated the agreed statement then lapsed into silence.

8.55 a.m. There was a long wait before Vicky's phone was answered and it was Emma who spoke. "Mum's not here, she's gone out."

"Do you know when she'll be back?" Tom asked.

"No, she was in one of her secretive moods. I'll tell her you called, gotta dash, I'm late for school." The raw pain of bereavement had seemingly mellowed and Emma sounded like any other sixteen-year-old.

Tom leant over and turned up the radio to catch the nine o'clock news headlines and the story was second lead and was almost over before it registered. "Traffic at Heathrow Airport is in chaos as the exit and entrance road tunnels have been blocked. The M4 and A4 approach roads are at a standstill and lines of stationary cars are building up on the exit lanes of the M25. It appears to be a deliberate action and not a result of accidents and has caused the maximum amount of disruption at the height of the rush hour.

"Police say they have little information on those responsible and are treating the incident as having a possible terrorist connection. Eyewitnesses, however, say that several women seem to be involved and there is some suggestion that it might be a protest linked to the Harrow disaster."

Tom held his head in his hands and groaned, "Oh no!" before grabbing his coat and hurtling down the stairs two at a time. His car was on a meter immediately outside the office.

Progress through Harrow was painfully slow but eventually his car screeched out of Northolt Road on to the A40 where traffic was flowing freely and he headed towards the M25. He felt a touch of irony as he passed the landing lights of Northolt Airport.

He pulled a pen and pad from the glovebox and dialled directory enquiries but after an interminable delay, the operator said she did not have a number for airport security so he settled for general administration and juggled the pad on his knee as he wrote down the number.

When he looked up, the boot of a white Mercedes was hurtling towards him in a blaze of stop lights and so he hit the brakes and instinctively swung the car to the right and into the outside lane. A pair of flashing headlights completely filled the rear windscreen and the shrill of an Italian car horn almost lifted him bodily out of his seat.

Tom's heartbeat had just about returned to normal by the time he reached the M25/M4 intersection but he had still not been able to get through to security. Traffic on the inside lane was at a standstill and flashing blue lights were everywhere as drivers were frantically being waved on to prevent them from stopping.

Tom took a circuitous route via Staines and finished up opposite the airport's cargo entrance but as he swung into it, he was met by a line of flak-jacketed police carrying semi-automatic weapons, all of which were pointing at him. Screaming down the perimeter road towards them were several armoured personnel carriers filled with soldiers in camouflage fatigues.

"Airport security, please. It's urgent," he shouted to the nearest policeman.

"You've found it," the man replied without smiling as he trained a machine pistol on Tom's heart. "Get out of the car."

10.30 a.m. Charles Astbury was in Birmingham at the invitation of the motor industry and had just finished a late breakfast in his hotel room, leaving sufficient time to go through a couple of despatch boxes before heading off for his tour of the Rover Solihull plant. There was a knock and his PPS entered carrying a mobile phone.

"It's the Home Secretary, Minister."

Astbury took the receiver: "John!" He listened in silence for a while. "Well, I have a general rule of thumb for situations like this – make life as difficult as possible for them." Again he listened and nodded. "Absolutely, it's got to be nipped in the bud. It'll frighten the daylights out of them. Thanks, John, bye!"

11.30 a.m. Tom had been escorted to a waiting room in the airport security offices but he had not seen the women nor had he been provided with any information about them. He had tried to conduct a conversation through a small hatch and eventually the duty sergeant reluctantly confirmed that they were being held but Tom's demands to see them had been ignored. "Wait there," was all he had been offered. He had tried being nice, followed it with outrage and had then become angry, demanding the personal numbers of the two officers on the other side of the hatch. The sergeant had hooked his thumb under his epaulette and shoved it towards Tom without saying a word whilst the PC sat at a desk and carried on writing, simply saying, "You can read!"

Tom had taken both numbers down with a flourish and as soon as he'd finished, the sergeant slammed shut the hatch between them. The waiting room was long and barren, one wall lined with brightly coloured plastic chairs with a gap where the hatch was situated whilst there was a door on each of the other three sides. One led to a lavatory, one led to the outside and the third, directly opposite it, seemed to lead to what was a rest room used by civilian airport security guards. One particular guard came and went several times and eventually had to acknowledge Tom's presence.

"Still here, then?" He was an enormous man, tall enough to play for the Harlem Globetrotters and wide enough to obscure the sun.

Tom was already on his feet, wandering around in aimless frustration. "Yes, 'fraid so. Have you got a minute?" The huge man stopped. "You don't know what's going on, do you, with the Harrow women?"

"No mate, sorry. Is that who they are, then? You their brief?"

Tom nodded and tried to turn the man's interest to his advantage, playing the sympathy card with a vengeance. "Yeah. I'm obviously worried because they all lost someone in the crash and, to be honest, they're in a bit of a state. They've been through real hell – it's hard to imagine what it must be like for them. Really, I don't know how they've survived. I don't think they know what they're doing themselves."

He wanted this man on his side because he probably had the one thing Tom was lacking – information.

"What was it then, some kind of protest?"

"Yes, exactly – at least that's my guess. Believe me, it certainly wasn't anything threatening!"

The huge man's interest was growing and as it did, Tom could feel the hostility draining away. "We heard a whisper that it was something like that but I'll tell you now, that's not how it's being treated. They've got the anti-terrorist lot in."

"You're joking!" That was not good news, Tom realised, and offered the man his card. "Just to show I'm legit. Look, I'm absolutely gasping, there's no chance of a cuppa, is there?" He wanted to stay as close to this man as possible.

"Hang on, I'll see." He disappeared into the rest room, reappearing after a few seconds and beckoned to Tom. "Not a word to anyone, right?"

The room was smoky, with a few chairs and a table strewn with used cups and an assortment of tea stains at one end, where there was a kettle. Three men were present in addition to the big one, who was referred to as Wally, and they sat at the table, ties undone, jackets open, cups of tea in front of them.

"Help yourself," Wally said.

As unobtrusively as possible, Tom made a strong black coffee. "Is it okay?" he said, gesturing towards an empty chair, and a couple of the men nodded without showing any real interest and Tom sat down.

"So what's it all about then?" one of them asked without challenge.

Tom gave them a quick rundown on the people involved in the support group, concentrating on their personal stories, in particular the experiences of the four women being held.

If the security men had harboured any suspicions at the start, they were soon dispelled. "Do you know what's happened to them?" Tom asked in a direct appeal to their privileged position.

"Sorry, mate, cops have taken over. No bugger tells us

anything," one of the men replied. "So they all lost someone, did they?" asked another and Tom confirmed it.

"Bloody shame, isn't it? Not like it even had anything to do with them, really. Bloody plane falls out the sky when you're minding your own business."

"Terrible," said Wally. "Mind you, I always knew one of those peanut planes would go down; we've been saying it for months, haven't we, Tes?"

"Matter of time, that was all," replied Tes.

"Peanut planes?" Tom looked quizzically at Wally.

"Yeah," the big man snorted, "that's what you pay to fly on 'em and that's what you get to eat – peanuts. Get it?" Tom said he thought he did.

"I don't reckon it's just that," added Pete, the quietest of the three. "It's the P11 – terrible plane, always finding something wrong with it."

"But it's not got a bad safety record," Tes chipped in.

Pete warmed to his theme. "I should bloody think not, it's nearly new but they're having to do a lot of work to keep it in the air. In the end it gets so you can't keep up with it all, something gives and it's wallop, goodnight, Eileen. I know for a start that some of the little airlines haven't got round to modifying the cargo door yet."

"You seem to know a lot about it," Tom said.

"Not really. I used to be a baggage handler till they made me redundant and you hear the maintenance crews talking – can't help picking up bits and pieces."

Tom drank his coffee and threw in the occasional question, allowing the tea break gossip to flow naturally backwards and forwards, unobtrusively steering it back to aircraft in general and the P11 in particular if it appeared in danger of moving elsewhere.

Pete obviously knew quite a lot about the P11 and in particular its rear cargo door. He got into his stride. "It's only a minor fault but when you close it, as well as the electronic closures, you have to put some muscle behind it before you turn the handles to the locked position. If you don't, it can look like it's properly secured but when the plane gets near to altitude the difference in air pressure sometimes causes it to spring open

– just a little bit. The safety catches stop it opening fully but you shouldn't have to rely on them."

Tom couldn't mask his interest. "Has it ever caused problems?"

Pete shook his head. "No, not crashes or anything like that. It's only ever opened a bit but there've been a few emergency landings when that's happened. It puts the shits up everybody, I can tell you. Problem is, these small airlines have to work their planes so hard they haven't got the time to carry out modifications properly – they're flying twenty-four hours a day, you know!"

"But they've sorted it all out now, I presume?" Tom enquired.

"That's what I was on about. The manufacturers issued a new maintenance instruction but until the airlines got round to carrying it out the pilots had to check the cargo door every time it was closed. It pissed them off, pissed the baggage handlers off and was just another thing that had to be remembered. Its pressure all the time – move, move, move – but I know there's still a few that haven't carried out the modifications. Ridiculous!"

"Varsity one of them?" Tom asked.

"I don't know about that. They don't fly from here. It's cheap charters mainly, from Gatwick."

"But you don't reckon Varsity as an airline?"

Pete wrinkled his nose up. "Cheap aren't they – cheapjack."

"So who would know if their aircraft had been modified or not – baggage handlers over at Northolt?"

"Yeah, possibly."

"Do you know any?" Tom looked to Pete for an answer and he could see from the man's eyes that he knew exactly why Tom was asking, that his interest was professional.

Pete got up. "No, long time since I've been over there. Right, better get going." He turned to Tom. "I don't want to be rude but you'd best go back outside before any of the others come in." He held the door open, allowing Tom to exit first, indicating there wasn't any option, and followed close behind him.

In a near-whisper Pete said, "The Gate, that's where a lot of the Northolt lads go. Pub on the corner of West End Road and

Cavendish Avenue on the east side. Lol Kumar's your best bet – mention my name, Pete Driscoll."

"Thanks," said Tom quietly.

Pete brushed past him. "That's okay. Sorry, but its paranoia fucking junction around here. Best of luck."

Tom again rapped on the hatch to the police office and it was slid open by the same sergeant. Tom did not give him time to speak. "This has gone on long enough and I want to see my clients; failing that I want to know what they've been charged with and why I am being denied access."

The sergeant stared back at him before answering curtly, "Have you finished? They're being held under the Prevention of Terrorism Act and under its provisions—"

Tom cut him off. "I know its provisions! Are they still here?" The policeman merely shook his head. Tom didn't even try to mask his anger. "Forget it; we all know where they're being taken… Give me a pass to get my car out."

He turned and left the station, hurrying towards the police car park pound to where his car had been escorted. Of all the possible outcomes he'd calculated, this hadn't been one of them.

Tom headed back up the M40 and on to the A40 towards central London, trying to remember which turn-off he needed to take for Paddington Green. Of course he missed it and had to continue along the elevated road into the start of the Marylebone Road and with every other street a no-entry, it took minutes to find the little crescent on the edge of the Harrow Road. For the country's top terrorist holding and interrogation centre, Paddington Green Police Station looked extraordinarily innocuous.

3.30 p.m. The only time Vicky, Sheila, Wendy and Bridie saw each other again that day was when they were bundled into a helicopter for transfer to Paddington Green. As they rose into the air, two bright flashes of light were visible from a deserted part of the airport near the perimeter below them and the sound of two explosions could be faintly heard above the clatter of the helicopter's rotor. They were followed by two dense columns of black smoke.

One of the policemen grinned an explanation. "That's bomb disposal redesigning your cars, ladies," he shouted above the noise of the aircraft and for the first time, Wendy cried.

"Don't worry, Wendy, he'll get over it," shouted Vicky and, without thinking, offered an explanation. "It's her husband's company car – he doesn't know she's got it."

Wendy responded through her sobs. "It's not that – I forgot to take his golf clubs out of the boot."

3.50 p.m. When the helicopter descended on to the landing pad at Paddington Green, Tom was already inside the police station demanding access to his clients. It was denied and he began the wait which he knew could go on for hours.

3.52 p.m. The four women were hurried, heads bent beneath the clattering helicopter rotor, into the station and were immediately separated, with Vicky being ushered down a series of corridors into the reception area where there was nothing overtly disturbing about the place but it wasn't normal. All surfaces of corridors and rooms were the same colour, an inoffensive matt-white. Illumination was by recessed bright white light which flooded every surface, and walls were free of any object which might break the monotony – not a poster, not a notice, not even a dirty mark and nowhere was there a clock. It was like being wrapped in formless cotton wool, all designed to deprive the senses.

The atmosphere was electric, with uniformed policemen and women scurrying backwards and forwards, and she could hear the rattling of keys from somewhere nearby and a loud clang of cell doors being slammed. Only one reassuring sound drifted up the corridor. "Ya gobshite!" It could be no one but Bridie and her words were followed by the bang of another door being forcibly closed.

Vicky's custody record was filled in quickly, her personal details recorded along with what property she had on her when arrested and she initialled the appropriate box. She noticed the tick box which indicated whether a solicitor had been requested or not but before she could respond to it, the sergeant spoke.

"Are you requesting a solicitor?"

"Of course I am, I've been asking for one since I was arrested."

"Right, that's noted – and the request is refused." He did not even glance up and for the first time Vicky began to feel afraid. She had been certain she could cope with anything they threw at her but suddenly felt horribly vulnerable, unsure of herself and alone.

The sergeant outlined why she was being held but the detail washed over her. "You have been arrested ... caution has been given ... major public order incident ... provisions of the Prevention of Terrorism Act ... do you wish to say anything in answer to the charge?"

She didn't even understand the charge and simply shook her head. She was then escorted to a holding room where a silent female PC stood watch over her and neither woman uttered a word. Eventually, Vicky broke the silence. "I want to go to the lavatory."

"You can't!" The WPC didn't look at her either.

"I want to go to the lavatory."

"And I've told you you'll have to wait."

Vicky could feel her anger rising and it felt better than fear. "If you don't show me to a lavatory, I'm going to piss on the floor – and that isn't a threat, it's a promise." She watched consternation flash across the woman's face and after only a momentary pause, she reached for a button, pressed it and within seconds, two female police officers entered the cell.

"She wants the toilet."

A sergeant took command. "Right, on your feet."

Vicky stood up and the sergeant opened a door on the far side of the small room and indicated to the lavatory inside. "In there!"

Vicky entered the cubicle and stood by the lavatory pan waiting for the woman to close the door but she didn't and the sergeant and one of the other women stepped inside the cubicle so they were within touching distance of her.

"Come on, for Christ's sake," Vicky implored.

"Just get on with it and if you even think about flushing anything down the pan I'll break your arm – have you got that?" Vicky could see the sergeant wasn't joking. There really was no option and she lowered her clothing and sat on the lidless pan while the two women watched her intently. When it was over she was returned to the main holding room to continue her wait.

She had no idea how long she had been there when they came to get her but it felt like hours. Again it was the formless corridor, a woman on either side holding her arms and hurting them, several men ahead leading the way, keys on chains, speed and urgency. A door was held open and Vicky was pushed inside but this time no one came with her, the uniformed officers remaining in the doorway.

The room was entirely empty except for a large, single sheet of white paper which covered the floor and Vicky's confidence had almost entirely evaporated as she viewed the unsmiling faces. "All this for causing a bloody traffic jam. It's pathetic." It wasn't much of a counter-attack but it felt good.

The figures around the door separated and two women dressed in hooded white boiler suits entered, with even their hands covered. One was carrying transparent plastic bags whilst the other held something that looked like folded brown paper – and still the uniformed officers remained in the doorway watching.

One of the white-clad women spoke sharply. "Take your clothes off one piece at a time and start with your shoes."

There seemed no point in arguing and Vicky removed one of her shoes whilst the second woman held out a plastic bag into which Vicky dropped it. The PC closed and sealed the bag and identified it by writing on a tag.

"And the other one!" Vicky did as she was instructed and the process was repeated over and over again with each piece of clothing. She did nothing voluntarily, waiting to be told which piece of clothing to remove next, but when she was down to her leggings and top she stopped obeying.

"Take the bottoms off!"

She hesitated, aware that one of the male officers was looking in from the doorway. It felt demeaning and her anger ignited once more, stoked by her vulnerability.

"I'm not undressing in front of them!" She said it with an authority she did not feel.

"Don't argue, take them off – or do you want us to do it for you?" said one of the boiler-suited women.

Vicky refused to move and the cell became silent, all eyes were on her, waiting for her response and the situation began to feel unreal, almost as though she was observing it from above.

"I want to see my solicitor."

"You're seeing no one."

"I want to phone my solicitor!" She felt much better when she hit back.

"He knows," the woman PC replied.

"How do you know?"

"Just take your leggings off." Vicky believed the woman's claim and with that simple little gem of information she felt the fear starting to ease – she wasn't alone!

"The leggings."

Vicky removed them and dropped them into a bag.

"And the tights."

"Oh, come on!"

"Take your tights off." The male officer was still looking on.

"Get that bastard away from the door." Vicky could feel herself losing control.

One of the other officers said something to him and he pulled back out of vision and Vicky concentrated on the wall ahead of her, trying to ignore the watching eyes, and found she was fighting back tears but she would not allow them to fall.

When she was finally standing in only bra and pants, one of the boiler-suited women tossed folded-up brown paper trousers and a top to her and Vicky gratefully put them on, still under the eyes of several police officers. The paper flooring was rolled up and removed – it was all over and the relief washed over Vicky.

The numbers of onlookers reduced and one of the boiler-suited policewomen took away the filled and tagged bags but the other remained. "Right, I want some samples now." Vicky's heart sank. "I want saliva, hair and hand samples and scrapings from under your nails and I intend to conduct an intimate body search."

"Go fuck yourself – you're getting nothing more from me."

*

7.20 p.m. For Wendy, the ordeal had been bearable up to the point that the boiler-suited women police officers instructed her to undress. Until then she had looked at no one and to every question put to her, she had responded quietly under her breath so that no one could hear, "Bastards!"

When the white-clad women had threatened to undress her if she did not follow their instructions, Wendy could see they meant it and the tears started. After that she did everything that was requested, including providing samples. These were taken on cotton buds from her mouth and the front and backs of her hands and then nail scrapings and hair samples were added to the collection.

8.30 p.m. "Who's the senior officer on duty?"

The duty sergeant looked at a chart beside him. "Superintendent Wade."

"This has gone on long enough, I want to see him." Tom was not feigning his anger.

"I think he's busy at the moment."

"Don't piss me about. You've got four of my clients in there, all completely innocent of any terrorist activities, and I want to see them. Get me Superintendent Wade, now, please!"

The desk sergeant knew it was important to play everything exactly by the book and phoned through. "He's coming," he reported to Tom.

A silver-braided officer appeared and headed towards him. "Wade! I was just coming to see you, Mr Harrison." Tom followed him to his office. "We've got a problem with a couple of your clients, I'm afraid; they're refusing to allow swabs to be taken."

"Who is it?"

"In fact it's three of them – Mrs Denton, Mrs Manders and Mrs Gallagher."

"I want to see them."

"Maybe, we'll talk about that in a minute. You know if they refuse to give swabs we can take them forcibly? That's not really in anyone's interests, is it? So if I did let you see them, it would help if you explained that."

"You can only use force with a magistrate's permission – and you want me to save you that bother by telling them to co-operate. Is that the condition under which I *might* be allowed to see my clients?" Tom now had his anger under control.

"That isn't quite what I said." Wade's smile was purely cosmetic.

"But it's what you meant. The only thing these women have done is to make a protest. It might have been ill-advised but they've done nothing worse than that and you have no right to detain them under the PTA and even less right to test them for explosive traces. There has been no explosion and no explosives have been suspected, let alone found. If, despite this, you insist on going ahead with tests, the very least I will expect is for my own forensic expert to be present. One thing's certain, I won't advise my clients to co-operate and I won't help you to breach their fundamental rights."

Despite the policeman's attempt at nonchalance, Tom could see he had shaken Wade and could almost hear his brain ticking over as he tried to formulate a response. He waited for the bullshit to be produced and it wasn't long in coming.

"The situation is still as yet unclear and I'm afraid I can't afford to be as sanguine as you about what might or might not be involved."

Tom cut across him. "You say three of my clients have refused to provide samples – that would imply that the fourth has given them, am I correct?"

"Yes, I believe you are."

"It isn't a question of believing – either she has or she hasn't. You're in charge, Mr Wade, which is it?"

"Samples have been taken from one suspect."

"Which one?"

Wade played for time by pretending to look at the notes in front of him. "Yes, it's Mrs Percival, Mrs Wendy Percival."

"And what was the result?"

Wade redeployed his smile. "It isn't that simple. You're probably not used to dealing with this kind of case but to get an accurate reaction can take time as there's some fairly sophisticated equipment involved."

Tom didn't respond immediately. He carefully removed a notepad from his briefcase, opened it, placed it on the desk in front of him, took a pen from his inside pocket and placed it on the pad.

"An explosives field test kit is neither complicated nor sophisticated as you well know and you get a reaction within minutes. You've already got the results, Wade; I'm not stupid. What reaction did you get from the ETK? And before you answer, consider this. I want everything that's been said to be recorded as a formal objection for the purpose of future litigation, is that clear? Right, what was the result?" He began to write on the pad, glancing at his watch before he did so.

Wade made no immediate response and when Tom had finished recording the details of their interview, he looked up at him, catching the man off guard and his face was a portrait of frustration and resentment. Wade knew he was being barbecued, and coughed nervously before speaking.

"In the case of Mrs Percival, the preliminary results were negative but they may not be conclusive; of course as we have no idea if that will be repeated with the other three..."

"No explosion, no explosives and no traces. Section sixty-two – release my clients, Mr Wade, release them now or face a suit for false imprisonment."

9.45 p.m. The only break in the silence was the regular clink as a cover on the observation panel in the door was pushed aside. Almost no sound penetrated the holding cell where Vicky, dressed in her brown paper clothes and wrapped in a brown paper blanket, sat and waited. She had no idea of the time but knew she would not be left alone indefinitely. Any unusual noise which managed to breach the soundproofing made her jump, made her fear that the inquisition was about to start again. Eventually there was a clatter and the door was opened by a woman PC.

"Come on, you're going home!"

CHAPTER ELEVEN

Tuesday, March 12th, 1991, 10.30 a.m. It was front-page news. Not every day did four women trigger a full-scale security alert at Heathrow and bring half of West London to a grinding halt and the press was going to play it for all it was worth. The first interviews, given immediately on their release outside Paddington Green Police Station, had made the late TV news programmes. The dailies had covered the arrests and the story of the tunnel-blocking, with aerial photographs of the ensuing chaos on the following day but the women's release had come too late in the day for the press to do it full justice, so they were still running the story two days later. *Government Accused of Harrow Cover-up*, one broadsheet shouted in splash type. The picture was of Wendy, Sheila, Bridie and Vicky standing outside Paddington Green. Tom could just make out his own image in the background. Vicky was in front, animated, arm outstretched, finger pointing. *"J'accuse!"* would have been the perfect caption.

"The Government is hiding the truth behind the Harrow disaster," claims Mrs Vicky Denton, whose husband, David, was killed when Flight 469 crashed on the London suburb. Speaking outside Paddington Green top security police station, used to hold the country's most dangerous terrorists, she said there is an urgent need for a public inquiry.

Visibly angry at having been held for several hours, she claimed that a major cover-up was taking place in order to obscure the damaging effects of Government policy and to protect the profits of Varsity Aviation.

"When a foreign oil tanker crashed on to the rocks of the

Shetland Islands without loss of life, a public inquiry was announced within forty-eight hours. When a plane crashed on to London killing hundreds of people, there is no public inquiry, only excuses. Why?"

The Government's denial of a cover-up was voiced through Charles Astbury and he tried to dismiss the women's claims as post-trauma reaction, irrational and ill-conceived. His quoted words were patronising but, above all, unconvincing and it was clear that the nationwide publicity afforded to Vicky and the others and the largely sympathetic coverage by the media had rattled him. Only the *Daily Despatch* blasted the women, accusing them of risking life and limb and damaging the British economy.

Tom tossed the newspaper over to Mike who was on his knees, grovelling in the bottom drawer of a filing cabinet. "Yeah, seen it. The old man had anything to say about it yet?"

Tom hadn't up till then been visited by his father but knew it could not be far off. When the phone rang he half expected it to be him but it was Miss Rush. There was a gentleman on the line who wouldn't give his name and Tom was immediately on the defensive.

"Hello," he barked. There was silence.

"Hello, Tom Harrison here, how can I help you?" It came out as a challenge.

"Mr Harrison?"

"Yes."

"You don't know me but I've seen what's been happening."

He sounded young, probably in his twenties with a thin London voice which verged on the ingratiating. It was not a confident voice and Tom felt sure something was going to be demanded of him.

"You've been asking questions about Flight 469."

Tom was suddenly alert. "Yes. Why? Do you know something?" The tone was pushy, demanding and he wished he had been cooler. There was silence. "Did you see something?" asked Tom, removing all urgency from his question.

"No, I didn't see anything but I heard quite a lot. Is it all right to talk?" He spoke as though he was looking over his shoulder and noise in the background made it difficult to hear his words.

"Absolutely fine, no problem. What's your name?" The caller ignored him.

"I'm a radio ham – d'you know what that is?"

"Yes," he replied, "an amateur radio operator."

"Right! I listened to Flight 469 before it crashed and it's not how they say it was." He went silent and Tom felt excitement welling up and tried to encourage him.

"How was it then? I know my clients would appreciate it greatly if you can shed any light on what happened."

"Well, the pilot gave out two distress calls. I was flipping the dial when I picked up the first one – he was giving a PAN call..." He stopped as though it should have some significance.

"I'm sorry but I don't know much about radio language – what's a pancall? You'll have to spell it out for me."

"P-A-N, PAN," replied the man.

"No, what I meant was, I don't know its significance – what it actually means."

"Oh! It's when something's wrong but it's not too bad, you can handle it and you don't want any assistance. You give a PAN call so people know you've got a bit of a problem."

"Well he did have a bit of a problem, didn't he? Quite a big bit of a problem – he was crashing."

"Exactly," said the caller, animated for the first time, "but he didn't think he was going to crash at that time. I kept tuned to him and about two minutes later he gave out another call but this time it was a MAYDAY. That's when he was in real trouble."

Tom knew that the word MAYDAY was the international distress call and it was his turn to go silent.

"Don't you get it?" the caller asked. Tom didn't get it at all. "Listen, if you whack another aircraft, that's an out-and-out MAYDAY. There's no piddling around. Either you or the other guy or both of you are in dead trouble, so you give a MAYDAY. So what was the reason for the PAN? I thought that might just be of interest to you."

Tom signalled frantically to Mike to pick up the extension phone, which he urgently tried to do but first fell over the extended filing-cabinet drawer and then ploughed into the pile of boxes belonging to the support group case.

The logic of what the whining voice was saying suddenly dawned on Tom. If Flight 469 gave out a PAN call two minutes before hitting the helicopter then something was already wrong at the time of impact.

"If you think the Government's not being truthful why don't you go public with this?" Tom asked. The response was a thin and humourless chuckle.

"Listen, mate, if the Government's telling porkies over something as big as this, what do you reckon would happen to someone like me if I stuck my oar in, eh? It wouldn't be a bouquet of roses they'd send me, I can tell you!" There was a clatter on the line as Mike finally reached the extension and juggled it from its rest.

"That's it, I gotta go," said the voice.

"Where can I get hold of you?" Tom sounded near to panic.

"You can't, but I might be in touch," replied the man and hung up.

"Shit, shit, shit," said Tom, in a rare outburst of swearing, throwing his pen across the room. "We scared him off." He turned to Mike. "He heard the last transmissions of Flight 469 and it didn't happen as we're being told. And now we've lost him."

"Sorry, Tom, my fault," said Mike, and immediately dialled 1471. A segmented, recorded female voice spoke. "Number 0171 229 1918 called today at 1 – 0, 3 – 9. To return the call press three." He pressed the three digit and heard a ringing tone. Tom picked up his extension and they both listened but it rang for several minutes without being answered. They were about to hang up when a gruff but tentative voice enquired, "Hello?"

Tom shook his head. It wasn't the man he'd spoken to.

"I've just been speaking to someone on this number, bloke who's a radio ham, is he there?" Tom asked.

"Gawd knows," the voice answered. "I was just waiting at the bus stop and heard the phone ringing."

"It's a call box?"

"Yeah."

"Do you mind telling me where?"

"Tooting Bec – hang on, there's my bus!" The line went dead.

Tom jotted down as much information as he could remember about the conversation with the ham and turned to Mike, who responded even before he spoke.

"I know, I know – a tour of the Tooting Bec phone boxes. Not sure it's going to tell us much – I mean, the bloke might have just been passing through."

"Possibly, but it could be that he lives around there, doesn't have his own phone line and uses the call box instead. Try the telephone supervisor – might give you the street address. Failing that, ring it again – someone's bound to answer so ask them the actual location. If not, start with Tooting Bec underground station and when you've found the phone, have a word with newsagents in the area. There are publications for everything these days so there's bound to be a wireless mag. See if anyone has it on regular order – he might even have it delivered. And find out if there's a ham radio club in the area."

"Problem is, Tom, there's all this stuff." He pointed to a pile of files. "We've just got Quality Windows' response to Ed Somerville's writ and he wants a meet to discuss it. Ronnie Mash is copping for the drink-driving but wants a plea of mitigation. And we've now got trial dates for Sandra Lockett and Henderson and before your eyes glaze over, there's five new cases here I can't handle. They're all legal aid and three are so late you need to seek adjournments. On top of that, Wings want an all-day session – and I can see you don't want to know about the conveyancing but here it is."

"Okay, okay, scrub Tooting for the time being but do it as soon as you can. I also want you to try and make contact with Lol Kumar – and mention Pete Driscoll's name. In fact, that's priority. And there's something else we need – someone who knows about airplanes." Mike picked up his files and left, shaking his head.

The phone had been ringing all morning and one call was from Ailey and Bernard Tate, who wanted to meet later – and Tom could guess what it was about.

Louise Watson was doing a story on the women behind the protest and wanted the solicitor's perspective, plus he and Vicky had a meeting with Edward Veezey and Nellie Ford later that evening over at Ruislip. It was all in danger of getting too much.

The biggest surprise of the day was the outcome of his call to Varsity Aviation. Although he had no proof of anything yet, the ham operator's call had flushed Tom with enthusiasm and he wanted to begin rattling the airline's cage to see if they were on the defensive or not. He had expected the brush-off and had prepared himself to issue a few veiled threats but their reaction had been surprising in the extreme.

Neil G. Fleishmann, Head of Legal Affairs, had taken his call immediately. "Hi, Tom. I guess you're right, it's time we got together. I had been expecting to hear from you."

The American accent wasn't strong and Tom guessed he had probably been resident in the UK for some years. Sincerity and reasonableness clung to his words with tenacity and Tom could visualise his body language – open, inviting, welcoming but above all disarming.

Varsity obviously did not like the publicity which had ensued from the Heathrow protest and their aim would be to prevent anything similar from happening in future. Tom thought this was probably why Fleishmann had been eager to meet so promptly – Friday in fact.

Tom could not go to the meeting without a clear negotiating line as any sign of weakness or doubt, any hint of incompetence or lack of purpose and they would eat him alive. He was desperate for an hour or two with no interruptions in order to clarify his thoughts and prepare.

1.15 p.m. "Two gin and tonics, please, Jenny."

Harry Harrison took the drinks over to where George Fraser was sitting at a small table by a window in the clubhouse overlooking the first tee.

"Cheers, George!"

"Cheers, old boy." It wasn't their first of the day.

"Turning into a bit of a bunfight, this inquest, isn't it." Harry was simply making conversation.

"Well, your lad is certainly taking it all a mite seriously and my officer's getting a bit testy with him to be honest. Tom's making demands that I've never come across before in all my time as coroner. Does he know what he's doing, Harry, because it doesn't seem that way?"

"To be honest, I'm not sure. He certainly likes to think he knows but then he thinks that about everything he does. Thing with Tom is, if he doesn't know something he'll damn soon find it out and if he gets it wrong at first, he simply shakes off the failure and comes back at it from a different angle. He's very persistent and determined when he wants to be, so don't underestimate him, George."

George became pensive and ummed as he looked into his drink. "You know he's trying to insist on a full hearing, with a jury?"

"No, he never mentioned it."

"Quite insistent! I wrote to him and tried to make the point that there's already a lot in the public domain and I don't think we need a full inquest at all but he wouldn't have it. So far as I can see, there's no obligation under the '88 Act to have a jury but this may depend on the outcome of the investigations. I suspect the causes of death will be quite straightforward in each case. It's ridiculous, Harry, he wants me to go through the whole process with a jury, full representation, the lot! An extraordinary amount of work and for what? Can't you speak to him?"

"He wouldn't listen, I promise you!"

"I think you should try because he's in danger of making your practice a laughing stock. I can't tell you how many parties there are involved in this thing and they'll all have to be represented. A waste of God knows how much time and money just because your boy wants his way. Believe me, he's got absolutely no reason for it. It's pure theatre!"

"George, I'm trying my best, honestly. I think there's a woman with a bit of undue influence over him, to be honest. She's a half-caste of some sort and seems to have impressed him and I hope I'm wrong but I suspect there might be a bit of playing to the gallery."

"Well, be warned, you're getting your name bandied about and these constant appearances on telly don't help.

Commercial clients don't like this sort of exposure – you know what I mean?"

"I know exactly what you mean." Harry took a long sip of his drink. "I am worried, I have to be honest, but you know Tom – he's always had this thing about the underdog. I don't know if I ever told you but when he was at prep school we had a complaint from his housemaster about the state of his clothes. Caroline nearly had a heart attack – she always sent him off looking like a new pin – so I followed him one morning, a good distance behind so he had no idea I was there. Do you know what he did? He went out of the front door and along the road but then doubled round the back of the house, through the back garden gate and straight to the shed. When he came out he was wearing his oldest, tattiest clothes and cap – he'd swapped them! Turned out the parents of one little chap were on hard times and he looked a bit scruffy – was being picked on and Tom wanted to stand four-square with him so he dressed the same."

George shook his head and smiled. "That kind of thing is fine for kids but it's a hard world out there for us grown-ups, Harry, not a lot of room for sentiment."

"I agree, George. Well, the ball's in your court so don't feel you owe me any favours because he's my boy. You do what you think is right but I have to be honest, though, I do admire him for his tenacity. When it's directed properly it makes him a very formidable opponent. He just needs a bit of direction."

"I can promise you one thing, Harry, there'll be no favouritism from me. Time for another?"

"Why not, I haven't got much on today."

2.15 p.m. Ailey and Bernard arrived and Tom knew by their faces that he would be expected to reach a decision about her offer. As ever, Ailey quickly skated over the formalities.

"It's not happening, Tom, it's just not happening. I don't want to lecture you on ethics but most of your people will do what you ask them because they respect you but a lot of them are uneasy. I know it's not your fault but you've got nothing to show them, nothing for three months of chasing."

Bernard could not wait to get his point across and Tom realised he didn't really like the man – he was an opportunist. "They're unhappy, Tom, because they reckon you're barking up the wrong tree. Most will do nowt without your say-so but I'm telling you now, they would sooner do it through the US courts because of the lack of action here – and the fact is, there's nowt on the horizon to give 'em much hope."

Ailey tried to steer the conversation away from the confrontation which appeared to be threatening. "I did try to warn you that this was a no-win situation without huge resources. It's no one's fault, it's just the way it is. You're gonna get nothing here in the UK and my offer to be our agent still stands. What about it, Tom? Together we can screw the mothers, I know it!"

Tom looked to the ceiling and tried to avoid being irritated by Ailey's patronising tone. He took his time before answering and the room fell into a very uneasy silence. He was genuinely considering what she had said but Bernard could not resist an opportunity to fill the void with one more comment.

"I'll be straight with you, Tom, there's a feeling that you're allowing one person to take control of the situation and you're making decisions for her and not for the majority."

If there had been any doubt in Tom's mind about what decision to take, that decided it. "The answer's no and in any case you're wrong. Most people want to keep the action here in the UK. Sure, a few will go with you but the majority won't – and I represent a group, not one person and it will be the group that decides so don't insult their intelligence."

He could feel a slight tremble in his voice and knew it was anger. With sudden clarity, it came to him why he was turning down the most lucrative business opportunity that had ever come his way – and it had nothing to do with Bernard's insulting little innuendoes. It was Ailey's outburst in Savoy Gardens.

She had shown her motivation to be compensation and nothing else. No matter how important or devastating any discoveries they made – even gross criminal negligence – Ailey would only view them as an aid to extorting greater compensation and thus upping her share of the winnings. If anything stood in the way of that goal it would be glossed over, ignored – even buried from view.

She looked genuinely disappointed at his decision and it was obvious she'd expected him to agree. He actually felt a little sorry for her and her response caused his anger instantly to evaporate; in fact it almost made him laugh.

"I'm not accepting no for an answer!"

It was like the petulant stamp of a foot, a toss of the curls and he had to respond. "You don't have any choice, Ailey," he said with a chuckle, reaching out to touch her arm in a gesture of intimacy.

She coloured and for the first time he saw her flustered. "What I mean, Tom, is please don't say no yet. I know I've put pressure on you but keep your options open for just a little while longer. I don't want to tell you why right now but I do have a reason, okay? Will you at least do that for me? Please?"

Tom could think of no reason not to, but in the forefront of his mind was the troubling thought that he could not ever share information with her, either now or in the future because their agendas were entirely different and contradictory.

"Okay, Ailey, we'll leave it on hold for a while – but don't get your hopes up." The phone rang. It was Caffrey.

"What?" Tom was incredulous. He turned to Ailey. "Did you know they were releasing most of the bodies for burial?"

"No, but I'm not surprised. You've got no more interest in them, have you?" In a rare slip of control Ailey failed to hide the fact that she was fishing.

Tom told Caffrey he would ring him back and without embarrassment asked Bernard to wait in reception and with extremely bad humour he left the room.

As soon as the door closed Tom put a proposition to Ailey. "All right, I'll be honest with you. You asked me for a favour and I agreed but now I need you to do the same for me. Please don't release the Baker bodies for burial."

"Why, Tom? They're not your clients."

"They might be significant. I'm asking the pathologist for a judgement."

"Hey, now hang on, buddy. That may give you the right to

see the pathology report but that's it – it does not give you the right to examine the body."

"I can request that right – and I will if necessary." He was banking on Ailey being ignorant of English law.

She went silent and tapped her foot before confronting him. "Don't bullshit me, Tom, I've been too long in this game. There's no way you can get at that body, not even if it was a homicide, so don't treat me like a moron – and before you even think of it, you try poaching the Bakers as clients and I'll fire off a letter of complaint to your Law Society with such a bang you'll hear the noise from here. Do you understand me? Now, what's going on? You've got a very big interest in the Bakers and I'd like to know why? No bullshit, just tell me the truth and I'll decide."

Tom knew the one thing he could not tell her was the truth because if Ailey thought another Baker post-mortem might reveal some proof of terrorism, something that might let Varsity off the hook, she would never agree. "Please trust me, that's all I'm asking," Tom said, with as much artificial sincerity as he could muster but it was clearly unconvincing.

"Crap!" She got up and moved towards the door. "All that 'trust me' bullshit means you don't want me to know your reasons and you haven't had time to think of an excuse I might buy. I'd like to help you, Tom, but you've got to level with me."

"That's a no, then?"

Ailey stuck her middle finger up at him but the smile was genuine. It was a lesson not to underestimate her.

"I'm fishing around, Ailey, I admit it. There are one or two glimmers but nothing very much. Baker is hardly even a distant glow and if we get access, it probably won't come to anything. It's called clutching at straws and to make matters worse, I've got a meeting with Varsity tomorrow and nothing to hit them with. Now I can't be much more honest than that."

"Mistake, Tom," said Ailey, without any rancour, "you should be going for Barcroft with me. Who you seeing?"

"Fleishmann."

"Top legal man and about as oily as an engineer's rag." She paused after opening the door.

"Flight 469 was flying under Algerian regulations. The reason it was scheduled to stop in Algiers was to change the flight crew because they'd already been working for nearly ten hours when they took off from Northolt." She smiled at him sweetly. "I can't see you go to the OK Corral without a gun, can I? Be seeing you."

Tom knew her information would be accurate. He also knew he was just the messenger and she wanted Varsity to get the message. That knowledge did not disturb him at all as he was just pleased to have something on them. He suspected it had no great import for Ailey but was just a first little shot to show Varsity that someone was on their case.

He returned Caffrey's call. "Why are you releasing the bodies now? I haven't finished my investigations."

"What's the matter, laddie, you saving them as Christmas presents?" Tom had forgotten how much he disliked that viscous but abrasive voice.

"I know I have no authority yet but I am in the process of obtaining it so while that's being sorted out I want you to hold on to Mr Baker's body."

"Which Mr Baker, laddie?" It wasn't the response Tom had expected.

"Station Road Mr Baker."

"Like I said, laddie, which Mr Baker?"

Caffrey was back in the driving seat and Tom loathed him for it. "I take it there's more than one Mr Baker of Station Road?"

"Aye, three to be precise! Now, if there's nothing else..." Caffrey hung up.

3.20 p.m. "It's getting a bit out of hand, isn't it, Charles?"

John Sturgis had never liked Astbury for even in a cabinet constructed from naked aggression and blatant self-aggrandisement, Astbury stood out as a master of both. His position as Minister of Transport would normally not have qualified him for the cabinet but his dual role as party chairman made it a necessity.

Sturgis could remember the personal struggle he had had over whether to support his appointment as chairman and in the end had voted for him – albeit with great reservations. He could not understand why but the party faithful loved the man. He did have great communication skills and was what people termed a good politician – he could lie convincingly.

"In what way, John?"

"These demands for a public inquiry. To be honest, I think they have a point."

"Do you now? They've already got a SAAIU inquiry." The two men lapsed into silence as the ministerial car headed towards Victoria.

"You're not suggesting you want the cabinet to reverse its decision, are you?" There was an unmistakable edge in Astbury's voice and John Sturgis detected it.

"It wouldn't be the first decision reversed by cabinet, would it? God almighty, it's becoming an everyday occurrence as the PM shifts his ground with every new breeze of discontent."

"There's one difference with this one, John."

"What's that?"

"I proposed it. I'm not in the habit of changing my mind as you may have noticed. You're not intending to challenge it, are you? Because if you do, I can tell you it won't succeed."

"Bit of an overreaction, Charles! All I'm saying is that these Harrow people are obviously not going to give up and if your intention was to protect public service policies from too close scrutiny, it's failed. Everyone in the country now knows what went wrong and I'm just suggesting it might be time to reclaim the initiative, that's all."

Charles Astbury opened his briefcase and removed some papers. "I wasn't aware that I'd surrendered it, John."

John Sturgis tried to control his irritation. As Home Secretary, his was one of the great positions of state and this junior minister did not even bother to hide his contempt and while he intended to let the subject drop, he could not resist a final jab. "Hope you're right, Charles, because it looks to me like that woman's determined to have your bollocks on a platter!"

He turned and looked out of the window as the car passed

the Cenotaph and thought to himself, *and yours will be the only ones, I'll see to that!*

4.00 p.m. When Louise Watson arrived, Tom was still frantically trying to make space in his day. Her breezy enthusiasm went some way towards restoring his equanimity and he suddenly became aware that he had never before really looked at her closely, as a person and not just a journalist. He took in her black, bubbly hair, wide-set cheekbones and big round, blue eyes, all of which looked decidedly Irish. She was slim-waisted, curvaceous and pretty, definitely pretty. But the real attraction was her eyes; they were a compelling blue and behind them seemed to sparkle a great deal of humour and warmth, even honesty. It was just a pity, he felt, that they had always met under circumstances where humour was the last thing anyone felt like exhibiting.

"You're not Irish, are you?"

"Mum was an O'Hannerhan – London Irish, never set foot in the old country but a Mick to her toenails."

Tom genuinely regretted that he did not have time for the interview but tried not to be dismissive. "What's your deadline for this story?"

"I've got a couple of days, why?"

"I can't do it justice today and it could be there'll be a bit more to tell tomorrow."

"Okay, but I can't make it until the evening; is that a problem?"

"No. Perhaps I'll let you buy me a drink." Tom had to make a decision as to how far he was prepared to trust Louise because although he could not fault the copy she had written so far, if it ever came to it, a good story might take precedence over everything else.

"What's your interest in the disaster – purely professional?" Tom asked but it came out as an accusation.

"Yes, of course, but it depends on your interpretation of the word professional, doesn't it." He could see her physically bridling. "What's your interest, Mr Harrison junior; is it unprofessional?"

"That's not what I meant." It seemed to Tom he was spending far too much of his time being verbally carved up by articulate and passionate women and it was almost certainly his own fault.

"No, I know it's not," Louise answered with directness. "What you were really asking was, will I do anything for a good story and say to hell with everyone else in the process? And the answer to that is no but I don't think you had any right to ask me. We're very similar, you and I, local born and bred, both affected by the disaster, both saw what it was really like and both, in our different ways, trying to find some answers. My credentials are as good as yours, Tom."

Tom reached into a drawer, pulled out some newspapers and tossed them in front of Louise. "You can't blame me for being just a little bit nervous." She didn't even look at them.

"I didn't write those. Try looking at my copy."

Tom took the papers back. "I have; it's all been accurate and principled and I apologise if you thought I was attacking you. The truth is, I need all the help I can get and if I hadn't thought of you as an ally I wouldn't have even raised it. I'm sorry – genuinely sorry because you're one of the last people I want to upset." He suddenly realised how sincerely he meant it.

"Sounds like you're on to something." Louise's nose for a story was proving stronger than her sense of outrage.

"Let's say there is a glimmering but it doesn't yet add up to much. What I really need is a bit of technical know-how. Do you remember a trade journalist who questioned Astbury about Flight 469 – right back at the start; I'm sure it was soon after the crash?"

"Yeah, I remember him well. In fact I've been in touch with him since to help with background info – knows his stuff. Anthony Berrens of *Jetstream* magazine."

"Got his number? I want to see if he'll talk to me – act as an adviser." Tom could see Louise's interest blossoming.

"Going to tell me what it's about?"

Tom felt he was now committed. "There was a technical problem with the rear cargo door on the P11 and it might have played a part in the crash." He could see the look of disappointment in her face.

"Old news, sorry. It's not public yet but I know Varsity is going to produce the maintenance records to show they had the modifications carried out – if it ever becomes an issue, that is."

Tom felt sick. It was one of the few leads he had and it was gone in one dismissive sentence. His purpose now was to save face and although he had not intended to mention the radio ham it was all he had left and so he told her of the phone call and as he did so, the possible sequence of events became clearer to him.

"Flight 469 had a minor emergency, just the kind of emergency that might have been produced by the rear cargo door slipping its main closures. It was well known to all P11 pilots that this had happened before and there was no immediate threat, hence the PAN call. But all that was holding the door shut were the emergency closures. What if they'd given way?"

Louise pondered what he'd said. "First you've got to show that Varsity hadn't modified the cargo door or that it wasn't done properly, then you've got to produce the air to ground conversation, then you've got to show it was the cargo door that gave way, then you've got to prove the emergency closures gave way, then you've got to show that an unsecured cargo door could cause a crash and..."

Her words petered out and she held her hands out, palms uppermost, but Louise was animated, her eyes shining.

6.00 p.m. By the time Vicky arrived, Tom had dismissed the cargo door setback and when she kissed him on the cheek he could smell her perfume and feel the warmth of her skin. It was always the same perfume and on the rare occasions when he detected it on someone else, it invariably produced an image of Vicky. He could barely admit it to himself but like a line from some Cole Porter song, his heart skipped a beat, or at least that is what it felt like.

"And before you say anything," she said, with a disarming smile, "no, I won't tell you when I'm next going to engage in a bit of direct action. Sorry."

Tom half thought about scolding her but reminded himself that Vicky had managed to produce more results than he had. He was about to say as much but Vicky cut him off.

"Shut up, please," she said, holding her finger up. "The reason I won't tell you is because it'll fill you with angst, you'll have sleepless nights and it'll compromise your solicitor's oath or whatever it is you swear when you finish your apprenticeship. But most of all, you'll try and stop me and I'm not having that, okay? Everything clear?"

"Perfectly," he replied, hoping that being arrested for terrorism and having her car blown up wasn't going to become a habit. They went to his car and began the frustratingly slow drive through West London.

When he told her about the radio ham, her enthusiasm was infectious. Arrest, detention and sensory deprivation appeared to have had no effect in blunting her determination. The journey suddenly became pleasurable; two enthused friends, happy in each other's company.

Tom could not bring himself to tell her about the release of the bodies for burial – David's body. In fact, it wasn't until they were approaching Ruislip High Street that he broached the subject and then presented it simply as a matter of fact and was surprised when she showed little reaction.

"That makes tonight's meeting a bit desperate, doesn't it – if you want to perform a post-mortem on Mrs Veezey?" Vicky's tone was even and she seemed untroubled by the news. Even more surprising, she indicated as clearly as she could that she knew precisely what Tom was thinking. "It's okay, Tom, it's not David, it's just his lifeless remains. I'm all right, honest."

He felt for her hand and held it for a moment, for a very long moment and felt the reassuring pressure of his fingers returned. Again Cole Porter did his stuff and Tom was angry with himself for even daring to allow this unprofessional indulgence with a client – but more importantly, a recently bereaved widow. He was disgusted with himself – but also excited.

He wrestled his thoughts back under control and forced his mind to concentrate on the purpose of their visit. "We always seem to be playing catch-up and, yes, tonight is important – and much more complicated than I'd like it to be. I don't just want to see the notes on Baker, I want our own pathologist to examine him."

Vicky perceptibly sat back in the car seat and spun her face towards him. "Is that allowed?"

Tom couldn't resist a smile. "No, not without consent and in any case I don't know which Mr Baker to examine; there seem to have been a lot of them at that address. You don't remember any initials or first names on the report you saw, do you?"

"'Fraid not. I just saw the name Baker."

Tom handed Vicky the *A to Z* and she began to look up Mafeking Road while he pulled the car into the kerb. "In a way, it's slightly irrelevant now that they're releasing the bodies because if tonight Mr Veezey asks us to act for him then this might enable us to request the path reports on all the Bakers. That's something but if we want to stop the burial, the only way I can do that is to get the surviving Baker or Bakers to also sign me up as their lawyer. Mr Veezey would then become redundant and we could leave the old boy out of it. I just feel safer covering both options because I do want to get that body – those bodies – examined."

"Ailey Newman's going to love you if you get the Bakers!" Tom noticed that Vicky never referred to Ailey solely by her first name, as if it were too intimate. She indicated with her hand. "Straight ahead, third right, second left."

Tom gave a wry smile and pulled away. "She's made it abundantly clear what she'll do if I try but more to the point, are the Bakers going to want their dead carved up for a third time? I doubt it." He negotiated the turnings and pulled into Mafeking Road. Vicky had gone unusually quiet.

"You all right?" Tom enquired but Vicky cut across him.

"As soon as we're finished here, drop me at home, will you, Tom?"

"Vicky … you're up to something?"

"Just don't ask!"

Friday, March 15th, 1991, 11.30 a.m. The opulence of the reception was mirrored by the lift, which was so smooth that Tom was barely conscious of it moving. As the doors glided open, Neil Fleishmann was waiting to greet him, hand outstretched.

"Tom, good to see you. Glad you could come." His

handshake could have cracked walnuts and the narrow-faced, balding, sallow-skinned legal executive adjusted his rimless spectacles and led the way down a wide corridor. "We're just round the corner here."

He led the way into a large and expensively furnished office based on the Japanese, minimalist school of interior design. About the only human touch was the framed desk photograph of a woman, presumably his wife, and three small children. Judging by the woman's clothes and Fleishmann's age, it was taken years ago.

The intimacy with which Fleishmann spoke to him set Tom's teeth on edge. Every word, every gesture felt designed to draw Tom into a cosy, confidential cocoon which bathed the two of them in mutual warmth and excluded the rest of the world.

Coffee was ordered, legal anecdotes swapped and at precisely the point when Tom thought the stage had been sufficiently set, Fleishmann asked, "Tom, you wouldn't mind if Chuck Cravits joined us, would you? He's our Vice President in charge of Corporate Affairs."

Tom did not mind and Charles Cravits responded to a buzz on the intercom by entering through a communicating door.

He could not have been anything but American as everything about the youngish man was wholesome, clean and deodorised. He looked remarkably like one of the Mormon missionaries who regularly canvassed Tom's flats and Tom could swear there was a faint aroma of Brut clinging to his closely shaved cheeks. His eyes, however, were bright, intelligent and unflinching – those of a man who knew his strengths.

Cravits immediately took charge and Tom could have written his script for him – a long and heartfelt expression of sympathy for those who had perished in the disaster, interwoven with a careful but unobtrusive positioning of Varsity Aviation in the 'not guilty' corner.

Tom knew all this was nothing more than the opening shot in negotiations which would doubtless drag on for months, perhaps even years. He was determined to give nothing away which, given the paucity of his hand, was not difficult. Fleishmann joined the conversation.

"As you must know, Tom, Varsity Aviation has an excellent safety record – second to none – and we want to be as open and as straight as we can with you. This is a dreadful situation and we're on your side, honestly, Tom. We feel for those poor people, for our own staff, for Christ's sake, who also perished, so just tell me what it is you want from us."

Tom had worked out his position and his approach but the more intimate Fleishmann became, the more formal Tom felt himself becoming and he cut through the niceties with his opening lines.

"Compensation, gentlemen, that's what I want. I am currently representing forty-seven clients, forty-two of them bereaved relatives and five who have suffered serious injury and I would like to know *your* intentions."

Cravits said nothing and Fleishmann's smile still clung to his lips but it was a thinner, weaker version of the one which had previously been there.

"Legally, Tom, we have no need to offer you anything. There is no suggestion that Varsity is in any way culpable in this dreadful affair…"

"Isn't there?" There was no threat in Tom's remark but the way it cut across Fleishmann provided the intended touch of theatre. Cravits showed no reaction.

Tom continued. "We won't really know the answer to that until the SAAIU inquiry is completed, will we?" His smile was totally benign.

Fleishmann relaxed. "We couldn't be any more confident than we are, could we, Chuck? Varsity is not in the frame."

Cravits ignored him and spoke directly to Tom. "Why should we pay you compensation?"

"Five hundred and twenty-three dead people killed by one of your aircraft – that's one reason. You have a massive public relations exercise to pull off if you want to retain credibility."

Fleishmann could not wait to get in. "Sorry, Tom, but you don't speak for the aircraft passengers. We have a contractual relationship with them and that will be handled separately."

Tom ignored his remark. "Our investigations are not terribly far advanced but there are already several anomalies and I'm sure you'll understand if I don't spell them out at this stage but we are concerned – let's put it that way." Fleishmann looked to Cravits as though to offer him the floor and Cravits accepted.

"I don't think this is the time to issue – well, shall we say – not very well veiled threats, Mr Harrison, because believe me, it isn't that kind of situation." The grey eyes remained focused on Tom and blinked not once.

"My apologies if that's how you interpreted my words, Mr Cravits; I wouldn't dream of issuing threats, either veiled or otherwise," Tom responded, summoning all the artificial sincerity he could muster. "It's simply that this could turn into a long and tortuous action in which every stone would need to be overturned. It could take years and I know there will be discoveries along the way that the public may not properly understand or may find disquieting."

"You know that, do you?" Cravits's question was just a little too abrupt and followed Tom's words just a little too closely, indicating he was not totally at ease.

"Oh yes." Tom said with an authority he wished was genuine.

Cravits forced his mouth to smile. "Do you have a for instance?"

Tom decided to deliver Ailey's message. "Yes, for example, I suspect that few members of the public are aware that you operate Varsity under Algerian flight regulations and the aircrew on Flight 469 had been working for nearly ten hours at the time of the crash..."

Fleishmann intervened as the temperature rose. "Absolutely nothing illegal in that at all."

"Mr Fleishmann," Tom said with great concern, "I wouldn't necessarily suggest there was – although I think we'll have to wait and see on that one. I'm simply saying that strict legality and public perception don't always sup from the same bowl." He had never used the expression before in his life and it sounded like his father speaking, but he quite liked it.

Cravits took over again. "If we come to the table to discuss some level of no-fault compensation, it won't be on the basis of buying off bad publicity. I hope that's clear. It will be to uphold our excellent corporate image and to make a gesture of compassion to the victims of this awful accident." There was a strong emphasis on 'accident'.

"But you are prepared to talk?"

Fleishmann's eyes flicked between Tom and Cravits before he spoke. "I think I can say ... er ... that's a possibility... I think we might be prepared to come to the table." Tom caught Cravits's almost imperceptible nod from the corner of his eye and Fleishmann relaxed. "Yes, we've always seen that as a necessary gesture to the people of London, haven't we, Chuck?" Cravits nodded silently.

Little else of substance was covered and eventually Tom excused himself, having established who would contact whom to set up the next meeting. He felt quite happy with the day as Fleishmann escorted him back to the lift.

Returning to his sterile office, Fleishmann met Chuck Cravits in the corridor.

"Not quite the hillbilly you led me to believe," said Cravits as he powered past.

When Tom arrived back in his office there was no word from Vicky, which surprised him, as there had been no contact from her since the previous Tuesday evening, following their meeting with Mr Veezey, a meeting which had been successful. Tom had carefully explained to the old man what was involved, in the least graphic terms possible, but he really wasn't sure that Mr Veezey had fully understood. The old man seemed to have withdrawn into death's anteroom and was waiting patiently for its big black horses to carry him off to be with his beloved wife once more.

It was his sister, Nellie, who had driven the decision along. "Of course you want to know *how* Lily died, don't you, Ed?"

"Do I?" he'd replied.

"Of course you do! You want to know if it was an accident, don't you, or if the buggers did something they shouldn't have done?" There was no suggestion that Edward Veezey was deaf but Nellie seemed to think he understood better if she shouted.

Money hadn't been mentioned until the end of the meeting when Nellie, who was as sharp as a knife, said, "Well, if you're expecting any money for all this you can whistle; Ed and I haven't got two ha'pennies to rub together." She raised her voice sharply, "Have we, Ed?" Ed was again lost in his own thoughts and didn't bother to reply. Vicky had immediately offered help from the support group in meeting the costs.

They left having got what they went for but Tom felt nothing but deep sorrow and took away with him the indelible image of a sad, old, beanpole of a man, in borrowed, ill-fitting clothes, sitting on a hard-backed kitchen chair, staring constantly into the distance, as though the past was the only surety of who he was and where he was. He found it difficult to concentrate on the conversation, perhaps afraid to let go of his thoughts in case his visions of Lily dissolved and disappeared like the smoke which had killed her and once dispersed, he may never be able to reassemble them. Afterlife or not, Tom hoped that Ed Veezey died very soon.

A quick knock and Mike's grinning face appeared round the door. He looked annoyingly pleased. "Lol Kumar, godfather of the baggage handlers, is ready to meet. He's not that keen so I reckon you're best striking while the iron's hot – like tonight! He's a bit wobbly because he thinks you might be trying to put the baggage handlers in the frame and you're going to have to persuade him that's not the case."

"What time?"

"Six thirty."

"Damn! Of course I'll go, it's just that I'd already arranged to see Louise Watson."

"Believe me, on the visuals front you'd be better off with Louise." Mike smiled as the phone rang and Tom answered it.

It was his father. "I'm afraid I can't at the moment, Dad, what about tomorrow morning? ... Nine okay? ... Fine ... Bye."

"So Mohammed's finally off to see the mountain, eh? It'll be a wrist-slapping at least, or maybe a Saturday morning detention and a thousand lines – 'I must not allow my clients to publicly shaft the Establishment.'" Mike chuckled to himself.

"It's bloody ridiculous, isn't it? I'm conducting a case that's huge by any legal standards and my old man wants to see if I've washed behind my ears. It can't go on Mike, can it?"

"You know what I think..."

The phone shrilled again before Mike could finish and Tom answered it. His reaction was one of unmistakable pleasure.

"Of course, Mrs Baker, I understand fully... To be honest, the answer has to be the sooner the better. Yes, tomorrow is perfect ... and, yes, ten's fine. Mrs Baker, you are approaching me entirely of your own volition, aren't you? I mean, no one has put you under any pressure and you're quite clear that I haven't solicited your business? The reason I say that is because I know you are presently legally represented and it would be unethical of me to attempt to persuade you to change lawyers. Good, as long as you're clear about it... I look forward to meeting you."

Tom hung up and looked at Mike in silence. Mike finally spoke. "New York's answer to Imelda Marcos is gonna want to spit-roast you!"

Tom cast his eyes to the ceiling. "*Que sera, sera!* Right, we've got to move because we need a different pathologist, a specialist."

"Not that again."

"I know which one this time."

"No prior knowledge of the Baker decision, of course?"

"Of course not, just good anticipation. Now listen, I want Sir Oswald Napier, champion of the old school, knight of the realm, so get on to Caffrey and make sure the three Bakers and Mrs Veezey aren't disposed of. I'll contact Napier."

Mike hesitated. "What is it you're looking for this time?"

"Explosives, old son, explosives!"

CHAPTER TWELVE

Friday, March 15th, 1991, 6.30 p.m. The bars of The Gate public house, and there were several of them, were large. The 1930s architecture had changed very little and neither had the decor – a polished oak and mirrored monument to art deco drinking.

It was fairly quiet in the largest saloon, the Flight Deck, with a few groups of mostly men standing drinking at the bar. Isolated on the far side of the bar, in the corner, was a sweeping curve of moquette-covered banquette seating where four men in working clothes sat at a low table, glasses in front of them.

There was no doubting who the leader was, for he sat in the centre and all heads were turned towards him. An unspoken message signalled the presence of Mike and Tom and the four men slowly turned in their direction but there was not one smile of welcome between them and their eyes were heavy with caution.

Lol Kumar's broad, clean-shaven face looked more Sinhalese than Indian and the blue cotton jacket hung limply down on either side of his stomach, like curtains waiting to be drawn over his bulging corporation. A shiny blue nylon tee shirt covered his protruding stomach, clinging as tightly as metallic spray paint, outlining every detail of his indented naval, and thin dark lines showed where the material had been sweat-stained by the damp creases of his skin. He was probably no more than forty years old yet carried himself like a modern Buddha. Tom barely noticed the other three men.

Power usually sits on people's shoulders like a mantle and Kumar was no exception. He sat immobile, appraising them, his hands resting on the seat at either side of him, one set of podgy fingers clutching an address book, the other a mobile phone. He looked like a man who was used to being obeyed.

Mike introduced Tom, and Kumar said nothing, simply inclined his head towards some low stools facing the group across the table. The two men sat facing Kumar and his entourage but Tom was in no rush to break the silence.

It was Mike who spoke first. "Drink, anyone?" There were two takers, although not Kumar, and Mike went to the bar. Silence continued and was broken by the ringing of a mobile phone with both Tom and Kumar reaching for theirs simultaneously; neither could resist a smile.

In fact it was Tom's call – Louise Watson. He made arrangements to see her later as peremptorily as he could and hung up, offering Kumar a card. "So you know who you're not talking to." He had to pitch it exactly right or it would sound aggressive. Kumar gave a single snort, his belly wobbled and Tom took it as a chuckle.

"So what have the baggage boys done wrong?" Kumar spoke the words with great care as though reciting poetry, in an accent which was distinctly middle class.

"Nothing," Tom replied. "I'm not interested in the baggage handlers, it's the airline I'm after. Do you know who was working on the Varsity flight, the one that went down?"

"I might," said Kumar.

"Anything you say to me is in confidence."

"And flash Harry here?" asked Kumar, nodding towards Mike as he returned with the drinks.

"Same applies to him."

"Baggage boys take a lot of stick – always have done. They're accused of blackmailing the airlines for more money, accused of restrictive practices, accused of damaging suitcases, accused of stealing from the luggage. Now what is it you're accusing us of? Not closing the door properly? Killing people? I hope not – " he looked at Tom's card – "Mr Harrison, I hope not!"

It had the ring of a threat but Tom let it ride over him. "I'm a lawyer, Mr Kumar, and I know that responsibility for the P11 cargo door wasn't the baggage handlers', it was the airline's. There is no doubt in my mind on that point – okay? What I'm interested in is whether the door on Flight 469 had been modified or not. Varsity claims it had."

Kumar gave a big, shaking chuckle which was as artificial as the dust-covered plastic flowers on the windowsill behind him. "What do you reckon to that, lads?" They took their cue from him and laughed mirthlessly.

"They treat you like shit, they tell you shit, big business is shit," said Kumar, leaning forward and taking a delicate sip from a glass of mineral water before returning to exactly the same, relaxed position. "Are you political, Mr Harrison?"

"Not overly," Tom replied truthfully.

"You should be! Politics is in the air you breathe, it's in the water you drink, in the food you eat and it's even in the bed where you make love. Politics made you what you are, Mr Harrison, and it made us what we are." Kumar threw out an arm to encompass his colleagues. "It is politics that sends young men to prison for stealing the things you take for granted, it is politics which allows capitalists to kill five hundred and twenty-three people and requires them not even to apologise."

"What do you know about the Varsity aircraft, Mr Kumar?" Tom had abandoned all niceties as he felt the only approach this strange man appreciated was directness and anything else would be seen as suspect.

Kumar turned to the man sitting next to him. "Tell him what you know, Chas." The thin-faced man was in his fifties, needed a shave and looked extremely nervous.

"Sure it's all right, Lol?"

"Tell him!"

As Chas spoke, his eyes kept flicking to Lol Kumar. "It was still stickered, for sure. It had the warnings on it clear as day, the same ones the other P11's had before they were changed. I dunno, but there was something not right about that afternoon. The only bloke I saw get off the plane was one of the cabin crew – the purser, effing and blinding away he was. Foreign geezer – could have been an Arab, spoke good English though. Moaning about how he was supposed to have had the day off but it was cancelled. Right pissed off he was, saying how he didn't like Northolt because of the security – you do get used to security over there, still officially an RAF place even though civvies fly from it. Treat you like shit too, the RAF police..."

"Concentrate on what you're saying, Chas – discipline." Kumar touched his temple with his forefinger.

"Sorry, Lol. Like I said, you get used to the security but there were some shady-looking geezers hanging around before that P11 arrived – always on the edges, just out of range of being able to see them properly. Felt like you were being watched, checked up on. Light was going when it came in – quickest turnround I reckon I've ever seen. Passengers were on, luggage loaded – it was all containerised – and away."

Tom spoke slowly and clearly. "And you're quite certain the rear cargo door hadn't been modified?"

"On my life!"

"Did the pilot, the first officer or anyone else check the door after it was closed?"

"No one. The plane was in and out quicker than a tube train. Flight marshal was doing his pieces – 'Move it, move it,' he kept shouting and hollering. They were heavy containers and I was having a real job getting one in the right position to lock it off. 'Time you were pensioned off, you doddering old fart,' he yelled at me. 'Fuck up once more and you'll be down the road.' I'm on a warning you see."

Tom tried to steer him back to the point. "I'm going to ask you again – did any of the crew check the door after you?"

"Flight crew didn't even get out of the cockpit – but it wasn't me that shut the door and that's the truth." There was real fear in Chas's eyes and a haunted look which Tom felt would probably follow him for life, certain he was the one who had closed the cargo door and clearly as much a victim as Tom's clients.

"That's all I wanted to know," said Tom, as reassuringly as he could. "I'm going to need to ask you to make a written statement, if that's all right."

"No, mate, I'm not putting anything in writing, no way!"

Tom looked to Lol Kumar for support and the man shrugged his shoulders. Then Mike looked to Tom for his approval to speak, got the nod and for his first intervention, leant forward to make eye contact with Chas.

"As far as I see it, you've got two choices, Chas. You can keep your head down and let them come for you – pick you off, pile the shit on you, make you the scapegoat, and believe me they will. They'll show you no mercy. Or you can get your retaliation in first; but one thing's certain – if you lie on the ground and shout, 'Look at me, I'm a doormat,' the bleeders will wipe their feet all over you, make no mistake."

Chas again looked at Lol Kumar, who held his glass of mineral water delicately in his hand, little finger crooked.

"The artful dodger knows what he's talking about, Chas."

Tom encouraged Chas with his eyes, trying to offer unspoken reassurance and finally the man said the words Tom had been waiting for.

"Yeah, okay, I guess you're right."

"We can do it now if you like!" Tom wanted his evidence down on paper as quickly as possible.

"No, no! I've got to go in a minute – I'll come and see you!" They had obviously pushed Chas as far as he was prepared to go for the time being so Tom immediately fixed an appointment and having done so, visibly relaxed. He was aware Kumar was watching him and returned his look.

"So, if you win this little battle, the world will be a better place, will it, Mr Harrison?" Kumar's cynicism surrounded him like an aura. "What about all the other Varsity Aviations, the huge national operators, the multinational corporations? Will they all fold their tents and disappear into the night as a result of your victory or do you think they might ignore you and carry on as normal?"

"I do what I can," said Tom.

"You may not realise it, Mr Harrison, but you have embarked on something that, by the time it is finished, whether you win or whether you lose, will change you. You will never be the same man again, so say goodbye to innocence!" The smile that Kumar beamed down on him was patronising and arrogant but brimming with certainty.

"Who the hell is he?" asked Tom as they strode across the nearly empty car park.

"From what I can gather, he's a sort of Trotskyite Buddhist organiser. Thinks the unions have sold out and he's become the Mr Fixit of Northolt – controls all the baggage handlers, cleaners and most of the caterers. He's got real power. He'll deliver Chas for us."

"Just so long as it suits him." Tom held his hand out, palm upwards, and Mike slapped it. "I think we've got our first little victory."

6.55 p.m. Inside the offices of the *Evening Chronicle*, the tempo was at its slowest. The last edition had been on the streets for a couple of hours and the newsroom had reduced to little more than skeleton staffing.

Louise Watson had no need to be there but she wanted some telling pictures to go with her feature on the Harrow women and there was such a huge volume to go through that time had drifted away.

She was surprised to see the editor still there and even more surprised when he headed towards her desk. Joe Hayes was a newsman and didn't often take a direct interest in features so long as they were legal and didn't contravene the paper's political stance. He flicked through some of her many prints. "Some good substance to the story?" he enquired.

"Plenty, believe me!"

Over Joe's shoulder, through the glass partition, Louise could see that a tall man wearing an overcoat had entered the newsroom and his hesitance showed he was a stranger. Several other men came into view behind him and as a group they walked over towards her and Joe.

The first man presented an official-looking card to Joe for inspection. "You Joe Hayes?"

Joe replied tentatively. "Yes?" and examined the card. Louise could see it was a police warrant card.

"You're the editor of this newspaper?"

"Yes."

The man looked at Louise. "And who are you?"

"Louise Watson; why?"

He ignored the question. "We have reason to believe you are

writing a story which includes information about the air crash on Harrow, is that right?"

"So?" Louise could feel her resentment rising.

The plain clothes policeman handed a typewritten and signed document to Joe Hayes. "You are required by law to hand over to us all the material in your possession which has any connection, either directly or indirectly, with the Harrow air crash. We have the right to search these premises and to remove any material which we believe might be pertinent to our enquiries."

Louise waited for Joe to respond but he said nothing and concentrated on reading the search warrant with ridiculous care. She still waited for him to say something, anything, to argue, to resist, but Joe kept his eyes down scanning the document and Louise ran out of patience.

"So, effectively what you're saying is, you can take anything you damn well please from anywhere in the building whether it's got anything to do with the Harrow disaster or not and we can do nothing about it. Is that right?" Louise challenged the man.

His smile was utterly false. "What a smart little journalist you are, miss. Now, let's start with your address book and list of contacts – computerised, are they?" As he spoke, other officers had started to arrive, bringing with them large plastic storage bins and Joe continued to read the document as though his life depended on it.

"Joe, for Christ's sake, say something!" He remained silently reading and so she turned back to the policeman. "It's Special Branch, isn't it? What the hell's this all about – and don't tell me national security!"

"My, my, I said you were clever. Got it in one. Now, your list of contacts!"

7.30 p.m. Tom dropped Mike in the High Street and made it to his office to meet Louise just in time to see her pressing the entry bell, walked up behind her and as she swung round he could see her face was a study in anger. "They've pulled my story; they've pulled my story on the women; they've searched the premises, treated me like shit... Can you believe it?"

"Hey, hey, just a minute. Who's pulled your story, who's treated you like shit?"

"The bloody Government, that's who. They've slapped a D-notice on it and Special Branch has been all over the offices like ants. They've taken all my pictures and research material and they even brought bloody plastic storage boxes with them and filled them like they were removals men. I can't believe it. There was personal stuff there and they just lumped it all in together. When I tried to take one notebook back – it had absolutely nothing to do with the crash, in fact nothing at all to do with work – one of the bastards grabbed my arm, forced me into my chair and said he'd break my wrist if I tried anything like it again. He hurt me, Tom!" There was disbelief and shock in her tone.

Tom put his hands on her arm to try and stop her from pacing up and down. "God almighty – what reason did they give?" His mind was racing as the implications of what Louise was saying began to register and was trying to work out if he should be doing anything and if so, what?

"National bloody security, that's what. 'Information that might assist an enemy of the state' or some such nonsense. Isn't there anything I can do, an appeal, a challenge, judicial review, something…?"

"You've got lawyers on the *Chronicle* – get on to them immediately, see what they have to say. They must have a lot more experience of this kind of thing than I have."

"They'd all gone home and Joe Hayes didn't even bother to call anyone out, can you believe it? They were so rude, so bloody arrogant and Joe did absolutely nothing, just flapped around like an old hen. The thing that really worries me, he didn't even look surprised."

"Get on to the dailies, the late night TV news, radio … go public on it?"

Louise shook her head. "No, with a D-notice involved they won't touch it and in any case I don't want it made public, there's a lot of rooting around still to do and the last thing I want is the whole of London pointing at me saying, 'There's that stupid cow who risked national security.' I think it's better if my face isn't splashed across the front pages and anyway, if anyone seriously thinks Special Branch is watching me they won't open their mouths even to breathe while I'm around. There's nothing I can do really, is there, Tom?"

Tom was desperately seeking an answer. "Well..."

"It's all right, save your breath, I know there isn't."

"Hang on, let's think about it."

"There's nothing that won't keep until tomorrow so you can buy me a drink. Anyway, there's something I want to show you and I'm sure it's connected. Come on, Tom, I'll get over it, I've calmed down now. It's all part of the job, I suppose."

They made their way across the street and into the first pub they could find and Louise's anger had subsided by the time they got their drinks and found a quiet table.

"God, I just fancy a cigarette and I haven't thought that for a long time," Louise said and drank from her spritzer. "Strange how things turn out, isn't it, Tom? So much death, destruction and misery and so many unanswered questions. Sometimes it seems I'm the only journalist who's willing to investigate and yet I end up with Special Branch clambering all over my office trying to shut me up. What does that tell you?"

Tom paused before replying but he already knew the answer. "It confirms my belief that Varsity aren't in this on their own..."

"Someone, somewhere, must be very worried, that's all I can say," added Louise, "but the question is, who? Who has access to Special Branch?" It was a rhetorical question.

"Well, I guess they got what they wanted so you're off the hook now." Tom didn't believe it but he wanted to put her at ease.

"They won't stop me, Tom." Louise spat the words out with total conviction. "I saw too much that night – the night of the crash." She sipped her drink. "I'm not really as tough as I make out, in fact I don't think I could have kept going if I hadn't been taking pictures. I don't need to tell you of the horrors, you know exactly what it was like but for me it became like a dream. There was nothing real about it. I was detached, like when I was a kid – when I knew I was dreaming and I could control what I did, what I said and even take the scary parts right to the edge because I knew if it suddenly got too bad I could wake myself up. But this time I couldn't wake up.

"The viewfinder was my get-out that night. If something was too horrible, too sickening, too unbelievably painful – I knew I could just stick the camera to my eye and cut it all down to size, to a two-dimensional, miniature scale. It dehumanised everything and the horror ceased to be real – that way I could handle it. That was my escape."

Tom could see the slight tremble in Louise's fingers and the tears in her eyes which were about to brim over. He went to put his hand on hers but decided not to interrupt her. He thought back to that night and the memories leapt out of locked cupboards in his mind with frightening clarity.

The floating trail of someone's cigarette smoke from the other side of the bar turned into the acrid sting of burnt human flesh. He had meant to leave Louise with the space to talk but found that it was he who was now speaking.

"I handled it by forcing myself to keep moving. I didn't think I could ever survive, mentally that is, after I had put Polly Bentham down in the station booking hall and held her hand while she died. She cried silently but I don't think they were tears of pain, they were tears of regret. She knew her life was over and she didn't want to go, she wasn't ready to go, but I couldn't do anything to keep her from it. She was going somewhere unknown and frightening and if I could have, I'm almost sure I would have slipped away with her. I have never felt so impotent, so useless ever in my life."

Tom felt a hand on his and raised his eyes to Louise's face and through misted vision he could see the tears cascading down her face, pouring out of her enormous blue eyes without self-consciousness. She smiled a little reassuring smile, wiped the tears from round her mouth then raised a hand to his face, brushing away his tears. Tom continued and Louise made no attempt to interrupt him.

"After she had gone I just wanted to stay with her because I felt responsible for her, as though to leave her would be a betrayal. I couldn't bear the thought of anyone else touching her, people who had not seen her when she was alive, but then I looked around and could see that so many other people needed help. So I started to do things – anything – and I didn't stop moving.

"That weekend I went back, around the streets, knocking on neighbours' doors until I found someone who knew her – that's how I discovered her name – but I kept asking questions about her; somehow I wanted to know her. I didn't want to walk away from them and sever the only link I had with Polly. Obviously I told the police but, dear God, I just wasn't expecting what came next. As all her family were dead, they asked me to identify her so I had to go to the mortuary and look again on her scorched little body. But it was the brown parcel label tied round her toe that completely broke me up. That's what she'd become, Louise, a number on a label. No longer was she an enthusiastic teenager who couldn't make her mind up whether to become a doctor or a dancer; no one knew that she had once adored her little brother; no one cared that she had once made great sponge cakes. A life full of promise snuffed out with just a label to mark her passing. I had to make a statement but I hardly recall what I said."

Tom looked up and found Louise's eyes and they held each other's gaze, warm and openly – understanding without embarrassment. When Louise slowly leant forward and placed her tear-wet lips on his it seemed utterly natural and right. It began as a kiss of consolation, a salty, gentle confirmation that she understood; a kiss of sharing and the tremble was almost imperceptible but it transformed it into a kiss tinged with wanting.

With a sudden movement, Louise separated from him and scrabbled in her handbag for tissues, laughing nervously. "Jesus, Joseph and Mary, mother of God, just listen to us now, wouldja!" She said it with an affected Irish accent, handing Tom some tissues as she did so. Almost immediately, she slipped back into a soft, confidential tone. "I've never spoken a word of this to anyone," she said quietly.

"Neither have I," and for the first time, Tom realised how much he had needed to.

"I saw you that night," Louise said, "you know, in the booking hall. I came up off the track and there you were and I could barely recognise you through the soot and grime but I knew it was you. I meant to come back and interview you but that was before I got caught up in the enormity of it all.

"I spent the whole night taking photographs, not necessarily because I wanted the pictures but because it was the only way I could cope. As the night wore on it turned into something oddly bizarre – there seemed to be all kinds of strange people about, taking notes, throwing sheets over things, and I just photographed them all. Half the time I didn't have a clue what was going on so I just kept clicking. Anyway, they've taken the lot."

Tom was wrenched back to the present and was glad of it. "Everything?"

"Every single shot – except these." She produced two glossy black and white prints. "I'd already put them in my bag to show you. Over the past few weeks I've been sifting through hundreds of prints but most of them didn't make much sense and I've got no memory of having taken them so I junked a lot. I was going to bin these too and stuck them in the reject pile but when I went to throw them out they were on the top of the pile and there was just something about them that bothered me but I couldn't put my finger on it. See what you think – they're both taken in roughly the same place."

She handed him the prints and Tom strained to examine them under the dim glow of the bar lighting. At first sight there was nothing he could decipher, simply remnants of what looked like burnt wood, the glint of water, unrecognisable pieces of charred metal and he couldn't transform the shapes into anything meaningful.

Louise moved her chair nearer his and began to trace the shapes with a finger. "That's the burned butt – look at that charred wood there – that's the chamber and that, I reckon, is the barrel."

Tom looked at her in disbelief. "A rifle!"

"Exactly! And I think this second print shows another one – there, disappearing out of the frame."

Tom was momentarily lost for words. "Where the hell did they come from? Someone on the ground or from the aircraft

– there's no way of knowing. Do you remember where you took them?"

"Not a clue. I would normally keep a log but not that night. By going back through the negatives I might have been able to place them from the shots on either side – but not now."

"And you're sure you haven't any more pictures anywhere, perhaps somewhere in the office where they might have forgotten to look? Have you lent any to anyone else, sold them to a picture library, sent any away for processing, entered them in a bloody competition? Anything?"

"No, I really don't think so." Louise stopped and looked at the ceiling. "God, how stupid of me, I've got some prints at home. I'd forgotten all about them – I took a load home to sift through weeks ago and never got round to it. They'll still be there."

"Did the Special Branch ask if you had stuff at home?" Tom asked quietly.

Louise thought for a moment. "No, I'm sure they didn't, they just said ... oh my God, that's what he meant! – the one who twisted my wrist – he said something like, 'Right now, everything you own belongs to us – and I mean everything.'"

They hurried to Tom's car and it took no more than a few minutes to get to Rayleigh Road and as they rounded the corner, Louise said faintly, "I knew it..."

Every light in her house was on and white-suited men were carrying coloured plastic storage boxes down the path, depositing them in an unmarked white van.

CHAPTER THIRTEEN

Saturday, March 16th, 1991, 9.00 a.m. Whenever his father rested both elbows on the desk and joined his fingertips together like the spire of a church steeple, Tom knew a lecture was in the offing. It indicated that all the pros and cons had been explored and neatly stacked in their respective boxes, that careful analysis had been applied and that a course of action had been decided upon. It was what Tom called his Solomon pose and when Tom had walked into his father's office dead on nine, that's how he had been sitting and Tom knew it was Salome he wanted to discuss.

"Sit down, Tom." Not a glimmer of a smile crossed Harry's face. "I think it's time we had a chat."

Tom also knew that if he had let Harry build up any momentum, stopping him would be like holding back a runaway train. One of two things was required – diversionary tactics or a pre-emptive strike, the former requiring tact and patience while the latter was much more economical of time and therefore the most appealing. And that's what he went for.

"She stays – as a client. I'm not arguing and I think it's highly unethical of you to even suggest it."

"I didn't suggest it," Harry complained.

"No, but you were going to! This whole thing is beginning to gel so please get off my back." Tom had not been in any way angered – it was simply a game which, played by the correct rules, was easily won. He had put Harry on the defensive and now it was time to toss him a sop, balm for his injured pride.

"Good news is, I had my first meeting with Varsity Aviation and they're prepared to come to the table. They're definitely on the defensive and thinking money so that's good, isn't it?"

It required an answer and Harry was being involved – being reeled in – and so it had gone on. Eventually, the whole point of the meeting had been forgotten as Harry proffered advice on the best negotiating stance.

At ten precisely, Mrs Baker had arrived and confirmed Tom as her lawyer. The three dead Bakers were apparently her husband, her elderly father-in-law and her brother-in-law, who had called round to help lay some pipework.

The moment Mrs Baker had mentioned plumbing, Tom's heart had sunk. "Do you know if they were using Yorkshire joints – the little soldered joints that you have to heat up with a blowtorch?"

Mrs Baker hadn't even needed time to think. "I don't know about little joints but they had a blowtorch. It made everywhere smoky, stank of burning metal, so I went to work early to get away from it."

In that instant, Tom lost all interest in the Baker case and found it hard to keep any enthusiasm in his voice. Blowtorches were invariably run from butane gas cylinders – exactly what Christine Olins had said could be the source of the shrapnel injuries. He checked if that was the case with the Bakers' job and Mrs Baker confirmed it was.

As soon as she had left the office, Vicky had appeared, unannounced. "Did I do good or did I do good?"

Tom had not been able to bring himself to tell her of the Baker discovery and feigned pressure of work to end the meeting quickly. However he tried to look at it, it was a blow and sapped the sense of discovery which had driven him for the past few days.

Sir Oswald Napier had agreed as a first step, to keep costs down, to read through the pathology reports on the three Bakers but only to perform a post-mortem on the one who was listed as having shrapnel wounds, although Tom couldn't help feeling that it was now probably immaterial.

The other two Bakers and Mrs Veezey would have to wait and would only be examined if the first post-mortem showed up anything of interest. It had suited Napier to do the work as quickly as possible.

Chas Newbold had made his statement about the cargo doors of the P11, even though a man who was working under a formal caution would have little credibility in the witness box, but it was all Tom had. He had hoped for corroboration but Chas had disabused him of even that hope. "They're mostly illegals down there – pop their heads above the parapet and they'll be deported." Tom knew he was right – no one would risk that. Chas dangled the hope of one baggage handler who was currently off sick but immediately removed it with his parting words. "But don't hold your breath!"

Tom knew he had been delaying lunch, waiting for the inevitable call from Ailey. The problem was of his making and it contained a dreadful irony – by accepting the Bakers as clients he had probably stirred up a hornet's nest that would bring all kinds of professional recrimination buzzing around his ears and it all now seemed utterly pointless.

When the call came, Ailey was calm, controlled but cold. "Are you in for the rest of the day?"

"Yes."

"And have you got time to see me?"

"Yes."

"Right, I'm coming over now. I'll be with you in twenty minutes."

She looked smart and attractive in a power-dressed sort of way and her reaction was not what he had anticipated. There was no string of New York Jewish invective, in fact everything about her was controlled, from the way she walked across the office to the careful crossing of her legs.

"Would you like to explain?" she asked, as though talking to a stranger.

"No, not particularly, there's nothing to explain." He felt guilty but he wasn't going to show it.

"Mrs Baker just happened to change her mind, is that it?"

"She rang me and asked me to act for her, end of story!" Tom saw the flash of anger dart across Ailey's face and registered the slight involuntary forward movement as she prepared for attack, then, just as quickly, it was gone.

"So it was just coincidence?"

"Ailey, it's not a situation I relish but I made no approach to Mrs Baker..."

"But you know a woman who did!" Ailey jabbed out the words.

"There are people in the support group who knew I had an interest and I can't speak for them but I did not approach Mrs Baker and I didn't ask anyone to do it on my behalf. And that's the truth." It may have been strictly true but Tom felt uncomfortable with it nevertheless. "I made a point of asking Mrs Baker if anyone had pressured her into asking for my services and she was adamant they hadn't. I don't mind if you approach my client and ask her." Tom almost laughed as he delivered the last sentence, knowing how antagonistic it was but he still didn't get the reaction he expected.

"It can't go on like this, Tom. If you're not careful, you're going to damage everyone's chances. Instead of us both fighting the enemy we'll end up fighting each other and that's not good – not good business, not good for the clients and sure as hell not good for us. Agreed?" She looked for confirmation.

"Absolutely, couldn't agree more." And he meant it.

"I think it's partly my fault. I've never really taken the time out to explain how I see a professional relationship between us working – and believe me it could work, to both our advantages. I'd just assumed you'd join with us because it seemed the obvious thing to do and I suspect that had it been almost any other solicitor in the entire goddam world, that's exactly what would have happened. No one has ever before rejected the offer of a professional relationship with Morton Gerrity, believe me. You're a bit of a pain in the ass, Mr Harrison."

The smile which accompanied her words completely threw Tom. It looked genuinely warm and totally unexpected and if she was using tactics, they were succeeding brilliantly.

Ailey continued, "As I'm tired of telling you, Morton Gerrity are amongst the biggest in the business at this kind of work and my senior partner, John Gerrity, is very keen to meet you." She threw an open brown manila envelope across the desk and it plonked down directly in front of him. "So what do you say?"

Tom extracted its contents – a return air ticket to New York on

Concorde and a booking advice for the Hotel Plaza on the Park.

Ailey smiled at him. "Out Friday morning – next Friday morning – and back Monday night. What do you say?"

Even while he was accepting, Tom could not help thinking what an incredibly smooth operator Ailey was.

Friday, March 22nd, 1991, 10.30 a.m. Eastern Standard Time
When they flew down the Hudson River and banked steeply to the left, Manhattan's skyline appeared in the tiny window next to him. It was the first time he'd seen it in real life and it was an incredible sight. His words were entirely involuntary. "Wow, just look at that!" and it made him sound like a little boy.

"Like it?" said Ailey, leaning across him to share the view.

"Amazing," said Tom.

"That's my home," she said proudly, leaning closely against him. The trace of expensive perfume reached him and he could feel her breast pressing against his arm.

A flight attendant requested their glasses and Tom drained the remaining champagne from his flute before handing it over. The morning had started with Buck's Fizz – had graduated to champagne with a touch of orange juice before becoming pure Bollinger.

He was feeling so good that he had even managed to stop thinking about the phone call from Sir Oswald Napier, which had come through just before they boarded the aircraft.

"I think your information was a little askew, Mr Harrison, none of the pathology reports mentions shrapnel wounds – sorry! It may have been on the notes but it certainly wasn't included in the final report."

It was another blow and Tom had tried his best to hide his disappointment. Napier added that the path report on Mr Baker senior, Mrs Baker's father-in-law, did contain a description of wounds which could conceivably fit that description but had not been described as such. The other two reports contained nothing much of interest.

Tom had given Sir Oswald the go-ahead to examine Mr Baker senior – there was nothing else constructive he could do. He was beginning to feel guilty at the ease with which he ordered other people's relatives cut up and if he ever had to justify it, it might prove difficult.

They were met at John F Kennedy airport by a stretch limo, bristling with TV and phone aerials and a uniformed chauffeur who treated Ailey with the utmost respect. As soon as they were settled in its black leather and chrome interior, Ailey produced an ice bucket and more champagne.

"Welcome to New York," she said as she poured. "Okay, today and tomorrow I'm going to show you my city and tomorrow evening, we're having dinner with John. I've set Sunday aside for any discussions which might arise out of that but if there aren't any then, hey, more fun!"

As they crossed the Triboro Bridge, Manhattan, on the far side of the water, began to take on its familiar shape, the shape he had seen in a hundred movies.

"Okay, a few survival rules. Don't ask a taxi driver to take you anywhere unless you give them the street reference – corner of West 45th and Eighth – that kinda thing. They probably won't even know where the Lincoln Centre is, they probably won't speak English and they'll drive you around for hours. Streets run across Manhattan and Avenues up and down, okay? Harlem's Uptown, the financial district's Downtown and you're staying near Central Park in Midtown. If you want to sound like a native, be rude to everyone, always be impatient and never say please or thank you. Have you got anything special you want to do?"

"No, just one old friend I'd like to look up."

"Well, that gives us plenty of time to have fun. Cheers!" Ailey raised her champagne glass and Tom clinked his against it. He looked at the string of yellow cabs and the soaring buildings and he didn't care how naive he appeared, he was going to do everything that tourists do: from riding to the top of the World Trade Centre to sailing round the Statue of Liberty; he wanted to stroll along Broadway and stand in Times Square and it was with sheer joy that he caught sight of the top of the Chrysler Building, sun glinting from its wonderful, reflective art deco curves. He was definitely going to enjoy himself, he decided.

Tom checked into his hotel – a monument to the Liberace

school of interior design. The foyer contained a most ludicrously flamboyant waterfall which tumbled, it seemed, from about three floors up. Lights that kept changing their colours turned the water different hues, most of them bilious shades of green and yellow. Hanging over the roaring water was probably the biggest chandelier in the world, its thousands of crystals cast to look like fractured ice. On the mezzanine level, the mood of the coffee shop changed to Hawaiian, with wicker tables and chairs interspersed with huge, drooping potted palms.

Tom's room was so disgustingly opulent he could not help but love it. Three sweeping curved steps led down from the entrance door, reflecting the semicircular shape of the room. Stretching out before him was a rectangular, glass-topped dining table surrounded by ten high-backed chairs, whilst round the perimeter of the room were three sofas and a selection of upholstered armchairs, each with side tables and a variety of broad-shaded, betasselled lamps. The drapes looked like something from the Royal Opera House and were remote-controlled.

Of course there was a bar with stools and through a doorway to the left a circular bedroom with circular bed and a variety of mirrors which reflected his image wherever Tom sat or lay. Beyond that was an L-shaped bathroom, the furthest leg of the L being taken up with an enormous Jacuzzi. Again mirrors predominated and Tom sat on the loo simply to test its view and could see some eight images of himself and found it extremely disconcerting. This was not a hotel to stay in if you were a graduate of the St Martin's School of Art.

Ailey called for him around twelve and Jaccuzied and refreshed, Tom was still flying high. Lunch was taken at a leisurely pace in a superb, bustling Italian restaurant in the Village where he had fresh asparagus cooked in olive oil and parmesan, followed by a wonderful penne pasta dish, lightly coated in pesto and pieces of fried garlic and topped with a moist sauce of freshly roasted vegetables from which the faint aroma of woodsmoke issued. The wine was an estate-bottled Sicilian red.

They took coffee in Ailey's offices at the Empire State, with Ailey's assistant Charlie, probably the tallest and least co-ordinated man he had ever met. Afterwards, Tom put in a call to Marc Olivier – a New York Haitian he'd met years earlier when he was on a lawyer exchange trip to London. They had spent a great year of total irresponsibility together.

"Sorry, Mr Olivier's out of town, back Monday."

From the moment they left Ailey's offices, New York became a mesmerising blur of sights and sensations. She was great company, outrageous at times and showed a fun side he had not seen before. New York was a musical memory land, reminders of great classic jazz tunes on almost every street. George Gershwin hit full volume as they crossed Tenth Avenue and down in the financial district, there it was, in real life. Delancy Street and he could hear Ella's voice – "*It's very fancy, on old Delancy Street, you know.*"

They passed Penn Station at almost exactly the right time – "Be at Pennsylvania Station at a quarter to four." When they went by subway – "the electric sewer" as Ailey called it – again Ella whispered to him through the urine-scented air – "... *where balmy breezes flow, to and fro.*" But The Duke had the last word as the A train rumbled through. It was like being on holiday and Tom knew he was being softened up.

Dinner was taken early and somewhere very high up and they did what they seemed to have been doing all day – clinked glasses whilst New York was set out beneath them, its myriad lights twinkling below like a fairyland, and Ailey followed his gaze.

"Pretty, aren't they?"

"It's unbelievable, it really is unbelievable." Tom shook his head and smiled.

"Know why they've got so many lights down there?" she asked and Tom replied he didn't. "It's to hide all the shit that's underneath." He was pleased that the old biting, cynical Ailey wasn't completely off duty.

Tom assumed they were on the way back to his hotel but the limo pulled up outside Carnegie Hall and he could see the billboards. *For the First Time in 20 Years – Thelonious Monk in Concert.* Ailey fanned herself with a pair of tickets, smiling at him as she did so. Tom leant across the limo and kissed her on the cheek. "God, I thought he was dead; how did you know? You're wonderful."

Even that wasn't the end of the evening and as Tom emerged humming, the limo again whisked them off, to the heliport near Battery Park. They donned headphones in order to hear each other above the clattering rotor and gently rose into the night sky. Twice the aircraft circled the floodlit Statue of Liberty, so close Tom felt he could almost reach out and touch her torch. It then took them on a circular trip of Manhattan, following the shoreline up the East River, across the Harlem River and back down the Hudson. As they watched the extraordinary pattern of lights from skyscrapers, street standards and strings of traffic – all white up one street and red down another – Tom found they were holding hands. The trip was all over in minutes but the spectacle would live with Tom forever.

When the limo finally pulled up outside the Plaza, Tom could honestly say he had had one of the best days he could remember and he told Ailey so. Again he leant across the back seat of the limo and kissed her, but this time it was on the lips. He kissed her in such a way that it could be interpreted as an extremely grateful thanks or something more inviting. Ailey chose the second and returned the kiss enthusiastically, gliding her tongue into Tom's mouth. The only sound was deep and gentle moans issuing from somewhere deep in Ailey's throat.

Suddenly she broke off. "Hey, I haven't seen this room of yours – they told me it was the super duper exec, once seen never forgotten. Aren't you going to show me?"

"Miss Newman, be my guest!"

When Tom showed Ailey into his palatial suite – The Fitzroy – she made straight for the bar. "Cognac?" He did not think he could face any more but said yes just the same. He gave her a conducted tour and they sipped their drinks as they went. When they reached the bedroom, Ailey ceased all pretence, put her glass down and moved gracefully up to Tom, placing her arms round his neck and covering his mouth with hers, kissing him hungrily, and he could detect the faint caramel taste of brandy. He returned her kisses passionately and again the moans began.

He broke free and removed his jacket and as he did so, Ailey stepped back, reached behind her neck to undo a fastener and her dress fluttered to the ground soundlessly. She was tanned and her lingerie was minimal, silky and very expensive. She moved back to him, undid his shirt and Tom could feel every swell and indentation of her body pressing against his – and he could see them both reflected in quadruple vision.

"Whoa, whoa, whoa – Ailey. This is meant to be business. I'm not sure this is very professional."

Ailey again found his mouth and spoke between kisses. "Tom, I'm not looking for lifelong commitment, I don't want your love and I don't want your babies – just fuck me, will you?" With that, she pushed him back on to the bed, straddled him and Tom offered no further objections. Two hours later, he felt he was about to die from exhaustion while Ailey still seemed full of innovative athleticism. He hoped she didn't remember the enormous chandelier suspended above the foyer waterfall.

John Gerrity came as a pleasant surprise and Tom instantly liked the man. He was big, with a mop of greying hair and a physique which looked ideally fitted to digging peat. He could be nothing but Irish American and his weapons were charm, warmth, humour and intimacy. There was something about him which hinted that, if all these failed, he would pluck your skull from your shoulders with his bare hands.

Business wasn't even mentioned until the main course and Tom had carefully watched his wine intake. John slid the Harrow disaster into the conversation almost seamlessly and he had started by running through some of Morton Gerrity's successes, which automatically led on to contingency suing. It was an impressive record and included some of the biggest international names, many of them based outside the US.

Eventually, he outlined how their relationships with foreign agents had been handled and what the outcome had been. He eschewed the heavy sell and left long gaps between business talk, filling them with anecdotes and increasingly humorous small talk. He didn't push, he stroked and smoothed and caressed.

Tom knew the pitch was coming to an end when John ran

through the claims that had failed. There weren't many of them but they all had a common theme – no local agent and conflict between local lawyers and Morton Gerrity.

"That's why there's always got to be a formal relationship – it concentrates the mind, makes people think about where their loyalties lie, but in the end, when there are losses, it's not us, the lawyers, who lose, we just move on to other cases and do it all again. No, it's the clients – they've got only one shot at it and if we let them down, their failure is permanent. When we pull together we win, when we pull separately, we lose – it's as straightforward as that, Tom!"

"I'm not sure it is as straightforward as that," Tom replied, measuring his response so it did not sound confrontational.

"I think it is." John smiled.

Tom thought for a moment. "Let me ask you one question, John. Are any of your London clients US citizens?"

John looked to Ailey but Tom could tell by his reaction that he already knew the answer but it was Ailey who responded.

"Just three, that's all, and all from the same family."

"Okay, I'm going to tell you what I think will happen. You'll chase those cases first because you know you'll get a result quicker and easier over here because they're US citizens. The British plaintiffs will go on hold and I'll be left trying to keep them happy because it could be years before you get round to them."

John Gerrity wasn't fazed. "Yeah, but that could also be an advantage. Once we get a result here it can obviously be used as a precedent for the UK claimants' cases."

"History's not on your side, John. As you know, the two systems work on different causation and a different interpretation of responsibility. If you get a result with the three Americans, it doesn't follow that the UK claimants will simply queue up and be treated the same. In fact, because there's so many of them, that's probably where the real battle will be."

It was Ailey who replied. "A precedent of the kind we're talking about has got to be a good thing as it sets the benchmark. In any case, we're talking much bigger money over here and that's got to be worth it."

"But you play for much greater odds – death or glory, win all or lose all. A UK suit may not come up with such big figures but at least it's likely to produce something – and that's a lot better than nothing. In the end, it's all going to depend on what you've got on Varsity or Barcroft." Tom gave a look of enquiry.

"We've got enough!" John Gerrity said it like a full stop and Tom knew that was all he was going to get but pressed on nevertheless.

"What if it turns out to be a terrorist bomb – where does that leave you? You're going to have to prove negligence and Northolt's still officially a Royal Air Force base, supposed to have some of the best security in the UK, so it's going to be difficult."

"Difficult but not impossible. We're not talking beyond reasonable doubt here, we're talking shit that sticks, okay? This is going to be an out-of-court settlement, no question about that." John Gerrity was animated.

Tom felt John had not told him anything he did not already know but as they went to the car, John dropped one last question. "Tom, have you made a decision in principle?"

Tom thought about it and answered honestly. "No. I really haven't."

"Then come to the office tomorrow; I'd like to talk detail, okay?" John shook his hand and leant forward confidentially. "You realise this could make you a rich man?"

Tom's laugh was completely involuntary.

John left separately and Ailey accompanied Tom in the limo. He could see Ailey intended a repeat performance of the previous night and as gently as he could Tom said he needed to sleep alone – he wanted to think, but above all else he needed to sleep. When he asked to be dropped off short of his hotel, Ailey said goodnight very perfunctorily and Tom watched the tail lights of the limo disappear amongst the Fifth Avenue traffic. He slowly wandered the rest of the way, past the last of the dejected-looking carriage horses alongside Central Park, waiting to take tourists on a night ride and the scent of horse dung smelt very homely and out of place in Midtown Manhattan.

Originally, Tom had had no intention of joining with Morton Gerrity but there was some truth in what John had said and so he tried to order his thoughts. What the hell were his options?

There was probably going to be a UK civil case but whether it got to court or not was another matter. Ailey and John would certainly file a US civil case but the chances of that reaching court were even more remote. He could be involved in either or both. A criminal case in the UK would be down to the prosecuting authorities, not him, and both the civil and the criminal cases depended on what the SAAIU report came up with. Problem with that was that none of his clients, all land based, were involved and the report might not be published in full anyway and God alone knew when that would be. Straight negotiations for compensation – certainly!

With the pressure building up, it wasn't out of the question that the UK Government would back down and announce a public judicial inquiry. If it did, there would be a lot of work. And then there was the resumed inquest, of course. Almost all these options could involve judicial decisions and if they did not go the way he wanted, he had to decide whether to get involved in the whole process of judicial review. And should he advise Vicky to sue for wrongful arrest? Life had been considerably more straightforward in the past!

When he reached his hotel Tom was still deep in thought but now it was of a personal nature. He knew he would not sleep yet and took the lift to the Lautrec bar on the roof. The desk clerk said it would be closing soon and so Tom guessed it would probably be quiet. It was, with just a few people sitting minding their drinks and looking out over New York. A grand piano occupied centre stage, its keyboard lid still raised, suggesting someone had only recently finished playing.

One phrase kept running through his mind. "Like a little lad in a sweet shop." It was almost certainly what Mike would have said and he was right. There were three women involved in the case and he had complicated his relationship with all of them. He hadn't planned any of it – it had just happened and so he looked at New York from on high and tried to rationalise his feelings. Without thinking about it he got up and walked to the piano, looking to the barman, who nodded back.

Tom sat down, ran his fingers gently over the keys and quietly slid into *Georgia on my Mind,* singing the words almost to himself. When he had finished he was startled by a solitary, slow handclap and looked to find a middle-aged woman had moved close to him, standing just to one side. "You play nicely, I enjoyed that."

She was very pretty and had probably once been beautiful but the slight puffiness in her face and the barely perceptible slur in her speech spoke of a need for drink. "Do you know anything else I might like?" The smile had grown even warmer and the invitation wasn't even subtle. Tom smiled back but the last thing he needed right then was someone else's desperation. He plucked a flower from the display on top of the piano, handed it to her and said, "Have a nice evening."

He slept surprisingly well but when he stepped into the lift of the Empire State Building to see John Gerrity, he still had not made a decision.

Sir Oswald Napier took his early morning coffee through to the conservatory and, positioning himself amongst the cushions of the wicker sofa, dictated into a hand-held recorder. Mr Baker senior had so many incisions that it took nearly half an hour to run through them but finally Sir Oswald concentrated on the area of greatest interest.

"Series of entry wounds numbering nine in all, distributed between the seventh vertical vertebra and the coccyx. Muscular penetration is total in all cases. One each is noted in the right and left *trapezius*, one in the right *deltoid*, two in the right *latissimus dorsi* and one in the left, one in the right *gluteus medius*, one in the right *gluteus maximus* and one in the left *gluteus maximus*. The distribution does not appear to be entirely random.

"It is difficult to speculate as to what caused the wounds as all traces of the penetrating objects have been removed from the body. They have not been recorded on previous pathology reports and no photographs have been taken."

Sir Oswald poured himself another coffee and stared out of the windows at the birds that were scrabbling for bread on the lawn. He raised the tape recorder to his lips again.

"The injuries are consistent with the violent and explosive

fragmentation of an anti-personnel device, possibly a grenade..."

Monday, March 25th, 1991, 9.00 a.m. Eastern Standard Time
Tom hailed a cab heading uptown and around 110th Street, New York started to change quite dramatically. Rows of beautifully renovated Victorian brownstone houses gave way to meaner terraces whilst numerous demolished buildings left rubble-filled gaps in their facades – gaping like missing teeth, like so many bomb sites from a forgotten war. Corrugated iron shacks selling cigarettes, beer and groceries hugged the sides of the road and shabby men in long, dirty overcoats slouched along the sidewalks or sprawled on benches and surreptitiously raised brown paper packages to their lips and drank from them.

Tom paid the driver off on 125th Street. The man had not wanted to bring him this far and made it clear that the only reason he was doing so was because Tom was white. Recognising his accent as English, he had three times asked Tom if he was sure he had the right address. As the cab drove away, Tom realised his was the only white face on the crowded thoroughfare, the main shopping street in Harlem, as busy and bustling as Oxford Street at Christmas.

He found No. 2438, wedged between an electrical shop and a cut-price clothes store, with stone steps leading up through a dimly lit stairwell to the second floor. As he neared the landing, two black youths came down the stairs towards him and their conversation froze. Tom had often seen the predatory look of men who live off and by the streets and both men had it but there was also dislike in their eyes, almost hatred, and they kept them focused on Tom as they passed in silence, moving pointedly to the side of the staircase as they did so. He found it disturbing.

Marc Olivier's big Haitian face beamed in welcome as Tom entered the law offices and Marc's hug almost squeezed the breath from him.

"Hey man, why didn't you let me know in advance? I'd have taken time off," and Tom knew he meant it. When the hugging and back-slapping had subsided and coffee had been poured, Marc showed him over the practice – four lawyers, a couple of secretaries, a receptionist and half a dozen jumbled rooms. It had the unmistakable feel of a legal-aid law firm, whatever the country, and a simple glance at the posters on the walls showed that Greenblat, Crone and Feldstien were the New York representatives of almost every liberation movement in the world.

To make the most of what little time they had, Tom accepted Marc's invitation to tag along with him for the rest of the morning and they navigated their way along the crowded pavements of 125th Street to Marc's car. Again, he became aware that his was the only white face amongst many black and a few Korean. He told Marc of his experience whilst mounting the stairs and he laughed and raised his voice above the noise of the traffic. "If you're a white guy on your own in Harlem you've gotta be a cop and if you're a cop you're tooled up and you won't hesitate to use it. That's why you weren't their favourite guy! White people see Harlem through the windows of tour buses."

They found the car and pulled away from the main street into smaller side streets, again marked by a rash of derelict and demolished buildings. "Why so many demolished buildings, Marc?"

"Not worth a cent to rent. Landlords often can't get their money and it costs them to get the tenants out so they torch the building. The only thing of any real value is the land and you can't destroy that. People die but ... it doesn't seem to trouble anyone."

Marc watched Tom's face as they cruised around and it had disbelief written large on it. "Surprised?"

"Jesus, Marc, it's like a third-world city – worse than some".

Marc smiled without humour. "Welcome to the ghetto, man! Once the black capital of America but now – unemployment, crap education, no welfare, no health care and not a lot of hope."

They headed across the Harlem River and into the South Bronx to check out a derelict building where two of his clients were supposed to have been dealing drugs.

The architecture changed to something resembling the most soulless parts of Eastern Europe and its stark, post-war brutalism; block after block of four-storey concrete flats and squeezed in between them, a few houses, some swathed in razor wire, illuminated by security lights and patrolled by snarling Alsatian dogs. Tom felt a pang of concern for his safety as they parked the car and began walking.

"Who the hell lives in those?" Tom asked, pointing to the besieged houses, still struggling with the shock of New York's darker neighbourhood.

"Ordinary people tired of being burgled, I guess."

"Marc, how does it happen? This is the wealthiest country in the world, for Christ's sake."

"The people here don't make the rules and they don't live by them. This is a dumping ground, man. Remember, I used to try explaining why I left Haiti – well Haiti's followed me here."

"It's just so fucking depressing!"

Marc smiled. It was the first time he had ever heard Tom use the word. "It's economics, Tom – money! There's now only one system on offer anywhere in the world and this is it." Marc swept his arm to encompass the whole area. "Money is King!" He placed his arm round Tom's shoulders as they walked towards the derelict building.

"The big guys own the park, Tom. They pick the team and pay them and they make the rules. If you can afford the ticket they might let you eat some popcorn while you watch the game. If you can't, then you're left outside and they don't even listen to your shouts of protest."

"So it just goes on like this?"

"Who knows? But when you've lived in a country where you're scared if someone knocks on the door at night, you see things a bit more starkly. When friends disappear because they've used the wrong words and you find their bodies, beaten and bruised, burnt and slashed, trussed up with wire and dumped on the garbage tip, you realise there's only two sides in this life. And whether you like it or not, you're on one or the other."

"They stepped carefully over the burnt timbers and fallen masonry of the derelict house and Marc positioned himself against a wall amongst discarded tin foil, matches and old syringes and began to check the lines of sight.

Ailey's world, it seemed to Tom, was a fifteen-dollar cab ride and half a world away.

Tuesday, March 26th, 1991, 9.30 a.m. GMT Tom flicked through the unopened letters looking for any that might be worth reading and when he saw the discreetly printed lettering of Sir Oswald Napier on one of them, he was almost afraid to open it. Before he could, Vicky arrived and as she was shown into the office Tom knew she was angry.

"Don't you think you should have told me?"

"No!"

"I'm your client but you don't think it's right to tell me that you're doing a deal that directly conflicts with my interests?"

Tom knew she had a point and he should have mentioned the US trip but he didn't feel conciliatory, got up from behind his desk and walked over to her. "You're not my only client so don't tell me how to run a case. I was invited to America, not to do a deal but to discuss the case with other lawyers who have a legitimate stake in it. I had to know if our interests coincided and if they did, how we could work together..."

"Christ, Tom, you sound like your father."

It stung him but he kept going. "I'll explain all the proposals that were put to me but my conclusion is that I think we're better off not joining with the US action, okay? But I had to explore it."

Tom surprised himself because he had been churning over the decision for two days without reaching a conclusion but now that he had refused Gerrity's proposition, he felt happy. He could see that his unequivocal decision had deflected Vicky's anger, but not entirely.

"You should have told me you were going! Why didn't you? What were you afraid of? Or wasn't it entirely a professional visit?" The meaning was unambiguous.

Tom could feel himself colouring but even worse was the sense of guilt which washed over him. He could hardly have felt worse had Vicky been his wife or girlfriend but she was his client, for Christ's sake! He looked at her and even before he could form the words for his denial, he was certain that she knew he had slept with Ailey and in that one glance was a wealth of understanding. Each knew precisely how the other felt. They had entered a world where hurt and regret combined but where neither could be acknowledged because it was unprofessional.

He broke the atmosphere by holding up Napier's letter. "Baker path report…!"

"Well, open it," Vicky replied tartly.

Tom ripped at the envelope and scanned through the pages before reading it out loud. "Dah de dah de dah… Hold on, here we go…" His voice trailed away before he slowly raised his eyes to Vicky's. "… He thinks it could have been an anti-personnel device…"

Tom immediately called Sir Oswald and asked why he'd reached that conclusion. The scientist answered carefully. "It appears that the wounds were caused by projectiles, which rather implies that they were the product of an explosion. Let us postulate that the explosion took place in a tank or some other enclosed container which was constructed of sheet or cast metal."

"Such as a Calor gas tank?" Tom interrupted.

"Exactly. The effect of the intense pressure caused by the explosion would be to expose the weaknesses in the metal, causing it to fracture along the lines of greatest weakness. The result would be fragmentation into pieces of an entirely random nature, some small pieces and some large pieces, all of an irregular shape. That is not consistent with the entry wounds on Mr Baker's body." Sir Oswald paused, waiting for confirmation that he'd been understood.

"So how is this different?"

"Well, the size of the wounds showed a degree of consistency and were all made by small pieces of flat metal – at least I presume it was metal – striking the body at different angles. For a metal object to break into these symmetrical shapes there would have to have been inbuilt fault lines. In other words, the metal was preformed into those shapes."

"What, like a waffle iron?"

"Exactly, or more probably the outer casing of a hand grenade."

"What happened to the pieces?" Tom asked.

"The Home Office report makes no mention of them and there are no photographs."

"Why not?" Tom could smell a trail unwinding in front of him.

"The old question, isn't it? Cock-up or conspiracy? It usually turns out to be cock-up!"

"What about powder residues – but that's not your field, is it?"

"No, but it's certainly worth exploring."

Tom hung up and briefed Vicky while he hunted through his address book. "Got it – Forensic Enquiry." He dialled the number. "Janet Moyes? Janet, it's Tom Harrison from a while back ... yes, that's right... Look, I have a body I'd like you to examine. Yes ... explosive traces!"

CHAPTER FOURTEEN

Monday, July 8th, 1991, 10.00 a.m. When Caffrey called, Tom was fully prepared to field his complaints about the Baker body but they never materialised. It came almost as a shock when instead he gave a date for the resumed inquest – Monday November 11th – and reminded Tom he had better lodge his written representations outlining the need for a jury rather sharpish. His only reference to Baker came at the end of the conversation.

"I was thinking, laddie, would you have any objection if the morgue fitted your corpses with zippers? It'd save an awful lot of time."

It was the first attempt at humour he had heard from Caffrey and Tom stifled a laugh but the proximity of real action at last produced genuine anticipation. There was pressure from every direction for results but at least he now had a focus for these demands.

Mike dashed into his office, full of urgency. "Quick, radio. Astbury's talking about Flight 469."

"… the cockpit voice recorder and data information recorder were eventually discovered amongst the huge volume of debris taken to Cardington. They were in an appalling state and for months now we have been using the very latest computer techniques in an attempt to decipher something, anything, from them but they were very badly charred. Although designed to withstand fire, the intensity of the inferno in this case was exceptional and it is with great regret that I have to report that all the efforts were in vain. The outcome is that we are still unable to add anything new to the limited information we already have."

The interviewer was abrasive. "Minister, we are now seven months down the line and we know almost nothing about the reasons for Flight 469's downing. Are there any preliminary findings from the SAAIU? It seems to have gone awfully quiet."

"If an inquiry is to be thorough it does take time. All I can say at the moment is that it is my understanding that nothing has yet been discovered to arouse suspicion. I know many relatives have questions about how their loved ones died and I'm very much hoping that the resumed inquest, which was announced earlier today, will provide just that opportunity."

"It is a very limited forum, Minister, and I'm sure we'd all be much more interested in the interim findings of the inquiry?"

"I'm afraid they are still some months away but the Special Air Accident Investigation Unit is, I know, aware of the urgency."

"And when they're available, they will be made public?"

Astbury's reply flowed seamlessly. "Of course SAAIU does not have the power to make public its report – that is not within its jurisdiction – but we are aware of the public's desire for information and that is very much in the forefront of my mind."

"Minister, thank you. Now we turn to the continuing problem of..." Tom pressed the off switch.

"Let him right off the hook." Mike screwed his face up in disgust. "What does that mean – 'very much in the forefront of my mind'? Sex is very much in the forefront of my mind but I'm not going to do it in public."

"Not what I've heard!" Tom smiled.

Back in his office, Astbury put in a call to Glennister on a secure line. "Andrew? Heard the broadcast, did you?" Glennister confirmed he had.

Astbury continued. "This is something of a political nightmare for us and the allegations of cover-up are not going away. I was given a fairly easy ride today but really, we need to defuse it now."

"And?"

"People need a focal point and you're the only one who can offer it." Astbury spoke forcefully.

Andrew Glennister took his time before answering. "You know we're in negotiation with the relatives' solicitors and that's all taking its proper course and we've indicated we're prepared to offer something. We can't do much more."

"For Christ's sake, man, I know what that means. You're going to start on the lowest possible figure, they'll reject it and make a counterclaim and you'll up your offer and so it will go on for years. Show some guile, man; make them an offer that's generous enough to create cracks in their solidarity because that's your biggest threat – solidarity. You should be working on two levels, public and private, and you have to try and weaken them, get a little dissension going."

"Charles, don't patronise me. We've been doing these kinds of deals for years and probably invented the divide and rule strategy. The only way these things are settled quickly is with a lot of money – and in this case we could be talking a hell of a lot of money and it's all being left to me! That wasn't the agreement, if you remember?"

"I want this settled. The contingency funds can only ever be there as a fall-back – in case the proverbial really does look like it's about to hit the fan..."

Andrew Glennister cut across him, "You're trying to shaft me, Astbury!" His voice was hard with anger. "And I don't take kindly to that..."

Astbury's voice barely changed its pitch but the threat was implicit in his tone. "Andrew, you and your company have done extremely well out of us over the years, just as you have out of our friends over the water. Don't jeopardise that, old boy, it would be such a shame..."

There was a long pause before Glennister replied. "So you're not making anything available to me?"

"Not at the moment, no – I think I've made that quite clear." There was no response from Glennister. "Now, we need to look ahead, don't we, Andrew, so don't brood over it, it's only money." There was almost a chuckle in his voice.

Eventually Glennister spoke. "I'm not happy but we'll let it ride for the time being. So, what's with this inquest?"

Astbury was dismissive. "Don't worry about that..."

None of Sir Oswald's other post-mortems produced anything of interest. He had looked at some of the Home Office pathology reports and had called for photographs in some cases but none had been taken. Tom was suspicious but Napier put it down to the large number of corpses or because the coroner wanted to save relatives from distress.

It wasn't convincing but there was not a lot Tom could do about it. As far as the grenade was concerned, there was nothing to indicate where it might have come from. Was it already in the house or had it come from the aircraft and had it played any part in the crash? Certainly not directly, as the explosion must have happened on the ground. Or had someone been threatening the pilot with it? The permutations were almost endless.

As soon as he heard that Janet Moyes had finished her tests for explosives, Tom headed down to her laboratories at Weybridge. A gravel driveway led up to the 1930s house, which was set back about thirty yards from the main road. The path then snaked its way round the side of the house and led into the back garden where a single storey structure resembling a granny flat provided the unprepossessing premises in which Janet did her work. The laboratories of Forensic Enquiry and its three scientists represented about one third of all the independent forensic scientists in the country – the hundreds of others in the business all worked for the prosecution.

She was a middle-aged, strong-featured woman with an open, challenging face who Tom knew well as she had provided her skills in other of his cases, not about explosives though. She explained her findings methodically. "First I took swabs from all over the surface of the body as well as from the skin surrounding the entry wounds – and I got nothing, nothing at all from the ETK. I then took swabs from round the edges and immediately inside the wounds and I'm afraid to say that they all came up negative –"

Tom felt like a prize had just been snatched away from him. – "with the exception of one." He stopped breathing.

"Just one of them produced a colour reaction – it wasn't strong but there was something there. Of course you can never be certain because you can get a false positive or spurious result occasionally because of certain interfering compounds – the sort of substances that are commonly found in the atmosphere.

"Naturally, I subjected it to a more sophisticated GCMS test over at Surrey University – sorry, gas chromatography mass spectronomy," she offered and handed him some paper printouts. "These show the retention times for different explosives."

Tom held up his hand. "Whoa, whoa, more simply, please."

"These printouts come from a machine which irons out any possible ambiguities. If there are any recognisable explosives in the sample, they're represented by a series of blips on a monitor. Each explosive has a different time lag so you can tell by how long it takes to get the reaction what substance it is. Anyway, I subjected the field test positive and I'm afraid it didn't come up with anything."

Tom felt his heart sink. It was a bitter disappointment. "Are there any explosives it can't detect – could anything have slipped through?"

"It's highly unlikely. This will pick up all the best-known constituents of PETN, RDX, EGDN, TNT and Ng.

"English, please!"

"Sorry. There are only a few explosives in common use and they're based on Semtex or nitroglycerine."

"So there was nothing you might have missed?"

"Not really. The only one we're not equipped to detect is TATP. It's hardly known here but has been used by groups in the Middle East but it's very unlikely it would be used as the explosive element in a hand grenade, it's much too unstable."

"Damn, damn, damn!"

"Sorry it's not better news."

"Not your fault." Gloom was etched into Tom's face.

As Janet Moyes filed her papers away she spoke confidentially. "That's my professional opinion, Tom, but I'll give you a personal one, if you like." She had his attention. "There was something odd about that body. I said there was nothing on the surface of the skin and when I say nothing, I mean nothing: no soot, no dried blood, no dried sweat – nothing. It had been comprehensively cleaned up and the same applied to all the wounds.

"I spoke to a couple of ex-colleagues at the Home Office labs and I know they tested for explosives on some of the bodies but I presume there was no mention of a positive finding in the Home Office report on Baker?"

"No – but you're losing me."

"For what it's worth, I think that body and the wounds have been scrubbed as clean as a new pin to try and get rid of explosive traces. It's quite hard to completely clean them from a flesh wound and I think I picked up a tiny remnant on one swab. I'm afraid it's not worth a candle because I can't put it in writing – but that's my opinion."

Tom was smiling again. "That will do for now."

He had been back in the office for only a few minutes when Fleishmann returned the call he'd put in earlier and they set up a meeting. Tom told Fleishmann he intended to bring Ailey Newman as an observer and having hung up, thought he'd better see if she was available and whether she wanted to attend.

Tom avoided saying he had already committed her and was relieved when she sounded pleased and agreed, but then came the question he had been dreading but was inevitable – had he decided to throw his lot in with Gerrity? He could sense the shock when he said 'no'.

"Why?" Ailey asked incredulously. "You seemed so keen in New York. Christ, Tom, I've even drawn up the contract. Do you want to explain why?"

"I haven't got an explanation, Ailey, it's more gut instinct than anything. I really did consider accepting but in the end I came to the conclusion I could best serve my clients by representing them myself. I know you're going to be annoyed but if it helps, I want to work closely with you so long as there's no conflict of interest, and this meeting seems as good a place as any to start."

There was no response from Ailey. "I'd like you to be there, Ailey, honestly." Nagging away in the forefront of Tom's mind was the night they'd spent together at the Plaza because it had immeasurably complicated the whole issue. He guessed Ailey must be feeling the same.

She was certainly angry and let it show. "Jesus, what's with you, Tom? You led both John and me to believe..." Tom stopped listening and the more her monologue developed and the more profound the accusations became the greater the resentment he felt. She and John Gerrity had unashamedly tried to seduce him, professionally speaking, because he had never even considered that their night together was part of the ploy. He was, however, acutely aware that the schmoozing and flattery had nearly worked and he was as angry with himself for that as he was with them. The biggest irritation, however, was that having made the offer, they were genuinely shocked that he should refuse it. People did not refuse John Gerrity and that was serious arrogance.

When Tom and Ailey met in the reception of Varsity Aviation three days later, the atmosphere wasn't warm although tolerable, but it worried him as it was important she did not view him as the enemy. They were called up to Fleishmann's office and just before the lift door slid open, Ailey said in a flat voice, "This is your party, Tom."

Cravits didn't join them, only Fleishmann's junior and his secretary to take minutes. Tom and Ailey accepted coffee and small talk until finally Fleishmann started on the preamble to what they both realised was going to be an offer.

The words were drawn from the lexicon of concern, punctuated with every conceivable disclaimer and Ailey contrived to make herself look as bored as possible, doodling on the pad in front of her throughout. Tom just wanted to know the figure and eventually Fleishmann got there but he first examined a sheaf of papers as though having to remind himself of the details.

"Varsity has always placed its public responsibilities above everything and we see our relationship with the people we serve as—"

"How much, Fleishmann?" Ailey cut in, then held her hands up in front of her. "Sorry, sorry, this isn't my show. Sorry, Tom." Fleishmann acknowledged her with a nod and got back into his stride.

"And of course where the people of London are concerned..."

"How much, Fleishmann?" Tom asked.

"Well..."

"How much?" He asked again.

"Completely without prejudice, we would be prepared to offer an all-inclusive sum of one million, five hundred thousand pounds Sterling."

Tom wrestled with a quick bit of mental arithmetic. Divided between his clients it would work out at a paltry sum. Fleishmann continued. "That will be full and final settlement of all claims worldwide."

Tom studied him for a moment. "I don't represent all claimants worldwide, just fifty-one people. That's forty-six dead and five seriously injured, all in Harrow, but you're telling me that this figure is to cover everyone affected, everywhere?"

"That's the offer. Of course that doesn't include the aircraft passengers – we'll be dealing with them separately." Fleishmann reclined in his chair, offer delivered, job done.

Again Tom grappled with the sums. "By my imprecise calculations I make that less than three thousand pounds a head for those who died. Is that correct?"

Fleishmann shrugged. "You can do the math any way you want, Tom, but the total is a million and a half."

Ailey rose, turned her back on Fleishmann and addressed Tom. "Can I just say one thing?" She did not wait for his agreement but walked to the door before turning to face the American. "Work it, Fleishmann! That's what I'd say if I was you, Tom." She exited the room with contempt billowing around her and closed the door far more noisily than she needed to.

Tom went silent and after a long delay, Fleishmann looked at his watch. "You don't have to make a decision now, Tom."

"I know. I was just trying to calculate how Londoners will react when we tell them about the state of your aircraft and what it was carrying. I think Ms Newman probably had it about right, Mr Fleishmann." He left but not before he had seen a distinct shadow of concern fall across Fleishmann's face.

Ailey's pace was remarkably fast for her size and Tom had to run to catch up with her in the street. She was still angry. "Jesus, the guy's not living in the real world. I can't believe him. It was like pissing on the funeral pyre."

"Hold on." Tom grabbed her arm as they passed a newsagent whose sales boards carried a screaming headline: *HARROW CRASH SLEAZE CLAIM*. He hurried inside and returned with a copy in his hands.

The story was to the point and carried Louise Watson's byline. *The Government is accused of compromising its inquiry into the Harrow disaster by secretly accepting money from Barcroft Holdings, Varsity Aviation's parent company.*

In a bitter attack on Government sleaze, a member of the Harrow Support Group claims that over £500,000 had been paid into party funds over recent years. Mrs Vicky Denton, widowed by the crash, gave details of the secret payments at a hurriedly convened press conference this afternoon.

Taking up a third of the page was a picture of Vicky, looking angry and determined. She was quoted as saying, "*No one pays out half a million pounds without wanting something in return. What Varsity has got for their money is a 'hear no evil, see no evil, speak no evil' trade-off from this discredited Government. We can have no faith in their so-called inquiry and can accept nothing less than a public inquiry.*"

Tom passed the newspaper to Ailey.

"Regular little revolutionary, your Mrs Denton. But she's sure as hell complicating my life."

"One thing I've learnt is that you can't fight these people by committee, Ailey. Vicky has rattled more cages than any of us."

When he got back to his office, Tom put in a call to Vicky but there was no reply. He knew that one of his most pressing tasks was to put together his submissions about the need for a jury at the inquest because without them it would be far from comprehensive. He delved into the pile of textbooks that Mike had obtained and poured over Section 8 of the Coroners Act 1988, which contained the words, *If it appears to a coroner, either before he proceeds to hold an inquest or in the course of an inquest begun without a jury, that there is reason to suspect…*

As Tom looked down the list of specified circumstances in which a coroner is obliged to summon a jury, he realised that none of them applied to this case, save one, 8 (3) (d) which read, *that the death occurred in circumstances the continuance or possible recurrence of which is prejudicial to the health or safety of the public, or any section of the public.*

That'll do nicely, he thought to himself but he also wondered if George, even without this clause, had the discretion to summon a jury if it seemed to him there was reason so to do. Tom spent the rest of the evening ploughing through numerous Home Office circulars in the hope of finding something to back up this suspicion – and he did.

Finally, with a sense of satisfaction, he relaxed and turned on the news to hear Charles Astbury again being forced on to the defensive and smoothly trying to defend the indefensible. His explanations for accepting secret donations had been well rehearsed over the years by numerous senior politicians but rang no more convincingly for all that. Astbury's repetition of the same old trite and discredited excuses did little for his public standing but knowing how transitory these *exposés* were, Tom felt no particular satisfaction.

It was approaching midnight when Vicky returned his call but he would not have cared what time it was. "Well, well, well, you've become a one-woman opposition, Vicky. And best of all, you've got right up Astbury's nose. How the hell did you get hold of the information?"

"It was unearthed by a couple of good researchers working on a docudrama about party funding. They had a leak from a Government insider who actually slipped them details of a special Solomon Islands offshore account into which money from overseas companies and individuals, including Barcroft, is being channelled. From there it goes to several sources – party funds and different right-wing pressure groups."

"What's your involvement?"

"I'm directing the drama elements. Oddly enough, the producer hadn't made the connection between Barcroft and Varsity but obviously I recognised the names."

Tom waited until they had extracted every ounce of pleasure from Astbury's and Varsity's discomfiture before he mentioned Fleishmann's offer and then held the phone away from his ear as Vicky responded. There was never any doubt that she would back his decision to reject the offer.

Tom wanted to keep her talking for personal reasons but there was legitimately plenty to discuss and he asked her to fix a meeting with the support group prior to the inquest. They needed to prepare themselves for giving evidence, what questions they would like him to ask, but also he needed to know what funds were now available from their money-raising strategies – both the pathologist and Forensic Enquiry would need paying soon but what he really wanted to say was, *Why don't you come over – right now?*

CHAPTER FIFTEEN

Monday, November 11th, 1991, 8.30 a.m. Tom leant forward to pay the taxi fare and caught a whiff of odour from beneath his shirt. It was no more than an hour since he had showered but his nerves were pumping adrenaline on overtime. It was not helped when he saw television crews and photographers clambering all over the steps of the Victorian town hall, and even worse, the rain was pouring down.

"What do you expect the outcome to be, Mr Harrison?" "What's your position on the collision theory?" "Are you going to be demanding a public inquiry, Tom?"

The questions battered at him and Mike as they climbed the steps.

"I'll make a statement after it's over, okay?"

"Just as well you bought a new whistle, isn't it, with all those cameras – can't have you looking shabby!" Mike spoke from the side of his mouth.

"You noticed then?"

"You look like an undertaker on a bad day! And the haircut – very solicitor-like!"

They made it through the ornate doors into the comparative quiet of the town hall vestibule.

"What room did Caffrey say we were in?" asked Tom, shaking the rain from his coat.

Mike checked his notebook. "Relatives room, 106. You're heading in the wrong direction."

What Tom wanted more than anything else was to be alone, to get his thoughts together and think through his approach. He knew he had to pull something out of the bag, but what? He had an unusable second-hand report of an air traffic control conversation; traces of an explosive he couldn't mention; a path report which talked of a hand grenade but which was far from conclusive and a body that seemed to have been scrubbed as clean as a butcher's block; possibly a couple of burnt rifles with nothing to say where they came from; and evidence of an unmodified cargo door which would be contested. To cap it all, he had had no advance disclosure from any of the participants and he did not know if George would even allow questions on any of the issues he wanted to raise or if he would agree to Tom's well-argued jury submission. He'd held better hands.

It was just after eight thirty, nearly an hour early, so he would have space to think but already people were everywhere. When they finally found room 106, tucked down a dead-end corridor, several relatives were waiting outside. "It's locked. Someone's gone to get the key," a voice offered.

It was another ten minutes before they entered the room and by then, the number of relatives had swollen to such a degree that they could only just fit inside the small space allotted to them – and more were arriving all the time. Intense conversations and raised voices were an indication of the tension people felt. Nerves were raw and they talked across each other in a volatile mix of thinly suppressed fear, pain, anticipation, and lurking just beneath the surface – anger.

A different group of relatives, people Tom did not know, pushed into the room and found places to sit on the windowsills, squeezed tightly together. Their wet clothes dripped on to the floor and windows steamed over thickly with condensation in what was becoming a damp, clammy and unsavoury little space.

Lawyers who had not been present at the first inquest made an appearance and tried to find their clients in the melee. And through it all Mike was busy with his new laptop, inputting additional personal details but the atmosphere was becoming intolerable as the noise levels increased and Tom realised he needed to take charge.

"Okay, okay." It wasn't loud enough and he raised his voice to a shout. "Listen to me! Everyone, please listen to me... Okay, that's better."

A voice from somewhere in the midst of the throng called out, "No one's told us anything yet, it's disgraceful." Her outrage terminated with an oath that was not quite decipherable but its profane meaning was nonetheless clear.

"I know, I know, it's bad organisation but I'm afraid we're in the hands of the authorities," Tom offered loudly, " but – it's important you listen because I'll try to explain what's going to happen, particularly for those of you who weren't at the last meeting."

Just as he thought he had exercised some minimal control over the throng of clients, a different lawyer appeared in the doorway, calling loudly. "Is there a Mr and Mrs Robb in here, Mr and Mrs Robb?" No one responded but he was not to be denied and called again, even louder.

"There are no Robbs in here, all right?" Tom snapped. "Okay, as I was saying, the procedure is this..." Ailey, Bernard and Vicky then appeared and pushed their way in, Bernard calling over the heads of everyone, "So there you are, I want a word with you."

"Not now, Bernard!" Tom shook his head in disbelief. "Right, ladies and gentlemen, can everyone hear me? Good. We'll all move into the council chamber, which is being used as the Coroner's Court today and the first thing that will happen is the coroner will open the resumed proceedings. He will then explain what the whole process is about and after that he will probably start by calling relatives to give evidence..."

Another lawyer was talking to three clients jammed in a corner and his grating voice kept cutting across Tom. "Excuse me, would you mind waiting until I've finished – it's very distracting." The man turned to face Tom, his voice shaking. "This is a public room!" and Tom knew he would have to battle through it.

"What you must decide is whether you want to speak or whether you feel your written statements are sufficient. How many of you think you would like to say something?" Only a few hands went up, one of them being Vicky's.

"For those who do want to speak, what you'll be allowed to say depends upon the coroner – the coroner is king and he calls the shots. He will ask questions first and then the other lawyers can cross-examine you if they want to – but I don't expect they will. I will question you last – and this is important – I will try to give you the opportunity to talk about safety, the failure of the emergency services, cover-up or anything else which concerns you. It might be allowed, it might not, but hold your fire until I give you the opening – don't let rip the moment you get into the witness box or the coroner will shut you up and then you might have lost your chance."

"How long is all this going to last?"

Tom couldn't even identify who was asking the question.

"As you can see, there are a lot of people and a lot of lawyers involved and I reckon at least ten weeks." There were audible groans but Tom pressed on. "As I told you before, I don't know what the other witnesses are going to say because the only things the coroner has let me see are copies of the Home Office pathology reports."

"Can we ask questions?" At last someone whose voice he recognised. It was Maurice Wreford.

"You'll almost certainly be allowed to ask questions of witnesses if they're giving evidence relevant to your deceased – but only *your* deceased – and please do it through me because it's important there's a co-ordinated approach. If there's something you want to ask, write it down on a piece of paper and pass it to me. I do have a plan and there might be questions which I think are better not asked until a given point, so please let me be the judge.

"Now back to the pathology reports. If you don't want to stay when the court is dealing with your relatives, you can leave at will. I can well understand if you choose to do so because the details will almost certainly be read out and may be distressing. Don't feel embarrassed, you're perfectly entitled to leave the chamber at any time you choose…"

A loud banging on the door preceded Mack Caffrey's head, which was already shouting before it was fully into the room. He drowned out Tom. "Would you all start moving through into the chamber, please? It's nearly nine thirty."

Tom ignored him. "Is there anything else you'd like to ask?

If you'd prefer to do it privately then make your way over to me now."

Caffrey was insistent. "Move through to the chamber – now, if you don't mind, ladies and gentlemen."

Tom wanted to keep speaking just to spite the man but it was time to get people out of the odious little room. "See them into the chamber, please, Mike..."

"Don't tell me, you're just going to the lav?" Mike knew him well and Tom's visit to the lavatory was essential before a hearing as nerves demanded it but also he never knew how long he might be stuck in the court room. He felt sure some big cases must have been won or lost because of a constricted bladder. Tom reached for his document case and again the smell of sweat wafted up through the material of his new suit and was getting worse.

There was one spare urinal and he juggled his zip between two lawyers who he guessed were barristers and they continued their conversation across him.

"Do you know Fraser?"

"Know of him, don't actually know him."

"What's he like?"

"Par for the course, I'd say. Bit of an old dodderer. Don't think he'll be giving you too much trouble." They both laughed.

No matter how hard Tom concentrated, nothing happened so in desperation he closed his eyes, looked towards the ceiling and thought of more pleasant surroundings, whistling silently as he did so.

"I said do you think you'll be long with the witnesses?" Tom realised he was being spoken to.

"Oh, forever, I should think."

"Oh, I see." The man didn't know what to make of the reply, buttoned his fly and left. Tom's problem was immediately solved and he eventually headed for the chamber, late but relieved.

He saw Caffrey and George Fraser ahead of him, halfway down the corridor and increased his pace to overtake them. They were walking slowly, reading a typescript, possibly a statement. As he caught up with them he heard Caffrey's question. "Are you going to read it immediately?" George registered Tom's presence and delayed his reply.

The greater space of the council chamber had solved the seating problem which bedevilled the old Coroner's Court and Tom even found a place with his name on it. Once seated, he looked around him and saw in every direction well-coiffured heads bent in earnest conversation, papers being extracted from cases and handed back and forth and through the mahogany and glass doors leading out into the marbled corridor, he could make out a janitor lazily mopping the wet footprints from the floor. At that particular moment, Tom would have given almost anything to change places with the man.

Tom scanned the court room trying to identify the barristers, who he would almost certainly have to do battle with, and identified the one representing the airline company, Varsity. He knew him to be Miles Beatty QC and watched as he talked intently with his client's representatives. He looked very old school and without even being able to hear him speak, Tom just knew that his accent would be tortuously ruling class. His longish, full hair ended in the nape of his neck with little curls and the cheeks were plumped with privilege. Beatty's mouth was small and tight and Tom wondered if it indicated a meanness of character; petty, picky, obsessed with minutiae and unable to grasp the broad sweep of this very complex case.

He reached for his document case to take out *Jervis on Coroners* and cold sweat engulfed him. His case wasn't there. Everything was in it, everything he needed for the inquest.

"Mike, I've lost my case," he hissed and Mike thought for a second. "Lavatory, you had it when you went to the lavatory, I saw you pick it up." As George Fraser entered the chamber, Mike slipped out.

Tom's brain was racing, desperately trying to formulate what to do if the document case had been lost. He could feel sweat trickling down his spine. What on earth could he say to his clients? How could he be so bloody stupid? It was, quite simply, the end of his career.

George Fraser waited irritably while Mike made his way quietly back into the room clutching Tom's briefcase. He then coughed a few times but did not have to call for silence as the chamber had already hushed itself in anticipation.

"Good morning, ladies and gentlemen. This is the reopened inquest into the deaths of five hundred and twenty-three people on the seventh of December last year."

Tom could feel a frisson of anticipation crackle through the chamber and George raised a piece of paper which looked like the same one he had seen the two men discussing in the corridor.

George continued. "In light of the situation and in deference to the public and of course in memory of the victims –" he had to be reading because he wasn't stuttering and fumbling – "I think there should be an evidential explanation." Tom felt the eyes of his clients burning into the back of his head and could hear their whispered questions but there was nothing he could say to them as he had no idea what was happening or what the old man meant.

"... I want to call Detective Chief Superintendent Markham to the witness box."

Caffrey, who was on his chair below the coroner's seat, saw Tom looking perplexed and leant back contentedly with just a trace of a smile on his fat face.

A uniformed policeman went on to the dais and stood in the section designated as the witness box. George Fraser led him. "Please tell us your rank and your station."

"I am Detective Chief Superintendent Markham of the Metropolitan Police, currently based at Harrow-on-the-Hill police station."

"And how long have you been in charge of this investigation?"

"From the beginning, sir. I was placed in charge of the investigation on the evening of December seventh."

"Have you visited the scene?"

"I have, sir, on numerous occasions."

George was still looking at his paper for prompts. "Were you responsible for all aspects of the investigation?"

"Yes, sir, all aspects of it."

"Do you have your notes with you?"

A scrap of paper was slipped into Tom's hand by Mike and

he saw it was in Ailey's writing. It simply said, "What the fuck is going on?" Tom wished he knew.

"Yes, sir, I have my notes with me."

"Has there been a specific investigation arising from this incident?"

"Yes, there has."

"What was the result?"

The policeman cleared his throat. "Sir, I have to ask you to adjourn this inquest."

Again, a burble of voices erupted from all parts of the chamber. Markham produced a sheet of paper which looked identical to the one George had been holding and read from it. "At seven thirty this morning, charges were laid against Mr Peter Thornton, pilot of the helicopter believed to have been in collision with Varsity Aviation's Flight 469. He has been charged with manslaughter."

George Fraser thanked Markham and dismissed the man before turning to the chamber. "As a result of this ... er ... particular development ... it would be customary ... it is customary, not obligatory, of me to adjourn as there must be no prejudice to the Crown's prosecution. I am accordingly adjourning this inquest *sine die* and consequently there is no immediate need for me to rule on the submissions about a jury."

Tom could hear Vicky's shout of anger and felt her hand clutching at his arm from behind; he could hear Ailey demanding to know what was going on and Bernard's flat vowels muttering, "Might 'a bloody well known it!" But before George Fraser could even rise from his seat, Tom was on his feet shouting to make himself heard.

"This is not only unexpected but unacceptable. We can only believe that this has been brought about through manipulation by Government agencies, stage-managed to prevent a proper inquiry—"

"This inquest is adjourned, Mr Harrison!"

Tom wasn't ready to stop. "I wish to register on behalf of all the relatives I represent my concern at the way this court has been manipulated and I want to express my clients' deep concern and anger that this court—"

"I have adjourned this inquest Mr Harrison... Sit down!"

"... that this court is being manipulated. There is clearly only one intention and that is to ensure it is gagged..."

George was trembling with fury and did the only thing he could think of to shut Tom up – he rose from his carved mahogany dais and hurried towards the exit with Caffrey scurrying along behind him.

Tom continued. "This is an outrage...!" but George Fraser had disappeared and Tom could hear the clamour from all around him. He turned to the relatives. "Would you all please make your way back to room 106." Mike marshalled them and their sense of disbelief whilst Tom led the way.

As soon as the full complement of clients had gathered, feeling irate and overwhelmingly stupid, incompetent and gullible, Tom began. "You heard what I said in court – we've been set up. It's grossly out of order and it has to be challenged." Voices from all directions demanded to know how. "Hang on, hang on!" He tried to remain calm in order to help calm those around him. "Unfortunately, under the coroner's rules, he does have the power to adjourn and we can't do anything about it for the moment but there are things we need to know. Why has the Director of Public Prosecutions decided to prosecute Peter Thornton and not Varsity Aviation and why has he chosen to announce it on this specific day? I'll tell you why – because Thornton's the fall guy. We might be able to judicially review that decision after Thornton's trial but in my view, Varsity should be in the dock defending a charge of corporate manslaughter. I know it's a controversial area but there have been a couple of other tragedies that have placed it right on the agenda and I think this reinforces our demand for a public inquiry in the longer term.

"Now, I'm afraid, we need to make a statement along those lines without prejudicing the trial so we need to think about it first. Do you want me to face the press?" The decision was unanimous.

Tom left the room and weaved his way through knots of people standing around in the corridor but felt someone pull at his arm and turned to see Ailey. "Jesus, this is like something out of Charles Dickens. Does Mr Bumble get a part in it anywhere?" She wasn't being humorous. "This is the biggest balls-up since Watergate and if you want to carry on fucking those people around for a bit of self-glory, fine. But I'm finished, you hear me? You're on your own Mr Harrison."

She spun away and walked off at speed, her feet almost breaking into a trot, high heels clacking on the marble floor. Tom exited on to the impressive stone entrance steps of the town hall and was besieged by journalists but ignored their shouted questions while he positioned himself so that he could be seen by all.

"I'd like to make a statement... If you'll just listen for a minute..." He managed to make himself heard and the microphone booms and tape recorders were thrust towards his face. He was conscious of Louise Watson in the front rank and automatically addressed his words to her.

"The support group can't accept what's happened here today. We believe that this court has been purposely gagged and this reinforces our demand for a public judicial inquiry into all aspects of this matter – and that's all I have to say." But it didn't stop the questions.

"You say you're being gagged – who by? And what do you think they're trying to hide?" "Who do you blame?" "How are the relatives taking it?"

Tom found it infuriating that the Thornton charge required him to remain silent but he had to respect it. "Any comment by me might risk prejudicing the prosecution of Peter Thornton and would amount to contempt or abuse of process and for that reason I really can't say anything further. That's all, I'm afraid." He began to make his way back into the town hall and as he pushed through the doors walked straight into Vicky.

"Another fine mess you got me into, Ollie!" she said, without smiling.

CHAPTER SIXTEEN

10.33 a.m. The fire door at the side of the building pushed open without resistance and the pavement outside was deserted of journalists. Tom and Vicky quickly blended in with morning shoppers as they walked with purpose, not bothering to look for a taxi.

"For God's sake, slow down, it's not a race!" Vicky grabbed his arm.

"Sorry! I'm just so pissed off. They're determined to stop us… We're not going to win this, you know that, don't you?"

"We're not giving up."

"Ailey might be right – take Varsity to the cleaners and forget everything else."

"Oh, shut up. We've had a knock-back, that's all." They continued in silence before Vicky asked, "Can I have another look at Napier's report when we get back? See – I'm still planning ahead."

"Great, but there's now nowhere else to go with this now."

"What about the judicial review?"

"Vicky, it's an outside shot!"

"We've got to keep going. It's been too long to give up."

Tom could hear steel in her voice and suspected that had she been on the *Titanic* she would be talking about suing White Star Line even as her lips were freezing over in the sub-zero waters of the North Atlantic.

"Talk to me tomorrow about what we do next and who knows, I might be out for blood again, but today I feel entitled to be totally negative and bloody miserable. I've been shafted, all right?"

Normally, being in Vicky's company worked liked magic on him but on this day, even by the time they had reached his office, he was feeling only a little more human. He held the street door open for her and a pony-tailed, leather-jacketed man exited, pushing past both of them. Tom was annoyed at the rudeness and was about to say something but changed his mind. He had had enough emotion for one day and was afraid that once he started, the man would get an unwarranted tirade of abuse.

The boring and slightly shabby offices which proscribed the greater part of his working life, and which he mostly ignored, suddenly appeared sad, insulting to clients who were required to pay not inconsiderable sums of money for the pleasure of engaging him in this depressing environment. He felt small and inconsequential and the fractional improvement in his mood that Vicky had produced evaporated instantly. Tom suddenly wanted to be anywhere but here; he wanted to be doing any job but the one he was. He felt like a fraud.

Purely through habit he checked for messages with Miss Rush, who viewed his thunderous face with deep misgiving. Her answer was tremulous.

"This has just been delivered for you, Mr Harrison," she said as she gave him a small package. Without a thank you Tom took it and marched up the steps towards his office with Vicky attempting to keep up with him.

Once there, Tom tossed Napier's report to Vicky to read and grabbed *Jervis* to check out what he should have done in court rather than ranting at George. His mood was not helped when he read Section 16 of the Coroners Act concerning adjournments and saw it provided room for him to make an objection. Fuck!

He was so frustrated with his own incompetence that he ripped open the newly arrived package with venom and found an audio cassette – not new and not identified in any way. He inspected it with distaste. "What the hell is this?" he said angrily to no one in particular as he searched for a portable player, found one and slotted the cassette into it, punching the start button as though he wanted to punish the machine.

Napier's report sat on Vicky's lap unopened as she silently watched his mood deteriorate. The player hissed and crackled but nothing intelligible emerged.

"Coffee?" He spat out as though it was an insult.

"No, thanks," Vicky replied. "I'm scared you might chuck it at me."

The humour went over Tom's head or he simply didn't hear as he charged into the kitchen in search of coffee. As he returned, the static noises abruptly reduced to background levels and a clearly identifiable voice burst into the room.

"... Roger, West Drayton control."

Tom and Vicky stared at each other.

"This is Flight Victor Alpha Four Six Niner outward bound from Northolt. I have a minor problem, possible slight depressurisation of the cargo hold. Request permission to return to Northolt. Please advise height and heading."

There was a joint intake of breath and "*Shit almighty!*" issued hoarsely from Tom as they dashed to the cassette player and positioned themselves in front of it while the scrambled sounds of static, indecipherable interference and distant voices hissed at them from the past.

"West Drayton control to flight Four Six Niner. Please confirm your present position."

"Flight Four Six Nine. I am twenty miles north-east of you, heading East, niner eight degrees. Altitude is twenty-thousand feet."

"West Drayton control. Turn right on to heading two six fiver degrees West. You are clear to reduce altitude to ten-thousand feet. Do you require assistance?"

"Negative, control. Turning right on to heading two six fiver degrees West and reducing altitude."

The static continued but the conversation came to an end.

"This is it, this is it! This is the recording." Tom grabbed Vicky's arm and was surprised to see how ashen she looked.

"This is the plane that killed David," she whispered and he felt like an insensitive moron.

The crackle of static increased and Tom fiddled with base and treble controls. "Is that it? It can't be!" They continued to wait and it was minutes before a voice again cut through the background noise.

"West Drayton control to flight Four Six Niner. Please turn left on to heading two four eight. Continue your descent at three degrees. You are one mile from the start of the glide path and looking good."

"Roger, control, turning left on to—" A noise drowned out the transmission – a sudden, sharp noise which was gone as quickly as it came. The same voice continued transmitting but fear had replaced the laconic technical exchanges and the man's slight foreign accent had become more pronounced.

"Oh my God ... West Drayton control, this is a Mayday – Mayday, Mayday, Mayday. The aircraft is not responding, I repeat, aircraft is not responding."

"Flight Four Six Niner, we have your Mayday. I repeat, we have your Mayday. Can you make Northolt? You will be cleared for immediate landing."

"West Drayton control. I am trimming and now have some control. I cannot guarantee to make the runway or to stay on it if I get there but I will certainly try."

"Northolt will be ready and waiting for you, Four Six Niner. I'm monitoring you all the way. Please let me know when you have made visual contact."

"Roger – not in sight yet."

"They will be standing by for you. You're looking good, Four Six Niner – stay with it ... and good luck!"

"Thanks, control."

Again the transmission was interrupted by a loud, unidentifiable noise and as it died down the pilot's voice continued but now on the point of panic.

"No control, West Drayton, no control at all. I've lost my heading. I'm going down. Control, I'm going down. Oh God, I'm going down..." The final English words were followed by a language which could have been Arabic and it could have been a prayer the pilot was repeating with feverish intensity.

The static cut suddenly, leaving a constant, droning background noise issuing from the little player on Tom's desk. Tom and Vicky looked at each other in silence as huge tears rolled down Vicky's face. The ring of the phone could have been a nuclear explosion for the shock it had.

"Harrison!" Tom shouted into it. "Sorry, sorry, Mike. Ring me back in ten minutes."

Vicky had her head in her hands and Tom put his arm round her shoulders. "I'm sorry, Vicky, I obviously had no idea what was on there. I am so sorry you had to go through that and have it all brought back."

She looked at him with a tear-stained face. "It's not David I'm crying for, you silly sod, it's that poor bugger flying the plane. He knew he was going to die. He knew he was going to die," she repeated, "and he could do nothing about it."

Tom swore to himself that one day he would get it right where understanding Vicky was concerned. He reached for the phone. "Miss Rush, who delivered that package you just gave me?"

"Why, the man you passed as you came into the office."

"Was he a courier?"

"I don't know. I presumed so."

"Did he say anything, leave any paper work? I mean, did you have to sign anything?"

"No. He just handed it to me and said something like, 'Give that to the bloke who's dealing with the air crash,' and left."

"Did he have a bag, anything written on his jacket – Speedway Couriers, something like that?"

"I'm sorry, Mr Harrison, I didn't really notice but I don't think so. He just seemed to be in a terrible hurry."

"Just a minute, Miss Rush." He turned to Vicky. "That bloke we passed in the entrance – did you notice if he was a courier?"

"I don't know. I don't remember a name or anything."

Again he spoke into the phone. "If you think of anything that might identify him, let me know, Miss Rush," and hung up. "If he was a courier he'd have wanted a signature so I think we've just seen the man who recorded this!"

"Well, at least you've got it!"

"No, I've got a bad copy and I can't authenticate it. We need a statement from whoever made it and we need the original recording."

Vicky went very quiet. "What do you think was happening on that tape?"

"I'm not sure. Can you bear to listen again?"

He called Mike to join them, they replayed the tape and Tom tried to interpret it as best he could. "We've obviously missed the PAN call – that's what must have alerted the ham to start recording – so the pilot's already said pan, pan or whatever it is and the first sign of trouble is twenty miles away from Northolt – and Heathrow, for that matter as they're only a few miles apart, so we can take it that this problem has nothing to do with Thornton's helicopter.

"Slight depressurisation of the hold he says. Could that fit with the cargo door having sprung its closures? I think the answer's probably 'yes' – it seems logical. Okay, now he's been given a heading and he's on his way back to Northolt so the situation's obviously under control and there's no panic.

"Right, this is where something dramatic happens – there! You can hear the noise – and he issues a Mayday." Tom stopped the tape. "There's no mention of a collision or perhaps he didn't see the helicopter. Anyway, he's one mile from the glide path, which must be east of Northolt because that's the direction he's coming in from. So where exactly does that place him? So far he's followed air traffic control instructions so he won't have gone veering off into a no-fly zone or we'd have heard them telling him. So where exactly is he? Probably where he should be."

He pressed the play button again. "Now listen to this – almost immediately after he makes the Mayday call – bang – something else happens and he's lost all control. Is that where he hit the chopper? If it is, then what was it that caused him to make the Mayday call in the first place? Whatever it was it was serious enough to threaten the aircraft. Or did he hit the chopper first, make the Mayday and this second bang was somehow connected?"

"Jeez, it's dramatic stuff, that's for sure," Mike said quietly, looking stunned.

"The trouble is," Tom continued, "we just don't know enough. We need some specialist knowledge – an expert. Hang on a minute, what was the name of that trade paper chap, the one who spoke at the original press conference? Remember him?" Tom checked his address book. "Christ, what was the man's name – Louise gave it to me. Yes, yes, yes – that's it, got it, under A for aircraft: Anthony Berrens. Mike, see if you can get an air chart, or whatever they call them, for the whole of Greater London. And when you've done that, get down to Tooting – we've got to find that radio ham."

Tom phoned Berrens and first sounded out how sympathetic he was to the support group and their attempt to get answers about the crash. He seemed understanding enough and volunteered his help when Tom outlined what he needed, clearly picking up on the urgency in Tom's voice, saying he would be over later that day.

Tom needed something more, some confirmation, just one snippet of knowledge to support his belief that they had hold of something extremely important, something which challenged the official view that was gaining ground – namely, that the collision with the helicopter was the most likely cause of the disaster. He kept Berrens on the phone because, with what scant knowledge they had, the recording did not necessarily disprove the official line but Tom's rudimentary calculations of time and distance gave him hope that somewhere on this tape was sufficient evidence to blow it out of the water. He wanted confirmation that it was worth Berrens's time in making the journey over to see him.

"Mr Berrens, where over London would you be if you were one mile east of Northolt's eastern glide path? Yes, from the start of it. Thank you very much; yes, I'll wait."

When Berrens came back with the answer, Tom's face transformed into something resembling that of an excited schoolboy. He turned to the others. "Flight 469 must have given out its Mayday somewhere over Walthamstow. The final emergency could have been no more than a couple of miles further west. That's a hell of a long way from where it hit Thornton's helicopter. The collision had nothing to do with its downing." He said the words with such satisfaction that Mike and Vicky applauded.

*

Tuesday, November 12th, 1991, 7.00 p.m. The atmosphere in the Caprice was exactly what one would expect from one of London's best restaurants – discreet, tasteful and deferential. When Charles Astbury was shown to his table, William Pennard, Editor of the *Daily Despatch*, was already there and had almost finished his single malt.

"Bill, sorry to have kept you waiting. Cabinet meeting overran. Oh good, you've got a drink." Before sitting down, he addressed the hovering waiter who had shown him to his table. "A kir!" There was no 'please'.

Astbury joined Pennard at the table and the two men phrased their conversation quietly and circumspectly as they selected their lunch yet there was something about the arrogance of their bearing which invited attention. Pennard's uncontrolled mop of white hair, flowing sideboards, hand-rolled scarlet silk handkerchief cascading from his breast pocket and the white rosebud in his lapel, which he was never seen without – were pure theatre that demanded to be noticed.

Astbury's expensive and superbly cut clothing, his well-rounded cheeks and the small curls at the nape of his neck somehow signalled the privilege of his class. But it was the confidence of his movements, the manner in which he held himself, the assurance with which even the most insignificant action was executed that screamed power and position. He was a man who had been weaned on self-importance.

By the time the first course arrived, pleasantries and domestic enquiries had been dealt with. The meeting had been requested by Astbury so Pennard was certain that a judicious touch of market trading was about to take place. He would, of course, never be so indiscreet as to ask Astbury what information he had for him outright but when the main course arrived, the man was ready to reveal it.

"Something that might interest you, Bill, considering how much attention you've paid to agricultural matters recently." Astbury checked the restaurant to see if anyone was within earshot. "Our mutual friend Baldry seems to have nailed his colours to the mast over OPs – organophosphates…"

"I know what they are, Charles!"

"Quite unnecessary really, but there you are. You may know he instigated a high-level inquiry into the effect they might have on those who use them regularly – farmers, particularly when they're used as sheep dip or in other concentrated environments."

"Yes, I did know. In fact Mark Edwards, our agricultural correspondent, made a submission to it."

"Yes, of course he did, I'd forgotten." He had not forgotten and it was this newspaper's interest in the subject which had dictated his choice of Pennard as the recipient of his inside information. "Well, one of the principal expert witnesses was Professor Roger Millichap of Oxford – he died a few weeks ago; remember him?"

"Yes, Charles, we ran his obituary."

"Quite. Well, it seems he told Baldry in no uncertain terms that the evidence was quite clear that even at low exposures, OPs attack the human central nervous system – quite seriously, apparently. All those shepherds complaining of the vapours weren't malingerers after all."

Pennard began to pay close attention. "Millichap said that? I understood he'd given OPs a clean bill of health so long as they were used according to the regulations and instructions."

"Exactly. That's what we all thought. After Baldry died, my information is that he had the minutes of their meeting rewritten, leaving out the bad bits and changing a word here and there – altering 'will' to 'could' and 'likely' to 'unlikely', that kind of thing."

"Good God, why would he do that? Actually, I can guess why but what's your version?" Pennard appeared shocked – as shocked as a man could be who spent his life revealing the machinations of the powerful.

"As you probably know, Baldry's constituency lies fair and square in the West Midlands, an area that has more sheep in it than people. But it isn't just sheep, there used to be a lot of cattle too, at one time. There are some extremely influential farmers involved who were already gunning for Baldry over the BSE fiasco, cost them an awful lot of money. Seems they gave him a clear warning that if he also upped their costs on sheep, they'd create a terrible stink and hound him out of office. They told him in no uncertain terms that outlawing OP dipping would wipe out the profitability of an industry that was already highly dependent upon subsidies."

"So Baldry cooked the report?"

"Exactly!"

Pennard looked thoughtful. "He wouldn't have dared do that without the okay from above, so who sanctioned it?" He had the scent of a major story in his nostrils and wanted to follow the trail as far as it would go.

"I don't know anything about that," Astbury answered dismissively and Pennard instinctively knew that what he really meant was, *Yes, of course I know who was ultimately responsible and it's them I'm really after*. "It's all in here, Bill, and I know you'll find it interesting – and useful." He pushed an A4 manila envelope discreetly across the table.

"It could be a resigning matter, you realise that, of course?" Pennard stated the obvious.

"Yes, I suppose you're right." Astbury adopted an agonised look which was as brief as it was false. "Trouble is, there's talk of a cabinet post for Baldry at the next reshuffle and I don't think that would be in the best interests of the country, do you?"

Pennard continued wanting to flush Astbury out. "But one of his principal sponsors has always been the Home Secretary. Without his backing Baldry would never have got where he has so it's not going to show Sturgis up in a very good light, is it? It'll weaken him considerably! In fact it could eventually end his ministerial career as well, couldn't it?"

Astbury smiled. "Oh really, do you think so, Bill?"

Pennard took the envelope and was reasonably satisfied. He hated running a spoon-fed story unless he knew precisely whose agenda it was serving and what or who was the intended target. Not to comprehend the detail made him feel as though he was being used, being manipulated. He felt pretty confident he had chapter and verse on this one and the only question still hanging in the air was why Astbury wanted the Home Secretary's head.

It was ruthless even by Astbury's standards, he mused, and to take both Baldry and the Home Secretary down indicated something very important and well below the radar as there were no vendettas in that quarter as far as he was aware. It was a good story by any measure and Pennard was happy with it so he sat back waiting for the *quid pro quo*, which was quickly delivered by Astbury.

"There is one thing you could do for me, Bill." He pushed another envelope at Pennard. "Here's a little story which I think is worth a fair bit of your valuable space. All absolutely true, totally fireproof and very important to me. Okay? And I think this might be only the first instalment as my instinct tells me we may well need to revisit it from time to time – but I know I can rely on you, Bill."

"I'm sure we can do something, Charles."

"And by the way," Astbury added as Pennard called for the bill, "don't use it just yet. Hold on to it for the moment and I'll let you know when the time is right."

Wednesday November 13th, 1991, 9.00 a.m. The telephone box was, as Tom had suggested, directly across the road from Tooting Bec underground station. Chances were, Mike reasoned, that the mystery ham had been heading for the station when he made the call. It went without saying that there was not a local radio club – that would have been too convenient and the theory of tracking the man through the magazines he might or might not have bought from a newsagent's turned out to be a nightmare.

Mike tried to work out logically the maximum size of the area he had to cover. East and west were no problem as he simply took the halfway point between tube stations, working on the basis that the guy would probably use the one nearest to his home. Between Tooting Bec and the halfway point to Tooting Broadway tube were a dozen or more small newsagents and it was a similar picture in the other direction, towards Balham tube station.

North and south were much more complicated as there was no tube in either direction. The nearest BR station of any importance north was Clapham Junction. South, there was nothing until Streatham. It could take days if all the little backstreet shops were included. Despite the scale of the job, Mike felt obliged to at least try for a result even though his hopes were low. Consequently, he plodded from one shop to another without enthusiasm and without success.

It was an area with a high ethnic population and many of the shops were owned by Tamils, some of whom spoke very little English. Trying to explain about radio hams and magazines at times became impossible and Mike was convinced that many of the negative responses he received may have been simply to get rid of him.

He'd established there was a radio ham magazine called *Wavelength* but every time he mentioned the name to a newsagent the response was a shake of the head or a blank look.

When he arrived back at Tooting Bec station for the third time, having done the east and west routes along Tooting High Street, Mike grabbed a quick cup of tea and headed up Trinity Road going north towards Clapham Junction. By the time he reached Nightingale Lane he'd had enough and flagged down a cab to take him back to his car. "Thanks, Tom, thanks a bunch, mate!" he said to no one in particular.

Berrens was fascinated by the tape and felt certain it was authentic. The problem was its quality – a much-used cassette, poor reception, faulty recording equipment – and for a multiplicity of reasons he said he needed the original if he was to carry out any meaningful analysis. He volunteered to work on the copy to see what he could establish but having only just acquired it Tom wasn't ready to part with it immediately.

With the aid of the charts Mike had bought from a hang-gliding shop, Berrens was able to confirm that Flight 469's problems had nothing to do with the helicopter. Tracing the aircraft's last minutes across the charts showed that it had been faced with three emergencies and all of them miles away from where the collision had taken place.

Berrens concluded that Flight 469 must have struck the helicopter after the final transmission, whilst it was plummeting to the ground, already doomed. If any of it could be proved, it would strongly support an application for a judicial review.

When Mike returned empty-handed it was a disappointment but Tom could not afford to give up on the ham as his was the best evidence he nearly had!

Ailey's call took him by surprise – but not her attitude.

"This is turning into a farce, Tom!" Space and time had clearly not improved her mood nor changed her intentions.

"So you said."

"I don't know what antediluvian legal hogwash is going down but I've had enough of it. I've stood by and let you play your truth games but now it's over for me."

"Ailey, you've already said all this. Is there some hidden threat here that I'm missing?"

"No threat. Your reason for keeping the case here in the UK is to keep control over it, to speed up the process because you think the US clients will get preference in the States. Well, I've just spoken to John and we're thinking of issuing a UK writ as well."

"Naughty."

"Coming from you, that's a joke. We don't intend to poach but if any of your clients want us to represent them we will, and it'll be a straight proposition – compensation!"

"And if Varsity declares bankruptcy?"

"Then we'll move it to the States and add them to the Barcroft action – that's not a problem. The real problem is lack of action here in the UK."

Tom wanted to shout at her, to verbally shake her – *Come and listen to this fucking tape, you moaning woman!* – but what he actually said was far more controlled. "I know you're annoyed with what's happened but it's not my doing and Varsity is talking so that's a start."

"Varsity is laughing at you, Tom, they're throwing you pennies."

He thought she was wrong. He'd done enough negotiating to gauge when someone was serious and was certain that the concluding position would be light years away from where they had started. True, it was difficult trying to hold the two positions – compensation and culpability – but that's what his clients wanted. One thing was certain, he would not be threatened. "If you're set on a UK action, get on and do it."

"Okay, so be it," Ailey responded and the line went dead.

Thursday, November 21st, 1991, 6.45 p.m. Tracey Yardley knew there was no point in waiting for Dean to answer the door because nothing would stop him from watching the football match on TV. Chimes rang again so she dried her hands and ran down the stairs but made no move to unhook the chain or draw back the bolt as, since the crash, Tracey had discovered insecurity. "Who is it?"

The voice was well spoken and ingratiating. "My name is Mr Collins, from the solicitors Hilldrew's and I'm not selling anything. Here's my card." An expensively produced visiting card dropped through the letter box and it was as he had said – Simon Collins, solicitor, representing Hilldrew's of Bond Street.

She opened the door on its chain and peered round it. Mr Collins, with his narrow shoulders, balding head and thick spectacles, did not look a threat so Tracey opened the door fully. "What's it about?"

"Well, I can honestly say it's something to your advantage. Could I please come in – just for a minute?"

"My brother's upstairs!" It was said as a warning.

"Good, because I would like to talk to him as well."

Tracey showed the man up to the flat and switched the TV off despite Dean's protests. Collins sat down and removed papers from his briefcase and his quietly spoken expression of regret at the loss of their family washed over Tracey. She had heard far too many meaningless condolences from people who did not know them and did not care.

"What do you want?" She had not meant it to sound as aggressive as it did but didn't particularly care that it came out that way.

"I represent Varsity Aviation...!"

Mr Collins talked at length but Tracey heard little of what he said. The words tumbled through her mind – imprecise, unrecognised but disturbing, dragging her back to where she did not want to go with only the occasional phrase registering.

Gradually, the numbness began to wear off and she started to listen to what he was saying.

"What do you want, Mr Collins – in simple, straightforward language?" Tracey cut across his flow.

"I am authorised to offer you a sum of money as compensation for the loss of your family. My clients have no legal obligation to do this and their offer in no way admits any liability whatsoever. It is what is termed 'no-fault compensation'."

"But we're suing you." Dean looked confused.

Mr Collins was careful about his choice of words. "That's not strictly true as no writ has been served but even if such a writ is served, I have to tell you that my clients will defend it vigorously. Any court case could take years and there would be very little prospect of you winning it. What they would like to do, however, is offer you a payment now, immediately, to help you build a new life, and I honestly believe it's a very generous offer."

"How much?" Tracey's question was demanding and without embarrassment.

"It's a figure of twenty-five thousand pounds."

Neither of them had worked since the disaster and although Tracey disliked Mr Collins, they were both desperate for money. A pile of brown envelopes in the bedroom was growing higher by the day and there were now so many that they no longer dared to open new arrivals.

Tracey went silent for a while and appeared to be deep in thought. "That's a bit under four thousand quid a piece for Mum, Dad, Beth and Wayne, Nan and Grandpa. Not a lot for nearly your whole family, is it, mister whatever your name is?" Tracey's voice was cold, hard, hurt.

Dean interrupted. "Hang on a minute, Trace, let's talk about it?"

Mr Collins quietly intervened. "I'm sorry, I don't think I made myself clear. That's twenty-five thousand pounds – each." He removed another piece of paper from his briefcase. "I can have a cheque for fifty thousand pounds or two separate cheques for twenty-five thousand pounds each, delivered to your bank first thing tomorrow. All that's necessary to complete it is your signature here." He held out a contract.

"Please, do read it. It's a standard agreement but there are just two clauses which I should draw to your attention. This one, here, which says that the payment is in full and final settlement. Basically it means you can't sue my clients in the future. And there's this one, here – my clients don't want these special payments to you to be seen as some kind of precedent by others and as a consequence they would insist you don't mention the settlement – to anyone. It's what people refer to as a secrecy clause."

November/December 1991 With an indefinite adjournment of the inquest, the remaining bodies were released for burial and Tom could see no further advantage in trying to delay it. Ideally he would have liked the resources and the permissions to subject all the corpses to forensic examination but in his heart he did not think it would produce anything further.

He had reluctantly come to the conclusion that the rifles were probably already on the ground – someone's trophies or even an arms cache – and similarly for the grenade. It was the only realistic explanation.

The possibility of a hijacker had been dismissed with the arrival of the tape as the pilot had not mentioned any threat and, prior to the Mayday, had been relaxed, his tone not that of someone with a gun under his nose.

In some ways it made life easier as all attention now focused on the technical shortcomings of the aircraft. Having rejected Varsity's offer, it certainly strengthened their hand for the next round of bargaining or for a civil suit.

After copying the tape, Tom had eventually allowed Anthony Berrens to have it and he had analysed it as best he could, providing a fairly convincing explanation of events. His scenario was that the Pan call was made after the first set of cargo door closures gave way – a problem but not a big one; the Mayday could have been caused by the second set of closures on the door also failing. Had that happened, it would have resulted in the cargo door opening fully, which would then certainly have led to rapid depressurisation of the cargo hold, which was sited immediately below the passenger cabin.

With the passenger cabin still pressurised, there would have been enormous downwards strain on the cabin floor and it was conceivable, in fact probable, that the outcome would be a partial collapse of the floor. The design of the P11 was such that many of its main computerised aircraft control systems – ailerons, flaps and rudder – ran through the floor and would certainly be affected.

The final act of the drama was probably caused by progressive deterioration – a further section of the floor giving way, completing damage to the controls. It was all technically feasible and consistent with the pilot's messages.

Tom had conclusive proof that Peter Thornton had nothing to do with the disaster but he could not use it. All he could use were two statements which claimed that the cargo door of Flight 469 had not been modified and no one had checked to see if it was properly closed. Without the original tape they were not very convincing so he desperately needed the radio ham.

When Vicky called and asked if he would like to be at David's funeral, Tom accepted but was uneasy as he had seen enough death, and the accumulation of grief that surrounded it, to last a lifetime. However, he did wonder if this act of closure might end Vicky's life of denial. Since the day she had walked into his office she had shown no signs of grieving and it was as though all her emotion had been converted into nervous energy, which drove her resolve to discover what had really happened. Tom half believed, however, that there might be another agenda – retribution.

Friday, December 6th, 1991, 11.00 a.m. In the event, it turned out to be a joint funeral with all the remaining members of the group who had not yet buried their relatives joining together. Vicky had not intended to have a religious service for David but out of solidarity with the others, most of whom wanted some kind of religious burial, she went along with them.

The final leg of the journey to the cemetery was down Braemar Street, a long, straight road of terraced houses which led off the main road with front gardens the size of pocket handkerchiefs. Each of the nine hearses rendezvoused at the end of the street and the sombre relatives silently took their position behind their loved one's hearse. One by one, the cortèges began their slow progress, a top-hatted undertaker in front of each, grieving relatives behind.

Slowly and inexorably, the street filled with its procession of misery but it remained just a scrap, a tiny fraction of the despair caused by Flight 469. As the first hearse neared the cemetery gates at one end of the street, the last hearse was just beginning its journey at the other end. Their engines ran almost noiselessly as they bore their brightly coloured, flower-strewn coffins to their final resting place. The only sound which accompanied the stream of silent, walking people was the gentle crunch of shoes as they ground the grit of the road beneath their soles. Drawn curtains at the windows of houses offered a token of respect and on front doorsteps, people stood quietly watching; a token of solidarity.

Tom walked alongside Vicky and Emma together with their relatives and friends. Emma sobbed silently and clung to her mother and Vicky offered all the support she could but from beginning to end, when the final crumbs of earth were tossed on to David's coffin, her face remained set, seemingly unmoved, and her eyes were free of tears.

When it was over and everyone filed into the Hollybush Hotel for sherry and sandwiches, Tom thought he had probably had all the emotion he could take for one day and went over to Vicky to make his goodbyes. She was deep in conversation with Emma and he remained at a discreet distance. He had not intended to listen and had, in fact, turned and started to leave but he wavered and there was no excuse for why he remained within earshot and purposely listened to their conversation.

"Can't you let it go now, Mum? We can't bring him back. Whatever you do we can't bring him back."

"I can't do that, darling; to me it would be like betraying him. Can I tell you something about your dad and me? I want you to listen, I mean really listen. I have never loved anyone like I loved him – not my parents, not my grandparents, no boyfriend, no one in the whole world..."

"I know that, Mum, you don't have to say it, it was obvious."

"Let me tell you, Em, it's important. When we met we were like chalk and cheese: different backgrounds, different values, different people. He was honest and straight and above all strong and I was none of those things. Your dad opened up a new world for me – one where people cared about each other, supported each other and tried to learn and progress and understand. He helped me to make life like that and the most essential part of it was the trust and honesty between us. Honesty can be very painful but it's what gives you strength and you deny it at your peril. We are being lied to, Em. People are lying to us about how your dad died. I can't accept that because to do so would be to betray him. How do you think he would have reacted if I'd been killed and someone lied to him about that?"

"He'd have gone ape-shit!"

Vicky smiled. "Well, I've gone ape-shit and I'm going to stay that way until I find out the truth. Can you understand that?"

"Of course I can, Mum. You're right. I know you're right, it's just that it's quite hard for me at times because it often feels like there's no room for anything else in your life."

"When I said I have never loved anyone else in the whole world as much as I loved your dad, there is one exception."

Emma put her arms round Vicky. "Don't you think I know that, Mum? Listen, I'm just a selfish, privileged, spoilt little brat but really I am behind you – all the way. Give the bastards hell!"

Vicky returned Emma's hug. "Well, as we're in the mood for being honest, there's a few other things I think you should know – I think it's important you should know… I've never lied to you, I just haven't told you the truth and I want to do that now because there's just the two of us left, Em, just you and me and the more you know about me the more you'll understand me – why I do the things I do, why I act in certain ways, why I can be such a hard cow…"

"You never are with me, Mum, never."

"All the same, we need each other and I want there to be no more secrets between us. You're going to find some of what I tell you upsetting and hard to take but try your hardest because with your dad gone, there's no one else who truly knows me and that seems wrong. I want you to know – Emma, I need you to know because I feel like I'm living a lie, betraying you and I can't live with that..."

Tom could not bring himself to eavesdrop any longer and walked away without saying goodbye, feeling a complete shit.

This final interment seemed to draw a line under the Harrow disaster and just for one brief instant the questions ended and the recriminations were laid to one side while a whole country paid its respects to the last of the dead.

Saturday, December 7th, 1991 The *Evening Chronicle* produced a special commemorative edition for the first anniversary of the crash. Centre pages were edged in black and bore the headline *Lest We Forget*. On eight pages it ran thumbnail pictures and brief biographies of all five hundred and twenty-three victims; families were grouped together, their smiling faces photographed in less painful times.

Tom did not read the paper that evening – he'd seen enough for one day and it was only chance that made him look at it the following day when, unable to find his daily paper, he took the *Evening Chronicle* to the cafe to read over lunch. As he sipped his coffee he turned to the pages of victims; pictures of those who had died on the ground were grouped separately to the aircraft passengers. Amongst the passengers he picked out a shot of the young man whose story had been published – the young man who had resigned from the army only to die before he took up his new, safer job. He looked every inch the soldier with his short hair and strong physique. Tom looked along the lines of pictures of the other passengers who were all male adults with serious faces and they jarred alongside the heartrending happy snaps of babies and toddlers, teenagers and grandparents who had died on the ground. In fact they looked something of a rogues' gallery – all unsmiling, fit-looking young men, short-haired, straight-faced...

As Tom leapt to his feet, the table lurched and clattered when he caught it with his thighs and his half-filled coffee cup went skittering across the table, spewing its contents everywhere. "They're soldiers, they're all bloody soldiers." He almost shouted it.

CHAPTER SEVENTEEN

Monday, December 9th, 1991, 9.00 a.m. "So what the hell was a planeload of soldiers doing on its way to Nigeria, pretending to be oil workers?" Tom had expected a more positive reaction from Louise and could feel himself gripping the phone in frustration. "You're assuming they're soldiers but you don't know." Louise was obviously determined to be objective.

"Have you got the pictures there?" Tom asked. "Just look at them. Even the four Americans – they're older but they're still obviously soldiers; look, their heads are almost shaved and I'll bet they're 'military advisers' or whatever it is they call them. I'll lay money on it! We finally have an explanation for the rifles and the grenade because where there are soldiers there are weapons – okay?"

"You can't assume it. You need proof." Louise was treating Tom's idea as the journalist she was, knowing she had to be able to make it stand up before it could be used and it frustrated Tom.

"Look, Louise, I'm supposed to be the lawyer and of course we need proof but let's begin by at least agreeing the proposition – could they be soldiers?"

"Yes! They could..."

"Thank you, that's a start. Now, will you do me a favour and find out what you can about Nigeria?"

"No problem, sir! A general, political, economic, military rundown, okay, Mr Harrison?"

"Exactly!" She had forced a smile back on to his face.

"On my way, captain! Quite the little detective, aren't we?"

He could not resist warm thoughts as they hung up. He called Vicky next and got exactly the reaction he'd expected from

Louise – positive and enthusiastic and the question he wanted to ask her had been burning a hole in him. "Vicky, have you got anyone in the support group who had a relative on the aircraft?"

"Do you know something, I'm not sure we have. I'll check and ring you back."

Tom had no sooner hung up than a call came through from Wings of Sonning. Bartlett the MD wanted their service contracts standardised as over the years, each time they had taken on a new client, the contracts had been modified to meet their individual needs. The outcome was a hotchpotch that was causing confusion – and in some cases financial loss, exacerbated by operating from their two different bases at Heathrow and Filton.

It was the last thing Tom wanted to think about but he did register that his father had only mentioned Heathrow. Tom asked for the paperwork and correspondence to be biked over and by the time he hung up, Vicky had come back to him and was on hold.

"Believe it or not, there's only one member of the group who had a relative on the plane. She's not been that involved in anything and has said very little to anyone, in fact I thought she was just one of the Friends of HSG – there's dozens of those. She's not involved in the claim for compensation or anything like that, which is probably why I hadn't noticed her."

"Who is she?"

"Quite an old woman – Mrs McNulty – Emily."

"Has she ever said anything about the crash, about her dead relative?" Tom asked.

"No, not that I've heard. She turns up to some meetings and chats small talk but she's never referred to her loss."

Tom looked to see if there was a McNulty in the memorial pictures but couldn't find one. "Is she on the phone?"

Vicky sounded smug. "I've already called her – she's in all day. Incidentally, I thought you ought to know that four of the claimants have withdrawn, said they don't want to pursue the compensation any further."

"That's got to be Ailey! Who are they?"

"Tracey and Dean Yardley; Troy Dawson and Des Niven."

"Did they give any explanation?"

"None, but they all sounded very guilty."

"It's got to be Ailey." Tom said it again as a statement. He was annoyed by Ailey's poaching and was still chewing it over when he raised the knocker on the door of Mrs McNulty's undistinguished terraced house which fronted directly on to the pavement of an undistinguished narrow street. The doorstep was red with Ronuk polish, a brass letterbox shone brightly and even the pavement looked as though it had been recently scrubbed.

A tiny old woman with newly permed, frizzy white hair opened the door. The freckles on her wrinkled face had spread and blended together to produce an almost mahogany-coloured mask and twinkling from deep sockets within it was a pair of the brightest blue eyes Tom had ever seen. There was nothing frail about the voice.

"What do you want?"

"Tom Harrison, I think you're expecting me. I'd like a few words if you've got the time, Mrs McNulty?" Tom consciously applied his reassuring voice.

"It's not going to cost me, is it?"

"No, I can promise you that, but I don't blame you for being cautious – solicitors – never trust 'em." The attempt at humour fell flat.

"Quite right, I don't trust lawyers."

"Sensible," Tom said with a smile, wondering quite where that left him.

"And don't patronise me. I'm not as feeble as I look, at least not up here," and she tapped her temple.

The front room was obviously the special occasion visitors' room. After space had been found for a piano, an overstuffed three-piece suite, a sideboard with candlesticks and framed photographs, there was not a great deal left. Leaves of the potted aspidistra atop its wooden stand in front of the net-curtained bay window gleamed with loving attention. Tom chose the sofa to sit on and Mrs McNulty perched on the front edge of a facing armchair like a sparrow waiting to take flight.

Tom took his lead from Mrs McNulty and decided he had to be straight with her.

"I don't want to stir up your personal grief but you had a relative on the plane that crashed, is that right?"

"Yes. Micky, my grandson. Well, he was like a son really. I brought him up from when he was ten. His mother – the trollop – she remarried and Micky didn't get on with the new man – they hated each other. He came to stay a few times and in the end never went back. She used to send me money but she never saw him again. Why am I telling you this?"

Tom could see several framed pictures of a fit-looking man in army uniform on the sideboard behind her. "Maybe because you've got no one else to tell, Mrs McNulty? Was Micky in the army?"

"Of course he was. Went in as a boy entrant at sixteen – seemed the best thing for him. Loved it, he did, it was his life."

"And was he still in the army – when he left for Nigeria?"

"Depends what you mean?"

"Was he still a soldier rather than an oil worker?"

"He might have been." Mrs McNulty sounded evasive and looked it but it was an evasion devoid of guilt, an evasion that said, *I don't trust you*.

Tom could not help smiling at the old woman, who was rocking backwards and forwards on the edge of her armchair, her mouth set in a tight little line and each time she answered his questions her eyes challenged him.

"Were there any other men who might have been soldiers on the plane with him?"

"Why do you want to know?" This time her eyes were penetrating, boring straight into him like gimlets.

"You know who I am and what I'm trying to do – find out why that plane crashed, why all the people on it were killed, including your Micky; why all those men, women and little children were burnt alive on the ground and why no one is telling the truth about it. To do that I need to know everything – every single thing." As had happened many times before, the moment Tom forgot about playing the part he thought was necessary and was forced to reach inside himself for the truth, he became believable, persuasive. He had not meant it to have such an effect but as he mentioned the little children he watched horror flit across Emily McNulty's face and knew he had reached her.

"I'm not supposed to tell you, you know. I'm not supposed to tell anyone!"

"Tell me what?" Tom kept his voice soft and low.

"It's a different life the army is. What did you say your name was?"

"Tom Harrison." He had not lost eye contact with her from the start of his questioning.

"Different loyalties the army has, Mr Harrison, different way of doing things – they expect different things of you. It's us and them and you don't tell tales out of school." She lowered her head and tried to twist a wafer-thin wedding ring on one of her puffy little red fingers but there was no slack and it refused to budge. "But he's dead now, isn't he, my Micky?"

"I'm afraid he is and I'm truly sorry for that – and is that where your loyalty ends?"

"I was only ever loyal to Micky, not them buggers."

Tom spoke gently. "Were there any other soldiers on the plane with Micky?"

Emily McNulty raised her head and looked at Tom, her moist blue eyes unblinking. "They were all soldiers, every one of them. Different regiments from all over the place – a few from here, a few from there, but all soldiers."

"Why, what for?" Tom had got the answer he came for but he was no wiser as to the reason.

"They were going to do what soldiers always do – fight."

"For what – against who?"

"How do I know? They don't tell you who or why, they just go and do it and when they've finished they come home again and train others and no one talks about it. You wait and get sick with worry but you never talk about it."

"You sound like it's happened before."

Emily McNulty gave out a short, dry little laugh. "You could say that. Three or four times, I don't remember now. I worry, I pray for my Micky to come back in one piece – and his mother doesn't even know what he's doing. Hard to credit, isn't it? He kept her name but she doesn't know anything about him."

"What was his name?"

"Flynn – Michael Sean Flynn." She said the words with gentle reverence.

"Micky's mum – she was your…?"

Again, Tom couldn't be sure if the bright blue eyes were misted with age or repressed tears. "My daughter, my youngest daughter!"

"And his father?" Tom asked because he had suddenly become interested in Micky, not just as a potential piece in his legal jigsaw but as a man whose life was a world removed from his own, a seemingly brave man.

Contempt was written all over Emily's face. "He just buggered off, never to be seen again. She certainly knew how to pick 'em, my daughter."

Tom knew he had to get back on track. "Why do you think we were told they were oil workers?"

"They have to have a story, don't they?"

"Remember, I don't know anything about this. Why don't you explain it to me from the beginning?"

"Where do you think our soldiers learn to fight? We don't have a lot of big wars any more so they fight other people's wars for them. When one of those foreign governments is in trouble – or they want to help get rid of one – they send some of our boys out, just depends which side our Government wants to win. After a few months the boys come back and can teach all the other blokes in their regiment how to fight in the jungle or in the mountains or wherever it is they've been."

"So being oil field workers was just a story, a cover?"

"They're very clever. All supposed to be volunteers so the lads have to resign a few weeks before they go off so if they're killed or captured no one can say they're British Army but they keep getting their pay, though – active service pay at that. Goes into a special account for when they get back home. Get paid by the foreign lot as well so they do quite nicely, thank you. That's Micky's, there!" She indicated out of the front window to a brand-new but dusty BMW sitting by the kerb. "That's his pride and joy, that is – was." As she transposed her grammar, Emily's head lowered and Tom could detect a catch in her voice.

"So he was a kind of mercenary?"

Anger flashed across the old woman's face. "My Micky was not a mercenary, he was a soldier – a sergeant. He was a proud, brave boy and he didn't do it for the money, he did it because it was expected of him. He thought a professional never said no."

"Sorry, Mrs McNulty, I didn't mean it the way it sounded." He leant forward and placed his hands on the wrinkled parchment that was her arm. "Why are you prepared to break your silence now?"

Emily McNulty got up from her perch, pulled open a drawer in the sideboard and took from it an envelope, passing it to Tom. There was only one piece of paper inside and he extracted it – a cheque for £100,000. "That's the silence money – that and the pension. If you're a young woman with kids that pension's your life, it carries you through to the end but say anything out of order and they suddenly find a reason why your man was a bad soldier. Even though he's dead they give him a dishonourable discharge and the pension stops. You're no longer entitled to it."

She took the cheque back. "That's what my Micky's worth. My boy is dead, Mr Harrison, and I will be soon as well so I don't need a pension. What can they do to me?"

Tom knew from experience that turning heartfelt admissions such as Emily's into usable statements was often fraught with complexity but it was why he had come. He delivered his words almost imploringly. "I need you to make a statement, Mrs McNulty. I need you to put in writing all the things you've told me about your boy, Micky. Will you do that? I know it won't help him but it will help us to expose those responsible."

"I've told you the truth, all I know and that will have to do you. I'm not saying anything else; I'm not doing anything else." She sounded utterly adamant.

Tom knew he had to keep trying. "Unless it's in writing and you've signed it, it's not much use to me, I'm afraid, because no one will believe it. Please – can I ask you to make a statement?" Tom tried to be persuasive without pleading and he was not sure he had succeeded.

"I don't know, I don't like signing things."

He decided not to push it any further for the moment. "Can I come back and see you again?"

"So you can get what you want?"

He decided there was no point in trying to deceive the old girl. "Yes!"

"You can try, Mr Harrison, but don't bet on it!"

Tuesday, December 17th, 1991 When the pile of paperwork arrived from Wings, Tom's heart sank as he had neither the time nor interest to deal with it. The stack of boxes connected with Flight 469 had continued to grow and additional administrative help was vital. Everything needed to be logged and filed and cross-referenced and much of it had to be put on computer – and that was another thing, the new computers! To justify the expenditure he had persuaded his father to shell out, much against his will, he was supposed to make them pay for themselves and that meant commercial success was essential.

Wings's problem was quite clear, that having started off with a standard, off-the-shelf contract, it had subsequently been amended and modified so many times that no one could remember which was the original. It had also been drawn up in a more leisurely age when turnarounds were not so quick and aircraft did not have to spend almost their entire life in the air to be profitable.

A new, standard contract would have to be framed to safeguard against some of the cock-ups which Wings had experienced over the past few years. Each of the old contracts was accompanied by a brief on what had gone wrong and any relevant correspondence. There was a massive amount of reading to be done before he could even begin drafting a standard service contract. Even by skim-reading, it was going to take hours simply to scan the material but he had to and Tom started with the oldest contract and worked forward chronologically.

He had lost track of time until he heard heavy footsteps clumping up the stairs and realised it was nearly seven o'clock. A weary-looking Mike shoved his head round the door.

"You realise my Charles Jourdan brogues are totally fucked?"

"All in a good cause, Mr Smith, but I can tell by your face

that you did not discover the crock of gold."

"No, I didn't even discover the bloody rainbow. Nothing – a big, fat, boring, blistering zero."

"Is that it now? Have you checked them all?"

"I dunno, I've done pretty well with the aid of Yellow Pages but it's a huge job, Tom. Today I did the bit down towards Streatham but there are so many back streets I might have missed some. Others have closed down but I've done the bulk, I'm pretty sure of that."

"Sorry, mate, a shitty job but well done. Might have worked." Tom could see that Mike was genuinely exhausted.

"So what now?" Mike enquired.

"No idea."

Mike looked at the pile of papers on Tom's desk. "That looks like fun."

"I've nearly finished for tonight. Fancy a drink, maybe a game?"

"A game would mean standing up, so no; a drink, yes!"

"Give me twenty minutes or so." Tom went back to his papers, had reached one of the most recent contracts and when he turned the cover page of the final contract for the day, two words leapt out and hit him between the eyes – Varsity Aviation. Wings of Sonning had, at some point or other, provided services for Varsity. Tom had no idea why he felt excited as there was no conceivable way in which a catering outfit would know anything about the maintenance of the aircraft they supplied but at least there was a connection, for what it was worth. What was it worth? Sweet bugger all, he decided.

Mike breezed in. "Ready?"

At that precise moment, Louise Watson rang to say she had the Nigerian information he wanted and Tom immediately suggested she come to the office and looked at Mike apologetically, who turned and walked away, talking to himself. "And what would you like to drink after your crappy day, Mr Smith? If it's all the same to you, Mr Smith, I'll have a Beck's – in fact I'll have several Beck's."

Louise arrived and planted a big kiss on Tom's cheek. "Hello, Sherlock, solved the case yet?"

"Elementary, my dear Miss Watson, elementary." Their laughter was spontaneous and Tom watched Louise as she settled down, took out her notebook and prepared to reveal to him her findings. Black, shiny curls were stuck to her forehead and her face was flushed pink, which seemed to accentuate her enormous blue eyes under the long and curling black eyelashes.

"You're going to like this... Excuse me, Mr Harrison, that's not a very solicitor-like look!" She laughed and flushed and Tom could feel his own face colouring. "As I was saying, you're going to like this because it all ties in. Right, there have been quite a lot of recent happenings that have been well publicised so you probably know about them..." Louise saw the blank look in Tom's eyes. "Oh dear, it means the long version then.

"Okay, in Nigeria, military juntas have come and gone like buses over the last decade or so and last year, the Chief of Army Staff, General Sani Abacha, was appointed Minister of Defence. Since then he has virtually ended democracy, surrounded himself with armed thugs and has been siphoning off around three billion dollars a year from the country but now we come to the interesting bit. A huge opposition movement sprang up and its focus is in Ogoniland, which lies four-square across the oil-producing region in the Niger Delta. It was led by a guy called Ken Saro Wiwa – you must have heard of him?"

Tom raised his eyebrows and Louise shook her head. "And I thought you were an intelligent man! He was a TV producer, writer and environmental activist – and he had very good reason to be an activist. They've been extracting crude oil in Ogoniland since the 1950s and for all that time they've been dumping massive amounts of toxic waste in the delta, causing huge environmental problems. Western countries simply kept their mouths shut but Ken Saro Wiwa spoke out and whipped up a huge following as president of MOSOP – the Movement for the Survival of the Ogoni People. Know how they dealt with him?"

Again Tom shook his head.

"Christ, Tom! They harassed him, arrested him, and harassed him some more, particularly when he devised an Ogoni Bill of Rights... Now, who are the principal players in Nigeria? Some of the biggest oil companies in the world – American and

British. In fact, the West is involved in Nigeria up to its eyeballs and despite all the concerns about the environment and the fact that they're hand in glove with a murdering, torturing kleptomaniac, they're still developing new oil fields. It's a mega-billion dollar project and as the industry grows so does local opposition and although Ken Saro-Wiwa advocates non-violence, others are looking at what's happening and the lack of progress and saying, 'This is getting us nowhere.' Armed rebellion may not be far away and they're certainly engaging in sabotage – and that could be extremely costly to the West and possibly close parts of the industry down.

"Now, you link a huge oil field with concerns about oil running out – oil that our economy is dependent upon – and you put that alongside a growing opposition movement that may perhaps one day take control and we've got a problem – by we, I mean our Government. They've kept their mouths shut about the desecration of the Nigerian environment and offered no support to the opposition so, if the opposition do take power, who are they most likely to be sympathetic towards? Not us, that's a given. The UK therefore has to do all it can to stop them gaining power – hence the soldiers, hence the secrecy, hence obstruction. It's all to prevent the electorate from knowing that our country is not just supporting a corrupt regime financially and morally but also militarily. QED." Louise looked at Tom with delight.

Tom did not have to feign being impressed. "Wow, brilliant, bloody brilliant. How come I don't know about all this?"

"Because you're a bloody ignoramus! Now listen – our foreign desk has been picking up all kinds of information from asylum seekers, business people returning from Nigeria and from the few good local journalists who dare to speak out. They know that British and US investment is still huge – and that's despite being in breach of world opinion and UN Resolution 591. If those soldiers were on their way to fight in Nigeria, our Government would walk over red-hot coals to keep the fact secret."

"They were soldiers, that's for sure!" Tom said.

"Definitely?" Louise questioned.

"Absolutely no doubt!"

"That makes perfect sense. Flight 469 was routed through to Kinneba not Lagos. It seems quite logical at first because Kinneba's in the oil region but the trouble is, there's not a fully equipped airport there and big planes only use it in an emergency. But if you want to keep prying eyes away, it's the perfect place to land. You certainly don't go to Lagos where everyone can see you. Jesus, Tom, no wonder you're getting stuffed by the Government – they're in it up to their necks. Now where's that tape you were going to play for me?"

"I'm afraid Mr Harrison junior is in a meeting at the moment but if you'd like to wait, I'll let him know you're here." Miss Rush's fingers fluttered back over her keyboard and Vicky sat down to wait.

"Mrs Denton...!" Harry Harrison appeared from his office and his smile was not in the slightest welcoming. "I was hoping to see you, do you have a minute?"

"For you, Mr Harrison, I have several minutes," she lied.

He showed her into his office with its dark mahogany, Rotary Club trophies and even a picture of Winston Churchill, complete with cigar. However, there was something distinctly ominous about his telephoned instruction, "No interruptions, please, Miss Rush." He then turned his attention to Vicky. "Er ... well, Mrs Denton." He fumbled with pens and paper on his desk and his eyes only alighted on Vicky in passing. He was making a very poor job of hiding his nerves.

"I think it's time we had a talk about how things are progressing – with your case. I'm quite concerned—"

"About what?" Vicky purposely cut across him as she tried to exercise control over the situation and there was nothing sociable in her tone.

"This is strictly confidential information, Mrs Denton, but conflicts of interest have developed which, quite frankly, threaten the financial viability of this practice."

"I didn't ask Tom to do it *pro bono*," she snapped, "that was entirely his decision."

"I am aware of that but it seems to have become all-consuming and recent developments have convinced me that we cannot go on as we are at present."

"You're about to ask me to take my case elsewhere, aren't you?"

Harry Harrison shifted and shuffled paper on his desk and went through a litany of concerns – the HSG case was a drain on their resources, it was occupying too much of Tom's time, it was moving into areas they weren't competent to handle. Vicky allowed him a free run because she wanted all the objections out in view before she responded.

He had long passed the point when everything necessary had been said but kept talking anyway, misinterpreting Vicky's silence as agreement. He began to relax and even offered a smile or two as the confrontation he had so feared failed to materialise. "Of course, Mrs Denton, trying to run a small practice isn't easy. Profitability isn't high and as you well know, there are an awful lot of very influential people in this area." It was an admission too far.

"Is that a fact, Mr Harrison? Why does that concern you?" The latitude Vicky had given him had produced precisely the honesty she was hoping for.

"No specific reason – just a statement of fact, really." He did not like the penetrating, unblinking, dark, dark eyes which were focused intently on him.

"Why would you even mention influential people in relation to my case?" Vicky persisted.

Harrison cursed himself for having said what he had but an answer was now required and he simply did not have one that was palatable to Vicky.

"It's simply a fact of life, Mrs Denton, nothing more, nothing less." It was the best he could do.

Vicky laughed but it was a bitter, sharp, cynical laugh that could have cut glass. "I am so stupid, so bloody stupid, I should have realised before – you're being leant on, aren't you, you hypocritical old fraud."

Harry Harrison got up from behind his desk and stormed to the door like an angry bull. "I won't be spoken to like that!"

Vicky also got up. "Try and bullshit me and I'll speak to you however I choose, you contemptible old bastard."

"If you can't control your hysteria then perhaps you should seek some help," he flounced out the words through pinked, blood-pressure-high cheeks as he took hold of the door handle.

Vicky was bitterly angry as she now understood precisely what it was all about. *Don't bluster. Five hundred and twenty-three people incinerated and you don't give a shit so long as your wobbly handshake still works for you, your little business still prospers and no one down at the club can accuse you of not playing the game*. She followed him to the door, placing her body against it so he could not open it and could see fear in his eyes but when he spoke it was transformed into anger.

"I don't want someone like you anywhere near my practice and certainly not near my son, do you understand?" He was trembling with the vehemence of his feelings.

"Someone like me? How like me? How like me, Mr Harrison?" She moved to within inches of him and Harry pulled back to preserve the space between them. "Someone who's five feet tall, someone who drives a Fiat Punto?" She pulled back the sleeve of her coat, "or someone who's a half-caste, a wog, got a touch of the tar brush?" The question hung in the air like something unmentionable.

"How dare you speak to me like that? I'm not prejudiced. I've never been prejudiced."

"No, of course not!" The laugh was entirely false. "I've met plenty like you, Mr Harrison, plenty; prejudiced up to their eyeballs. They try and keep you out of their streets, out of their shops, out of their schools, but the funny thing is, it never stops them from trying to screw you."

"I won't have foul language in my office, particularly from a woman." Harrison knew he had entirely lost control of the situation by ceding it to the small, bitter, angry and terrifying woman in front of him.

"Foul language? You think that's foul language? I'll give you some foul language, Mr fucking Harrison. Go fuck yourself, you pompous old arsehole." She knocked his hand from the door handle and exited.

Vicky moved quickly past Miss Rush, whose head lowered

and typing speed increased as she did so, bounded up the stairs and entered Tom's office without knocking and saw his surprised face and that of Louise Watson looking up at her.

Tom smiled. "Hi, Vicky, what can I do for you?"

She leant on the door frame. "You can get fucked too!"

The smile never left Tom's face. "That's nice. You've met Louise Watson, haven't you? Of course you have! Come in, I'll tell you the latest – it's really all coming together."

Vicky shook her head and chuckled a cynical-sounding chuckle but entered the office anyway and sat down. Tom started to give her a rundown on the Nigerian situation when a loud, crackly voice suddenly filled the room and all three heads turned towards the cassette player.

"This is Nightingale, this is Nightingale. Signing off and listening out. Speak to you next week, Sparky."

Tom leapt out of his seat. "Yes, yes, yes! That's him; that has to be the ham. That has to be his voice."

"Who, for Christ's sake?" asked Vicky, still trying to subdue the turmoil generated by her confrontation.

"The miserable little sod that holds the key to everything! That's the recording of the ATC flight conversations but I forgot to turn it off. He obviously used one of his old tapes and recorded over it to obliterate irrelevant stuff but he's missed that last bit. That's him signing off from a conversation and I'll bet that's his call sign – Nightingale. It's got to be!"

"Great," said Vicky, "he could have left his phone number!"

CHAPTER EIGHTEEN

Tuesday, January 14th, 1992 "Come on, the five dog – come on, you five dog!" Vicky nearly lost her balance as Tom pressed forward, urging his greyhound on. "I don't believe it, drifted right out on the corner." Two other dogs had gone through on the inside and Tom's greyhound came in third.

"That'll be the manicurist," Mike said with a grin.

"The what?" Vicky looked bemused.

"It's Mike's insider knowledge. I'm sure he makes it all up but he reckons they've got ways of making dogs lose that doesn't involve drugs..."

"It's gospel – on me mother's life!" Mike crossed his heart.

"Why the manicurists?"

"Well, they clip their toenails, don't they, just before the race. Dog racing's a bit of a carve-up and the money's not made by owning a good dog but by knowing which one's going to win. If you've got a blinding favourite and a passable second favourite, all the dosh goes on the favourite – short odds, like buying money, not very profitable. Now, if you can nobble the favourite, you're in business. Wet day like today, cut the toenails, vet won't notice and the doggie loses a bit of grip on the corners and drifts out just like matey did then."

Vicky was fascinated. "I hope you don't apply similar little wrinkles to the law, Mike."

"Don't let him corrupt you," Tom said, "he's got lots more little gems like that."

"Such as?" Vicky asked Mike.

"Well, you've got your cotton club and your pudding club. With the cotton club, they tie a little piece of cotton tight round one of the dog's toes – it's hidden by the hair but irritates the dog and takes its mind off the racing. Or they give it a big suet pudding not long before the start so it's like running with a cannonball in its belly. Very devious little game this."

Lights on the track had dimmed and runners in the next race were being led into the parade ring. "Quick visit to the bar?" Tom asked.

"I just want to have a word with Eveready – see you in a minute." Mike pushed his way through the crowd towards where the bookies were operating while Tom and Vicky went in the opposite direction, to the bar. They ordered drinks and found a space near the windows which overlooked the track.

"Thanks for bringing me along – boys' night out and all that. I appreciate it."

"Looked like you could do with some light relief."

"So, you ready for tomorrow?" Tom felt there was something distant about her, that she was using words simply to fill the silence and had no interest in his answer. He was certain a judicial review was the last thing on her mind.

"Not really. Mrs McNulty has become really obstinate – won't make a statement and we can't find Nightingale to authenticate the tape. But I'll do the best I can. Were you really telling me to *eff off*?" Tom enquired, his voice low.

"Yep! Sure was!"

"Do you want to tell me why?"

Vicky at first looked reluctant but eventually decided to speak. "After the mouthful I gave your father I didn't think it would be possible to carry on working together. But then, when I honestly looked at things, I realised that wasn't the whole reason. We're not really getting anywhere, are we?"

"I thought I was the Job's comforter – the gloom merchant."

"Have you ever really thought about the magnitude of this case?" Tom read it as rhetorical and simply raised an eyebrow. "You're taking on the whole bloody establishment and that's much bigger than just the Government because it trickles all the way down the line," she hesitated, "right the way into your own office."

"I'm not with you."

"How well do you know George Fraser?"

"On and off I've known him most of my life. He's like a very distant uncle." Tom looked concerned.

"Everything that man does, his whole reason for living, it's all handed down to him from above. He didn't get where he is by being brilliant, the best in his field, he did it by keeping his nose clean, joining the right clubs, knowing the right people. He is the establishment, Tom…"

"Come on, Vicky!"

"… and so is your father! They are the foot soldiers for people with real power. They're totally reliable, completely dependable and to win this, you've got to beat them and I'm not sure you can because you don't even recognise them for what they are – subversive little yes men."

Tom didn't respond immediately but took a drink, placed his glass carefully on the bar and then turned to Vicky, putting his hands on her upper arms. He pulled her towards him and looked into her eyes and he could see apprehension there.

"You may well be right and that's one reason you're important to this case. I'm a product of the same influences as them and I need your help to keep me straight. I shouldn't be saying this, but if you leave, it will not only be a weaker case but my life will be a much emptier place. Gone will be one of the few pleasures I get out of all this. Vicky, I would miss you."

He knew what his eyes were saying and for a brief moment he felt sure he saw something similar reflected in hers.

"This looks serious. You're not allowed to have barnies on a night out." Mike breezed up to them.

"Got a tip for the last race, Mike?" Vicky asked with a smile that disarmed the situation.

"If you want a bet, you'd better get moving cos they're taking them up to the traps now," he replied.

He and Tom allowed Vicky to go first and as she did, Mike took Tom's arm and hissed, "You're bang out of order, Tom, she's a client and don't forget it."

"No lectures, Mike!"

"You stick your hormones away for another day, mate, cos you can't afford them. If you're going to get struck off, let it be for being a bit devious in nailing Varsity but not for nailing Vicky." Tom tried to ignore him but knew he was right – he also knew he would take absolutely no notice of Mike's concerns.

They placed their bets and waited as the lights went up, illuminating the huge green oval just before the electric hare started its run to a whirring of wires. Dogs in the traps and even those in the kennels began to bay and bark in excitement. An odd little tipster, who all evening had been trying to sell tips for the next day's racing at Kempton Park, ran along the front of the crowd in his Union Jack top hat shouting, "Watch the three dog, Ernie knows the winners, watch the three dog."

As the hare passed the traps, the gates flew open and the three dog, Littlehampton Lady, came out in fourth place. Within a hundred yards she was lying second and on the first bend went through on the inside to take the lead and stayed there, winning by several lengths. "That's what they call 'one for the track'," said Mike, throwing his slips away in disgust.

They began to move off the terraces with the rest of the crowd and Mike was back in jolly mode. "As a bloke, I've always thought the last place on earth I'd want to live is Littlehampton, maybe followed by Hampton Wick. I don't think I could live with the innuendo..." His voice trailed away before he stopped short and almost shouted, "It's not because he sings on the airwaves at night, it's because he lives there. Nightingale! It's bloody Nightingale Lane, I'll lay money on it, the one road I never checked."

The following morning, Tom decided to walk to work as he needed a long, brisk, cold interlude to mull over what lay ahead. The key to any action now depended on the somewhat spurious prosecution of Peter Thornton and until that was over, everyone was in limbo. He decided to telephone the solicitors representing Thornton to get the date of his first appearance and this caused him to wrestle with a rather knotty problem – should he be handing over information about the tape to the defence or prosecution, or both?

*

Monday, January 20th, 1992 "Mike, I don't care if you have to camp out on Wandsworth Common, we've got to find him."

"Nightingale Lane is only a theory, remember." Tom could hear the desperation in his voice.

"Yeah, I know and I am looking for another radio ham to try and make contact with Nightingale over the airwaves but my money's on you – I'm convinced you're the best bet. Drop everything and get on with it."

Mike started his renewed search at the beginning of the lane, opposite Wandsworth Common. It was unlikely territory – a parade of expensive shops and restaurants leading into a road a mile or more long, lined only with terraced but pricey houses. He walked the length of it, scanning pedestrians for long hair as he went.

By the time he reached the end of Nightingale Lane, he was no further forward and felt pretty desperate. He walked round the corner into the traffic flow of Balham Hill, tried to get his bearings and then saw Clapham South tube station almost next to him. The realisation dawned instantly.

It was served by the Northern Line and that line went to Tooting Bec via Balham. What if Mr Nightingale had gone to Tooting Bec on the train and was actually leaving the station when he made his phone call, not going to it – perhaps having travelled from Clapham South? With no newsagent in Nightingale Lane, the most convenient place to buy his magazine would be near the tube station – and there it was, a newsagent's almost next door to it.

"Not the biggest seller in the world," the shopkeeper said, referring to *Wavelength* magazine.

"But you sell it?" Mike asked.

"Just one – special order."

"Delivered?"

"No, the bloke calls in."

"Tall, long hair, leather jacket?"

"Yeah, that's him."

"And you don't know where he lives?"

"Sorry, haven't got a clue. We get the mag on sale or return so it's no skin if he doesn't turn up."

"It's not here now is it – the magazine?"

"No! Not due in for about a week."

"Do me a very big favour, would you – give me a ring as soon as it arrives – and I mean as soon as it comes off the van – and that's for your trouble." He pushed a ten-pound note into the man's top pocket. "And there'll be another after I get the call."

The man looked worried. "There's no bother, is there? I don't want trouble."

"Kosher, mate, no trouble – on me mother's life!"

Saturday, February 8th, 1992 Mrs McNulty's face was blank when she first looked at Vicky but as recognition dawned she broke into a smile. "Hallo, dear, come in, please." Vicky followed her into the little terraced house. "Did that Mr What's-his-name, Mr Hartington, send you?"

"Mr Harrison? No, he didn't, Emily; in fact he doesn't know I'm here." Vicky saw a little confusion in the old lady's face as she showed the way into the front room.

"Well, dear, what can I do for you?"

Vicky's eyes never flinched as she looked into the old lady's. "You can sign a statement swearing that all the things you told Tom Harrison are really true – that's if you genuinely want to help me."

"Well, you don't beat about the bush, do you?" No shock or resentment emanated from Emily, just strength and interest.

"No, not usually, Emily, I don't."

"Well, I think this probably calls for a cup of tea."

Vicky waited patiently while Mrs McNulty disappeared to the kitchen and looked around her sparse little home. When she returned with the tray, Vicky could tell by the set of Emily's face that she had been doing some thinking but said nothing and waited while the old lady poured out teas using a tea strainer to retain the leaves. After she had declined sugar, Vicky spoke, having decided there was only one way to handle the situation.

"It's not enough, Emily!"

"Yes, it is enough!" The old lady's face was set and she was adamant. “I thought about it afterwards, after he’d gone, and I realised there were too many other people involved. I don’t care about me – they won’t touch me and if they do, so what? It’s the others I’m worried about because I don’t know what effect it will have on them – mostly women with little children. That’s why I keep telling him I won’t sign anything.”

“They’ve beaten you! You tried to stand up to them but in the end you’ve let them beat you!” Vicky watched as the old lady’s eyes glistened with anger.

“You just listen to me, madam – no one’s ever beaten me, no one!”

“You were beaten from the day you were born, Emily. Not because of who you are but what you are.”

“You think so, do you?”

As she had anticipated, Vicky could see from Emily’s agitation that she was furious and so spoke quickly, leaning towards the old woman with a clear sense of intimacy just in time to forestall the outburst.

“I’ll tell you about your life, shall I? About the house where you were brought up, the house with one fire to keep you all warm even through the coldest winter. It wasn’t successful, was it, and you shivered at nights even with all the clothing you could find piled on to the bed. And when the coal ran out and there was no money for more, the indignity of having to try and borrow from neighbours, or even worse, the humiliation when your mother had to prise off her wedding ring with soap in order to pawn it for a few lousy shillings.”

Vicky watched the old woman’s eyes intently and saw the shadows which flitted across them. She knew she had struck a seam of recognition. “The first time was the worst, of course, and after that it became progressively easier until she couldn’t get through the week without a visit to the pawn shop. And then there was the day when she couldn’t afford to redeem it so she left it until the next week, and then the next and the one after that. But the longer it went on the more impossible it became until eventually a brass curtain ring took its place on her finger.”

All challenge had deserted Emily and she listened quietly, making no attempt to intervene. She did not look shocked or outraged but strangely passive, as though listening to a radio play. Vicky continued.

"It wasn't living, it was surviving, wasn't it? And when the men were sent home without work and took their sense of futility and failure out on you, it became a battle for survival, didn't it? Desperate people locked together in bitterness with no escape but anger. You knew you had the worst of everything, the worst schools where they took pleasure in beating their morals into you; the worst houses where damp and rot made them not worth even half the few shillings' rent they charged. You only had to give your address for someone to look down their nose at you, to categorise you, to write you off – and none of it of your making." Even if the detail wasn't entirely accurate, Vicky knew she was ploughing a furrow that Mrs McNulty recognised vividly.

"How did you buy your clothes, Emily, when you had to have something new and not miserably second-hand – a wedding, a christening, a funeral – how did you buy them? Was it the Provident cheque? Of course the few shops that accepted it traded on your poverty, didn't they? The worst choice, the poorest quality and twice the price that anyone else charged. And most of the other people in the shop were poor like you, weren't they, ashamed of the humiliation when you had to produce that little piece of paper which screamed out loud – *Here's someone who doesn't count, someone you can treat like shit.* And that's exactly how they did treat you, wasn't it, those superior, snotty people?

"Oh yes, let's talk about the people. Shall I tell you about the people, the ones with collars and ties who tried to speak with better accents – the doctors and school teachers, the people in the labour exchange, the housing clerks, those responsible for giving you your hand-outs and those who dared to pretend they knew what was best for your children and your grandchildren ... the unforgiving bastards from the social." Again a shadow clouded Emily's eyes but Vicky didn't pause – but then, she was no longer really talking to Emily.

"They were the ones whose every word reminded you of who and what you were – that you amounted to nothing, you were of no consequence because you were poor – just that, no other reason, poor and a nuisance. Even your most oppressive fears that came to torture your mind in the middle of the night, they didn't even care about those. Because you were poor you were a whinger. Because you were poor you deserved anything and everything that happened to you and so well did they do their job that whatever happens subsequently in your life, no matter how warm the central heating makes you, no matter how much money accumulates in the bank, there's a part of you that still believes they're right, that thinks you are of no consequence, that you do deserve little or nothing.

"You think your daughter is hard and unfeeling –" the movement was involuntary as Emily started forward in her chair – "but is it any wonder? You never needed to carry the guilt for that because it wasn't your doing, it was the legacy the bastards have bequeathed you, Emily, and they're still taking advantage of it.

"The people responsible for killing Micky and my David and all the other innocent people don't agonise over whether they deserve the things they have, they believe it's their right. They probably don't even lose sleep over the death of our loved ones – it was just a commercial setback. You or I couldn't live with the thought but not them. They expect you to accept what they're prepared to hand out to you – just like the benefits people and the social workers – only this time it's truth they're being mean with. If you want anything else you've got to demand it and if you don't, you will never find out why the grandson you loved so much was killed. That's why I say they've beaten you."

Mrs McNulty looked tense, defensive, and ill at ease as she shuffled around on the edge of her overstuffed chair.

"What do you think those responsible for the disaster want you to do, Emily?" Mrs McNulty looked away but her eyes were focused on nothing for there were too many thoughts bothering her. "Look at me, Emily, look at me!" The old woman caught and held Vicky's gaze. "What do you think they want you to do? I'll tell you! They want you to keep your mouth shut and sign nothing – and that's what they expect you to do otherwise they would have been to visit you by now. That's how arrogant the bastards are. They think they've got you. Have they, Emily? Have they got you? Jesus Christ, I hope not because this one time in your life you have a real chance to show them all that you are worth something. That you're worth an awful lot!"

The two women looked into each other's eyes in silence for a long, long time and it was Emily who eventually broke it.

"I'll tell you something, madam, you're not who you pretend to be!"

Wednesday, February 12th, 1992 Tom had discovered that the date for Thornton's committal for trial had been set for June so it was imperative to continue pursuing the tape for he needed to obtain a statement from Nightingale and get his hands on the original recording. He and Mike had paced up and down the northern end of Nightingale Lane, discreetly talking to postmen, milkmen, window cleaners and anyone else who called at the houses, describing their quarry in as much detail as they could remember but it was useless.

Even the radio ham that Tom had employed could raise no word from Nightingale. He had put out calls nightly, asking the man to make contact and requesting other hams who knew him to get in touch, including Sparky, who was also mentioned on the tape. Some did return his calls but they were from distant parts of the world and 'London' was about as close as they could offer in terms of an address.

Vicky was unhappy with the lack of progress and it seemed to deepen her growing sense of futility and to make matters worse, work had dried up – the dramatic reconstructions she had been asked to direct had quietly been taken away from her.

"I would love you to do them – no one would do them better, I know that, but you have rather compromised yourself." The producer had been embarrassed but it was out of his hands, he claimed. "Of course, had it been left to me it would have been a different story…! Upstairs think it's a – well, not to sound too grand – a kind of betrayal of trust, if you know what I mean. I think they're peeved you didn't tell them what you intended to do with the privileged information you obtained – from us – about the fact that Barcroft, the holding company of Varsity, was contributing to Tory party funds. Left them unprepared – made them look a bit amateurish. There'll be other work, Vick, don't you worry."

In fact, there had been no other work and having spent some of her anticipated earnings on buying Varsity Aviation shares, her financial situation was precarious.

Tom advised her to sue the Metropolitan Police for false imprisonment as no charges had been laid against her and it seemed increasingly unlikely they would be. The four women in the Heathrow protest had huge popular support and that carried with it a kind of immunity and so she told him to start preparing the papers.

He had also heard nothing from either Ailey or Fleishmann, who had both also gone to ground, failing to return messages he had left. Unless something happened soon, he decided, he would advise his clients to issue a writ against Varsity even though he felt they did not yet have enough evidence for it to succeed.

Tuesday, June 16th, 1992 Thornton's committal was an old-style 6.1 paper committal based solely on witness statements with no witnesses called. Tom attended and was surprised to find that people recognised him; even the silk for BALPA, the pilots' union, representing Thornton made his way over and talked briefly. That was a first! It also seemed that whenever he looked in his direction, the defence team's outdoor clerk was watching him intently.

He still hadn't resolved the dilemma over Nightingale's tape but if he did get his hands on the original, as an officer of the court, Tom knew he was ultimately obliged to hand it over as evidence, especially if it could in any way help Thornton's acquittal. If it could and he didn't produce it, he could be in all sorts of professional trouble but worse, he might be responsible for a miscarriage of justice. If he did produce it, he would have sacrificed one of his most powerful pieces of evidence, allowing the opposition months to undermine its credibility.

Tom watched Thornton closely throughout the committal

and it became quite clear that the man was nothing more than a scapegoat, a useful tool to prevent any further enquiries into the downing of Flight 469. He was certain that the outcome was not in doubt and that Thornton would be sent for trial. And so he was – it was to be a jury trial at the Old Bailey, the Central Criminal Court.

The decision killed Tom's appetite for work as there was a sense of things slipping away. He had made some important discoveries but others, the really important ones, were still just out of reach. Thornton's committal was a major obstacle as he would not come to trial for at least a year and no matter what Tom unearthed in the meantime, he would not be able to use it, although he would have to consider handing it over to either the prosecution or the defence. He was caught in a trap and somehow knew it wasn't accidental. The year ahead looked to be bleak and frustrating.

It seemed almost poetic when Mike, bubbling with enthusiasm, grabbed him on his return to the office. "He's rung; the newsagent's rung! The latest issue of the mag is in and he's going to keep it under the counter. When our man asks for it, he's gonna tell him to call back tomorrow and I'll be there waiting. I think, I hope, I pray we're going to get him."

Mike got the call he wanted the next morning, was prepared to stake out the newsagent's on the following day and informed Tom.

The prospect of being hobbled for at least a year was getting to Tom and he barely responded, simply carried on sifting through his mail without enthusiasm. When he came to a plain piece of typed paper without letterhead or address and saw the words 'Peter Thornton' it was seconds before it registered. It was a part, just a small part, of Thornton's statement – a couple of pages – but a couple of pages that had not been produced in court. He reached for the phone.

"Listen to this, Mike! 'Visibility at the time of the collision was reasonable and although the light was fading, I could still see clearly. I believe it was the wing tip of the P11 which impacted with the rear of the fuselage and tail rotor and its effect was to spin the Jet Ranger in an almost complete 360-

degree circle. Although we were gyrating wildly, I had a clear view of the other aircraft for perhaps two or three seconds and it appeared to have no commercial or military markings by which I could recognise it – certainly not on the tail plane, which was the part of the aircraft I could see most clearly.'"

"Purposely blanked out?" Mike asked.

"It's a possibility!"

"What about our baggage loaders, wouldn't they have seen it?"

"We'll ask them."

"Who do you think sent us that?"

"It's clearly someone on Thornton's team doing us a favour – and my money's on the outdoor clerk. There was definitely something bothering him in court. Perhaps someone in this whole bloody mess has a bit of a conscience or perhaps, as the guy on the bottom rung of the ladder, he's fed up with being crapped on." Tom suddenly sounded enthusiastic. "Mike – get that bloody radio ham, will you!"

Mike was outside the newsagent's at seven thirty sharp but it was after nine when a tall man with a ponytail and wearing a leather jacket loped towards the shop from Nightingale Lane. Mike got out of his car, strolled across the pavement and casually looked in the newsagent's window as the man reappeared clutching his magazine. Mike allowed him to get several paces ahead before following.

He did not go into the tube station but walked back towards Nightingale Lane and after passing a few houses, turned up a garden path. As he felt for his keys Mike caught up with him. "Excuse me, mate, I wonder if you can help me." The radio ham turned but said nothing.

"It's Nightingale, isn't it?" Before he could reply, Mike handed him a card. "I reckon it was probably easier to find the lost chord than it was you."

Nightingale was cautious. "What do you want?"

"In my book, you're probably the most important person in the whole world right now."

Nightingale fiddled with the front door, trying to fit his key into the lock and then, with a surprising burst of speed, thrust the door open, stepped inside and tried to slam it after him. Mike winced as his foot was crushed. "Jesus, that's the Gucci's done for." The words were strangulated, issued through clenched teeth. He tried to take the pressure off his foot by putting his shoulder to the door. "It's not going to close, mate, so you might as well talk to me." The man put his weight on the door and Mike winced again but kept his foot in place, speaking through gritted teeth.

"I know you're scared but you'll be safer if you talk to us. On your own, they can pick you off whenever they want and no one'll be the wiser. I'd be scared too if I was you. Look, I just want to talk, nothing else." The man still hesitated. "Come on, you tosser, we're not going to let you disappear now, are we? Once the information you've got is public you're safe, can't you see that?"

Gradually the pressure on his foot eased and the door edged open but Mike kept his foot where it was until it was wide enough for him to step inside.

Nightingale's appearance was nondescript verging on the unsavoury – long, lank hair and a pallid complexion contrasted with the red rash of minor skin eruptions.

"Right then, lead on, squire, and if you have a sudden urge to stick the kettle on I won't argue." Mike extended an arm in invitation.

Nightingale led the way up the uncarpeted stairs. "What do you want? I gave you the tape, there's nothing else."

"Yeah, there is – and by the way, what's your name? I can't go on calling you Nightingale – makes us sound like a couple of transvestites." Nightingale did not reply.

Electrical equipment dominated his room while a small table and electric cooker took up one corner, a wash-hand basin another and a sagging settee occupied the long wall facing the window. The entire window wall comprised trestle tables wreathed in wires, dials, keyboards and VDUs and a couple of canvas 'director's' chairs were set in front of the equipment.

Mike chose one – conveniently close to a pile of papers and opened envelopes which, without embarrassment, he glanced through, looking for names. Nightingale was, in fact, Barry Morris.

"You're not the bloke in charge, are you?" Barry asked jumpily.

"No, Baz, I'm not, but he'll be on his way over here in just a minute. You've been brilliant, mate, I mean that, but we need just a bit more – then we're finished with you."

"Like what?"

"Like the original tape."

Barry Morris reluctantly produced a Sony reel-to-reel and Mike felt himself exhale with relief. "You beauty, Bazzer. You're going to hand that to me now and then you're going to make a statement to say what it is and when you recorded it. After that you're in the clear, you're no longer a threat to them, okay?" Barry nodded nervously.

Mike tapped out a number on his mobile. "Tom – there's a man here wants to sign something!"

Friday, July 24th, 1992 "I can't do it with you hovering over me," Anthony Berrens said with exasperation. "It might take days – and I'm going to have to involve other people. It's quite complicated."

"But it's important, can't you speed it up?"

"Tom! I'll do it properly and you'll get the results as soon as I'm finished, okay? This the original master tape?"

"Yes. I've taken a submaster which is in the safe. So how long do you reckon?"

"It's going to be a couple of days – I can't even start until tomorrow."

Tom had no option but to leave him to it but it was with reluctance. When he got back to his office, Maurice Wreford was waiting for him and this normally dignified man was agitated and angry and for once not terribly coherent.

"It was outrageous ... buying me off ... he was putting a value on every one of my family ... sign here and shut up, that's what he was really saying. You must do something about it! It's disgusting – outrageous. He offered me ten thousand pounds for each member of my family and when I rejected it, immediately increased the offer. It was like bartering. You must stop him, Tom." Maurice thrust a card at him.

Tom eased the man's hurt as best he could. Hilldrew's

negotiator, Simon Collins, was the person responsible according to the business card. "I'm sorry, Maurice, but I'm afraid it's perfectly legal so there's nothing much I can do about it."

"I was so unprepared for it – I had no idea they could do that."

Tom felt a touch of guilt for having blamed Ailey for his defections – it was obviously Varsity and it would account for why they had been ignoring him. Clearly, they were trying to peel away as many clients as possible both to weaken his hand and to create an atmosphere of defeatism in the group.

Tom continued trying to put Maurice at ease and agreed he should call a meeting to inform the whole group about Varsity's tactics. After Maurice Wreford had left, Tom began to review the case solely in the light of a civil action and decided to prepare the paperwork. It was time to take Varsity on.

It was three days before Berrens contacted him and when the call came, Tom dropped everything. Arriving at Berrens's house, the man looked pleased but would reveal nothing. "I wanted you to actually see what I'm talking about," he insisted as he showed Tom through to his study.

Tom was desperate for any information he had. "Does it tell us anything we don't already know, please, that's all I need...!"

"It tells us plenty but I'll talk you through it." He would not be rushed and slotted a tape into a player surmounted by twin monitors. "Okay," Berrens said, "everything which makes a noise makes its own series of sound waves. It's all well documented so we're not on the cutting edge of technology." He appeared to be entirely relaxed around gadgetry and when he started the player, a series of moving lines appeared on the screens in the form of peaks and troughs. There was no sound but Berrens pointed out a pattern that was fairly repetitive.

"See that there? That's the aircraft's background noise – engines, air conditioning and so on. It is, in fact, a jumble of sounds that combine together and come across with considerable consistency. Now see that? That's where the pilot speaks – a clearly sharper and different set of waves and even without knowing anything about it, a sound expert could look at that and say – 'human voice'. It's like a fingerprint.

"Now, look at it, it's gone crazy and see the patterning, it's spread over a period of several seconds and obviously loud but the peaks are still on the screen. That's the first noise interruption which led the pilot to give his Mayday."

"Yes?" Tom waited for an explanation but it didn't come and Berrens twiddled some knobs to clarify the images. "Fascinating, but what does it mean?"

"I'm coming to that. Okay, now this is the really interesting bit – look, right here! This is the second noise and just look at these impressions – huge peaks, going absolutely bananas, right off the screen and all over in a second or so. Classic stuff that!"

"Anthony, I'm a lawyer not an engineer – tell me what's happening, please."

"Okay, I'll go through it again…"

"No, just tell me!" Berrens ignored him and rewound the tape.

"This time, I'm going to add the original soundtrack to the oscilloscope images – honestly, it's worth it, absolutely mesmerising." Tom stopped objecting so Berrens could do it his own way.

The sounds on the master tape were much clearer than the cassette and the effect was chilling. As the pilot spoke, the scope's images formed sharp mountainous formations in direct response to his words and when air traffic control responded, that also made a pattern but a different one. Berrens interrupted the recording. "See, those voices have been transmitted by different equipment and take on a slightly different form."

Tom wanted to scream with impatience.

"Now, there, that's the first noise and you can see the peaks are rounded with a measurable distance between each one. This is the second noise – see how sharp the peaks are, how close together and how they jump about all over the screen?"

"So what the hell are the noises?" Tom couldn't contain himself any longer.

Berrens smiled. "There's absolutely no doubt. The first set of patterns is of rending metal and other materials. If the floor did collapse, as in our original scenario, this is exactly the sound trace you would expect to see."

Tom could feel his excitement growing. "And the second?"

"There's no doubt about that either – it's an explosion – of some considerable force!"

Tom whistled. "Would this stand up in court?"

"Absolutely!"

"What's your rationale?" Tom asked.

"Probably the same as yours," Berrens answered. "The emergency closures gave way on the cargo door and eventually the primary closures gave way as well. There was depressurisation resulting in a floor collapse, and that probably triggered an explosion in the military equipment in the hold. None of it had anything to do with the helicopter, that's for sure."

"Got you, you bastards...!" Tom punched the air as he said it.

CHAPTER NINETEEN

Thursday, September 24th, 1992, 2.00 p.m. Varsity Aviation's offices in the Strand were not perceived as a suitably impressive venue for the Annual General Meeting and so the Jonson Room of the Palace Hotel was chosen. As Tom and Vicky headed for it, Tom tried to make himself heard above the rattle and clatter of the tube train.

"The trick is to put them on the defensive but not give too much away."

"I'm not stupid..."

"It's important, Vicky, so listen to me. We've got information which they don't know we have and I want to be careful how much we let out, okay? The Thornton case is *sub judice* but it's focusing only on a failure to observe regulations so we must avoid making any mention of soldiers or arms and ammunition and that's important. And just as important is the tape – I really don't want them to know we've got it. Are you clear about that?"

Vicky showed her exasperation. "Is there anything we can bloody say? I think it's probably best if I leave you to do the talking as my legal representative, how's that...?" It wasn't said as if by someone ceding control but more from petulance.

"That's good, that's very good." And he hoped she meant it but was not convinced.

From at least a hundred yards away they could see the press gathered outside the hotel and as they approached, TV lights blazed into life and cameras began to flash.

"Why are you here, Mrs Denton?" "What questions do you intend to ask?" "What are your concerns about the company?"

Tom turned to make a statement and came face to face with

Louise. Her smile was disarming and he found himself involuntarily smiling in return as he spoke to the assembled press.

"Mrs Denton is a shareholder in Varsity Aviation and on her behalf I will be asking the company's chief executive some questions pertinent to the death and injury caused by Flight 469." As the journalists started clamouring, he raised his voice. "We'll answer any questions after the meeting." As he turned to leave, he spoke confidentially to Louise. "Are they allowing you inside?"

"They sure are!"

"Good, you should find it interesting."

A doorman opened the doors self-importantly and they entered the comparative quiet of the hotel and walked the long corridor to the Jonson Room in silence. It was an imposing place, with its neatly laid out gilt and maroon plush salon chairs, which were already beginning to fill up. Most shareholders were female and elderly and it was like looking over a sea of well-groomed, silver-grey, permed waves.

Tom knew these were the little people, the amateur capitalists, happy to think they were playing genuine Monopoly but probably unaware that even if they all joined together they could never win a vote – not even to change the locks on the company's lavatory doors. The real power brokers – City financial institutions, pension funds and corporate brokers – never bothered to attend an AGM for they did their dealings behind the scenes and Andrew Glennister was sitting on his dais with a pocketful of their proxy votes – enough to carry any motion he chose.

The noise levels increased as the press filed in and when they were settled, the meeting got underway.

Debate over presentation of company accounts was interminable with every line queried by someone, while others were so eager to please they would have voted for compulsory euthanasia for the over-60s if Andrew Glennister had proposed it.

Vicky was clearly growing impatient. "For Christ's sake, say something, will you!" she hissed at Tom.

"Not yet!" he said calmly.

The vote to accept the annual accounts was about to be taken when Tom rose, finding that the nervous tension that always preceded a court appearance was entirely absent.

"I've listened to this debate and the many words spoken by shareholders and executives with disbelief. For those of you who haven't seen it, I would like to read out the apology at the top of page five of the annual report. It sums up my concerns." Tom projected his voice so there was no doubt that everyone could hear.

"It says. 'We would like to apologise for the drop in profitability and the fact that this was reflected in reduced interim results. This was due to unforeseeable, one-off circumstances and we anticipate returning to full profitability within twelve months.'

"Could I remind this meeting that those 'unforeseeable, one-off circumstances' were the deaths of five hundred and twenty-three people caused by one of this company's aircraft? Does anyone intend to address this issue?"

Andrew Glennister cleared his throat and waited for the whispered conversations to die down. "At this moment in time we are debating the company accounts. Would you please confine yourself to that topic?" He was clearly disconcerted.

"Where else on the agenda is it listed?" Tom asked.

"It is not an agenda item. We anticipated it would arise from the floor," Glennister lied.

"The worst air disaster in Britain's history – in your company's history – and it was not considered worthy of debate unless someone raised it from the floor? Is that what you're saying, Mr Glennister?"

"Please confine yourself to the company accounts, whatever your name is." Tom ignored the elderly voices hoarsely whispering for him to sit down, terrified that his intercession might stir up sufficient controversy to lower the half-yearly dividend.

"Harrison!" Tom offered. "My name is Harrison! Mr Glennister, do you propose to offer any apology to the injured and the relatives of the dead? Perhaps more importantly, do you intend to offer any explanation as to why it happened?"

The voices of complaint increased in volume.

"I won't be barracked like this at my own AGM!" Glennister's face began to flush and he turned scarlet. "Of course we regret what happened and offer our sincere condolences – as I have done on numerous occasions in the past – but we cannot offer any explanation until the SAAIU inquiry into this disaster is completed. We will now move on to item four on the agenda..."

"Mr Glennister..."

"Sit down or I will have you removed!"

Tom was delighted and had one eye on the journalists. It was time to give them a story so he remained on his feet. "I have a question which is pertinent to these accounts." He raised his voice to be heard above the increasing noise. "If you can't offer any reason for the crash of Flight 469, how can you give the assurance that you –" Tom read from the annual report – "'anticipate returning to full profitability within twelve months?'"

He could feel Vicky pulling at his jacket and could hear her voice, rasping and insistent. "For fuck's sake, I didn't come here to discuss the company accounts!" He kept going.

"How could you write those words when you know that any finding of culpability would produce so many lawsuits that Varsity would be wiped out overnight – unless, of course, you have information that the report will exonerate you. And if you do know that, perhaps you could tell the meeting how you know."

The voices calling for Tom to sit down were growing, but other, louder voices were calling, "Answer, answer!"

Tom had done what he had intended and Glennister was almost shaking with fury. While he was still stumbling over his reply, Tom raised his voice to such a pitch that its sheer authority stilled the commotion in the room.

"Why, Mr Glennister, will you not admit that your aircraft, Flight 469, was not carrying oil field workers and its cargo was not ordinary luggage?"

There was a palpable gasp as Glennister stood facing Tom across the plush and gilt room full of expectant people, all waiting for him to answer. He looked lost and floundering.

"That is a lie – that is an outrageous lie..." He paused for breath and then gathering his wits, in measured tones he reminded everyone that the matter was *sub judice* at present owing to the prosecution of the helicopter pilot. "I would be most obliged if restraint and circumspection could be exercised."

Vicky leapt to her feet and before Tom could intervene held an object in the air as she shouted at Glennister. "You're a liar, Glennister, you're a liar. I've got proof of what really happened, and you know it's—" She was screaming and about to blurt out what they had discovered when Tom pulled her down.

He was furious. "Just shut up – it's premature and prejudicial." Despite this potentially damaging interjection, Tom was determined to get his question answered – at least while the journalists were still present – and again leapt to his feet.

"I repeat my question, which does not breach the *sub judice* rules – who and what was being carried on your plane?" Silence momentarily descended while the packed room waited for a reply from Glennister.

"Stewards, stewards, clear the room. I want this room emptied. Clear the room." Glennister strode from the dais, his face a mask of fury. Chairs were knocked over, people shouted at each other, one woman swung her handbag like a mace at a protesting shareholder and TV crews recorded it all to a flurry of camera flashes.

As Glennister tried to exit he was mobbed by journalists demanding to know if there was any truth in Tom's accusation, while others demanded to know if he thought terrorists were involved. Glennister was unable to leave and above the turmoil Tom could hear him yelling, "Call the police – get the police in here now."

Journalists surrounded Tom and Vicky, their interest focused on the cassette. "Was that an audio cassette, Mrs Denton?" "What's on it?" One particularly astute reporter asked, "Is that the missing air traffic control conversations?" but his voice was lost amongst others. "What proof have you got that the passengers were not oil field workers?" Tom felt like the conductor of some discordant symphony.

His eyes were drawn to one person who he had not

previously noticed and who sat silent and immobile on the end of the front row of chairs, almost as far distant from Tom as was possible. She watched him with sad eyes, he nodded in acknowledgement and a small smile, a flicker of sympathy, he thought, crossed her face. Esther Vine adjusted her posture and wheeled herself towards the emergency exit.

"What were you holding, Mrs Denton?" Again the question came and Tom knew he needed to act.

"Don't say any more, Vicky – nothing! Do you hear me?" He turned to the journalists. "We will be making a statement in due course but have nothing more to say at the moment!" As he spoke, he ushered Vicky out of the room, parrying questions as he went. As he passed Louise Watson, she put her mouth so close to his ear that her lips brushed it and whispered, "I want an exclusive, Tom Harrison – you owe me!"

"My office in an hour!" he whispered back and as he and Vicky left the room it began to fill with blue uniforms.

"Are you going to say nothing *all* the way?" Vicky asked. Tom ignored her as the train rattled its way into Maida Vale station.

"I've been a naughty girl, all right? Slap my wrist and have done with it but don't give me the silent treatment." There was nothing contrite in her tone.

"You were stupid and petulant. You only said one thing and it was the very thing I asked you not to say. You just couldn't resist it."

"I don't need this, Tom."

"Well, try apologising!"

"Go screw yourself!"

"You fucked up. Apologise – it's not that difficult!"

She didn't answer and they remained silent until the train was approaching Harrow and then Tom spoke. "Right, I want your assurance that you won't make any further statements about any of this without agreeing them with me first. Okay?" She didn't reply. "Okay, Vicky?"

"Yes, o-bloody-kay! I didn't actually say it, did I?"

"No, but you nearly did. The dailies will be on to it tomorrow but I'm giving Louise an exclusive and she'll break it this evening. She'll be the first out and that will allow us to set the agenda so don't speak to anyone else, all right?"

"All right, Stalin!"

"No press interviews, no television, no publicity stunts. Got that?"

"Yes, *obersturmbhanführer*!"

"Good." They got off the train and walked towards the station exit but Tom was still not smiling. "Do you want me to give you a lift home?" It seemed to be spoken more out of duty than consideration.

"No, I feel like walking."

"Okay. I'll probably give you a ring later." He walked towards the car park then turned and called after her. "What was on that cassette, Vicky?"

She pulled it out of her pocket and held it in the air. "Sting's Greatest Hits."

He shook his head and walked away but after a few paces he heard her voice, now devoid of antagonism.

"Tom!" He looked back over his shoulder. "Sorry, Tom!" They smiled.

5.00 p.m. "What the bloody hell were you thinking about?" Charles Astbury was so agitated he could not keep still and marched backwards and forwards within the narrow confines of the St John Street office. Five paces to the window and five back again to the door. "Calling their bluff, calling them liars – then having them thrown out; what on earth possessed you?"

"Make no mistake, Charles, you've got some serious shit on your hands. The guy obviously knows what was on the plane. It was a knee-jerk reaction, what else could I do? I'm sorry."

"He might suspect, Andrew, he might even know, but can he prove it? That's a very different proposition entirely. And as for serious shit, I spend my life dealing with it, that's why I'm a Government minister – that's what Government ministers do. All you had to do was to stay confidently *schtum* using the contempt of court ploy – it's as simple as that!"

"How are you going to handle it?"

"If you'd done what I told you to do and bought these people off instead of playing penny-pinching, stupid bloody games with them, none of this would have happened. I warned you, I told you it was a potentially damaging situation and you still quibbled, trying to save money. You could lose the lot now, you realise that, don't you?"

"It's not going to come to that," Glennister answered morosely, desperately seeking reassurance.

"No, it's not – at least not while I've got anything to do with it." Astbury continued his pacing.

Glennister shook his head. "It's unbelievable. I just refuse to be shafted by a conveyancing lawyer and a hysterical half-caste."

"That's being dealt with too!" Astbury looked at his watch and picked up his briefcase. "Now, if you'll excuse me, I have to go and piss on some rather important flames."

6.15 p.m. So rarely did she do the walk that Vicky had forgotten how far it was from the station to her home. *Pompous sod*, she thought, and told herself she had only apologised to keep the peace – but she did not really believe it. Whatever she had done wrong, she could not take her actions as seriously as Tom seemed to. She had almost – slightly – transgressed the *sub judice* rules but so what? Big bloody deal. Did it really matter? And the information about the soldiers and the flight recording – so what if she had almost let the cats out of the bag a bit early – Varsity were going to know about it sooner or later anyway so it was all a bit pathetic, she felt. In reality, she knew she was trying to minimise the importance of what she had done because that's what she always did when accused of anything – it was instinct.

The look on Glennister's face when she held Sting in the air was worth it, she decided, and smiled inwardly, wondering why her life had always been a series of confrontations. Did they just happen or did she go in search of them? Again she smiled – she sought them out like a pig roots for truffles!

Vicky walked up her garden path and tried the latchkey and when it refused to turn she knew instantly she had been burgled and the burglar had dropped the catch. She walked quickly round the house to the back, hoping it was not true but there was a broken window and the kitchen door stood wide open.

Believing the burglars might still be inside, she phoned the police on her mobile and then shouted through the open door. "The police are coming, you bastards." When no one came running out, she went into the house and wandered slowly from room to room. There was no great mess, just a few things thrown around and she guessed she had probably disturbed them as TV, video and CD player were all still in place.

The dining room cum office at first looked as though it had been trashed but it was mostly papers thrown around and her computer was still there. Packaging and paper, floppy disc jackets, CD covers, cassette covers and disturbed files were everywhere but she didn't touch any of it and after having checked out the ground floor, was aware of just how little, if anything, was actually missing.

It angered Vicky that the staircase, which she normally ran up and down without concern, had been turned into something threatening and she hated the greedy young bastards who were responsible, who didn't care what effect they had on their victims.

I won't be anyone's bloody victim, she thought as she climbed the stairs slowly, apprehensively, nervously looking into each bedroom in turn. Her room seemed untouched, the spare room was certainly okay and Emma's room also seemed to have escaped, except that when she looked closer she could see that her duvet had been disturbed.

The smell was unmistakable – a gagging, cloying stench of ammonia and a large orange stain all over Emma's duvet cover that could only be urine but what chilled Vicky more, and made her almost too afraid to turn round, was the stabbing, slashing, frenzied knife attack that had shredded her daughter's bedclothes.

CHAPTER TWENTY

Friday, September 25th, 1992 Louise Watson's story was necessarily inconclusive. Her interview with Tom had not been a briefing but more like a series of instructions on what she could and could not publish. In the end, she was left with a punch-up at an AGM and not much more. Whichever line she said she wanted to take, Tom sanctioned it with *sub judice* cautions and there was little corroboration for what remained.

Without Tom's censure, the dailies had not been so constrained and had cobbled together some outrageous pieces of speculation which trampled all over Thornton's legal protections. Louise had had a head start but because of Tom's caution, she had lost it.

The *Daily Despatch* used Vicky and her AGM outburst as the lynchpin for their story, providing a good personal interest angle, although the picture of her was not flattering and made her look demented. The impression was heightened by their concentration on her 'struggle for survival', the mental anguish she'd been through and her months of 'despair'. It was a thinly veiled piece of misogynistic stereotyping as an hysterical female.

Public reaction was almost unanimous that a public inquiry should immediately be announced and one newspaper had picked up a comment by a paramedic involved in the rescue operation and had run it as a strapline under the main headline. "I knew we weren't being told the truth." It seemed to fairly reflect the public mood.

It was dangerous stuff and Astbury knew it had to be controlled. He had purposely reserved his response until the day after the story was broken by the *Evening Chronicle* so he could gauge the public mood and prepare accordingly. His first interview was with Whitemore, who had moved over to the lunchtime news show and it set the tone for the press conference and all other radio and TV interviews which were to follow. But Whitemore was out for the kill.

"It's a pretty pickle, isn't it, Minister, when a support group of ordinary people has to do the Government's job for it?"

"What the Harrow Support Group has done is highly commendable and I'm the first to congratulate them – but I'm not sure it amounts to having done the Government's job. We also have to be aware an incident such as this does attract those people who are looking for a cause and also, unfortunately, the damaged and unbalanced – a sad but simple fact of life. We have to be absolutely sure of the ... stability, I suppose, is the correct word, of anyone who appears to have an axe to grind." As usual, Astbury appeared totally relaxed and there was no trace of concern in his voice. "As you know, we are awaiting the results of an investigation and a trial is pending, which seriously limits what I can say. I'm afraid I have to leave it at that."

"Well, you seem to have lost the air traffic control recording and there is some speculation that the Harrow group have found it. Bit embarrassing, isn't it?"

"There is absolutely no verification of what some group or other has obtained and if anyone, I repeat, anyone, has any material pertinent to this case, they should immediately hand it over to the SAAIU or the prosecuting authorities."

"Many of the reports in today's papers do imply rather serious investigative oversights. Doesn't that concern you?" Whitemore's avuncular criticism dripped with wearied disbelief.

"Everything about this dreadful affair concerns me but there are two issues here. Again, the only way we can be certain that evidence has any value is for the inquiry to examine it. But we must also remember that a man is facing charges connected with this disaster and we cannot jeopardise his trial with idle speculation. I really have to stress that most strongly."

Whatever question Whitemore put to him, Astbury used one or other of his two excuses to parry it. Whitemore began to sound as though he was hectoring a responsible and concerned minister and the frustration began to show.

"All right, Minister, I'll accept your position on these issues but who were the passengers on Flight 469?"

"What has that to do with the causes of the crash?" Astbury replied sharply. "I'm not prepared to sit here and engage in a wide-ranging debate about tittle-tattle."

"Who and what was on the plane is hardly tittle-tattle, Minister, and cannot be difficult to answer unless there is a discomforting, perhaps sinister, explanation."

Astbury answered the question carefully and Whitemore knew he had donned kid gloves. "I wish I could answer but the *sub judice* rules are paramount. The team at Cardington have performed an extraordinary job in sifting through literally hundreds of tons of debris but because the tragedy struck ordinary houses, it follows that mixed in with that debris is all manner of things. Many of them, seen in their correct setting, are easy enough to identify – a cassette player, a tape recorder, even a central-heating timer. But take those same objects and mix them up in the wreckage of an air crash and you have a frightfully difficult situation.

"I would imagine that Varsity Aviation has been contacted on numerous occasions to clarify the particular make of a certain part – simply to eliminate it, particularly those items which might at first sight be capable of more than one interpretation. Once the prosecution has concluded and the SAAIU has completed its task we will all be in a position to make authoritative determinations."

Whitemore knew he would get nothing further from this extremely slippery and overtly plausible minister. "And no public inquiry? There appears to be a lot of public support for one."

"Well, of course there would be if people were to rely on the press reports for their information. It has been highly irresponsible, you know, Gordon, the way a few unconfirmed allegations have been whipped into a froth of hysteria. I really dread to think what this is doing to the victims and bereaved of this appalling accident."

"Well, they seem to be the ones calling for the investigation."

"A very small proportion of those who were affected, I can assure you."

"No public inquiry then?"

"I've made myself abundantly clear on numerous occasions. We have chosen what I believe is the right approach and I can see absolutely no advantage in a further forum which, of necessity, would not now report for far too long. It really isn't an option."

"Thank you, Minister!" Whitemore sounded frustrated and reluctant to end the interview. He knew there were nuggets buried somewhere deep beneath Astbury's evasions but time had ended his digging.

"What did the police have to say?" Tom paced slowly alongside Vicky as ducks scurried from under their feet.

"Well, if you want it paraphrased, they said 'buy a new duvet, fit an alarm and claim all you can off your insurance'. I know I was in a bit of a state last night but it was horrible. It felt so personal, like it was aimed specifically at me. You don't mind me dragging you out, do you, Tom? I just couldn't bear to stay in the house."

"Not at all," he replied and meant it. They sat on a bench overlooking the park lake while unconcerned little children threw scraps of bread to scrabbling ducks. "So this is what normal people do at lunchtime – sit in the park, eat sandwiches and lead a civilised life. Did you work out what's missing?"

"It's all video tapes, computer tapes, CDs, floppy discs, some paperwork – nothing of any value at all. Police weren't that interested to start with but when I gave the detective the list, you could see him mentally wiping the slate clean – like it wasn't even worth investigating."

"Doesn't surprise me." Tom said as they sat looking ahead across the sparkling water.

"Do you know what he said about the duvet? He reckoned that some burglars get so excited by breaking in that they have to go to the loo. Can't help themselves. That's it, that's the explanation for the piss on the duvet!"

Tom spoke tentatively, as though the words were being

dragged from him. "Vicky, you were very upset last night and I didn't want to hype it up but..."

"You think it was a warning, don't you?"

Tom hesitated before answering. "'Fraid so."

"It's repulsive! I hate the bastards!"

"It was also a bit of a fishing expedition, see if you'd got anything of interest to them, maybe even a copy of the ATC tape, but the real purpose was to frighten you."

"They wouldn't do anything, would they – to Emma, I mean?" For the first time since he had met her, Tom realised that Vicky was nervous, perhaps even afraid. He didn't reply but threw the crusts of his sandwich to the ducks. "Would they, Tom?"

"Question is, Vicky, who are 'they'? Is it Varsity doing a bit of freelancing? Military? Security services – who?"

"Who do you think?"

"It's complicated. I've been looking back at some unsolved headline cases and believe me, it's a shadowy old world out there. Foreign involvement is big so MI6 will have their oar in there somewhere – could be getting MI5 to act for them?"

"I can't believe they'd do something like that – slashing a child's duvet and urinating on it. It's sick!"

"Worked though, hasn't it?"

"It's not going to stop me!" She almost spat the words out.

"It attracts the nutters, you realise. Jobs like yours are farmed out, apparently – to shady little private security firms – two men and a dog, that sort of thing, but with connections to someone or other in the security services. Some operators have been exposed in the past and can be really gross people – paedophiles, thugs, psychopaths. No one gives a damn and if they get caught, they can't be connected to the security services. They're dealt with as straightforward burglars."

"You didn't answer my question."

"What question?"

"Whether they'd do anything to Emma?"

Tom turned to face Vicky and took one of her hands in his and paused for a long time before answering. "If I'm honest, yes, I'm afraid they might!"

*

"Which do you want first, the bad news or the bad news?" Mike met Tom on the stairs.

"I reckon it had better be the bad!" Tom didn't interrupt his stride and continued towards the office while Mike fell in behind.

"Well, our lovelies from Northolt reckon they didn't notice if Varsity's markings were blanked out – hard to believe, isn't it? Said they were working right under the belly and the light was going and anyway, they work on so many planes there's no reason to notice."

"Damn!" Tom threw his briefcase to one side as they entered his office.

Mike kept with him. "Apparently, blanking out a tail plane isn't that unusual. Lots of planes are chartered from one company to another and the first thing they do is cover up the name and when they've got time, paint their own over it. So that's that!"

"Each bit of the Varsity picture is fairly innocuous on its own but will they all eventually add up to make a bigger picture of some kind?" Tom didn't sound sure.

"The other bad news is the pile of civil stuff waiting for you, you realise that, don't you?"

"I don't want to know, Mike!" Tom raised his hand dismissively, flicked through his messages and found nothing worth acting on. "Do you fancy making a little book, Mr Smith?"

"Always willing! What on?"

"I reckon we'll get a call from Ailey and from Varsity – neither will be able to resist it because they'll both want to know exactly what we've got. Question is, when will they phone?"

Mike thought for a while. "Well, Varsity won't want to look too keen so I reckon about five days. Ailey, now she's dead keen. When do you reckon?"

Tom screwed up his eyes. "Varsity three days; Ailey tomorrow."

"Nah," Mike shook his head, "Ailey today! Tenner?"

"Done!"

The phone rang and Mike answered it. "Tom Harrison's office... Yes, just a minute." He handed the phone to Tom, smiling whilst rubbing his thumb and fingers together. "It's for you – Ailey!" and tiptoed out of the office.

"I just wanted to tell you, we've decided not to initiate proceedings in the UK. We're sticking to our original intentions of going for Barcroft in the US. I was genuinely annoyed by the inquest but I shouldn't have been so aggressive."

"It's okay!" Tom wasn't quite sure what he was meant to say but felt certain that the Plaza Hotel – or rather what didn't follow it – also had as much to do with her actions.

"You seem to have unearthed some good stuff. Does it stand up?"

"More so by the minute."

"Could we meet?" At least Ailey was straightforward. The rest of the sentence, which she didn't bother to finish, would have gone something like, *because I want to get my hands on your evidence for our US case – is there any chance?*

"There's a support group meeting next week, come to that. I think we should keep everything formal, and yes, if the group approves and so long as it doesn't conflict with anything we've got going, we might be willing to disclose our stuff to you."

He heard her laugh down the line. "Jeez, I think you've been on what I'd call a fast learning curve."

"So what have *you* got – anything?"

"Actually, Tom, we've got a pile of shit on them but it's still mostly whispers. We've people working on it literally all over the world and as soon as we can substantiate any of it, I'll let you know. Are you looking for a trade-off?"

"No, I'm trusting you to let us have anything which might help our case."

"Sure, Tom, goes without saying." She hesitated as though expecting him to speak. "Anyway, it's good to talk. Mike obviously knows you well."

"How come?"

"When I spoke to him earlier, he said you'd be okay about it – suggested I ring immediately."

"Did he now?"

Saturday, September 26th, 1992 Tom felt almost physically sick when he read the *Daily Despatch* next morning. Their story of the previous day had been the softener; this one went for the kill. The blows, as they were delivered on the front page, were brutal.

Harrow Victim's Life of Misery

The strapline beneath the headline fleshed out the bones:

Abused and beaten, raped and assaulted – Vicky's secret life pushes her to the brink

Again, the chosen picture was of a barely recognisable Vicky, but someone wild of eye and manic of face. Tom wondered how many hundreds of photographs they'd sifted through to find this one. The story seemed incredible.

Mrs Vicky Denton, founder of the Harrow Support Group, has lived with a terrible secret since her childhood.

She has been one of the Government's most vocal critics since the crash of Flight 469, constantly accusing it of secrecy and cover-up. The dreadful irony is that her own life has been exactly that.

A Despatch *Special Report has discovered that Vicky Denton, under her maiden name of Vicky Brearley, was part of a child prostitution ring operated by her own mother. She was only rescued from her life of hell when Manchester Social Services took her into care at the age of 15.*

For months, Vicky refused to say anything which might incriminate her mother and only after careful counselling did she eventually break down. Her confession shocked even experienced professionals.

Often beaten and abused as a small child, she was eventually raped at the age of 13 by her mother's boyfriend. Soon afterwards, she was being used as a sex lure to entrap wealthy and influential Levenshulme business people who were then blackmailed. Vicky was only one of several children involved in this despicable and sick racket.

The Despatch *says, Vicky Denton's case is not a product of some distant dark age – such things still happen today. There is no doubt that the scars of her experiences will live with Vicky throughout her life and require the support and understanding of every one of us. She is as much a victim of life as her husband who was killed in the Harrow disaster. We must all try to be understanding of her often irrational and uncontrolled outbursts. Who amongst us would not act the same after such an appalling and damaging childhood?*

The report traced Vicky's life up to the present and dripped with concern for her mental state after having been subjected to so *many cruel and crushing blows*. The knife was twisted by a highlighted box in the middle of the piece. It was headed,

The Despatch *Doctor says...*

Anyone who has been subjected to experiences similar to those of Vicky Denton will continue to pay a price long after the physical wounds have healed. Having spent her early life in a web of lies and deceit, it is no wonder that she sees them wherever she looks. A strong bond between abused and abuser is common and, unable to exact revenge on her mother, Vicky is probably seeking retribution elsewhere.

It is possible that this sense of injustice has played a part in her vociferous condemnation of any official connected with the Harrow disaster. It almost certainly motivated her to carry out her extraordinary disruption of Heathrow Airport and subsequently to sue the police simply for carrying out their duty. It is a chain of unreasonable actions which have their origins in other unreasonable actions in her past. It is a chain likely to continue until Vicky Denton is provided with the medical care which will allow her to come to terms with her childhood.

Tom screwed the paper up and threw it across the office and without even thinking what he was going to say, called Vicky.

"Are you all right?" He still sounded outraged.

"You've seen it, then?"

"Aren't you angry?"

"Yes, sure I'm angry. I'm angry that we've got some of the worst press anywhere in the world; I'm angry that people are so easily corruptible; I'm angry that we're all lied to on a daily basis – but I'm not going to cry over it."

"Sue the bastard, that's what I say!"

"Funny, Tom, you haven't asked me if it's true. Frightened of the answer?"

"I don't know why but I assumed it was probably true – or rather based on truth. Is it?"

"Yes, it's fairly accurate. Overhyped of course but the essentials are about right."

Vicky's lack of reaction worried Tom; it was not what he had expected but then he rarely got it right where she was concerned.

"I'm on my way over…" He hung up before she could say anything.

The cafe was one of those which either aped the gentility of a time past or was simply still stuck in it. The waitresses were elderly, wore little aprons and spoke like hospital visitors. Tom ordered a pot of coffee and some home-made biscuits. "I'm not expecting you to say anything – I just thought you might need some company."

"That's nice of you, Tom, but it isn't necessary." He realised she found it hard to admit need in case it opened up a chink somewhere – a weakness that someone might take advantage of.

"What about Emma?" Tom enquired, half fearing the reply.

"Until a few weeks ago, I'd never told anyone anything about my past, only David. He never asked any questions and I only told him what I thought was pertinent. He knew that was the only way I could handle it. It was at the centre of our relationship yet unspoken for most of the time. Strange, isn't it? For all I know he might have believed something very different about some of my past."

The coffee and biscuits arrived and, sensing the intimacy, the waitress worked quickly and quietly and immediately withdrew to the kitchen.

"The first person I've ever told was Emma – after the funeral. She was wonderful. The formality of saying goodbye to what was left of him made me realise how important David had been to my life. Not just because he loved me but because he accepted me with all the wrinkles and warts and tantrums – and violence. Oh yes, I could be violent when I was younger – although never, ever to Emma!"

Tom listened to her with a mixture of sadness and guilt. He was being allowed a privileged insight into the intimate world of someone he desired yet the more he was allowed to see, the more he felt excluded. It was a process which had started at the funeral and was now being completed. As the complexities of her life and relationship unfolded, Tom realised that his own interest had been comparatively simple, not to say basic. He had kidded himself that it was only his professional oath that stood in the way of a relationship developing between him and Vicky but the realisation came swiftly and without pain that friendship was probably the best he could hope for. If he was honest, it was perhaps the only thing of real value that Vicky either needed or wanted from him. He would have to settle for that but desire still played little tunes of hope in his consciousness.

"Isn't there anything we can get them on?" He was still enraged at the way her life had been ripped open simply to discredit their cause.

"Not really, Tom. I'm sure you don't want all the details but they've got enough right to make it impossible. The rape was more like forceful seduction, with money and alcohol as the persuaders. And the blackmail? I was ignorant of that. Yes, I did have sex with a few older men but – I was manipulated, told it would help to keep my mother out of prison – that kind of stuff."

"Someone's been seriously digging into your past."

"It's made me realise I've got every reason to be scared because I think they'll do whatever they see as necessary. They've also defused me because if I make any allegations against anyone now it'll be put down as hysteria. They've almost got *carte blanche* to say what they like in future. We've taken on some powerful people, Tom. Did you hear Astbury yesterday when he said that he had to be absolutely confident about the stability of any witness? That was aimed at me; he has to be behind this or at least he knows who is."

"Possible."

"There's one consolation. He's scared as well – we've got him on the run."

CHAPTER TWENTY-ONE

Wednesday, September 30th, 1992, 7.30 p.m. It was never going to be an easy meeting, Tom knew that. The well of resentment in so many members of the group had slowly been filling – drip, drip, drip – with every piece of disinformation and Government ruse to avoid conceding control and it was inevitable it would overflow at some time.

It was equally frustrating for Tom, for as orchestrator of their campaign, he was the only person on whom relatives could focus their resentment. He kept telling himself that it wasn't personal – but it didn't help much. When they weren't shouting at him, they were forcibly arguing with each other and wherever he looked he could see eyes that were bright with anger – the eyes of people who have been backed into a corner and have nowhere else to go.

"But you've got all this stuff on them, there's got to be something we can do with it. It shows them for what they are, murdering bastards…!" Bridie Gallagher was almost trembling.

"I'm afraid it's not conclusive." Tom tried desperately to keep his voice level and devoid of passion for he knew if he did otherwise, the meeting would become uncontrollable.

"It's just so much bloody pussyfooting…" Bernard offered and puffed on his empty pipe.

Maurice Wreford was one of the few who remained calm and analytical. Tom could think of occasions when this English reserve would drive him mad but on this particular day he clutched at it like a lifebelt.

"Maurice is trying to make himself heard – please, he has the floor."

"I just want to be absolutely clear about the situation we've arrived at. You're saying that the evidence we've amassed would not secure a conviction if we were to take action ourselves against Varsity?"

"That's my opinion."

"What if we were to hand it all to the Director of Public Prosecutions? Surely, there's enough for him to instigate an investigation and perhaps add to what we've found?" Voices were immediately raised in protest but Maurice simply stood, head bowed, waiting for the noise to subside. When it did, he looked up and continued without once raising his voice. "Is there any chance he would instigate proceedings?"

"In a word, no! I think everything would disappear without trace. I suspect he would say what I've said – that there's insufficient evidence and he would hand it all over to the SAAIU inquiry for them to examine."

Maurice battled on. "And do you believe there is any chance that the inquiry would act on it?" The hoots of derision were unkind but if they hurt him, Maurice did not show it.

"I think we've got more chance of winning the pools!" All evening Tom had been aware of how quiet and restrained Vicky had been and even as he tried to keep the lid on the emotional cauldron he was aware of her, standing near the front, watching, her face set, revealing nothing.

"You have to remember that the inquiry was instigated by Government – a political inquiry – and if you analyse Astbury's statements you'll see he's never said that the results will be published and the reason is – they won't be! The country will be fed spoonfuls of its findings, the uncontroversial, uncritical bits which are palatable and the rest – anything awkward – will never see the light of day."

Again the calls of anger filled the room and again Maurice waited. "So where does that leave us now?"

Bernard Tate stepped out from a small group of people. "I'll tell you where it leaves us – no bloody where. It's the end of the line. I said from the start we should forget all this nonsense and go after them in the States. We should have done it then, we should do it now! End of story!"

There were more mumblings of agreement than Bernard had ever received before but Tom still believed they were wrong.

"That's one option but there are others. We can continue to deploy bits of the material we have amassed in the compensation negotiations with Varsity. Not the whole picture, just enough to worry them. Then there is the Peter Thornton trial and with your permission I am considering whether I should offer his defence team some of the same information. That might bring it into the public domain and increase demand for a public inquiry – that's if they use it. We also don't know what's going to come out of that trial and there may be something that helps us. After the trial, we could launch a judicial review of the decision to limit the prosecution to Thornton rather than tackle the corporate responsibility of the company. That would certainly put the results of all our enquiries out there and turn up the pressure. And don't forget the inquest which will have to reconvene at some point – we're probably looking at some time next year..."

"Wait another year, you mean?" It was Hetty Mackay, close to tears. Tom looked to Vicky for a counter-voice but it wasn't forthcoming.

"I know you're doing your best, Tom, but it's ridiculous." Bridie's anger was less raw now. "I'm not shouting at you, it's just the situation. It seems that everything's stacked against us and you've only got sops to offer. We're not eejits, Tom."

The words stung him and for the first time he spoke exactly as he felt.

"And I'm not treating you like idiots. I said at the start of all this that you had choices – money or truth. That's still your choice. I said it might take years – and it might. I said I would do everything in my power – and I have. If you're angry then be angry at the system not at me because it's the system that's taken you on. Be angry at the power of money but not at me for trying to play by the rules.

"You want to attack Varsity – so do I. I've prepared the papers for a civil action in case our no-fault compensation claim is unsatisfactory – you've already rejected five million and I believe it will be considerably increased. We're now getting into big figures and high legal costs, including theirs if we lose.

"We've achieved wonderful things but now it's crunch time! Bernard wants you all to go with Ailey Newman and look for compensation in the States and if that's what you want – do it, you'll have my full support. There's no compromise for me – I want to know what really happened so I won't be joining you. Let me know what you decide. I'll be down in the bar."

Tom walked away feeling totally defeated and Mike followed him, saying nothing but quietly ordering drinks for them both.

"Cheers, guv!"

"Cheers, Mike!" Tom could see from Mike's expression that someone was behind him. He turned to see Vicky.

Mike quickly put his glass down. "I've just got to make a call – see you in a minute."

"Can I get you a drink?" Tom asked.

"No, thanks. There are a couple of important things I want to tell you."

"Now's your time – everyone else is doing it!"

Vicky ignored the comment. "You've done brilliantly, Tom and you're right, it is a choice – money or truth – but I've got to move on. I'm going to sue Varsity on my own."

"What?" He was utterly disbelieving but in the next breath the lawyer took over. "Who's going to do it for you?" Tom could hear his voice but he wasn't conscious of stringing the words together. He felt breathless, like he'd been kicked in the solar plexus.

"It's someone I met at a friend's; runs a big City commercial firm. It's no criticism of you, Tom..." She didn't complete the sentence.

"Then who is it a criticism of?"

"No one in particular..."

"Don't lie."

"Okay, Tom, I'll tell you. I trust you, in fact I'd trust you with my life, but ... it's your father. I have no faith in him – at all."

"He's not on the case, Vicky."

"No, but he's in the office..." It was clear what she meant. "I've made my decision Tom ... sorry! Can we have a drink together, perhaps tomorrow?"

"No, Vicky, perhaps in a week or two."

"Okay, but I will keep in touch."

"That's it, is it?"

"Only if you want to see it that way. Bye, Tom, and thanks for everything." She stretched up and kissed him but he didn't move his face towards her but stood immobile and then watched her as she walked out of the pub, quelling the desire to run after her.

"You look like shit!" Mike quietly reappeared. "What's happened?"

"Nothing – just got too close to someone, that's all."

Before Mike could make any comment, Bridie appeared from the meeting room above. "Could you come back, Tom, we'd like a word?"

He climbed the stairs wearily and at that moment had no interest in what they had to say but was surprised to find the room remarkably quiet. Maurice stepped forward and shook Tom by the hand in a strangely formal gesture. "Would you continue to act for us, Tom? Well, most of us! No one could have done more than you." Tom found it strangely comforting.

The idea only occurred to him at the end of the meeting when he passed the payphone near the entrance doors. Without agonising about it, without exploring his reasons or his motivation, he called Louise and simply said, "Fancy a drink?" She accepted without hesitation and it was only as he hung up that Tom allowed himself any pang of guilt. He knew he was using her, hoping she would, for a few hours at least, help to dull the pain he felt.

Tuesday, October 20th, 1992 Nigel Eastrich had the unmistakable stamp of a charmer about him. He was much too eager to smile and everything he said was subtly designed to flatter and stroke. He had an aversion to plain speaking and a love of verbosity, as though the sound of his perfectly modulated voice was more important than what he had to say.

When Vicky finally left his expensive offices in Holborn she was confused. She didn't like the man on a personal level but kept reminding herself she wasn't employing him to be her lifelong friend. This was a strictly professional relationship and in that respect he seemed the right person for what she wanted – an impressive record of successes, highly recommended and enthusiastic.

He spelt out clearly what he believed to be the strong points of her case and said he believed it was well worth pursuing. It was almost with embarrassment that he had asked for a deposit – "purely to establish your *bona fides*, to show your seriousness and, of course, to comply with this firm's long-established custom and practice. You don't have any objection to that, do you?"

She had written out a cheque for £3,000 with some trepidation as she didn't really have the money. Work was non-existent and David, wonderful man that he was, had shaken off financial responsibility like a dog sheds water and had had no personal insurances, no pensions and no company hand-out on which to rely. Responsibility was always going to come tomorrow. Both their careers had been slow to take off and it had been his intention to do something about the future – in the future. As a result, she had received nothing as a consequence of his death.

Nigel Eastrich had reassured her that the £3,000 would probably be enough. "Because of the nature of this case, we'll – how shall I put it – we may rob a few corporate Peters to pay your litigious Paul." It had to come out of the £15,000 she had raised by remortgaging her house – money which was meant to provide a cushion until she either received a settlement from the police for false imprisonment or work began to come in again.

She urgently needed to talk to Tom about her case against the Met but if he no longer wished to handle it – and she could understand perfectly if he did not – then she guessed Eastrich would probably take it on. Every time she thought about her rejection of Tom in favour of this suave new solicitor with his expensive suits and placatory words, she found herself humming involuntarily, as though that simple, tuneless, pointlessness of the act would drown out the embarrassment and sense of loss she felt. It didn't.

Vicky went directly from her meeting with Eastrich to a copy shop to proof the press release she had written. There was so much angst and personal investment involved in pursuing Varsity she wanted the whole world to know about it. She also wanted Varsity, or whoever was pulling their strings, to know that they hadn't succeeded in intimidating her. Much as she hated even thinking it, she felt confident that her change of lawyer, from a high street unknown to one with a higher profile would send exactly the right signal to them.

Having faxed and posted the release, she had dinner with a producer and began to court work, something she hadn't had to do for a long time.

Monday, October 26th, 1992, 10.45 a.m. "Shit, shit, shit!!" Tom kicked at a cigarette butt on the pavement as he strode away from the offices of Durrant and Dawes. After the tense support group meeting, those clients who remained had agreed with his proposal to approach Thornton's defence solicitors. He had decided to offer them a copy of the tape and it wasn't just that they had turned it down, it was the manner of their rejection – utterly dismissive.

"Mr Harrison, we're not interested in flights of fancy or convoluted conspiracy theories, they have absolutely nothing to do with our client's defence. He is accused of manslaughter as a result of a failure to observe regulations and we have an adequate response to that. We have no desire to muddy the waters with allegations that are simply not relevant to the charge."

Tom had tried to raise the public interest angle and was almost laughed at. "We're not being paid to defend either the public or their interest, we're being paid to defend Mr Thornton and we're not going to turn this into some kind of politically correct circus! If you have got concerns, I suggest you explore them through the proper channels or, dare I say it, initiate your own litigation."

The implication of those last few words had been clear – he was not up to such a challenge either intellectually or on the strength of the evidence he presently held. On the other hand, the dilemma was slowly distilling into an unpalatable single option. Should he just hand the tape over to the SAAIU or the police and be done with it? He could give them a copy and keep the original provided by Nightingale. That way they would realise the game was up but would not be able to destroy the evidence. But of course, they would immediately demand the original, just as he had. It would, however, absolve him from any allegation of non-disclosure should there be a perverse finding against Thornton.

He gave a single chortle out loud and shook his head. Yes, it would absolve him of any responsibility and put his career on to safe ground but did he, honestly, think that having the recording would constrain these people – honestly? It would simply hand them the only ace he held.

He knew he sometimes played a bit fast and loose with codes of conduct and had been prepared to trample with hobnail boots over the one that forbade intimacy with a client. It was a different age when Benjamin Disraeli had come up with that little beauty as part of his equivalent of the doctors' Hippocratic oath for lawyers. It placed a demand on lawyers to ensure that justice really was truth in action. Did he also see that as from another age, outdated and capable of being ignored if he so chose? Tom didn't need to give it any thought because he knew he had a powerful belief in justice. He tried to analyse his motivation and was convinced his dilemma over the tape and what to do with it was not about gaining his clients an advantage but about getting at the truth. Although he shrugged it off in front of Mike, a sense of duty sat heavily on his shoulders – very heavily – and he needed time to work this one through.

He kicked a Coke can and it clattered noisily across the pavement and fell into the gutter. He was aware that only part of his anger had been fired by Robin Dawes's rejection – the rest was a result of Dawes's inadvertent confirmation that the charges against Thornton were a sham.

The solicitors defending Thornton were so bloody straight that by default they were aiding the Government. They knew there was no case against him but rather than enquire why this sham had been initiated, they were keeping their heads down, avoiding confrontation, maintaining a low profile. They had excluded any broader investigation of the crash itself. The purpose of it all could not be clearer – the Government knew that prosecuting Thornton would head off any criticism of inaction and provide at least twelve months' delay. They also knew that the flames of passion burn less fiercely with time and they were buying that time. The problem, as Tom saw it, was how to keep the flames stoked up.

He found his car and climbed in but did not drive away. What the hell hope could he offer them? He sat and racked his brains, aware that he needed something to save face as much as anything else. Perhaps he could get Terry Lewis to raise a question in the House to try and flush out Varsity or Astbury or their paymasters, whoever they were.

It would have to be something extremely forthright and he composed the question as he thought. *Can the minister confirm that the passengers aboard Flight 469 were not oil field workers, as previously claimed, and that the cargo was not ordinary luggage?*

Before he had even finished phrasing it, he had also composed Astbury's reply. *I have to tell my honourable friend for Harrow Central that I am in no position to provide a response to that or any other question which must await the outcome of current criminal proceedings and a SAAIU investigation. I know he will understand the reasons why I make this response and I also know that his own concerns for national security, which he has voiced frequently and eloquently over a number of years, will ensure that he accepts it with his normal courtesy and understanding.*

Paraphrased – *If you ask that again, you can kiss goodbye to any chance of a knighthood – understand?*

He would have to try it, if only to stir the pot a little. He would also keep up the pressure for a public inquiry but that was difficult because it was entirely out of his control. All he could do was to make demands and encourage others to do the same. But it was highly likely the Government would continue to refuse.

That was one possible approach but it would need something more than he currently had – perhaps a local campaign involving not just the support group but London people generally? Did anyone have the energy or resources to organise it?

The inquest? What about the inquest? It had still not been held and had been adjourned *sine die* – indefinitely – so it would have to be reconvened and concluded at some point. There was nothing to say it could not be reopened the moment criminal proceedings were out of the way.

He had not endeared himself to George Fraser but at least he knew him, he was a local and therefore subject to local pressure. He certainly would not want a full inquest with a jury and would try and sneak by with a formal one – but was it possible to influence his decision? Even before the thought had properly materialised, Tom began to reject it.

He turned the ignition key, nosed up Kingsway and headed for the Marylebone Road. He would need some strong support – a powerful voice with weight behind it. George Fraser would have to be softened up and public pressure was the best pummel. Even as he itemised the needs, Tom was aware of his own inadequacies – it would take much more than him! So where to start? No sooner had he thought the thought than the answer followed. He pulled over and dialled a number.

"Louise Watson." Her voice sounded extremely professional.

"I was just saying to myself that what I need is someone with weight, someone who's strong and who has a powerful voice. And who did I immediately think of?"

"Bullshit!"

"Oh dear! It sounds like I don't have your absolute trust."

"I wouldn't trust you if the Pope himself recommended you – come to think of it, particularly if he recommended you." Tom could hear just a trace of humour lurking beneath Louise Watson's answer.

"It's interesting – what I've got to tell you ... really interesting!"

"It had better be."

"It's just after twelve, what time can you be free?"

"If you really have got something worthwhile – I'm free whenever."

"Great. I'm in the Marylebone Road – I can be with you in less than ten minutes."

"I'll see you in reception." Louise didn't sound entirely enthusiastic. "And can I get one thing straight, Tom, is this business or pleasure? It's just that I'm getting a bit pissed off with your double messages."

"It's both! See you in a minute or two."

In fact, when he pulled up outside the *Chronicle*, Louise was waiting on the pavement. He stole a reserved *Chronicle* parking space and together they walked the short distance to a simulated rustic wine bar where they sat at an outside table between potted pavement palms – an exotic touch amidst London's traffic fumes.

"I've come to a dead end." Tom loosened his tie and allowed the warm autumnal air to sneak beneath his collar. "No public inquiry, no compensation yet, no end in sight to the civil action against Varsity and no disclosure of our material at the Thornton trial – they just don't want to know! You realise that this bloody trial has blocked off every single avenue? Absolutely nothing will happen now until after it's over – nothing at all!"

Louise sounded defensive. "The *Evening Chronicle* has pressed as hard as it can for a public inquiry but we've lost it – the Government just isn't going to budge. And you have to remember, when push comes to shove, the *Chronicle* is a loyal Government supporter. It will only go so far before backing off."

"I'm not criticising you or your paper, Louise, honestly, but where do we go now? I don't want you to laugh before you've given it a bit of thought but what do you think about pushing for a full inquest to be reopened once the Thornton case is over – once they've lost their last fig leaf?"

"I would have thought it was about as effective as a sticking plaster for a cut throat. But keep talking."

"We simply don't have anything else. Is there any chance the *Chronicle* would back such a demand if I went public with it? It's not as politically contentious as a public inquiry and it doesn't need Government approval. It's simply down to one silly old fart – George Fraser – a much easier target. He'll resist it, I know, and try and get away with a formal inquest with a token presence but if we keep going at him we might embarrass him into it."

Although the idea had started to formulate only minutes before, the more Tom talked, the more he liked it. Perhaps it was clutching at straws but at least it was positive action.

Louise didn't react immediately. "Not the stuff of high drama, is it? What do you expect to come out of it? No, I'll rephrase that – what do you want out of it?"

Tom went silent and traced rivulets through the condensation on his beer glass with a fingernail. "The words 'fuck' and 'knows' immediately spring to mind. What *can* we get out of it? Well, the jury can use their own words but are advised to bring back one of four verdicts – an open verdict, accidental death, death by misadventure or unlawful killing. That's it. That's the sum total of the prize we can expect; that'll be the extent of our victory – the culmination of all our heartache and commitment. Pathetic, isn't it?"

"What if you get a verdict of unlawful killing? Won't that have some impact? At least it will say that someone was to blame."

"Oh sure, but no one will go to the Tower!"

"Mixed messages again, Tom. Do you want a bloody inquest or not? Make a decision and stop faffing around!"

"Yes, of course I do. It's like asking Captain Oates if he wants a cup of hot cocoa."

"Right, here's to it then." Louise raised her glass. "You work on George Fraser and I'll have a go at the editor. I reckon I can deliver you the *Chronicle*." Tom played the game and clinked glasses with Louise.

"You should set Vicky loose on Fraser! Frighten the life out of him," Louise added with a wry smile.

"Vicky's moved on." He was aware he hadn't said the words naturally. Some of his confusion had sneaked out and affected the delivery, pushing it up an octave.

"Moved on where? You make her sound like a travelling circus."

"She's gone to another solicitor. She's suing Varsity on her own."

"Oh, I knew that." Tom's jaw dropped as Louise fished in her briefcase and produced a copy of Vicky's press release. "It was faxed through earlier – she's holding a press conference tomorrow. I thought it was all part of your grand plan. I didn't realise it was a solo event but it's all right, isn't it? Doesn't threaten the campaign in any way? Christ, you made it sound like the end of a marriage." Louise turned her head and watched the passing traffic unseeingly as she sipped her drink.

"Why?"

"Why what?"

"Why did she go?"

"Who knows?" Tom tried to sound disinterested.

"Well, it would account for quite a lot, wouldn't it?"

"Like what?" He was praying her response would be confined to professional matters. Louise did not oblige.

"Like how I'm suddenly getting phone calls from you; like how you've suddenly turned into Prince Charming; like how we're suddenly having drinks together regularly." There was a tartness about Louise's words and Tom did not want her to continue but she did. "Do you want to know what I think?"

He did not want to know. "I think you're going to tell me whatever I say."

"I think you're besotted with her, aren't you, and she's not playing ball so you're using me as a distraction. Don't forget, I've seen you together."

"She was my client, Louise. You're not allowed to have affairs with your clients."

"Well, isn't that fortunate, she's an ex-client now!"

"And you're not allowed affairs with ex-clients, either."

"Bet there's nothing in the rules to say you can't bloody fancy your client, though, is there?" Louise swung round on her chair so that she was side on to Tom and he felt a desperate need to rescue the situation.

"Okay, confession time. Yes, I did 'fancy' her and yes, it was stupid to allow that to happen but we fought a lot of battles together and out of that came friendship. I guess I wanted it to go one step further."

"Did she feel the same?"

"I haven't got a clue." It hurt him to say it but it was the truth. "More to the point, I'd like some of your company right now, if that's all right?"

She looked at him for a long time before answering. "I don't like being used, Tom, so watch yourself. You met Vicky before you met me and I can understand why you'd find her attractive. Shit, even I find her attractive. I like you, Tom, God knows why, but I do." Her smile belied the gibe. "I'll give you time to get over it but you're not going to use me, is that clear?"

She turned towards him, placed a hand on his arm and put her face very close to his but her eyes were unsmiling. "I'm not very good at playing second fiddle, Tom. I've got a lot of passion to give and ... well, let's just say passion for the moment. I'm not going to waste it on someone whose interests lie elsewhere." She took a drink and when she spoke again it was with a mixture of threat and promise. "If you want it you're going to have to earn it – not with words but actions. You've got to show me – because words come too easily to you."

She leant back from the table and finally gave Tom a broad smile. "Now, I think that's going to cost you an extremely expensive dinner! Cheers." She raised her glass and Tom realised he was extremely happy to buy her dinner – and he didn't care about the expense.

Not having a car was becoming a bore. By the time Vicky had got through a day of meetings and finally arrived at the tube station, the evening rush had long since ended. There were plenty of seats on the Watford train when it pulled in and as the automatic doors hissed shut, a big man wedged his shoulder between them and with a supreme effort forced them apart. They thudded shut after him and he looked around for a seat.

Vicky was in one of the long row of seats which have their backs to the windows and facing her was a similar row, empty apart from an old lady in one corner. Despite the wide choice available, the man chose a seat directly in front of Vicky and sat down, his bulk appearing to take up three seats, his feet almost touching hers as he sprawled his legs out.

She lifted her *Evening Chronicle* but was conscious of being stared at and did not look up for fear of making eye contact. The feeling of being watched grew stronger and Vicky was aware she was simply looking at words on the page but not reading them.

At Kensal Green, the old lady got off and on the pretext of checking her route, Vicky raised her eyes and looked at the long map above the windows, directly over the man's head. As her eyes glanced along it she allowed them to stray to his face and he was staring at her without blinking, his eyes utterly dead, lifeless – brutal and compassionless.

Without signalling her nervousness, she surreptitiously checked the carriage to see how many passengers it held and there were just a handful. She went back to the *Chronicle* but she knew his eyes were still boring into her. If the intention was to intimidate, it was working.

Vicky tried to think through her options. All she had with her was her briefcase and handbag. The handbag was in her lap but the briefcase was on the seat next to her. She put her paper down and placed her hand round the handle of the case. It was at least something she could wield if necessary.

The train pulled into Wembley Central and when the doors opened, two people exited but no one joined. Again, Vicky pretended to check her destination but when she heard the shouted "Mind the doors," she waited just a fraction longer and as the first hiss of compressed air preceded a rumble of the closing doors, she was on her feet, bags in hand, and as the gap between the twin sliding doors diminished, she leapt through them on to the platform. The trailing briefcase was clamped firmly by their rubber jaws as the doors came together with a thud. She wrenched at its handle but it was immovable, as though held in a vice.

The man rose from his seat, smoothly and leisurely as though he had all the time in the world and strolled towards the trapped bag. As he reached it, the doors hissed again and parted, freeing the briefcase so abruptly that Vicky almost fell backwards. He stepped through the now fully opened doors on to the platform and the smirk on his face brought no life to his still dead eyes.

Vicky's delay in leaving the train had ensured that all the disembarking passengers had already scurried through the station exit and the platform was almost empty. She could feel the fear rising and without looking at him, she walked quickly down the platform, clutching the bags and fighting off an urge to run.

She passed a carriage with several people still in it and as the doors again began to rumble shut, she stepped through them and back into the train. They thudded to a close behind her and it seemed an eternity before she heard the 'click' as the motors engaged and the train began its whining acceleration.

The man stood on the platform watching her disappear but if he felt cheated, it was not reflected in his expression, which remained implacable. When the train pulled into Harrow-on-the-Hill, Vicky's heart was still pounding, her mouth dry, and she grabbed her breath in shallow little sips. Fear increased as she alighted from the train and no matter how logically and how persuasively she told herself that the man could not possibly be waiting for her – it had no effect.

As she exited into the dark of the station forecourt she searched desperately for a taxi and not until she was sitting inside it did she feel safe.

"Next one on the left!" she said to the driver. "If you pull into the drive, you can reverse out and go back the way you came otherwise you'll have to go all round the houses."

The taxi swung into the drive, illuminating the front of the house and without even realising she was doing so, Vicky checked all the windows and doors to see if the house had been broken into. Everything looked normal but hanging from the knocker of the front door was what appeared to be a bag. It could not have been left by Emma as she was away.

Fear was still at work and she asked the driver to wait until she had let herself in. Within a pace or two of the door, under the brightness of the taxi's headlights, she could see it was not a bag but something black from which a liquid dripped. As she stepped in front of the headlights her shadow was thrown against the door and the object disappeared into darkness but as she moved to one side crippling fear washed over her. Vicky could clearly see the present left for her: it was a black and white cat – Minouche, a neighbour's affectionate little she cat

– and it was impaled with a kitchen knife to the white woodwork of her front door – one of Vicky's kitchen knives. The still dripping blood showed that whoever had done it had only recently finished their handiwork.

When a deep voice sounded close behind her Vicky's heart almost stopped. "You all right, love?" The taxi driver's approach had been drowned out by the noise of the clattering diesel engine. He surveyed the door. "Oh my good God, that's out of order; there really are some sickos around. Do you want me to call the police, love?"

"No. Thanks, but no." She shook her head as though to shake away the image. "Could you take me to Manley Court, please?" Without even thinking, she gave Tom's address and it was only when the cab pulled up outside that she wondered if she had done the right thing.

When Tom answered the entryphone, she knew immediately he had someone with him and had it been any other night she would have walked away.

"Is it important, Vicky, only I've…?" His voice petered out.

"It's important, Tom."

"It won't keep until tomorrow, will it? I'm in the office all—"

"Open the fucking door, Tom!" She hadn't meant to shout.

The buzzer sounded and she pushed it from the retaining latch and for the first time since the tube train she began to feel secure.

Tom met her halfway up the stairs and had it been another time and another person it would have been almost amusing to watch his embarrassed attempt at nonchalance. As she came out of the shadow of the stairwell on to the dimly lit half-landing, she saw the expression on his face change.

"Jesus Christ, Vicky, what's happened to you?"

"Something horrible," was all she could say.

As she entered his flat she caught sight of herself in the hall mirror. She had no memory of doing so but she must have touched the cat and bloodied her fingers for blood was streaked all over her face. She continued into the living room.

The picture was cosy. Ella sang softly, the bottle of wine was almost gone and two pairs of shoes were abandoned in the middle of the carpet. Louise – of course it had to be Louise! The young journalist looked at Vicky and her concern only just outweighed her resentment.

Vicky felt lonelier than she had done for many years and knew she had no right to feel jealous. "He's got shit taste in wine, hasn't he?"

CHAPTER TWENTY-TWO

Friday, November 13th, 1992 The Peter Thornton trial was at least seven months away so Tom knew he still had breathing space before deciding whether to hand over the tape to the DPP. Whenever he turned his mind to it he never reached a conclusion but just went round in ever decreasing circles. One thing was for sure – whatever the decision, timing was the essence and it almost felt like the last throw of the dice.

He realised there was no point in going to the wire over an inquest with George Fraser and that it would have to be a war of attrition. Tom worked on two fronts – never missing an opportunity to soften up his father by playing the civic duty card, hoping it would worry away at his conscience and he, in turn, would relay some of it to George.

Then there was George himself. On the occasions when Tom did see him, he simply evaded any questions or comment about inquests, either in particular or general and if pushed, he was non-committal and made it clear he would not even contemplate a decision prior to the end of the Thornton trial.

Tom could not work out if he was simply a duplicitous old bastard or whether he genuinely thought the trial was important and hoped that something revelatory might come out of it. Either way, it was stalemate for the time being.

Tom was quite straightforward about what he wanted and told George that he would be officially asking for a full inquest to be reconvened once the Thornton case had been disposed of. George smiled patronisingly and Tom could read his thoughts through his rheumy old eyes. *It's going to take more than you to make me!* Wisely, Louise had decided to hold back from launching the *Evening Chronicle* campaign until after the trial for there was little point in going into battle whilst the other side had a perfect excuse not to fight.

The group had been divided over the plan in an obvious three-way split. The three perspectives hadn't altered since day one, just the proportions had varied but in truth, they didn't have much option but to support Tom. The only ones who really worried him were those who felt they could not face having the embers of their pain fanned back into life for if they withdrew their support his moral strength would be seriously attenuated.

Nevertheless, the overall effect of having a target, a plan and majority backing was positive and he again felt he was riding at the head of the cavalry rather than slogging along with the poor bloody infantry, being sniped at from behind every bush.

The change in Vicky had been dramatic the evening she had arrived at his flat. It was only with reluctance that she had accepted a brandy; having called round for help and support she spent her time refusing both. Like a mother hen ushering her chicks to safety beneath her feathers, she had tried to scoop up her fears and hide them from sight, camouflaging her obvious concern with nonchalance and by becoming progressively more brittle.

One moment he had wanted to put his arms round her and tell her gently that everything was all right, that he'd protect her – but that would have been the response of a lover and he was not her lover. The next moment he wanted to shake her and tell her it was okay to be scared, that she could let go and no one would think any the less of her. But he knew she would never do that in front of Louise and probably not in front of him, either. He had even thought of asking Louise to leave but had immediately dismissed it as being unfair and cruel. The choice was Vicky's – both he and Louise had wanted to help her and she had to accept or reject it but he certainly could not write the script for her.

In the end, he had insisted they take her to the police station and from there they had gone back to her house, while the police did a search, and then on to Wendy Percival's, where she was to stay the night.

When Louise had asked Vicky if it would be okay to run a news piece on the story, her response had been a curt. "Do what you like!" The shutters had completed their descent.

Louise had rung Terry Lewis and suggested it would do him no harm to offer Vicky the use of a car from one of his lots – considering what had happened it was eminently newsworthy. *When a journalist rings and wants to cast you as the hero in a local story only a fool would decline*, thought Terry, and immediately found a small and ageing trade-in for her. Okay, it had seen better days and yes, it did have a few electrical faults but it was the thought that counted – and the coverage it got in the *Evening Chronicle*.

Daily newspapers all ran stories on Vicky's intention to sue Varsity but there had been a quantum change in their attitude towards her. No journalist referred to the *Daily Despatch* story directly but it informed the tone of every line of copy. Vicky had been transformed from a seeker after truth to something of a nutter but gnawing away at Tom was genuine concern for her safety. She was still a formidable opponent and seemingly had the ability to compromise people almost at will. It went without saying that whoever was targeting her felt similarly.

Tom had found her withdrawal from his action extremely painful as Vicky was one of the most extraordinary women he had ever met. However, he had to let go and if she made a balls of things, that was her business. He hoped her move to Nigel Eastrich would work out but he had his doubts.

She had kept the umbilical attached by asking Tom to continue with the false detention claim against the Metropolitan Police but even their legal team had noticeably changed their attitude to the case. They had begun with a clear intention to settle speedily but were now dragging their heels and the reason seemed obvious – Vicky no longer had public support and the sum they were prepared to offer, if they were to offer anything, had clearly diminished greatly. Tom would never forgive the *Daily Despatch* for that.

Patience was not something that came naturally to him but he knew he was going to need it if he was to progress the routine work of the practice. Mr Henderson had received a nice out-of-court settlement; Geordie Wilson was officially no flasher, just a urinator; and Sandra Lockett had been given three months for her fifth shoplifting spree. On the desk were a pile of other Hendersons, Wilsons and Locketts and when Tom looked at them his heart sank. He picked up the phone. "Fancy a game, Mike?"

The road out of Brighton was almost at a standstill and Vicky had purposely delayed returning home until late in order to miss the Sunday evening, nose-to-tail jams that inevitably followed a sunny weekend but it seemed everyone else had done the same. She didn't know if it was going to be like it all the way to London or whether there was an accident up ahead, after which it would probably clear but by the time she had reached the Henfield turn-off, the going was still slow and she decided to take the country route through Horsham to Dorking, hoping it might be clearer. It was and she was able to make good progress. The further from Brighton she travelled, the clearer the roads became.

The light had almost gone by the time she left Horsham and she turned on the headlights and felt for her night-driving glasses in the glove box. Having found them, she glanced in the rear-view mirror and could see headlights closing on her at speed but whoever it was would find it difficult to overtake on the narrow road.

The lights kept coming and she watched with concern as they bore down on her, seemingly with no intention of slowing. At what must have been the last possible moment the headlights dipped as the driver slammed the brakes on immediately behind her, so hard that the front of his vehicle dipped down towards the road surface. The same lights continued following her just inches from her rear bumper, their full beam reflected in the driving mirrors effectively blinding Vicky.

She accelerated to increase the distance between them but the other car matched her, maintaining the same proximity. Her heart began to race. *Yobs, just drunken yobs after a day out at the seaside*, she told herself as the car remained close behind. Ahead, Vicky could see a lay-by and as she approached it, slowed down and pulled off the carriageway, giving the car behind a chance to overtake.

She realised her mistake too late. The big, four-wheel drive vehicle drew alongside her car and then slammed into the side of it. With a grinding of metal, it crunched down the entire length of her vehicle before steering sharply across the front of it, crumpling the offside wing and forcing her car into the hedge.

Vicky was powerless to prevent it but was just able to swing the steering wheel to the left and with only inches to spare, missed a large grit bunker. The Fourtrak wasn't so fortunate and piled into the solid concrete obstacle, coming to an abrupt halt, its bonnet flying open in a clatter of shattered headlight glass.

Vicky wrenched at the driver's door to get out but the impact had buckled and distorted it, making it impossible. She could see two men in the Fourtrak, one of them big and bulky, perhaps even big enough to take up three tube-train seats and her eyes were riveted to the men as she wrenched at the door, over and over again.

The men appeared to be dazed – they had probably hit the windscreen and may well be hurt but they were recovering. Vicky put her shoulder to the door but it would not move. The big man was shaking his head as though to clear it and it could only be seconds before he opened his own door. She prayed for a car to stop but none did – they were both in the lay-by, obstructing no one.

Vicky struggled across into the passenger seat and tore at the nearside door handle and felt a surge of relief as it clicked open, but it was short-lived. As she thrust the door outwards it hit resistance – and opened no more than a few inches. Panic engulfed her but the harder she pushed against it, the harder the door seemed to bounce back and the dread realisation dawned that it was hawthorn branches; the car was firmly wedged in the middle of a hedge and neither of its two doors could be moved.

The smaller man had got out of the Fourtrak's passenger door and approached her. She could see his face clearly and the smug look which appeared on it when he realised she was trapped. He called to the big man, who was still in the driving seat of the other car. "Start her up, make sure we can get out of here."

Panic had given way to a numbing fear and Vicky scrabbled back to the driver's side, desperately feeling for the electric window controls, moving the rocker switch backwards and forwards, backwards and forwards but there was no movement from the window. Fighting against the terror which was swelling in her, she tried the passenger window control and it also refused to move but each time she pressed it, the unit gave out an electronic 'click' which it had done since she had been given the car. Sometimes it worked, sometimes it didn't.

The Fourtrak's engine burst into life and its driver reversed it away from the grit bunker and as soon as it had stopped, the smaller man opened the tailgate, removed a can and walked back to her car where the big man joined him. Vicky could see both their faces clearly and there was no doubt that it was the man from the tube train and he was smiling that same, cold, compassionless smile.

Her fingers continued frantically to work the rocker switch and with each forward movement the window gave a dull click but refused to open.

The smaller man flicked open the top of the can and began to slosh its contents over Vicky's car. The smell was unmistakable – petrol. With a sudden whirring, clunking sound, the electric motor sprang into life and the window next to her began slowly to descend but very slowly as if reluctantly.

The men had withdrawn some distance from her car and were almost invisible in the darkness until a cigarette betrayed their position and when they applied the lighter to a rolled-up newspaper, their faces were perfectly illuminated.

The window was still continuing its slow, downwards travel and Vicky waited – waited, waited, waited, waited, staring at the widening gap, willing it to open enough for her to clamber through it. The whirring stopped and she saw the burning newspaper describing a glowing arc through the night air towards her car.

She thrust her head and shoulders through the now wide-open gap and grasped at branches, pushing with her legs at the same time and the inch-long thorns buried themselves deep in her hands with a burning, throbbing pain but she refused to let go. She could hear herself crying out, screaming with pain and fear – pulling, grabbing, groping her way through the hedge. She also heard a 'whoosh' as the petrol ignited, momentarily felt its searing heat and saw the night light up.

Hard earth knocked the breath from her and the heat on her face was cooled by the hedgerow plants as she fell amongst them. She rolled over and over into the field – away from the fire, away from the men, and she could hear them shouting to each other above the noise of the burning car.

Vicky got to her feet and tried to run but fell back on the grass as her legs failed her, and so, on hands and knees she crawled and scrabbled until she was able to take control of the fear that was paralysing her, and then she was on her feet, running.

The field sloped uphill and she could see a copse surmounting the top, lit up by her burning car, and she ran towards it but could not resist the urge to look back and again terror flooded over her as she could clearly make out the silhouette of a man against the flames. He was in the field, running fast towards her and she could hear herself moaning, screaming, shouting words with no meaning. Her foot slipped from beneath her and she fell forwards forcibly into something wet and cloying and she could sense the man was closing on her.

Still twenty yards distant he stopped and looked back towards the road as the big man called him, "Come on, for fuck's sake, they'll be here in a minute – leave her!" Vicky became aware of flashing blue lights moving towards them from the direction of Horsham and could just detect the distant sound of police sirens. The smaller man paused and looked first in one direction and then the other, between the rapidly approaching police lights and her, and she instinctively knew that he was desperate to finish the job.

"Forget about her!" Again the big man's voice barked out in the night air and the smaller man reluctantly turned and headed back to the road. Shortly afterwards, the Fourtrak roared off without lights towards Dorking.

Vicky lay where she was and watched the lights approaching but they did little to assuage her fear – the vile, cruel bastards who wanted to murder her must have been following her all day; they knew about Brighton and therefore they must now know Emma's supposed place of safety!

Her face burned with the acid sting of nettles and the stench of cow shit, which covered her hands and legs and filled her nostrils. She laid her head on her folded arms and, for the first time in years, cried. Vicky Denton felt utterly defeated.

CHAPTER TWENTY-THREE

Tuesday, May 11th, 1993 The day felt unusually heavy. Time seemed handicapped and sounds drifting up from the street below were dull, almost muffled. Even when Geoff Tinsley dropped the clattering roller shutter on his fruit and veg display the noise was not intrusive.

Tom knew it must be four thirty because Geoff always closed his shop at four thirty – always. It was a stark reminder of the suburban confines of Tom's life. He glanced at the files piled up on his desk – a never-ending production line of people's worries and concerns, each vitally important to the people whose names were on the covers – but in the grand scheme of things…?

He lifted the cover of the top one, peered inside and then closed it. He retrieved three Quality Street wrappers from the otherwise unused ashtray, separated foil from cellophane and with the top of a ballpoint smoothed each piece of coloured foil into a neat rectangle on the blotter pad in front of him, carefully crumpled one of them up as small as he could make it, wrapped it in the second and subsequently the third until they formed a reasonably symmetrical ball. He flicked it with his forefinger, the aim being to get it into the lidless barley sugar tin which housed his paper clips. It pinged off the tin and scuttled across the desk.

"Ha… Ha… Ha… Ha…"

The distant sound which came through two walls was deep and barely audible. Tom knew it was his father being charming. He flicked the ball again and it ricocheted off the files and plopped in amongst the paper clips.

"Ha… Ha… Ha… Ha…"

He could almost time the gap between each component of the laugh. It had all the spontaneity of a royal wedding.

Tom had totally forgotten until his father had reminded him earlier that it was the anniversary of his mother's death. After work they would go through the annual ritual of placing flowers on Caroline's grave together and then going for a drink. Harry had initiated it as a way of keeping her memory alive, he said. They were supposed to talk about her, about old times, to resurrect memories and share them. In fact what would happen would be the same thing that happened every year. They would place the flowers and Harry would then talk about work. When that had petered out they would sit in silence for a while and then Harry would excuse himself and go to the golf club.

Tom was rather relying on him to stay true to form because Louise had rung him earlier and offered to buy dinner. She was pleased about something. They had been seeing quite a lot of each other over the past few months. No one had spoken of commitments, of permanence or even of love. It had been a time of great enjoyment, a lot of laughs and, as promised, a fair bit of passion.

But first, before Louise, he had the trip down memory lane. It was difficult to remember his mother clearly. He recalled all kinds of anecdotes and shared experiences but when he tried to visualise her face it always seemed to turn into the photograph on Harry's desk. God, how different to his father she had been. Completely off the wall!

It had always been something of a lottery to introduce new friends to her because he never knew what he might find. It wasn't that she was daunting or rude, far from it – she was just unpredictable. Perhaps eccentric was a better description.

He remembered Janet Brophy, belle of the tennis club. Long slender legs with enough family money to ensure they were always suntanned and a face so beautiful he believed he would never, ever, meet anyone so stunning. Janet was not strong on ideas or conversation but it was neither of these which attracted Tom.

She was eighteen, he was nineteen and trying to capitalise on his victory as the club's singles champion. Janet's interest in him blossomed the moment he'd held aloft the silver salver. He knew she had a short attention span and he had to work quickly. A couple of days later he whisked her off home when the house was supposed to be empty. It wasn't.

As he slotted his key in the lock, the door developed its own momentum and opened inwards. Holding the latch was his mother. She had recently developed an intense interest in do-it-yourself and had decided that wall lights would enhance the hallway. With a cold chisel and club hammer she had begun chasing channels in the wall to take the wiring conduit. The old lime plaster was powdery and each thwack with the hammer and chisel produced a cloud of fine plaster dust and little, stinging projectiles.

Caroline's logic was faultless – she needed to protect her eyes, stop her hair from becoming matted with dust and protect her lungs from the lime.

What confronted Tom and the lovely Janet Brophy was an apparition of a spectacular nature. Caroline had enclosed her hair in an old felt hat and pulled it tightly down over her ears. A bunch of artificial cherries dangled from the side. She had on a pair of padded pilot's goggles and her mouth and nostrils were protected by a sanitary towel, attached at the back of her head by its loops. She was covered in a layer of fine white dust, including the glass of her goggles through which she could barely see. When she spoke, the sanitary towel wobbled up and down and her words were completely unintelligible.

His moment with Janet Brophy was gone forever.

His mother should have died while scuba diving off Tobacco Quay in the Gulf of Mexico, despatched instantly by a great white shark. Or from a parachute malfunction while skydiving over Florida's Zephyr Hills. Sadly her death had been much more prosaic – cancer while she was still comparatively young.

"Ha... Ha... Ha... Ha..."

Tom didn't have the heart to deny Harry his memoriam outing even though it felt increasingly artificial.

He had never been able to fathom out what it was that had attracted his mother to his father. A handsome, unemotional pedant and a loving, over-the-top loopy. Perhaps it was just that he was handsome. Maybe he was one hell of a lover. Somehow Tom doubted it. Perhaps like Vicky, Caroline had her own secret past which she was prepared to trade for security and respectability.

With Caroline's diagnosis, Tom's life changed. All the old certainties were stripped away and he was forced to confront the prospect of death for the first time. Harry quite clearly could not cope with death. He refused to speak about it, appeared to be largely unaffected by it and it apparently altered his routine not one jot.

Tom would never forget the moment when all hope was shattered. His father sat one side of Caroline's bed, Tom the other, but it was Tom who was holding her hand. The surgeon was quite extraordinarily matter of fact, yet kind and understanding at the same time.

"I'm afraid it's not very good news, Mrs Harrison. Although none of your arteries were obstructed, the cancer has spread to your kidneys and liver and I suspect to your lungs as well. I'm not going to recommend chemotherapy because I think it would be pointlessly distressing. I honestly suggest the best thing you can do is to put your affairs in order as soon as possible, then forget about them and make the most of your life."

Caroline shed no tears but simply looked at the bed cover and said quietly, "Oh dear, that's a pity!" She had just listened to her own death sentence and it was "a pity". The Harrisons seemed to be masters of understatement.

Six weeks later Caroline began to slide into unconsciousness. Tom sat with her as much as he could and was constantly at the hospital for the last twelve hours or so. Harry popped in from time to time, patted Caroline on the hand, said some consoling words and then left.

When his mother could no longer return the pressure of Tom's fingers and her eyelids remained closed over the mustard yellow of her jaundiced eyes, he knew it could not be long. The rattle of her breathing became progressively more laboured as she fought for breath, the gasping punctuated by a regular mechanical hiss as morphine was injected directly into a vein in her wrist. Tom went to see if anyone could ease her departing and when he returned Caroline was dead.

As Harry seemed incapable of sharing his grief, Tom hoped he had been coping in whatever way he could. When he discovered that Harry had spent the last hours of Caroline's life umpiring a golf competition, a fundamental change took place in their relationship. For Tom, a part of his father also died that day.

"Ha... Ha... Ha... Ha..."

Harry's laugh again reached out through the walls. Tom flicked the foil ball and it rebounded into his lap from the file marked *Styleasy versus Wotherspoon*. The rap on the door was tentative but still it made him jump.

"Come in!" The door edged open and very slowly a hennaed head of hair eased into view.

"I suppose a cup of tea's out of the question?"

"Vicky!" He hadn't seen her for months.

"Aren't you going to ask me in?"

Tom was genuinely pleased to see her.

"Have you made me rich yet?"

"We're getting close. The way I hear it, the Met's top people have told them to settle it quickly but there's still some wrangling over the final figure. It shouldn't be long. How are you?"

She smiled wanly. "Broke!"

Suspecting the worst, Tom plugged in the kettle and waited for her to talk.

"It's been a disaster. Mr Nigel bloody Eastrich has, in a phrase, cleaned me out. He's presented me with a bill for thirteen thousand pounds and has done precisely nothing for it. I've had to drop the action!"

He shook his head. "What you need, Vicky, is a good lawyer!"

She laughed but it was forced and there was then a long silence while Tom busied himself with cups and teabags, wanting to say something welcoming to her but feeling once again the sting of rejection that had taken so long to cease hurting. Vicky broke the silence.

"How's the case going?"

"Well, it's going but that's about all." Again they lapsed into silence until Tom reached for something to fill the void and he was not sure if he genuinely wanted her opinion or whether it was merely a convenient subject on which they could both focus. "Actually, I have a bit of a dilemma." Vicky said nothing, merely inclined her head. "It's really something I have to make a decision on but you might like to give me your view."

Tom realised before he even spoke that he would not be swayed by whatever Vicky thought but he did feel the need to talk about it. "It's a professional problem and I've been mulling it over for months – the tape and what I should do with it. The Thornton trial's coming up in July and it's clear the case is being litigated on a very narrow basis and the defence seem to want to keep it that way. It's like neither side want to turn their heads and see what's beyond the blinkers, like they've sorted it all out and already know what the verdict will be."

"A set-up?" Vicky asked.

Tom thought before answering. "Yes, that's exactly what I think ... but if I'm wrong...! I can't just stand by with this material if it's genuine and allow a potential miscarriage of justice ... can I? And besides, as an officer of the court I'm obliged to hand it over to the DPP. We all know the implications of the radio transmissions – that Lloyd, the helicopter passenger, died because the plane was in trouble long before it smacked into him and whatever mistakes the pilot made, he wasn't the cause of death. The recording is central to the case."

Vicky looked bemused. "Why now, after all this time? Have you told Mike?"

"Nothing like a trial for focusing your mind and yes I have mentioned it to him briefly but we haven't actually discussed it."

"Why not?"

"Because deep down he's a bloody puritan and I know what he'll say."

"So you only want advice that confirms what you've already decided?"

"It's a bit more profound than that. If I can get the clients to agree, I could send a copy of the tape to the prosecution in the Thornton case for onward forwarding to the police. Of course, I'll let them know I still have the original and that two further copies are going to the SAAIU and the coroner – this way they can't ignore it or pretend to lose it. I'll enclose a note for George explaining why it's obviously relevant to the 'how' question. Whatever he thinks of the tape he'll still have to address it if only to allay rumour and suspicion. I also think it might ensure an inquest takes place."

Vicky raised an eyebrow. "Well ... you certainly seem to have thought it through. All pluses the way you describe it so why the hand-wringing?"

"I dunno! There's just something that bothers me – apart from almost certainly losing my job if I don't. In fact there's a hell of a lot that bothers me."

"Such as...?" Vicky asked.

"It's all too nebulous. I need to think about it more."

"You need to discuss it with Mike." Tom was surprised by the forcefulness of her words.

Tom and Harry sat at the same table, side by side, backs against the wall, looking outwards into the saloon bar of the usual post-graveside pub. Harry had a whisky and water in front of him, Tom a pint of lager but it was only Tom who was drinking. Harry was even more taciturn than usual and sat in silence, head inclined forwards, staring at his untouched drink, ignoring Tom's attempts at conversation. When he did eventually speak it was quietly, introspectively.

"I envy you, Tom." The words were delivered with heavy regret, a sentiment he had never before associated with his father.

"Really? Why?"

Finally Harry looked up from his drink and there was no anger, no challenge in his eyes and Tom wondered if this was the way most fathers looked at their sons.

"Because you're confident, you're intelligent and you know what you want out of life – the opposite of me..."

"Oh come on, Dad," was all Tom could think to say but his father wasn't listening – he had gone somewhere else and wanted to talk about it.

"When I met your mother, I was out of control. I was angry, resentful, frightened and had no boundaries, but the worst thing was I didn't know why. I thought I could find the answer in a bottle, with women, but it just made everything worse. You probably don't want to hear all this but I need you to."

Tom did want to hear it – but he would have preferred another day when his mind was not so full of Vicky Denton. There was absolute silence as Harry continued.

"I met your mother and it was as though just by being her, she was the antidote. She didn't admonish me, lecture me or offer advice – she simply carried on being who she was and that lovely, warm, positive manner of hers simply enfolded me. I loved her, Tom, with all my heart, more than you can ever conceive and I know you thought me heartless when she died but it was the only way I could cope. As she drifted away so did the major part of me. I died with her, Tom.

"I know you find my ways irritating, even laughable – my routines, my timekeeping, my adherence to old-fashioned values – but they're a construct, Tom, the boundaries I never had as a young man. I knew if I was to retain your mother's love I could not betray her faith in me by retreating into those destructive days. My routines gave me boundaries I would not cross, they gave me contentment and self-belief and they were the means by which I held on to the love of a beautiful woman. Oh yes, she did love me, Tom, even though you may find it hard to believe. And now she's gone, it would be so easy to revert to the man I once was but I won't. I will keep on being the old duffer you think I am as my homage to Caroline, to all that she did for me."

Harry raised his glass and said, "To Caroline – to your mother, Tom."

"To Caroline, to Mum," Tom said as he raised his glass and saw his father crying for the first time in his life. He wanted to reach across the table and take his arm but a lifetime of not being able to do so prevented him. It was too late. He knew that what his father had said was in some ways momentous and Tom was angry with himself as he had absorbed it with only half his consciousness. The other half was occupied by someone else.

*

Tuesday, May 11th, 1993, 8.00 p.m As soon as Tom saw Louise waiting in the bar of the restaurant he knew something was pleasing her but his heart did not soar with warmth as it should have done. "Hallo, Mr Lawyer, have I got news for you."

"That's nice," he said tersely, forgetting to kiss her. He ordered a drink and asked for the menu, which he read in silence.

"Well, aren't you going to ask me what it is?"

"Sorry, I was miles away."

Louise moved close to him. "I can't believe how long it's taken to get hold of it – every door slammed shut the moment I started asking questions. I've had our stringers on it all over the world."

"Hold of what?" Tom could hear the irritability in his voice and saw the smile on Louise's face wane.

"No need to be like that!" He had taken all the fun out of her news and she continued in a matter-of-fact voice. "Varsity aircraft have been involved in at least five incidents when the cargo door of a P11 has sprung its closures. I've got chapter and verse."

"Any of them give way fully – any crashes?"

"No. Doesn't look like it."

"Doesn't take us any further forward then, does it?" Again his voice was unnecessarily sharp.

"Sorry I couldn't arrange for one of them to crash for you, Your Highness. Stupid of me but I thought it helped establish the first part of your proposition that the door might have sprung free."

"Yes, I suppose that's true."

"Oh thanks! I thought you'd also like to know that Varsity's supposed crash-free safety record isn't quite what they claim." Tom genuinely paid attention for the first time. "A plane went down near the Libyan coast four years ago. It was reported as being an Intercon aircraft but in fact it was on long-term charter to Varsity and was being crewed and operated by them at the time of the accident – or whatever it was."

"I remember that – wasn't it shot down or something?"

"Yes, it crashed in the sea outside Libyan airspace but the Libyans claim it was well inside when they fired on it. Said it had refused to acknowledge their radio requests to identify itself and because it was dark they couldn't visually ID it so they had no option but to shoot at it. The Yanks, of course, said it was an unprovoked attack on an aircraft in international airspace by an evil terrorist state run by a madman and immediately issued invitations to World War Three."

"Which one was true?"

"I've no idea! There was eventually some suggestion of navigational error."

"Not sure that helps us much either." Again it came out dismissively.

"Jesus, Tom. What's with you? I'm not running this bloody case, I'm just trying to provide you with information that might be useful. Do what you want with it but don't be so bloody ungrateful. It's quite obvious if an airline is so crap at fundamental maintenance and it can't keep its navigational equipment functioning properly, it doesn't say much for its standards generally, does it?"

"Is that what it came down to, poor maintenance?"

"I have no idea, no one probably has any idea, but it clouds the water somewhat, doesn't it, and I thought that's what you wanted. Sorry I wasted your time!"

Tom could see her annoyance was turning to anger – the first time he had seen her angry since their meeting in his office shortly after Flight 469 went down. He was genuinely sorry and tried to mollify her. "Sorry, you know I've just come from the cemetery – all that mournfulness has made me a bit touchy." He couldn't believe he was using that as an excuse and it felt disloyal to Caroline.

"Oh, really, Tom? Whatever's on your mind it's not that."

"No. Not just that. It's a combination of things – the Thornton trial ... you know...?

"No, I don't know."

Over dinner, Tom managed to placate her and all seemed fine until they ordered coffee. He knew he had been feeling nervous since he'd arrived. Louise broke the silence.

"You're feeling guilty about something. What is it?"

As soon as Louise put it into words, he knew that was precisely what he was feeling.

"Nothing," he lied, "absolutely nothing."

Louise scraped the last piece of cheese from her plate even though she didn't really want it. "Well, if I was prepared to give you the benefit of the doubt, I'm certainly not now. Something's been wrong all evening. What is it?"

"I'm just on edge. Sorry, Lou – it's the trial." His excuse may have been partly true but in truth, he did not know why he was feeling so shaky. It was only when the realisation dawned that he needed to tell Louise that Vicky was back on the scene, as they would meet in court, that reality hit and he was subsumed with embarrassment. His attempt at nonchalance failed dismally.

"You're not going to believe this but I've had a disaster client return to the fold. Vicky Denton has been ripped off by her fancy lawyer and she's asked me to represent her again."

Louise looked as though she had been slapped. "Oh, I believe it, Tom, make no bloody mistake, I believe it! And of course you've accepted her back and if you weren't a vegetarian no doubt you'd have killed the fatted calf as well." Louise rose from her seat and Tom could see tears welling up in her eyes.

"You're wrong, Louise, it's over. It's all over for me!"

"How come your words tell me one thing but your actions, your attitude, your body language, even your stupid bloody crooked, guilty grin, tell me something else entirely?" She threw her napkin down and hurried from the restaurant.

Monday, July 12th, 1993, 9.30 a.m. Tom defied anyone not to be intimidated by the Old Bailey. It wasn't a venue for judging life's minor indiscretions – it was the legal equivalent of grand opera even though the Thornton trial was in one of the smaller courts.

Tom could have sworn he'd told Vicky they would have to sit separately but if he had, she had obviously forgotten. "You mean you sit up near the front while I'm on the public benches at the back? Charming!"

All Vicky's old confidence seemed to be back in force. She had tackled the threat to her and Emma's life in the best way she could. In some sense she saw it as a defeat but in reality what she had decided to do was nothing more than a ploy. She had taken the precaution some months before of writing to every media outlet in the country informing them that she proposed to make no more individual statements about Varsity. It seemed a strange communication but the more perceptive journalists knew exactly what lay behind it – she was removing herself from the spotlight and hopefully from danger. It appeared as though she was throwing in her hand and Vicky knew the message would reach those with an interest in her. Her return to the Harrow Support Group showed that she hadn't given up but she was sensible enough, she claimed, only to engage in joint action from now on. Bridie had moved in with her and a careful security scheme had been worked out with other members of the group. Emma was also back home as Vicky had rationalised that they would find her, if they wanted to, wherever she went to live. She worked on the basis that Emma was only any good to them as a threat because to harm her would ensure that Vicky would never give up her battle. Tom hoped she was right.

Once he might have given in and gone on to the public benches with her but not now. "That's the way it is, I'm afraid. Perks of being a member of the club."

He took his seat in probably the most famous court in the world to witness a case of enormous public interest and, he suspected, of almost no consequence. The press bench was filling up but so far did not include Louise. She had refused to take his calls and he felt increasingly desperate to talk to her.

Of all the drama and tension-filled cases which must have enthralled that mahogany and stained-glass court over the years, the Thornton trial was not one of them. As it was about to get underway, Tom heard a noise behind him and turned to see Louise sliding on to the press bench, her timing making it impossible for him to go over to her. She avoided looking at him and Tom felt his heart lurch as the gravity of the situation struck him. He looked at the dark curly hair and desperately wanted her to focus those huge eyes on him, to acknowledge him, to smile at him. She did none of those things.

Thornton sat motionless in the dock in the old part of the building underneath the familiar cupola which bore the scales of justice. There was an abrupt knock on wood and the usher announced briefly, "All stand." The judge entered and took his seat upon a leather-bound, high-back chair. The court clerk sat below him with a row of robed and wigged barristers just to his right-hand side in the well of the court. Tom thought of Ailey and what her caustic reaction might be. "Would the defendant please stand." The clerk then read out the charge of manslaughter, to which Thornton quietly replied, "Not guilty."

The case against Thornton was technical and unexciting and required only a couple of hours of the prosecutor's time. It began with simple identification details by an air traffic controller and a fire officer, who confirmed the location of the ditched helicopter. A day later, the evidence against him was brought to a close and Tom knew that his original concerns about a cover-up were accurate. There had barely been mention of Flight 469 and the death of its passengers and not even a passing reference to deaths on the ground. A couple of expert witnesses had rattled through the functioning of diverse control systems, the different interpretation of their operations and a whole load of technical gobbledygook.

When the defence presented its case, the aim was obviously to portray Thornton as one of the country's unsung military heroes. Had he first fought in Borneo when, as a junior officer in the Fleet Air Arm, he had flown a Whirlwind helicopter? Yes, he had! And had he carried Royal Marines into mountainous jungle clearings so dangerous that it had been a 'volunteer-only' mission? Yes, he had, and yes, he had returned safely! Had he acted on his own initiative and landed ahead of a group of escaping terrorists and captured them single-handed? Yes, he had! And had he been awarded a Military Cross as a result? Yes, he had! And so it went on. Thornton had flown Sea Kings in the Falklands conflict and had again been decorated, after which he became a successful commercial helicopter pilot.

If Peter Thornton was to be found guilty of anything, it would attract no more than an extremely apologetic slap on the wrist.

On the third day of the trial they finally tackled the important issues. The real meaning of the charge against Thornton was that by allowing Lloyd to fly above the ceiling stipulated by Heathrow Control, he had jeopardised the life of other aircraft passengers. And it was to this that Tom's ATC tape was directly relevant and would have established Thornton's innocence beyond doubt. For the first time Tom had serious doubts about his non-disclosure.

Thornton's defence was simple. The essence of teaching someone to fly is to allow them to make mistakes – but mistakes which do not threaten safety. He had been instructing Lloyd to hold a constant heading on the journey home from Battersea heliport. The particular no-fly zone they had entered was there for precisely that type of occasion. He knew their position exactly, knew how far they had penetrated the zone and had not gone beyond the normal allowable tolerances.

As soon as he believed it was time to return to their course, he had attempted to take control and exit from the no-fly zone. At that point Lloyd had become abusive and had refused to cede control and in his professional judgement, it was more dangerous to fight for control of the aircraft than to continue on that course. As soon as he was able to retake control, which was very soon afterwards, he had done so and was almost back on course when he was struck by Flight 469.

Towards the end of the fourth day, after final speeches and a sympathetic summing-up by the judge, the jury went out and returned after a recess of only fifteen minutes with the verdict that everyone expected – not guilty. Tom gave a huge sigh of relief, which was quickly replaced by anger. He spoke with authority to the waiting press pack. "For the last year or more we've been saying that nothing could happen until this trial was over. Well, it is over so now it's time for action."

He'd wanted to say it to Louise but as on every other day of the trial she had left the court before him. He had regularly left messages for her, had written and had called round several times but she had not responded. In his heart Tom knew why. She was waiting not just for words of apology or explanation but a few simple words of commitment – one short sentence, exchanged between lovers since time immemorial. And he wanted to say it but didn't know if he could.

Vicky went her own way and when Tom reached his offices he sought out Mike to discuss the outcome of Thornton's trial. Mike barely looked up from what he was doing and spoke with his head down as though studiously studying the papers in front of him.

"I gather you had some last-minute wobbles."

Tom didn't bother to ask how he knew as the answer was obvious. "Yeah – an attack of conscience."

"But you ignored it, yeah?"

"Yes, I did." Tom sensed that Mike was unhappy as his voice seemed to issue through almost clenched teeth.

"Was that the brightest idea you've ever had?"

"Probably not, Mike, but on balance I think it was the right decision."

"I see. You've totally ignored your obligations as an officer of the court, if it comes out you've probably fucked any chances of getting an inquest and pissed all over your career, and from where I'm sitting, that don't seem like brilliant decision-making to me." Mike swung towards Tom and Tom could see anger in his face but more than that, he was hurt. "Why the fuck didn't you discuss it with me, Tom, or ain't it worthy of the office boy?"

Tom felt his face colour and anger surge through him – anger born of injustice. "Shut up, Mike, shut the fuck up… Don't you ever dare say anything like that to me again. Yes, I know I've put my career on the line and the reason I didn't discuss it with you is because I didn't want to screw up your future too. If the shit hits the fan you can honestly say you played no part in it. And that's the truth, whether you believe it or not." Tom watched some of the tension drain from Mike's face.

"Why? Why did you do it, Tom? Why did you put yourself in such a fuckin' stupid position?"

"Okay, let me ask you a question. Does this case stink of cover-up to you or not?"

Mike went silent for several seconds. "Yeah, of course it does, you know it does."

"So why did I do it? Because if we're both right and there is a cover-up then that tape would have given – whoever it is – the only trump card we've got, given them lots of time to rubbish it, to find an explanation for it, to emasculate it. As far as I'm concerned, I partly met my obligations on disclosure by offering it to Thornton's defence—"

"But they ain't the DPP..." Mike chipped in.

"I'm aware of that but Thornton's trial wasn't affected – not one bit. He was acquitted just as we knew he would be so no damage was done..."

"And you reckon that might go in your favour – if they try and crucify you."

"I don't know, maybe, but anyway, I'm not relying on that. If we can expose what really happened to Flight 469 – whatever the fuck it is – and we can expose the fact that there has been a cover-up, then I stand an outside chance of arguing that I had good reason for not disclosing the tape."

"No pressure then, mate?"

That evening, on the late news, it was announced that the SAAIU would be releasing its interim report the following day. It had already been printed and had been delayed to await the outcome of the Thornton trial.

Friday, July 18th, 1993 Tom was almost completely devoid of excitement when he opened his copy of the report and read the official interim version of the crash of Flight 469. There was no blame attached to anyone and the cause of the crash was stated as 'unknown', exactly as he had expected.

George Fraser raised his glass of gin and tonic. "Good health, Harry!" He had hardly had time to sip it when he saw Tom Harrison making his way across the clubhouse, weaving his way round the crowd of early evening drinkers.

"George!"

"Tom, my lad! Perfect timing, it's your father's round." Neither man got up from his bar stool.

"Not for me, thanks. Heard the news, George? Thornton trial – it's all over – not guilty."

"Bad form, Tom, old chap. No business allowed in the bar!"

His father literally wagged a finger at him.

"I thought you might like to see this – wouldn't want you to miss it." Tom handed him that day's copy of the *Evening Chronicle*. The headline read, *NOT GUILTY – BUT WHO WAS?* It was a strident call for a full inquest to be reconvened. Louise might not have been talking to him but she had certainly kept her part of the campaign strategy alive.

Tom watched George's mouth set as he glanced over the article. "Watson – local girl, isn't she? Might have had the decency to talk to me first."

"Quite a friend of yours, Tom!" His father's words were heavy with innuendo.

Tom ignored him. "What are your thoughts, George? It's all down to you. The whole of London's waiting to hear what you've got to say."

George called over to the bar. "Jenny, get the lad a drink, will you, there's a darling. Dry white." He turned to Tom. "That's right, isn't it?" Tom didn't bother to argue.

George waited for the drink but showed no inclination to respond. When he did it was with obvious irritation.

"You know I can't discuss this with you. If you want to talk about the inquest you must address me formally in court. And that's an end of the matter. What I will say, as your father's friend, is that two and a half years have gone by and memories fade quickly. I had a case this week – the mother couldn't even remember when she'd last seen her son. Three months, that was the best she could manage, sometime in a three-month period. It's impossible. Memories will have faded, Tom, take my word for it. And what will an inquest do? Drag it all up again, open the wounds. Stressful business, you know."

Tom knew he was pushing George but both men had drunk plenty and he reckoned George could take it. Anyway, it was worth a try. "It's the relatives who want it reopened."

George snorted. "What people want and what they need are very often different animals, aren't they, Harry?" He turned back to Tom. "Emotional havoc – that's what it'll wreak, emotional havoc. What do you think, Harry?"

"I think you've summed it up perfectly, George. But Tom

here's got a bit of a bee in his bonnet about it, haven't you, Tom? The only person I know who thinks inquests serve any purpose." He suddenly remembered he was talking to the coroner and gave a big whooping laugh. "Sorry, Georgie, no offence, old chap."

George chuckled with him.

Tom waited for the laughter to subside. "Come on, George, it's what local people want. The reason I came here is to tell you I'll be submitting a formal application for a reconvened, full inquest. I thought it might give you time to think about it."

George again ignored him, put his empty glass down and turned to Harry, "Are we playing a round or not?" Harry took the hint and got up. As the two men made their way across the clubhouse, George paused before turning to face Tom.

"I'll see you in court but I have to tell you, I'm disinclined to grant your application."

Tom watched them go out to the first tee and tried to control his exasperation. As they prepared to drive off, he lost the battle.

"Shoes, Tom, shoes," his father shouted as Tom joined them on the tee. "You must wear golfing shoes to come on the green."

Tom ignored him and spun George round by his shoulder so they were facing each other. "Listen to me, George. Five hundred and twenty-three people are dead. It's torn apart this city in a tidal wave of grief and pain and suffering. There are parents who've lost their entire family, there are children who still can't sleep at night and there are others who'll be having plastic surgery for years to come.

"A full inquest isn't going to reopen their wounds because their wounds have never healed. They've been prised apart every single day because no one will give them answers; no one listens to their calls for help; no one cares about them. Remember all those sad words when it happened, George? Remember them? Bullshit – pure bullshit and you're aligning yourself with the bullshitters – an airline that doesn't give a damn, a Government that wants to protect itself and now a coroner who thinks it's all too difficult or too expensive. We're dealing with negligence so huge it takes your breath away."

George began to fiddle with the driver he was holding and Tom snatched it out of his grasp and with a huge swing he sent it flying down the fairway.

"Listen to me! You've got the power to help these people begin their healing and if you don't use it they'll never forgive you – the people of London will never forgive you and I sure as fuck won't. I'll hound you out of office in disgrace and piss all over your reputation. That's a promise. Be brave for once in your life, George – justice is a concept not a sinecure."

Tom turned away, barely conscious of where he was walking.

"Get off the green, man. God almighty, don't you have any manners?" A tartan-clad golfer stood in front of him waving him to one side.

"Bollocks," was all Tom could think to say – and then kicked the man's golf ball as far as he could. He suddenly felt a little better.

Tuesday, July 27th, 1993 Ailey had continued to fly backwards and forwards across the Atlantic and Tom had received reports of regular sightings but he hadn't seen her for months. It was therefore something of a surprise when he found her waiting for him in reception at his office. There was no animosity in her smile when she saw him.

"Tom, I'd like to say you look good but truth to tell you look like shit." She hadn't changed.

He led her across the road to the cafe and bought coffees. By the time they were seated and stirring their cups, most of Tom's frustration had dissipated.

Ailey obviously had something to say and she started straight in. "What's happened about the inquest, I understand you're trying to get it reopened?"

Tom gave a hollow laugh. "I think I might have just blown it– it's not every day a lawyer tells a coroner that he's going to shaft his reputation. But, we'll just have to wait and see. I'll be making a formal application – probably next week."

"Well, you've got some good stuff, it should be interesting."

"That's if he'll let me use it. If he wants to be awkward he can make everyone stick to establishing the immediate cause of death and by immediate, I mean immediate. Was it trauma, asphyxiation or burning – and refuse to call witnesses who aren't pertinent to that."

"Jeez, your system sucks," Ailey sipped from her cup, "and so does your coffee. Well, if it does get off the ground, we've picked up some interesting material. You may not be able to use it at the inquest but it will sure come in handy at some time."

Tom couldn't help but signal his interest. He would have made a lousy poker player.

Ailey continued. "The one thing that's always bugged me about your soldier theory is that it could let Varsity off the hook as far as culpability goes. You can hear them now – *We chartered that plane in all good faith, we had no idea it was going to be used for military purposes, we would never have allowed explosives on board* ... and so on and so on *ad nauseam*. They'd point to the paperwork, which would sure as hell support them in every detail. That was a big problem." She took another sip of coffee, turned her nose up at it then looked straight at Tom. "But I think we've got them!"

Tom had lost interest in his coffee and Ailey became animated as she leant towards him and spoke quickly but confidentially. "Tom, this has cost us a fortune. We've had to grease every outstretched palm between here and Timbuktu, via Tripoli and Baghdad. We've bought, threatened, corrupted and entertained just about every guy in the Middle East who's entitled to wear a uniform, from car park attendants to death-dealing generals – plus a fair assortment of officials and government ministers as well. But we got it – in the end we got it! And what's more we can prove it.

"Do you remember four years ago, an airplane was shot down over Libya—"

"An Intercon plane on charter to Varsity –" Tom interrupted and the shock on Ailey's face was almost amusing – "something to do with poor navigational equipment."

Ailey rediscovered her enthusiasm. "Exactly, that's one of the stories that was doing the rounds. Bullshit! That aircraft flew a perfectly normal course until it got close to Libyan airspace and only then did it suddenly supposedly go off course. But it intruded on Libya's airspace in a very specific way – very specific. It followed the coastline exactly and it couldn't have been visual because it was dark. It was navigating it." Ailey paused, more for dramatic effect than anything.

"And?" Tom encouraged her.

"We can prove that sitting fifteen thousand feet above the Intercon flight and about twenty miles outside Libyan airspace was a military AWAC –" Tom looked uncomprehending – "an advance warning aircraft – one of those modified 747s with a huge great mushroom detector on its back. The Varsity plane was triggering the secret Libyan air defence radar posts into action; one after another all down the coast like a goddam pinball machine – ping, ping, ping. And the AWAC was quietly sitting up there charting them, every single one of them so they could later be taken out by strike aircraft if necessary.

"The Libyans knew exactly what was going on and would have shot the plane down immediately if it had been a military one. In the end they decided they had no option and took it out anyway, passengers and all. Do you see the importance of this, Tom?"

Tom shook his head in disbelief. "So, Varsity was prepared to gamble with the lives of innocent passengers for military purposes, relying on the Libyans wanting to avoid massive international condemnation. It put Libya in a no-win situation. If they did nothing they would give away the positions of their air defence system, enabling America to bomb the shit out of them at a later date with impunity. And if they did react, they'd face global condemnation. I suppose they figured it was worth it just to save some radar sites from being fingered."

"Yeah, exactly," Ailey said excitedly, shuffling forward on her chair, "but the real point is, Varsity can't claim ignorance when it comes to their aircraft being used by the military. Once something like that has happened, you make damn sure it never happens again – if you're innocent, that is. It's like being arraigned for receiving stolen goods. The first time you might put up a defence by saying, 'Hey, I had no idea, I believed the guy when he said it belonged to his mother.' But you can't do that a second time; the second time ignorance is no defence."

Tom mulled over the importance of what Ailey had said. Either Varsity carried out the operation willingly, in which case it placed them very close to the military, or someone had so much shit on them that they were essentially blackmailed into it.

"Did they jump or were they pushed?" Ailey, it seemed, had read his thoughts. "I can tell you, buddy, they jumped. Last year Varsity was exposed by a French journalist for breaking the sanctions blockade on Iraq – but it was all hushed up. We've established for sure that it wasn't the only occasion. In fact they'd been running regular flights into the country – not medicines and food for starving kids but engineering equipment, luxuries, even champagne."

To Tom, the two incidents seemed to contradict each other, the first placing them on the side of the military, the second placing them in direct conflict with it. "That doesn't make sense to me."

"It would if you understood the crappy politics of the Middle East." Her smile was close to patronising. "Why do you think the whole goddam world invaded Iraq a couple of years ago?"

Friday, September 10th, 1993 Tom finally gathered his strength and his wits together to face the support group. This proved onerous because the original impetus had waned and many had not appreciated the full significance of what had happened at the trial. Some had simply given up, some had been bought off, some had taken the Ailey route, others stayed with it out of courtesy to him and now only a very few nurtured the flame of hope. Tom found his feet and thoughts dragging themselves to the room in the pub where the meeting was due to take place. Given half a chance he felt confident he could get the show back on the road.

Sure enough, there were only a handful of people waiting and unlike the old days the meeting was surprisingly mute. There were just two questions asked by one relative from one of the few Jamaican families in Harrow who had never spoken before – Wesley Jordan. "If we go down the judicial review route, how much will it cost and how long will it take?" The answer said it all, so they chose the inquest.

*

Monday, January 10th, 1994, 9.30 a.m. Tom's bitter words to George Fraser came back to haunt him when he sat in the council chamber in the town hall surrounded by all the parties involved in the crash of Flight 469 and their representatives. He knew he was the only one who wanted a full inquest with a jury and alienating George Fraser, if that's what he had done, was not the most sensible action of his life, nor the most professional. But there wasn't much he could do about it now.

Because of his outburst on the golf course and the subsequent fear that the application might go pear-shaped, Tom had managed to restrict the number of people attending from the support group. In fact, Vicky and Bernard were the only ones present and he made no mention of his brush with George but suspected that most of them would have supported him had they known. The only other person to accompany them was Mike. His reinstatement was tenuous but Tom's view was that possession was nine tenths etc. etc... It had been the worst conflict ever between him and his father.

Harry had brought in Mark Ratcliffe on a short-term contract to complete the Wings work and Mike had tried, not too discreetly, to get him to look into the Varsity connection. Harry must have briefed Mark to expect something like it and he had immediately reported Mike's efforts to Harry. The outcome was inevitable.

After he had been given the news about Mike's dismissal, Tom had instantly crossed the road and stormed into his father's office. From the look on Harry's face he could see he was expected and Harry pre-empted Tom.

"It's no use looking like that, I've made my decision and it's the only possible decision I could have taken." Tom had decided on his tactics and allowed Harry his run. "It is a clear breach of the Law Society's Code of Conduct and we would all risk being struck off if I responded in any other way. I know you like the man, although God knows why, but this is a transgression I cannot ignore..."

"I told him to..." Tom spoke very quietly.

"I beg your pardon?"

"I told him to do it!"

His father was completely lost for words as the gravity of what Tom had said sank in. "I told him if he didn't try and point Mark Ratcliffe in the right direction I would sack him. He refused at first, said he didn't want to do it but I insisted. Mike's innocent, it's me who should be disciplined."

"You're lying!"

"No, I'm not. And I want you to withdraw the dismissal."

"I wouldn't dream of it."

"If you want to save my career and this practice from publicity that will destroy it, I recommend you think again. I've already advised Mike that if you insist on going ahead he should register a complaint for unfair dismissal with an industrial tribunal." Tom watched as the import of his words registered and then he produced the final blow. "And I've assured him I will act as his principal witness if he chooses to do so. He has said he will."

It took almost two hours to resolve the situation. Harry knew he was being shafted but had eventually clutched at the compromise rapidly cobbled together on the hoof by Tom. Mike would be given an official written warning, which would show Ratcliffe that something had been done about his complaint. A full inquiry would be held into Tom's actions immediately following his application for a full inquest or, if it was granted, after the inquest proper. Tom felt himself colour when he thought how Harry would have reacted if he had known about Tom's failure to disclose the tape. Such thoughts were best avoided.

It was all bullshit, they both knew it was bullshit, but any time lag would dull the raw nerves that currently jangled. Without debating it, they also both knew that the word 'inquiry' was a euphemism for confronting the long-avoided debate about their working relationship. In his heart, Tom knew that the father and son team that was Mappin, Jones and Harrison was near its end. Even more depressing was the fact that the one piece of information which could have nailed Varsity was out of his reach and was almost certainly going to remain there.

*

There was almost a weariness about the courtroom and again Tom cast his eyes over the numerous participants as they shuffled around from one conversation to another, the purpose of the Inquest subsumed in self-importance. He spotted the posturing Miles Beatty and could hear sounds emanating from his little mouth but could not identify their meaning.

George opened the hearing and straight away launched into a statement about his powers and obligations. Citing Section 16 (3) of the Coroners Act 1988, he made it clear that it was solely his discretion whether to resume an adjourned inquest! He'd only do so if there were 'sufficient cause to do so'. Tom was gripped by a cold reality – perhaps George wasn't even going to have an inquest, never mind a jury. Two thoughts occupied his mind – the end of his reputation and the end of his campaign.

"I need to hear representations from all of you on this point," continued George. "I already know what you all have to say about a jury, were I to hold an inquest. What you have to consider is whether there is presently any purpose until SAAIU has completed its investigations, which I understand is ongoing and which is bound to have a bearing on the key question in the inquest.

To no one's surprise, Tom was the only lawyer who had been pressing for a resumed inquest as well as a jury. So the focus of the whole chamber was on Tom. Their annoyance at his time-wasting was palpable.

"The public has been denied any investigation into the deaths caused by the crash of Flight 469. The inquest was adjourned for more than a year so that a criminal case could be heard against the pilot of the helicopter in the hope that it would provide answers. I attended that criminal trial and the dead of Harrow were not referred to once, not even a mention! There was no exploration into their deaths – neither the immediate causes nor the contributory factors. I believe there was never any intention to do so. It is clear that only a full and transparent inquest will uncover the truth and allay rumour and suspicion."

Tom knew that last phrase would ring many bells for George but he did not expect such an immediate response. "I'm inclined to agree with you, Mr Harrison. There is a measure of sense in what you propose."

There was tangible surprise from some at this unprecedented accord between George and Tom – and consternation from others.

George announced October 1st for the preliminary hearing to consider a resumed inquest before he realised he had not consulted any of the other parties. "Any objections, gentlemen?" – (even though one was a woman).

None was forthcoming.

Caffrey called, "Court Rise!"

CHAPTER TWENTY-FOUR

Monday, 22nd November, 2004, 3.30 pm. "I am William Bailey and this is *Tough Talk*," the interviewer said to camera before turning to face a different one. "Flight 469 crashed in Harrow on the Hill in 1990; very many died and the world hung its head in sorrow. There have been other, more terrible tragedies since then but this one simply won't disappear and the man who has made it his life's work to ensure it doesn't is solicitor Tom Harrison. Mr Harrison is the representative of an eponymous band of people who operate under the title Harrow Support Group and which, with him at its head, has been seeking an inquest into the disaster for almost longer than most of us can remember – and not very successfully I might add.

"It has all gone very quiet over the last ten years but prior to that Mr Harrison and his team were rarely out of the news. The last hurrah, as I remember, was a refusal by the then coroner, one George Fraser, to accede to his request for a full inquest. Is that correct, Mr Harrison?"

Throughout Bailey's meandering introduction Tom's mind had wandered elsewhere and he questioned why the hell he had agreed to the interview in the first place. It was when he found himself remembering a younger, more naïve Tom, on a chill December afternoon, cradling in his arms the incinerated schoolgirl Polly Bentham, that he knew the answer with clarity.

Tom replied with a 'yes' but before he could expand on it, Bailey interrupted him.

"Surely to God that was the time to throw in the towel, wasn't it?" Bailey lent back on his chair and extended his arms outwards as if in supplication.

"No it wasn't. My clients still had no answers and the SAAIU report into the crash was wholly inadequate ..."

"I see; always someone else at fault?" There was spite in Bailey's words.

"I don't need to defend myself but you're right, we didn't accept the Coroner's ruling and challenged it by filing an application for leave to seek a judicial review."

"And for those of us who live in a different world to you, in simple terms, what is a judicial review? Asking to have the High Court look at George Fraser's ruling to see if it stood up?"

"Correct, to see if it was judicially sound. We lodged the leave application in late 1995 but it was months before it was granted and then we had to wait a further twelve months, practically into 1997, before it was heard."

Bailey sounded almost interested as he responded. "I don't have any strong memories of that review – was there no publicity, simply done on a nod and a wink?"

"It got very little publicity, which is a shame because it was quite a dramatic three days."

"Who represented you?"

"It fell to me as I knew the case better than anyone."

Bailey shook his head. "High street solicitor, petty disputes, conveyancing, neighbour disputes – bit of a leap of faith, wasn't it?"

"Apparently not. Their Lordships found the trial of the helicopter pilot was an irrelevance as far as the crash of Flight 469 was concerned. They were satisfied that the evidence we unearthed was directly relevant to the causal chain and that the coroner had failed to take this into account. In fact no one had involved the families. On the basis of the Wednesbury principles, the case was remitted to the coroner with an order quashing his ruling and requiring him to reconsider resuming an inquest with a jury."

For the first time since the interview began, Bailey showed real interest. "The Wednesbury principles?"

"They apply in judicial reviews and are all about decisions having to be reasonable."

"That was 1997 and—"

"... there was a change in Government, when Tony Blair won

his landslide victory." Tom interrupted. "I think the Government were nervous that something might emerge from the inquest that would embarrass them – so they made sure it was delayed."

"But it is now 2004 and still no inquest – why not a private prosecution?"

"No inquest so no determination of the causes of death and without that, you can't prosecute."

Bailey again threw his arms out dramatically. "Dear Lord, why didn't you just accept a normal inquest? It would have all been over by now."

"Yes, it would, because we wouldn't have been able to ask any of the questions that needed to be answered nor present any of our damning evidence. It would have been a verdict of Accidental Death. I'm not going to allow multinational corporations to build their empires on the backs of incinerated school children!" Tom was surprised how anger still lay just below the surface even after all this time.

Bailey feigned disinterest. "We still have seven years to account for, Mr Harrison, seven years!"

"I guess the judicial review finding must have come as a shock to George Fraser because he was rushed to hospital with breathing difficulties and heart complications and was subsequently ordered to rest. So we were well into 1998 by the time George was back in charge."

"That's still six years ago – am I going crazy or have we stepped into a world of mad hatters and vengeful queens?"

Tom attempted a joke. "Vengeful queens are the one element this case has lacked so far, but I wouldn't rule it out for the future." At least Mike would like it, he thought.

"The truth is, George Fraser had far too much to deal with and an antiquated system with which to do it so I think he just tried to buy himself some time by setting a date ten months into the future."

Bailey mused momentarily. "If my maths is correct, that takes us into 1999. So there you were – nine years after the event, a coroner with a dodgy heart, no foot soldiers and a collection of very annoyed people. Well, we know it wasn't resolved to your satisfaction or we wouldn't be sitting here now, would we? So what went wrong this time?"

"Sadly, just two months before the inquest was due to be held, George Fraser died." Tom was surprised that he felt almost regretful about the old boy's passing.

Bailey's long, extended, "Ahhhhhhhhhh," had little to do with sympathy. "Back to the drawing board then? One assumes there are procedures in place for this kind of thing – after all, those enquiring into death are not immune from it themselves, are they?" He seemed quite pleased with his observation. "There must be deputies, associates, stand-ins or similar?"

"In this case the deputy wasn't considered experienced enough." This was all part of Tom's working life but sitting in a television studio, watching disbelief spread across the ample jaws of a professional cynic, he was becoming aware of how ridiculous it all sounded. "Please tell me what happened – I can hardly bear the suspense," Bailey implored.

"Well, finally, in 2000, the Lord Chancellor appointed a coroner who was –" Tom paused. The word he wanted to use was *sympathetic* but he searched for something more neutral – "accommodating!"

"You're saying he was on your side?" Bailey laced his words with synthetic incredulity.

"No, I'm saying he approached the whole inquest in a spirit of enquiry – he seemed to want to get at the truth."

"So where is he now?" Bailey bellowed. "Didn't produce an inquest, did he?"

Tom couldn't resist smiling as each step of the extraordinary process was unveiled. "He did try, I promise you. There were long delays while he tried to find a suitable venue but the only place big enough was Harrow Town Hall and it was undergoing repairs!" Again, Tom couldn't help but smile. "But there was something else…" Bailey raised an eyebrow. "It was decided that this inquest should use the very latest IT technology which would have to be installed and tested before it could be let loose on us. The timescale was – generous!!"

"Please, Mr Harrison, put us all out of our misery. What went wrong this time?"

"The coroner was moved to Hull!"

"Oh dear Lord," Bailey implored, jettisoning aggression in favour of bemusement. "Why, why, why, please tell us why? Did they offer ANY explanation for banishing the erstwhile coroner to the edge of the known universe?"

"Well, we were approaching 2001, the year of—"

"... 9/11!" Bailey boomed as though answering a quiz successfully.

"Precisely, AND the next general election!" Tom replied, now enjoying himself. "The re-elected Government did say that because of the inquest's importance, they were considering the unusual option of appointing a High Court judge, but they obviously had other priorities, like the so-called War on Terror."

Bailey studiously ignored the politics, asking, "So how did we get from there to where we are now?"

"There was another delay because of a shortage of suitably qualified judicial volunteers."

"How long a delay?" Bailey asked.

"Over two years!"

"So we're now into 2003 and still no coroner. Was this something personal against you, Mr Harrison, or is this how England's much-vaunted system of justice works when no one is watching?"

"Perhaps a little of both—"

With hands gesticulating, arms imploring and voice booming, Bailey cut across him. "In the name of common sense and sanity, why, why, why did you persevere? Why, Mr Harrison, why?"

"Since 2000 the law has changed because of the Human Rights Act..."

"No, no, no, not the EU riding to the rescue to the sound of the *Marseillaise* or *Deutschland über alles*??"

"'Fraid so! Once it was incorporated into our domestic law, it had a dramatic effect on the procedure at inquests. The whole concept of causation has been reinterpreted to accommodate the right to life provision under Article Two and establishes procedural safeguards for a full, independent and transparent investigation which should involve the family, ensures accountability and looks at causation in a broader context."

"Would it be too inconvenient to translate that into English so we can all understand?" Bailey asked with heavy sarcasm.

"We're now able to look beyond the simple cause of death – suffocation, drowning and so on – to look at what *led* to the suffocation or drowning."

Bailey responded. "So we are now where we are and you finally have a coroner – one Lady Helen Galsworthy – and you can now ask potentially embarrassing questions about why the aircraft was where it was and what caused it to crash?"

"Potentially but I've no doubt her Ladyship will have her own ideas of what's permissible and what isn't."

"I think that is more than enough for anyone of a normal constitution. The inquest opens in exactly three weeks so no doubt there are yet more episodes to come in this, the longest-running legal soap opera of all time. Mr Harrison, thank you."

Tom felt confident of his performance but was still wondering why the hell he'd agreed to the interview in the first place. He doubted it had done anything to reignite public interest, which was what he had hoped, but had instead confirmed people's cynicism.

"Ah well," he said to Bailey, as the studio filled with technicians. "Onwards and upwards." And felt utterly stupid for having done so.

CHAPTER TWENTY-FIVE

Monday, 22nd November, 8.45 a.m. The mood in the large but improvised courtroom was a world removed from the heady days of the past. It was muted, without enthusiasm, apprehensive and suffused with a sense of *here we go again*. Even Ailey, who had flown over from the States, was not her normal, ebullient self but Tom thought that might simply have been age, maturity. Her jokes were delivered without their usual bite.

"Has anyone been home since ten years ago, or whatever it was, or do you all live here?"

"Of course – another of our quaint customs. Don't tell me you came over here just for this, Ailey; your interest is long gone, along with most of my clients."

"Yeah, but didn't they do well? I couldn't see you go into battle without cheer-leading from the sidelines."

"Naah, Ailey, that's not you, there's nothing in it for you!" Tom said the words jokingly and without spite.

"Okay, I do have a case but... I timed my visit to coincide with your inquest. How do you think you'll do?"

"Well, I've lost most of my personal witnesses..." Ailey inclined her head as if to say *c'est la vie*. "But they all knew they'd have to sign a gagging clause. I've no complaints."

"So how will her Ladyship behave as coroner – make your life easier?"

"I somehow doubt it. And she's a deputy coroner," Tom said with a smile, knowing the effect it would have on Ailey.

"Deputy, deputy – why, what's wrong with her, she not paid her dues?"

"The guy who took over after the one after George is the

coroner but he is not up to the job, so she was appointed."

"And Mr Micawber is the coroner's officer – sorry, the deputy coroner's officer! You guys! Did you at least manage to raise anything new?"

"Not really. You remember the question of whether the cargo door had been modified or not?" Ailey nodded. "Well, with a bit of subterfuge, Mike discovered that all Varsity's servicing and modifications were carried out at Filton, in Bristol. He went up there and got an admission from a senior manager that the door hadn't been modified."

"Well, that's better than a poke in the eye!"

"But I can't use it, it's only verbal."

"Subpoena the guy!"

"We can't, this is an inquest not a trial. It's all down to the DC!"

Ailey deployed her usual line in incredulity. "Jesus, your system sucks!" As she was disappearing off into the growing crowd, she paused and in a voice raised above the noise said, "What happened to the specs?"

"Lasered them away," Tom smiled as he recognised the old voice – as though she had swallowed her words, driven them up an octave, shoved them through a nutmeg grater and then delivered them down her nose. And then she was gone.

He looked around the court and for the first time in his life was conscious of his mortality. Everyone whose face he recognised bore the marks of time. Creases had appeared where flesh had once been young and smooth, grey hairs had sprouted here and there; those who had been grey were now almost white and hairlines on many had raced backwards. But not his own, Tom was pleased to note.

Mike appeared out of the throng and Tom noticed for the first time, because of the time warp he momentarily inhabited, that his partner had also matured – mellowed, was perhaps a better description. His style was still as sharp as a razor but the gleam of mohair had given way to something less reflective, less eye-catching and his shoes looked capable of being walked in.

"Do you need me, squire? I was going to run through a few things with our witnesses."

"No, I'm fine. Had more preparation time than the second coming!" Again it reminded him that he was not the enthusiastic thirty-something anymore and he found a poignancy in the absence of many who had been there at the start. Bernard had taken his money and gone. Maurice Wreford had died many years ago, a sad and very lonely man. George was dead and so was his Tonto, Mack Caffrey. Maurice's parting was extremely sad but even the others, who he didn't particularly like, had been important players in events that had defined Tom's career – his life, even – and so their departure also carried with it sadness. Not least his father who, despite their many disagreements, was the last of his small family to die. Tom found himself an orphan at forty-five.

He had done everything he could and was not particularly thinking about the inquest, merely allowing a sense of calm to assert itself as he looked from face to face of those who surrounded him as they milled around in muted anticipation. It was like identifying milestones that charted a course through most of his adult life.

One of the most important was Vicky, who had just entered the court with her usual enthusiasm and spontaneous laughter, hugging people, kissing them, making them feel special. Her presence increased his introspection while at the same time dissolved the fourteen years that had passed into just a handful. She was the one person he had seen regularly over the intervening years. He felt little different to how he had felt when he first met her. Now, here he was, with middle age beckoning to him from over the horizon and he was still in awe of her. He had no regrets about his professional life, few doubts about his abilities as a solicitor but it was his private life that was chaotic, if he allowed himself to think about it – which was hardly ever. Procrastination had become a way of life.

Vicky saw him and came hurriedly over, beaming, arms open to hug him. "I just wanted to say – and I know I've told you this a hundred times – but whatever happens I think you're brilliant." Tom hugged back. "Just wanted to say break a leg," Vicky chirruped. "I'll see you later!"

"A one-off, that Vicky, isn't she?!" Mike said as he suddenly appeared alongside Tom. It wasn't the words he used but the way he spoke them – a shorthand reminder of the censure he'd regularly voiced over the years. Mike did not approve of Tom's affair with Vicky. Yes, she was a very different woman – harder, more self-protective, more complex than most. He knew it was a complexity formed by damage, a scarring that made her who she was – a woman who could never really trust anyone, for whom relationships had to be entirely on her terms, always holding back, never casually off guard, suspicious, cynical, doubting, disbelieving and of the overpowering belief that the only person she could truly trust was herself.

In the early years, he had tortured himself with self-doubt over her marriage. Whatever had existed between Vicky and David, Tom was certain he had never been able to replicate it and that had made him feel inadequate. He was convinced he had failed miserably to find that special something which Vicky needed and which her husband had provided. In truth, he had become tired of looking.

Mike had painted a scenario for him which, he claimed, was the true test of love. *Imagine*, he'd said, *you're on a two-week holiday in the Welsh mountains in a caravan but you're broke and the wind and rain never stop. Would your relationship stand the test?* Tom knew that the answer in Vicky's case was an absolute no. Death was the most likely outcome.

As Tom continued to scan the faces he was surprised and delighted to see one he had once known so well. Sitting on the edge of the crowd, the place where she always seemed to be, was Esther Vine. She had shrunk into a little shell of her former self and her wheelchair seemed almost to engulf her as though it was part of her. When she spoke her voice was frail with age. "Mr Solicitor – you're nothing if not persistent!"

"It's been a long, long time, Esther! It's lovely to see you. How are you? You've never responded to our letters – I thought..."

"No, not yet – there's a week or two left in me but God knows why." She looked at Tom suspiciously. "And I'm only here to look, to watch, to listen, so don't get any ideas."

"No, Esther, I wouldn't dare! I'm sure I asked you this question many years ago but what do you hope to discover? Anyhing?"

"No, nothing, Mr Solicitor, I made all my discoveries a long time ago. For this ... thing ... I thought I am either with you or I'm against you and I decided it was better I am with you."

The first glaring reminder of how much things had changed had been the airport-type security scanner Tom had been ushered through as he entered the building. As he took his place in the courtroom it was a different world to the earlier hearings – a world full of high-tech equipment. TV screens adorned the walls and would display the rolling transcript of proceedings for the benefit of the jury, relatives and the public; benches were no longer cluttered with files and legal tomes but wires proliferated to the laptops in front of every lawyer and journalist; even the coroner had her own designated screens. The result was a constant buzz of machines and the tapping of keyboards. The documentation called up by the lawyers was found by a specialist court technician and displayed on separate screens for witnesses and the rest. Most cross-examined via laptops but some, like Tom, still preferred to work from paper. The personnel had changed just as dramatically with many more women advocates and black ones too, younger and probably tougher, he guessed. The genteel air of previous centuries had been almost entirely erased.

"Be upstanding!" The voice of the coroner's clerk filled the court – a female voice, a comparatively young voice. It was followed by Lady Helen Galsworthy's entrance. No wig but a stylish head of well-coiffured blonde hair and a smart designer suit in place of the traditional gown. This was Tom's second encounter with the formidable lady and he hoped it would be the last.

A large number of potential jury members filed into court and the tedious selection process began which Tom could only watch as he had no right to challenge. The coroner asked each one if they had any connections with the disaster and some were excused on the grounds they knew people who had died and others because they had been working in the emergency services and so on. In the end, an eleven-strong jury comprised a mixture of men and women, some middle-aged or older, with one Asian man and a couple of what looked like students and a youngish professional-looking black woman.

Formalities and jury-swearing were completed and the coroner spelt out to the jury the meaning of an inquest, the fact that it was not a trial and that she was responsible for deciding on all witnesses and advising the jury on legal matters, including their narrative verdicts. She went on to explain that because the day-to-day running of such a vast inquest involved a large amount of data and many witnesses, she was to be represented in the court by a team of solicitors and barristers, led by Mr Robert Hopkirk QC.

Tom had already briefed his clients that it was the QC who would call witnesses relevant to the crash itself – eye-witnesses, police, ambulance personnel, medical witnesses and so on – and would question them. After their evidence in chief, Tom would be allowed to cross-examine them. He had supplied a list of his own witnesses to the coroner and Hopkirk would call them and follow this same procedure, providing the coroner thought their statements were relevant. There were many relatives who were not represented by Tom but the procedure would be the same.

There was a potential problem over relatives who had died subsequent to the crash as agreement was required for their statements to be read out. Tom had been determined that Maurice Wreford's statement should be one of those and had extracted such an agreement from the coroner and, unusually, had been granted the right to read it himself rather than by Hopkirk. He knew the QC's delivery would be stripped of all passion. There was no gamesmanship involved but Tom was adamant that the jury should gain at least a small sense of the despair and agony that had driven Maurice when he had made it.

Tom rose and suddenly felt an onerous need to be truthful to Maurice. "'My name is Maurice Wreford and at the Harrow Morgue I identified all the members of my family who died on that day. They included my wife, my daughter, my son, my daughter-in-law, my son-in-law and my three grandchildren.'" Tom read each of the eight names carefully and with as much reverence as he could muster before continuing with the rest of Maurice's statement.

"'It was a birthday, a family get-together, and we had run out of ice cream. Beatrice thought we had some in the chest freezer in the shed so I searched for it but couldn't find any.'" Tom remembered clearly when he had taken the statement from Maurice how, the moment he had begun to speak he had left the confines of Tom's office and was back in his old house, treading carefully through his memories. "'In some ways it was better because I went to each of the children, asking them which flavour they would like. That way I could buy exactly what they wanted.

"'Actually, I forgot to write it down and when I got to the shop I let someone else go ahead of me while I tried to remember, and then I heard this noise – a dreadful, dreadful noise and the funny thing is I knew immediately what it was. I knew it was an aircraft crashing – it couldn't be anything else.'"

Lady Galsworthy sounded almost brutal in the way she cut across Maurice's words. "I think I should point out to the jury that the location to which we are referring is this point here." She pointed to a model of the crash site with a polished wooden rod. "I'm sorry, Mr Harrison, please carry on."

Tom was irritated and tried again to reach for sympathy. "'It all happened so quickly but I started to hear other noises over the engines – crashing, crunching noises which seemed to get louder and then there was this dreadful, deafening crump and the whole shop shook and trembled. I watched as tins fell off the shelves. I knew what it was but I didn't move. Just for a fraction of second – it couldn't have been more than that – everything seemed to go quiet and all I could hear was the sound of a car alarm wailing and I thought, *That's not going to do you much good.*'"

When Tom had taken the statement he had written it almost exactly as Maurice had spoken and had made no attempt to edit out the digressions because they had been important to the old man.

"'Then there was a great whooshing sound and everything lit up. I knew an aircraft had crashed and I knew it had burst into flames and I was paralysed.'"

Tom was no longer addressing the words to a coroner but was himself elsewhere, outside the courtroom, with the stench of fire and burnt flesh in his nostrils. He was oblivious to the dozens of faces which were turned towards him, oblivious to the silence into which his words fell.

"'I tried to run back to my house but my tired old legs wouldn't carry me and my lungs ached and I could only walk. I wanted to run, to fly, to speed like a young man and I could barely walk. It seemed the faster I tried to go, the more my chest hurt and the heavier my legs felt.

"'The sky was ablaze – for as far as I could see, it seemed. And I knew my house was somewhere under it, beneath that roaring, crackling, raging inferno with its great, hungry fingers of red and black flame leaping up into the night sky. But I tried to pretend that it might have missed us and even if it hadn't, everyone might have got out, they might be safe. But they weren't, they'd all gone, all of them, every one crushed and burnt.'"

Tom was unaware but his voice had ceased to sound like that of a solicitor reading someone else's words and had dropped to little more than a loud whisper. Absolute silence reigned in the court as everyone strained to hear what he said.

"'I reached the flames and I tried to keep walking, tried to find a way round them but a man, I didn't know who he was, took hold of me and kept saying, "You can't go in there, mate, you can't go in there." I said 'Please let me go,' and I kept on saying it, on and on until he did let me go.

"'I went back towards the blaze and all I wanted was to see my family, my wife, my children, my grandchildren, I wanted to be with them. I wanted to walk through the flames, I didn't care what happened to me but before I got anywhere near the house the heat began to burn me and I stopped...'"

Tom paused, just as Maurice had done when his speech was interrupted by racking sobs. Tom raised his eyes and looked around the court. Everyone present could read in them the same emotional horror that had been in Maurice Wreford's eyes.

"'I wanted to go on and I couldn't. I tried once more and the heat took my breath from me and I turned back again. I should have been with them and I wasn't; I couldn't do it, I wasn't brave enough, I failed them, I failed my family.'"

Again Tom paused, looked up and continued but without reading from the statement, letting the pages hang by his side.

"'I was a coward. I was nothing but a damned coward. They died and I lived because I was afraid of the flames. I was nothing but a coward.'"

Tom seemed to hold his breath but finally continued. "'It was a very, very long time before the ambulances arrived—"

Lady Helen interrupted. "Mr Harrison, I would be obliged if you would confine yourself to the immediate causes of death, as agreed."

Tom's heart sank – a brand-new coroner, a brand-new European ruling but the same old obduracy. He decided to let it go for the moment. Was she going to attempt to restrict the inquest to the most basic enquiries, ones which would allow Tom no scope to explore the wider issues? It was probably too soon to confront her.

"Mr Wreford wanted to say one last thing to the court. 'I have been a law-abiding man all my life and I have tried to be a good citizen. In the last few years I have witnessed so many cheap, tawdry, unprincipled things that I am ashamed of my country. You are our last hope. Please don't let us down.'

"This statement was made eight years ago." Tom sat down.

Vicky was next to take to the witness box and answered Robert Hopkirk QC's questions in a clear, level voice. His questioning was confined to identification and, bizarrely, the state of David's health prior to his death. None of the other legal representatives took the opportunity to question her and so Tom stood and began to pose questions about David's rescue and the time taken before he received treatment. As Vicky began to talk about the cuts to services and the inadequacies this produced, there was no hesitation from Lady Helen and she intervened.

"I'm afraid this isn't relevant to the purpose of this inquest, Mr Harrison. It may well be that everything Mrs Denton says is accurate but it falls outside the remit of an inquest."

Tom saw the change in Vicky's stance, saw her tense involuntarily and watched as the upper part of her body moved almost imperceptibly forward to do battle and she was still angry after all these years. Before he could stop her, she had turned it into bitter, abrasive words.

"I am talking about how David died. Isn't that why we are here? If the emergency services hadn't been so emasculated, David wouldn't have died. There wouldn't even have been an inquest into his death." She leant even closer towards the coroner, reducing the gap between them. "Are you telling me that's immaterial?

'Your husband dies because of incompetent and cynical policymaking, Mrs Denton, but that can't form part of an inquiry into his death!' Is that what you're telling me?" Vicky's voice was strident and other, equally angry, voices called out from the body of the chamber in support. It was exactly the spark that Tom wanted but Lady Helen appeared unmoved by the outburst and did not respond immediately, as though deciding how best to deal with it.

Tom leapt to his feet and filled the gap as Vicky stared at the coroner, waiting for a response. "This is a matter of enormous public interest and you, M'Lady, have the power to make recommendations with regard to public safety. I would implore you to use that power and allow me to ask the relevant questions. May I remind you that we obtained a ruling that this was a new inquest and therefore comes under the European Convention on Human Rights and as such extends the ambit of causation, and allows the jury to bring in a narrative verdict. To do that it needs to hear all circumstances that bear upon the death of those who are the subject of this inquest, and therefore lack of emergency care must be part of the chain of causation."

It was a confrontation Tom had hoped to avoid but had suspected it would happen. In the end, no matter how persuasive he was, Tom knew the decision would be Lady Helen's. If she decided to keep the lid on this inquest there was nothing anyone could do about it. The prospect was appalling but Tom believed he could see doubt in her eyes and it was important he gave her a way out.

"Please, M'Lady, could I refer you to page 404 of the Coroners Act, Section eight, subsection three..." As he spoke, Tom metaphorically had one eye on the jury and one on the press benches. Angry calls from the public continued and they were exactly what he wanted as they provided Lady Helen with the reminder she needed – that she was teetering on a very insecure tightrope of credibility. He realised this was probably the most important submission he had ever made and if it was denied, the inquest was in danger of turning into a shambles. He kept from his voice all trace of the desperation he was feeling.

"It begins with the following words, 'If it appears to a coroner there is reason to suspect –' and if I could draw your attention to pages 177 and 178, M'Lady, there is a commentary on that phrase…" Tom paused while Lady Helen reached for her copy of the Act and turned to the relevant pages before continuing. "… If there is reason to suspect – in other words, if there is information apparent to you at this stage, which there is – indicating that the circumstances surrounding this death could be prejudicial to the health of the public, or a section thereof, then you have the power to cast your enquiries much wider than the immediate cause of death…"

Varsity was again represented by an ageing Miles Beatty QC and he was quickly on his feet. Tom conceded and sat down. He guessed Beatty was as ignorant of inquest procedure as he had once been but the man was astute enough to know that if Tom won this general point, it would make life very difficult for Varsity later in the inquest.

"We are dealing here with speculation, nothing more, nothing less." His voice had become deeper, even more ponderous and superior over the years. "There is no firm evidence to suggest, none at all, that these deaths were caused by anything other than an accident. And I suggest to you, M'Lady, that had this accident taken place in any city anywhere in the world, their emergency services would have been overwhelmed. There are many people present here today, all involved in this inquest in one way or another, and this political witch-hunt which has persisted for more than a decade, has nothing to do with them – nothing whatsoever. I submit that this is entirely the wrong forum for such a broad-ranging review of social policy."

Lady Helen turned to Tom but before she could invite him to

respond, Tom was on his feet. "I will repeat, M'Lady, if it appears to a coroner there is reason to suspect that the circumstances surrounding a death could be prejudicial to the health of the public, or a section thereof, then you do have the power to seek wider information. Quite clearly, inadequate local emergency services are prejudicial to a section of the community, namely those who live in Harrow. And as for my friend's caution that there is no firm evidence to support such a contention, may I point out that the Act specifically states – " Tom read from the Act – "'Where there is reason to suspect' – it does not require evidence, simply suspicion." Tom looked around the chamber. "And there is an abundance of that.

"My client has amassed a great deal of evidence to show that the failure of the emergency services contributed to her husband's death. And there are many other experiences like hers – fire engines that stood idly by waiting for instructions, ambulances turned away from hospitals, superficially injured people being given preference over those with life-threatening injuries. All this quite clearly has great relevance to the health of a section of the public. The submission I am making is on the regulations set out in the Coroners Act prior to the adoption of the ECHR and its much wider obligations."

Tom waited as Lady Helen silently read the section and he reminded himself that although a high-ranking High Court judge, she was not an experienced coroner and he almost certainly knew more about the procedures than she did. On the other hand, he hoped he had not rubbed her nose in it because whatever the law said, that way lay defeat.

She seemed to reread the passage several times before looking up. Eventually she spoke. "Very well, Mr Harrison, but please keep it brief. I will be listening carefully and if I believe you are straining the patience of this court I will stop you. Do you understand that?"

Tom could feel the tension draining away. "I understand perfectly, M'Lady!" It was half a victory and Tom suspected she would allow him latitude in this instance but not necessarily in the future.

It was at that point, that Tom noticed a figure on the press benches – Louise – and curbed the desire to shout across the court to her. He turned back to Vicky and the irony of the situation did not escape him. He led her through the failures that had resulted in David's death without further interruption from the coroner.

One by one, the bereaved took the witness box over the following weeks and the same themes kept recurring – slow ambulance response, too few of them, too few hospital beds, too few trained trauma specialists, poor organisation and obstructive military and police personnel. Although Lady Helen tried to hurry things along, the testimonies were delivered.

Esther Vine turned up every day, sat in her wheelchair but neither Bridie nor Sheila was alongside her and Tom suspected that the woman with her was a carer and Esther was probably now in a care home. Tom made a point of looking at the press benches every day in the hope that Louise would acknowledge him but she never did. He noticed that on some days she did not complete a full day in court, leaving at around 3.00 p.m. and he guessed she was collecting children from school. When the coroner adjourned court at lunchtime one day, Tom positioned himself outside the court exit and waited for Louise. He was surprised to find his heart was pounding and he was breathing shallowly. She didn't see him immediately and turned to walk away but he quickly caught up with her, walking alongside. "Hello, stranger!"

"Tom, hello. Impressive performance."

"It's been a long time," Tom replied.

"Certainly has. How are you?"

The pleasantries continued for a while and Tom could feel slight panic as Louise had not slowed her walk, had not turned to face him, had not said how pleased she was to see him, and he could feel the opportunity disappearing with her rapidly moving heels. He hadn't known what to expect, how she might react but everything about her response was politely bland, as if he was a distant neighbour.

"Blimey, I can't keep up with you. Tell you what; let's have a coffee – if you've got time, of course."

Louise looked at her watch and then hesitated before replying without any real enthusiasm. "Okay, but a quick one."

They found a cafe and sat down with their coffees and Tom sensed there would be few questions from Louise and so he chit-chatted away, asking her this and that. Yes, she was back with the *Chronicle* on the news desk as a part-timer but was hoping to go full-time soon. She had two kids, which Tom knew anyway, and her husband was on the international desk for CNN in Paris. There was something about the way she said it that made Tom suspect everything was not running smoothly.

"That must be a bit difficult," he offered, hoping to hear more.

"Well, that seems to be my lot, doesn't it? Difficult relationships." For the first time she looked Tom directly in the eyes and the words were said forcefully. Tom knew they were not directed solely at her husband and was shocked that such depth of feeling should still exist after all this time.

He did not reply immediately but a sense of loss washed over him. Gone was her lovely sparkle, gone was her enthusiasm but most of all, he had not once heard the light, infectious, beautiful laugh that had replayed in his mind every time he had thought of her over the years. Something had been stripped from her and he had helped to erase it. He had no response.

Louise eventually filled the silence. "I was sorry to hear about your dad's death."

"Yeah. I'm glad he opened up to me before he went. It sort of transformed how I saw him. I was able to grieve properly. In fact it was the day ... we last went out..." Tom felt guilty resurrecting the memory. Louise did not react immediately but when she did, she again looked directly into his eyes.

"But it wasn't that which caused the problem, was it...?" Again he was silent. "Has anything changed, Tom?"

Words would not come and when they did he was surprised by their import. "Since I stopped seeing you my professional life has been pretty good – successful. My private life has been ... confused; Mike thinks it's a mess."

"You're not blaming me, are you?"

"Of course not, I'm totally to blame."

"You should listen to Mike more often! You're a lovely

man, Tom, but you're like a little boy in a sweetie shop, not knowing which one of the goodies to grab. I'm not sure you'll ever change."

Again it was there, that same old criticism. "I know it's time I got myself sorted out. He paused. "Just sitting here with you drinking a cup of coffee has made me happier than I've felt for … I dunno, probably years. I was trembling when I was waiting outside the court for you. Please can we do it again?"

Louise smiled at him with what appeared to be as much disbelief as warmth. "I'm not the same woman, Tom. I've changed but I'm not sure you have. I've gotta go." She gathered her bag and moved towards the door but turned before exiting. "See you, Tom!" He grabbed hold of that simple phrase and tucked it safely away to be recalled later.

The process of giving evidence by the bereaved was something of a catharsis for them but by the eighth week, Lady Helen had clearly heard enough. "I don't propose to call any more relatives but I do have their statements and I will read them."

Tom rose. "I realise this is a lengthy process but it is a vitally important one and I would request that you call all the relatives." From the corner of his eye he detected movement and in the now silent courtroom Esther Vine's wheelchair moved slowly forward towards the coroner's dais. A little husk of an old lady looked up at the coroner.

"Please, I would like to say something."

Tom could see the exasperation on Lady Helen's face. "I should have said, just one more witness, M'Lady. Mrs Esther Vine, mother of Rachel Vine. She is the last I would like you to call." He implored her with his eyes.

"Very well but Mrs Vine will be the last."

Lady Helen led her through the process of identification and finally handed over to Tom. Esther did not wait for him to question her.

"I don't want to take up your time, M'lady. You have listened to many people and you have seen many tears – more misery than is good for anyone. I just want to mark my Rachel's passing. She was no Einstein – far from it – but she must be remembered. I've kept my sorrow to myself for fourteen years and every single day, I have asked myself why. Until today I had no answer. Maybe I still don't have answers but I feel much closer to them.

"I have listened to so many people whose hearts, like mine, are breaking but through their pain I have seen pride – pride in the ones they lost. My Rachel blessed my life for thirty-two years. She gave love unconditionally and without limit. Her life overflowed with happiness and because of that, so did mine. The ending of her life stripped mine of its meaning. This is all that's left – what you see here in this chariot of inability: a filleted, gutted, empty old woman who no longer even functions properly.

"Am I proud of my Rachel? For sure I am, even though for thirty-two years I was made to feel ashamed. My Rachel was what they now call Downs Syndrome. Now someone has taken her – no, no, I must be honest, they have killed her. They must answer for that. If accident it was, I will forgive it. But nothing else will I forgive."

Esther swept her arm to encompass the rows of other silent seated people. "We will not allow you to build your empires with the bricks of our sorrow."

Without waiting to be questioned, she slowly propelled her wheelchair backwards to her position near the doors and unthinkingly took a cigarette from its packet and placed it in her mouth. Without a word, her carer wheeled her outside.

"We have heard at great length from the relatives of those who died and having established who died, we must now look at the causes of death. Many pathologists were involved and in most instances I believe it is sufficient to rely on their statements. I do, however, propose to call Sir Oswald Napier."

Hopkirk's questions were perfunctory and there was nothing particularly profound unearthed by the other lawyers who took it in turns to question him. But what alarmed Tom was Napier's apparent desire to be compliant, to readily agree with the propositions they put to him, propositions that tore the legs off his original position. As so often happened with experts, their forthright views offered in private frequently became generalised and stripped of certainty when in the witness box. He was almost in danger of becoming a hostile witness and Tom was angry.

He began carefully, gently, taking Sir Oswald through his findings. When he reached the section which said that the skin of Mr Baker, the deceased, had been thoroughly cleaned, he could see he was embarrassing the man.

"Are you saying that Mr Baker's skin could have been purposely cleaned of explosive traces?"

"I didn't say that."

"No, I'm aware of that. What I asked was, could it have been purposely cleaned?"

"That is a possibility."

"Other parts of the body were not so thoroughly cleaned?"

"That is correct."

"Who could have been responsible?" Sir Oswald was the first witness to begin the process of discovery and Tom banked on Lady Helen not wanting another confrontation at this point so he pushed for answers.

Napier looked irritated. "I can't possibly say."

"Who performed that post-mortem?"

"I'm afraid I can't remember his name."

"But it was a Home Office pathologist?"

"Yes, I believe it was."

"Someone who is not here today because he claims to be ill. Is that correct?" He didn't need a reply – he had sown the seeds he wanted. "Sir Oswald, what do you believe could have caused the pattern of wounds on Mr Baker's back?"

Sir Oswald paused before answering as though considering the facts. "It's possible it could have been caused by an explosion of some kind."

"An explosion of some kind? What kind, Sir Oswald? An explosive device perhaps?"

"That is a possibility."

"It's a bit more than a possibility according to your statement, isn't it? In fact it's a probability, isn't it?"

"It could have been an explosive device."

"An explosive device?" Tom said the words slowly and carefully. He could sense that Beatty was desperate to interrupt but couldn't as he knew the questioning was relevant. "A hand grenade, for instance?"

"Possibly."

"Possibly or, as you put in writing, probably?"

"It certainly could have been a hand grenade." Napier said the words reluctantly.

Tom sat down and waited for Beatty to question his witness. "Sir Oswald. Could the wounds on Mr Baker's body have been caused by something other than an explosive device, something other than a hand grenade? Considering you have offered no conclusive proof of either, I would ask you to deliberate very carefully before answering."

Napier did precisely that. "It is conceivable they could have been; there are few certainties when dealing with—"

Beatty cut him off. "Could the cause have been something else? Please answer me with a simple yes or no."

"Yes, I suppose it could but in my opinion it is unlikely."

"And did your examination reveal whether this device which caused the injuries – this device which could have been something other than an explosive device – did it reveal whether it had anything whatsoever to do with aircraft?"

"No."

"So it could have been something already in the house, perhaps something normally quite innocuous but transformed into something deadly by the unique circumstances of an air crash?"

Napier paused. "Well, I'm not certain about that..."

"I didn't ask you for certainties, Sir Oswald, I asked you if it could have been?"

"It's conceivable but personally, I haven't come across many exploding waffle irons or chestnut roasters." At last, the neat and ageing scientist had hit back.

"Thank you, Sir Oswald." Beatty sat down.

After the pathologists, Lady Helen called the public service representatives – fire, police and ambulance – and Tom questioned each one, feeling certain he had made out a convincing case for criminal negligence. In reality, because of the way in which budgets were controlled, the responsibility would ultimately fall on local government, which seemed grossly unfair as they had been the people shouting most loudly about the cuts.

As week followed week, the amount of preparation needed reduced so Tom and Mike increasingly found time in the evening to have a drink together.

"I had a coffee with Louise a few days ago," Tom said, almost guiltily.

"I know you did. Why wait till now to tell me?"

"Didn't occur to me... Anyway, how do you know?"

"I had a drink with her myself a couple of days ago."

"You didn't tell me!"

"You didn't tell me, either," Mike replied with a smile.

There was a long silence as each took a sip from his glass and Mike knew that Tom wanted to know more but for whatever reason wasn't asking.

"You screwed up big time there – you know that, don't you?" Mike eventually said.

"What? What do you mean?"

"You know exactly what I mean."

"That's all ancient history," Tom replied as he returned to his drink, considering it very thoughtfully before turning to face Mike once more. "What did she say?"

"Not a lot! How did you let it happen, Tom, how did you let her slip away? You know she was genuinely stuck on you."

"It just happened, Mike. Don't go on about it."

Tom didn't want him to, didn't need him to, because he was fully aware of the complications and failings of his life, his capricious emotions. The truth was, every time he had heard Louise's name mentioned over the intervening years, it was as though he had taken an instant tonic that produced a smile and he always wanted the conversation to linger a little longer than was probably appropriate.

There had been occasions in the distant past when he had surreptitiously hung around the *Chronicle*'s offices in the hope that he might bump into her but it had never happened. The times he had seen her were always unexpected, on the high street, at a party and twice when she had come into his offices in pursuit of a story. They were surprises that momentarily snatched his breath away. There had been a few occasions when he had arranged to see her to talk about aspects of the case where she might be able to offer some help but these were contrived.

He finally accepted that he had absolutely no right to emotionally hover over her like some proprietorial godfather once she had had her daughter, Maisie. He knew he could not continue flitting in and out of her life simply to remind himself of what might have been, because the few meetings between them had clearly had an impact on her too. He was messing with her peace of mind, disturbing her. Problem was, he could not resist exploring whether there were still a few glowing embers that might possibly be fanned back into life.

The reason he had eventually stopped trying to see her was Maisie. He had seen Louise with her in the street not long after her birth and had crossed to speak. The chat was short and strained and when he looked into her eyes there was nothing there for him. They were alive with love for her baby and there was no longer even a glimmer of interest for anything, anyone else. She had finally moved on and the realisation hurt him far more than he could ever have anticipated – and he didn't think it was simply ego.

"I might be wrong," Mike added, "but I'm sure I saw the faintest little glimmer of interest when your name was mentioned, although Christ knows why!"

When the former Varsity airline's operations manager, Patrick Kennedy, was eventually called to the stand, there was silence. Tom listened to the man's testimony with impatience as Hopkirk posed his questions. He found a note suddenly pushed into his hand by Mike. It simply said, *He is not the organ grinder he is the monkey, yes? You know what to do with his nuts. Esther.* Tom looked up to see her smiling brightly through yellow teeth, the first time he had seen her do so.

Kennedy outlined Flight 469's route to Nigeria and no

questions were put to him about the cargo doors nor what the aircraft might be carrying in the hold. Kennedy spoke with such apparent honesty that Tom believed he probably did not know anything. Finally the questioning got round to the events immediately prior to the collision with the helicopter.

"We've got no way of knowing exactly what happened. The black boxes were destroyed and so we have no record. Unfortunately, all crew members and passengers perished so we also have no witnesses either. Under these circumstances I expect it would be normal to rely on air traffic control's recordings but apparently there was a machine malfunction so that option is also denied us. As far as we know, there is nothing to suggest that anything other than the collision with the Bell Jet Ranger – Mr Lloyd's helicopter – caused Flight 469 to crash."

Hopkirk's handling of the witnesses was infuriating.

"Mr Harrison, is there anything you would like to ask Mr Kennedy?" the coroner enquired.

Tom rose to his feet. "Were the passengers on the aircraft truly oil field workers?"

"Mr Harrison, would you please confine yourself to relevant questions."

Tom's heart sank – so this was where Lady Helen was going to begin the obstruction.

"It is entirely relevant!" The words spat out of Tom's mouth. "To establish who died is part of the verdict the jury will be expected to return and in the context of this disaster, 'who' must include what they did for a living. I will show later that this is entirely relevant."

Without waiting for the objection to be resolved, Kennedy replied. "They were oil field workers." Tom was convinced that Kennedy believed that to be the case and let it ride.

"Why, Mr Kennedy, was the aircraft where it was when it collided with the helicopter—"

"Mr Harrison," again Lady Helen interrupted, her voice heavy with weariness, "the remit of this inquest, as you very well know, is to establish the cause of death. I must ask you to confine your questions to that and that alone. You may disregard the question, Mr Kennedy."

"My question is pertinent to establishing the cause of death. The reason why the aircraft was forced to return to Northolt—"

"I will say it again – it is irrelevant to the cause of death. Do you have any other questions?"

"Yes, I do. What was the aircraft carrying, Mr Kennedy, in the cargo hold—"

"Mr Harrison! I have been extremely lenient with you so far as it is not my intention to stifle this inquest but I will not allow this line of questioning. Do you understand?"

Tom could hear the angry and outraged voices of relatives beginning to swell again and particularly Vicky's. He knew if he confronted Lady Helen now there was likely to be pandemonium so he indicated to them to calm down and retook his seat. Kennedy left the stand and Leslie Betts, fire officer in charge of rescue operations, was called. He gave a long testimony as to the extent of the fire, its nature, building damage, water supply problems, the numbers of appliances involved and the condition of people who were rescued.

Tom stood before Lady Helen had even invited him to question the man. "Mr Betts, did you discover anything unusual at the scene?"

"Ignore the question, Mr Betts. Mr Harrison, I don't intend to keep telling you this but for the last time, will you please confine yourself to questions directly relevant to the causes of death?"

Tom turned away from the woman, fighting to control his temper. He faced her again. "If that aircraft was carrying explosives which caused it to crash, it's as relevant to the cause of a person's death as the particular brick which hit them or the fire which burned them. To say I can't look beyond the immediate cause is like saying that the victims of the Holocaust died from gas poisoning and it's irrelevant as to who put them in the gas chambers or why—"

"That is offensive and inappropriate, would you please sit down."

Tom remained standing. "As we have already established in the High Court, you have the power and the responsibility to look at the wider picture in terms of causation—"

"Mr Harrison, sit down."

Still he remained on his feet. "I believe I can show that Flight 469 crashed as the result of an explosion and I must be allowed to pursue that line of argument. In pursuit of that, I would like to submit this statement." He held it in the air. "It is the statement of Mr Barry Morris..." Tom had to shout to make himself heard above the growing noise in the chamber and Miles Beatty's objections.

"Just a moment, Mr Harrison." Lady Helen cut him off then looked down at her papers but Tom could tell she wasn't reading them – she was playing for time. She looked at her watch and eventually spoke. "As it is very nearly lunchtime, I'm going to adjourn proceedings. We will pursue this when we reconvene at two o'clock." With that she rose and left the court.

Over lunch, Tom was surrounded by relatives. Their voices merged into a jumble of angry questions. It was some time before he could make himself heard. "She's playing it by the letter. I thought we'd won this point earlier but obviously not. She's trying to stifle discovery and all I can do is try and shame or embarrass her into taking a broader view. Her Ladyship is entitled to do almost anything she wants but if explosives were the cause, she has no option but to let the question in. I've just got to keep plugging away at her."

When the court reconvened, Tom was on the edge of his seat, waiting, and as soon as Lady Helen took her place he was on his feet. "I would like to submit the statement of Mr Barry Morris, a radio ham at that time who recorded conversations between Flight 469 and Heathrow air traffic control."

She did not reply but glanced through the papers on her desk and so Tom continued, his tone becoming increasingly demanding. "This witness is absolutely central to the proceedings. He is a witness to the last conversation between the pilot of Flight 469 and the ground and as such is pertinent to the cause of death. These are the last words spoken by the aircraft's pilot before it crashed."

Because of her delay, the coroner had turned a simple request into a superb piece of drama and Tom could hear whispering everywhere and could see the frantic scribbling of shorthand reporting. Lady Helen looked increasingly uncomfortable and eventually spoke but quietly. "Very well, Mr Harrison."

"I'm sorry, M'Lady, I didn't quite catch what you said."

Lady Helen knew she was being baited. "I said let me have your statement and I will then decide whether to admit it or not. Why did you not submit it before?"

"It was purely out of concern for security, which you will understand once you've read it."

"Very well, I will read it now." The coroner's officer moved almost apologetically across the court, took the statement from Tom and handed it to Lady Helen, who adjusted her glasses and asked for patience.

Mike went in search of Barry Morris, who was waiting in an unmarked room on his own. Vicky approached Tom. "What's happening?"

"She's caught between a rock and a hard place. If she won't let me follow this line and we can show that explosives were involved, her decision can be judicially reviewed and she knows it."

Mike appeared with Barry Morris at the side of the court as the coroner looked in Tom's direction, peering over the top of her spectacles. "I haven't warned this witness that he may be called – what is his availability?"

"He has just entered the court, M'Lady!" Tom replied, trying to hide a smile.

"In that case I will call him."

Tom trod carefully. "Do you also intend to play the recording referred to in the statement – I believe all the necessary equipment is to hand?"

Miles Beatty rose. "I would like to object. My client has had no opportunity to see the statement and knows nothing of any recording—"

Tom didn't wait for Beatty to finish. "I, also, have not seen many statements, Varsity's included, despite having made many requests over a period of years. This is nothing more than a level playing field. Could I urge the court to allow the statement and the recording into evidence?"

The coroner looked at Tom. "I may be prepared to consider your request if you can give me your assurance that this is not just a fishing expedition."

"You have my assurance. I would now like to play the recording referred to in this statement."

"Very well." The coroner did not look happy.

By the time Mike had produced the player and positioned it carefully, the court was so silent that the only sound was an occasional stifled cough.

It was some time since Tom had listened to the recording and he had forgotten the appalling drama contained in it. Again, the dreadful conversation between a dying man and an impotent air traffic controller hissed and crackled out, far more riveting than any theatrical production. It finished playing and Tom switched it off. The almost total silence which followed continued for several seconds before a hiss of whispering erupted. The coroner cut it short by calling Barry Morris to the stand.

Tom took him through the technicalities of how and when he had made the recording and what equipment he had used. Morris answered as briefly as possible. When Tom had finished, Beatty took over and wrapped his questions in scathing disbelief, challenging Morris in any way he could.

"Why have you never supplied a copy of this recording to any Government agency – not to the Director of Public Prosecutions, not to the Department of Transport and not even to the SAAIU, charged with investigating the crash? Was that because you knew its authenticity could be challenged?"

"No, it was because I didn't trust them!" Morris was forthright, seemingly not in the least intimidated by either the circumstances or Beatty. He had aged well and looked comparatively smart.

"You didn't trust the Government? Well, I can understand why *you* might distrust authority but I'll come back to that later. You have produced a tape which we have no way of authenticating and we're expected to take your word for it?"

Tom rose. "I have not yet submitted it, but I do have supporting evidence in the form of a statement from an expert witness."

Lady Helen looked at him in exasperation and then at the Varsity QC. "Please continue." As Beatty turned again to Morris, Tom was handed another note by Mike. *What do you call Jewish penicillin? Chicken soup! Esther.* She was smiling at him once more and Tom found it hard not to laugh – not at her humour but her bizarre timing.

Beatty continued. "So, we have a recording which is many years old, which has never been submitted for analysis, which has not been authenticated in any way and we have only your claim that it is what it purports to be! Would that be a fair summary of the situation?"

"It's the last conversation of Flight 469." Morris's delivery allowed no room for doubt.

"Mr Morris, you have several criminal convictions, I believe. Perhaps you would like to tell the court what they are?"

Morris was completely unfazed and ran through a list of petty theft convictions, mostly taking electronic parts, and all many years ago. He topped it with an admission that he had also been convicted for non-payment of his poll tax. There was nothing apologetic in the way he spoke and he finished with a smile directly at Beatty. "I haven't got any convictions for lying, though."

Beatty ignored it. "With a record like yours, why should this court believe you?"

"Because I know my stuff, that's why."

"And what stuff is that?" The question was put with heavy emphasis on 'stuff'.

"Electronics and the like – I've got a BSc in radio engineering and a Master's in microwave communication. I'm also now a university lecturer in electronics." People didn't try to hide their laughter. Morris was asked no further questions.

Tom watched Barry Morris step down from the witness box and walk nonchalantly out through the court's doors and felt an overwhelming sense of anticlimax. This was the jewel in the crown, the revelation that he had nursed for more than a decade, for which he had put his career on the line, and it was all over comparatively quickly and the world just kept on turning. Sure there had been sounds of shock and awe from those in the chamber and he guessed that the revelation would receive splash headlines in almost every newspaper and top the running order for TV news but… There had to be more. There had to be a reaction.

He knew his feelings were merely his own peculiar reaction and there was still much to do. He turned back to the coroner. "It would be appropriate to call Mr Anthony Berrens, who has subjected this tape to scientific analysis and can reassure my learned friend as to its authenticity. He can also explain its relevance to the crash of Flight 469."

Beatty moved as though to object but Lady Helen waved him back into his seat. "I'm going to allow it, Mr Beatty, so reserve your energy. I suspect you will be needing it." And then in an aside which Tom could barely believe, she added, "I suspect we all are!"

With that, the coroner adjusted her spectacles and gathered gravitas round her like a cloak. "I am not at all happy with the direction in which this inquest is going – the direction in which you're pushing it, Mr Harrison. It is not a criminal investigation and neither is it a public inquiry, both of which would be more suitable forums for this kind of exploration. I'm not at all happy and I'm inclined to disallow your request. However, let me see his statement."

CHAPTER TWENTY-SIX

Again Tom had contrived to see Louise when the court adjourned and she had agreed, a little more enthusiastically this time. There was no brittleness and on two or three occasions he had heard the melodic laugh that was Louise. They had even ventured tentatively down the road of nostalgia with *Do you remember when...?*

He had cautiously introduced a question about her husband and the change in mood was instant. Louise's face hardened. "It seems to be my lot always to be the spare party in a *ménage a trois*, only this time it's not another woman but work and ambition. Determined to go places is Adam, even at the expense of his wife and children." She paused and sipped from her coffee. "Actually, that's not fair, Tom. I think the ambition is a product of other things being wrong and this way he doesn't have to face up to them, doesn't have to talk about them."

Almost without pausing she added, "Mike tells me you still see Vicky from time to time even after all these years." There was almost allegation in her voice and Tom was sure he could still detect an underlying trace of hurt, carried forward from the past. It was obvious that he and her husband had been jettisoned into the same recycle bin.

Tom wanted to reply *past tense* but it wasn't quite true and as he had made a promise to himself never again to deceive Louise or even to use partial truths, he let it pass and tried hard to return to less painful subjects but the mood never quite recovered and then his efforts were stopped short.

"What do you want from me, Tom? I'm married, I've got children. You can't talk as though none of these exist. I'm a different woman, we're both different – although on second thoughts I'm not sure that's true where you're concerned. What is it, Tom, what do you want?"

All he could say in response was, "I want to go on seeing you," and he was aware he had not given the answer she sought. But at least it was honest. The conversation got no further and after leaving Louise he went to his office and felt a surge of relief when he found Mike there, who clearly read his mood.

"Past six, mate – something about yardarms and all that. Come on, I'll buy you a drink," Mike offered in a way that assumed acceptance.

They closed up and wandered the few yards across the road to the pub opposite where they took seats on stools at the far side of the bar, looking back across the optics and glasses and out through the etched glass Victorian windows. The pub was busy with after-work drinkers.

Tom felt almost embarrassed to say it but he did. "I've just seen Louise again."

Mike didn't immediately reply but when he did, his voice was quiet and serious. "You ran one hell of a risk and you know what, it could still come back and bite you on the arse even after all this time."

"What, Louise?" But Tom knew precisely who and what he meant.

"The power of sex, Mr Harrison, the power of sex!"

"I doubt anyone would give a damn now but I couldn't have been more discreet, Mike, so bloody discreet that I felt like a married man having an affair, never letting dare slip who I was seeing, avoiding certain places, always pretending, always hiding."

He knew Mike was right. Sex had been the driving force between him and Vicky. It was passionate but always, at the back of Tom's mind, was his knowledge of Vicky's past. A combination of her unpredictability and fervour in bed had the effect of making Tom feel almost permanently insecure. Being with Vicky was like walking through quicksands, never knowing when stability would give way to danger and never being sure that she would extend a saving hand to help him from the quagmire.

The realisation came suddenly that whatever traits and attributes Vicky was searching for in this life, Tom did not possess them. The realisation didn't upset him.

"So what should I have done, Mr Smith?" In matters of law Tom was self-confident but in matters of life, he deferred to Mike.

"It's a bit bloody late to ask that, isn't it? How long have you been ... intimate ... with Vicky – ten years?"

"No, eight – seven – I don't remember; it was well after George died. It just happened, Mike – it just happened..." Tom's voice tailed off.

Mike took his time in responding. "Listen, my friend, you go through life and if you've got half a brain you pick up experiences along the way. If they're good ones you repeat them, if they're bad you avoid them. Don't get me wrong, I love Vicky, I think she's a great woman. I'm in awe of her but the combination of you two scares me – not for her sake but yours. In my honest opinion, you should never have gone there but having done so, you should never have gone back.

"Look at you, you sad, ageing bugger. You're forty five, you still live in that same shitty little flat, no kids, no regular girlfriend and, my old son, you're getting grumpier with each passing year because you're throwing yourself into work as a diversion and the more you do it, the more two-dimensional your life becomes. I don't think you're a very happy bunny because you have an addiction – actually, not so much an addiction but an obsession, and that's a very jealous emotion; it won't allow space for anyone else."

"Fuck me!" Tom pushed himself back on his stool. "You stop playing the field and pay your dues by getting married and having kids and just because you've done it, we're all supposed to do it." There was no real animosity in Tom's words.

"Yes, I did stop playing the field but not reluctantly, not just 'paying my dues' as you put it. I met someone I didn't want to lose, someone who meant something special to me, someone who was a bit – well, a bit *more*, if you know what I mean. I fell in ... well, I fell in love. See, it's a simple word to say. Demons don't appear out of the woodwork and tear pieces of flesh from your body with red-hot pincers. It's nice, Tom, very nice for however long it lasts and you've denied yourself that." His voice became suddenly serious. "You can't do to Louise what you did before. Stop seeing Vicky, she's not good for you!"

Tom knew without doubt that Mike was right because he had already made that decision. He felt Mike's arm across his shoulders and when he spoke it was warm and intimate. "Look at that, Tom, take a damned long look at it!" Mike was pointing out through the pub's window to something beyond.

"What – what am I supposed to be looking at?" Tom asked.

"The sign," replied Mike.

"What sign?"

"What sign? That sign – *Harrison and Smith, Solicitors*! Wouldn't be the same if it just said *Harrison, Solicitors*, would it? And as for *Smith, Solicitors*, well, just don't cut it, does it?"

Tom looked long and hard at the large letters opposite him which were already beginning to show the first signs of ageing and had no need to consider the question.

"No, Mike, it wouldn't be the same. One more before we go?"

Tom tried to read Lady Galsworthy's body language as she entered court, head down, looking at no one, refusing to raise her eyes from her papers. When she did look up it was with all the imperiousness she could muster and spoke without preamble. "I have given a great deal of thought to the request for me to admit the statement by Mr Berrens..." There was a long pause and Tom detected something different in her demeanour and heard Mike whispering in his ear.

"Something's happened, mate, and I'm not sure I want to know what it is."

After what seemed like an inordinate delay, the coroner spoke. "However, I have received representations from the Attorney General's office with concerns about national security – concerns that evidence presented in this court might jeopardise public safety and be of benefit to potential enemies. Clearly this is a serious situation which by its nature has to be treated with the utmost gravity. As a consequence, the Attorney is minded to issue Public Interest Immunity certificates regarding some aspects of this inquest and accordingly I have requested a hearing to establish the scope and nature of the public interest." The coroner paused as she perused the documents in front of her.

"The bastards," Tom whispered in fury.

"Does that mean what I think it means, Tom?" Mike hissed. "That when she calls the witnesses we want to question – anyone who works for the state – they've got the Government's full permission to refuse to speak. They needn't say a bloody word. Please tell me that's not what it means! That they've screwed us!"

"That's exactly what it means!" Tom replied but something told him to get the entire picture before allowing his anger full rein. He waited in silence.

The coroner continued. "I will, of course, be unable to proceed with this inquest until I have heard *ex parte* submissions from the Attorney."

Tom rose quickly and the coroner acceded by inclining her head. There was no preamble and those who knew Tom could just detect a quaver in his voice that indicated profound anger. "This inquest has been fourteen years in the making and most of the written statements have been available for at least ten years." He raised his voice. "Why, why, why were these matters not canvassed prior to the start of the inquest as is the recognised and accepted practice? Why now, after all this time, has the Government suddenly seen fit to invoke national security in order to prevent disclosure of material that has been available to them for years?" Even as he was speaking Tom knew, without doubt, that the reason was Morris and Berrens. Morris had been sprung on them but without Berrens's corroboration, Barry Morris's evidence could be trashed.

The coroner held her hand aloft to stop him. "Mr Harrison! If you will allow me, Mr Harrison," she spoke the words like a displeased school teacher, "I cannot answer your questions because I do not know the nature of the concerns and whether they are related entirely to these historic events or whether they are as a result of recent happenings that might or might not have some relevance to the proceedings in this court. I simply won't know until after the private hearing that has been requested."

"'I', Your Ladyship, or 'we'? I am making the assumption that all of us who represent clients in this case will be invited to attend!" Anticipation hung in the air whilst the coroner moved her position but looked no more comfortable when she had rearranged herself.

"I would not make that assumption, Mr Harrison; in the first instance it will only be my counsel at the hearing—"

"What?" The word exploded from Tom's lips. "You cannot allow this miscarriage of justice – after all that's happened? It will make our system of inquest a laughing stock. I urge you to resist this demand!"

"No, Mr Harrison, I will not resist what I am instructed to do because I do not know the seriousness of the Government's concerns. Unlike you, Mr Harrison, I will reserve my reactions until I know what we are dealing with..."

"This is unacceptable..." Tom shouted the words, momentarily forgetting the requirements of court decorum.

The coroner cut across him. "I am adjourning this inquest until Friday morning at 9.30 a.m." With that she rose and was gone. Tom turned to Mike. "Why, Mike, why? This Government wasn't even in power then – you'd think they'd latch on to anything to embarrass the Tories!"

Mike was as calm as Tom was irate. "No, no, no, mate, doesn't work like that! On the big issues, like I said before, they all piss in the same pot!"

Tom stood alone in the deserted chamber, allowing everyone else to stream out, not feeling like conversation. Vicky appeared back through the large doors and joined him. It was some weeks since they had been alone together. "Well, you look about as comfortable as a lorry driver at a feminist rally. Cat got your tongue?" Her smile was only a shadow.

Tom had been avoiding her eyes but now looked directly into them and they remained like that for some time, Vicky looking up at Tom, he looking down at her diminutive figure, immobile, unblinking. He was shocked to see Vicky's eyes slowly fill with tears and then overflow as they trickled down her cheeks. As they did so, a wistful smile gently spread across her face but still nothing was said by either and Tom knew that he was responding similarly.

Eventually he tried to speak. "Vicky..."

She raised her fingers and pressed them lightly on his lips to stifle his words and shook her head almost imperceptibly. Finally she spoke. "It's okay, Tom, I know. I've known for some time. It was just a question of when – of when you could find the courage." Wistfulness gave way to sadness. "It's the right decision for both of us but particularly for you and it's only now – that it's happened – I realise how much I'll miss you. But no regrets, Tom!"

It was a statement not a question but Tom considered it anyway as he looked at the powerful, incredibly attractive woman who had been a part of his life for so long – long enough for little creases to have surreptitiously made an appearance round her eyes where before there had been none. A part of him wanted to cancel out the scene, allow things to go back to where they had been just minutes before, but an even larger part of him dismissed the proposition. With the finality of his decision he could feel a sense of relief slowly expanding within him – relief tinged with genuine sorrow. "I'll miss you, Vicky!" he whispered.

"Actually, Tom, just one regret. That you never did realise quite how much I cared for you."

"No, I didn't – but perhaps I do now. Does that compensate?" They pressed cheek against cheek and remained like that for long, long seconds.

The court fizzed with anticipation as the coroner entered but immediately faded to absolute silence. She spoke immediately. "Following submissions from the Attorney General, I would like to hear arguments from all parties before I reach a decision on whether to be guided by the PIIs or not. Would the jury please leave?"

The jury, which had remained entirely silent so far, as was expected of them, had barely warmed their seats before being asked to exit the court once more. The jury usher accompanied them outside.

Tom had no idea if Lady Galsworthy was genuinely looking for guidance or whether it was a charade.

One by one, legal representatives of each interested party made their submission but each was short and whatever their choice of words it amounted to the same thing – they would leave the decision to Her Ladyship. Tom came last. He tried to hold the coroner's eye while he was speaking but she was not having it and looked away. "I have sufficient evidence to reveal the truth behind the death of these people. It is all here in this court and you have the power to allow it to be heard and it requires that you resist censorship – by anyone. If you don't, you will effectively deny truth."

The coroner took her time before speaking. "As Public Interest Immunity certificates are only advisory, the final decision on whether to accept them or not is mine. In this instance I believe that the concerns raised by the Government are outweighed by those of public interest and I have therefore decided not to be guided by them and I rule that there will be full disclosure at this inquest..."

Noise erupted in the courtroom and Tom smiled at Mike. "Quite a lady, our Galsworthy, Mike. She's just told the Government to go get stuffed! Is Berrens on standby?" Mike indicated he was. "Get him here as quickly as possible – along with his equipment."

"Ten minutes," Mike replied.

"I would now like to call Mr Anthony Berrens." The coroner turned to Tom. "I gather a different kind of playback equipment is needed to assist this man's testimony; do you have it – are you able to play the tape?"

"I am M'Lady." The air seemed almost to crackle with expectation as Berrens was called. Tom looked around the faces in the chamber, some expectant, some overlaid with trepidation. Even Lol Kumar was on the public benches, smiling at him smugly, even more rotund, folds of flesh threatening to engulf him.

Berrens's oscilloscope and voice recordings lost none of their impact in the tense courtroom despite the long passage of time. As he had done before, Berrens knitted the two recordings together – the exchanges between the air traffic controller and the oscilloscope readings – in a macabre technical obituary to the dead of Harrow. Again there was complete silence when the tape finished. It was broken by Tom.

"I would like you to summarise your findings."

Berrens responded with the enthusiasm of a circus artist being asked to perform. "The voice recordings and the readings are consistent with a technical problem which was progressive. It fits the scenario of a partially opened rear cargo door springing from its main closures and causing a collapse of part of the cabin floor which in turn triggered an explosion in the cargo hold."

Tom wanted the jury to be in no doubt. "Are you telling this court that the oscilloscope readings resulting from the second incident aboard Flight 469 indicate, beyond any doubt, that the cause was an explosion?"

"Absolutely correct, there is no doubt about it whatsoever!"

"And are you also saying that this explosion took place many miles away from where Flight 469 collided with the helicopter?"

"That's precisely what I'm saying. When Flight 469 struck the helicopter it was already doomed and was heading for the ground out of control. I am convinced beyond any doubt that the downing of Flight 469 was as a result of an explosion on board." Berrens could not have been any more adamant or convincing. Tom immediately looked to the jury and he could see incredulity in their faces.

Beatty tried hard to challenge Berrens's interpretation of the sound waves, but it was fruitless.

The coroner then called an extremely nervous Arthur De Witt, the air traffic controller on duty the night of the crash, and established the basic details of his responsibilities. Every person in the chamber was aware that only one person had questions to pose which had any real meaning, certainly they were the only questions in which anyone had any interest. Tom was also aware of it as he stood before Arthur De Witt.

"You have now heard a copy of the tape recorded by Mr

Morris and you have seen the interpretation placed on it by Mr Berrens. Mr De Witt, was that your voice on the two tapes?"

"It's very difficult to say, it was such a long, long time ago."

"It sounded like your voice, didn't it? A younger you?"

"It sounded like a lot of voices I know."

"Would you say that what you heard was an accurate reflection of the conversation you had with Flight 469 on the night it crashed?"

"I had about thirty conversations that night and thousands subsequently; I can't remember."

"How many of those 'thousands of conversations' have been with an aircraft that has subsequently crashed and killed five hundred and twenty-three people, dreadfully injured hundreds more and demolished a large chunk of London?" De Witt didn't reply. "How many Mr De Witt – ten, twenty, thirty?

"No ... only the one."

"Only one, only the one, and you can't remember it? Let's make things easy for you. Did you have a conversation with Flight 469 of any kind?"

"Yes, of course I did."

"And was everything all right?"

"I seem to remember it had some problems."

"What problems?"

The silence in the council chamber was almost deafening. De Witt made no reply and looked down at his feet.

"What problems were you made aware of during your conversations with Flight 469?"

"I'm not sure."

"You're not sure. The only crash you've ever dealt with and you can't remember what the dying pilot told you—"

There was an interruption as counsel for air traffic control took to his feet. "Madam Coroner, I have been very patient but this is now little short of bullying. My client has said he doesn't remember—"

"And I am saying it's not credible," Tom cut across the barrister.

The coroner was looking directly at De Witt when she spoke. "And I am inclined to agree with you, Mr Harrison. Please continue!"

"Okay, let's go back to the beginning and try the opening question again, Mr De Witt. Did those tapes, as far as you can remember, record an accurate account of the conversation between you and Flight 469?"

Tom saw De Witt's lips move but could not hear his reply. "Would you repeat that, please?"

This time the man's voice could be heard clearly. "Yes!"

"Thank you, Mr De Witt."

As Tom sat down, Mike passed him another note.

Roses are reddish,
Violets are blueish;
If the Pope wasn't Catholic
He'd surely be Jewish. Esther.

Again Esther was grinning at him from her prime position near the door. Tom felt increasingly like he was playing a part in some bizarre, surreal drama to which the Queen of Hearts, the Mad Hatter and a White Rabbit would suddenly make a contribution.

De Witt was followed by Chas the baggage handler and Tom felt his heart sink. This was the one witness he had not been looking forward to – but ironically, of course, it was one of his most important. Varsity had known since the judicial review that Chas was to give evidence and there was no doubt that Beatty would be well prepared. Although not employed directly by Varsity, Tom knew that Beatty would have full details of Chas's disciplinary record, his personnel files, any political affiliations and all criminal convictions. As soon as Tom had finished with the witness, Beatty would attempt to demolish his credibility, his reputation and, with absolute certainty, his testimony. Tom intended to raise the negatives that Beatty would try to rely on and spoil their impact.

Chas's evidence provided the first step in the chain of cause and effect and placed Varsity firmly in the frame. To have delayed carrying out the modifications to the cargo door and then to have lied and said the work had been done, made the company culpable, even if it was impossible to prove that Varsity knew the aircraft was carrying military explosives. Even in the coroner's newfound co-operative mood, there was no way she would allow Tom to introduce the background information which Ailey had supplied. So, the least credible of Tom's witnesses carried the greatest burden of proof.

Charles 'Chas' Henry Newbold took the witness box and Tom felt even sorrier for him than he had years ago. He was another witness who had visibly shrunk but such was this man's loss of weight, his stooping posture, that Tom was certain he had become an alcoholic and possibly worse. Hopkirk quickly led him through the basics of his statement before giving the floor to Tom, who began his questioning slowly, his voice gentle, undemanding.

"How long have you worked around aircraft, Mr Newbold?"

"I dunno, quite a few years – maybe twenty." His shaving hadn't quite worked and little tufts of bristles sprouted between nicks and sore patches, his shirt wasn't quite clean and there was something very unsavoury about the man – rather pathetic. "But I don't any more; I'm retired, on the sick."

"Although you had previously faced a disciplinary hearing and were subsequently dismissed by your employers at Northolt, you still have a fair knowledge about the ways of airlines at that time, I presume?"

"Yeah, I guess so."

"And you had worked on the P11 aircraft before, perhaps many times?"

"Yeah, quite a few."

"Had you ever seen any carrying what are referred to as 'stickers' on their rear cargo doors – instructions that the door must be closed under the supervision of the captain or first officer or must be inspected by them following its closure."

"Yeah. Not these days of course cos that's all in the past but you used to see them from time to time."

"Was Flight 469 carrying such stickers?"

"For sure."

"In your experience, are the stickers ever left on after the modifications have been carried out?"

"No. Never. It wouldn't happen. They have to be inspected after they've been modified and the inspectors would automatically remove them if the engineers hadn't; but they wouldn't be missed. It'd cause too much hassle anyway with the ground crew pulling the pilot out every time they wanted to shut the door. There's no way that would be allowed."

Miles Beatty rose to his feet. "Mr Newbold was a baggage handler, madam, and he is being asked to speak about technical matters which must have been outside his experience..."

Tom had not bothered to sit and spoke before the coroner could reply. "I've finished with that line of enquiry, Your Ladyship. Mr Newbold, how can you be sure that Flight 469 carried the warnings on its cargo door?"

"We hadn't seen any for ages; it must have been one of the last P11s that still hadn't been modified. You can't help but notice them."

Tom's voice took on an even quieter, more intimate tone. "And of course, there were the particularly terrible circumstances surrounding that flight, weren't there? I suspect that after all these years you have mulled over in your mind anything which might have been relevant?"

"You're not kidding. You can't help it – even now."

"What were your feelings when you first heard of the scale of the disaster? When you knew how many innocent men, women and little children had been killed?"

Chas looked down and his voice became quiet. He obviously didn't want to speak about it and his words were delivered begrudgingly, in staccato groups, a few words at a time. "Well ... how do you think you feel...? You've worked on it ... you've put the baggage on ... you've been inside that plane... It was just another job ... then it's crashed ... people died. That's not a good feeling."

"Did you then or since ever think about your actions and what effect, if any, they might have had?"

"You don't think of nothing else... Over and over in your mind... Did I do this...? Did I do that...? It don't stop."

"Whose responsibility was it to close the door?"

"The gang leader – but that wasn't me, I wasn't the gang leader; I was even on a caution, there's no way they'd let me near it." Chas delivered the words in a rush, his head swivelling from side to side of the chamber as though looking for favourable reactions.

Tom kept his voice low and intimate. "What effect did the crash have on you? Do you still think about what happened?"

"It never leaves you, does it?"

"When is it worst – at night?"

"Yeah, you can't help thinking. You've seen all those faces looking at you out of the newspaper and you know they didn't look like that when they were found. You listen to all the stories and they keep coming back to you just when you're not expecting it." He looked directly at Tom and Tom encouraged him with his eyes. "Sometimes I think I hear their screams, even now, they won't leave me alone. There's times when I think they're real – the screams – and they're sent to punish me ... but I'm not guilty, I'm not, I promise I'm not." Chas looked urgently over to the relatives. "It wasn't my fault, I didn't do it, it wasn't me who killed them."

Tom could just make out the first small tears running down Chas's face and hated what he had to do next. He raised his voice and his words came out hard and brittle. "Mr Newbold, your memories are clear and horrifying because of what you think you might be responsible for. You were the last person to touch that cargo door. It was you who closed it, wasn't it, and that's why you'll never forget those stickers? They are your constant reminder of what went wrong. They will live with you for the rest of your life, won't they? They are the memorials to the hundreds of people who died?"

"Please, Mr Harrison, less invective and one question at a time," interposed Lady Helen.

Chas's response was almost lost in the great, racking sobs which issued from his bent and scrawny frame. "It wasn't my fault, he told me to close it, I was on a warning, I couldn't refuse or he would have sacked me ... he told me to do it... 'Close the fucking door, you useless old sod,' ... that's what he said. I had to do it..." His voice was swallowed by his tears.

Tom spoke in a softer tone. "Mr Newbold, you are not solely responsible. There are many people who carry the blame." Tom knew his words were useless because he had thrown petrol on Chas Newbold's constantly smouldering guilt.

"Is that a question?" Lady Galsworthy remarked sharply.

Tom sat down, suspecting he had destroyed what little was left of a man's life. He felt Mike's hand on his arm, his fingers squeezing hard. No words were necessary.

Mike went over to Chas and helped him from the witness box. Tom noticed that Chas's exit was followed intently by the eyes of many of the relatives, some of whom were also crying, and the faces of the jurors looked equally as ravaged. He felt tears in his own eyes but for very different reasons – his complicity in the sadness. But he now knew that whatever Miles Beatty threw at Chas when he returned, no matter what records Varsity produced to show that modifications had been carried out – records that Tom was prevented from exposing – there was not a single person in the court who did not believe that Chas had closed the unmodified doors incorrectly. Tom knew he now had Varsity squarely in the frame.

Beatty essentially threw Chas a lifeline by offering him hope that the doors had been modified and that something else must have caused the aircraft to crash and Chas grasped at it like an alcoholic being handed a bottle of Scotch. With eagerly nodding head and a repetition of "Yes, sir"s he tried to resurrect some vision of innocence – but for himself, not the court. Tom suspected that everyone apart from Beatty wanted it to be over, for the empty husk of a man to be gone, to cope with his crushing burden of misplaced guilt.

When he stepped down, Mrs McNulty gave evidence about the passengers being soldiers, and the death of her grandson, Micky, clearly and with transparent honesty, despite her fragility, that Tom would not have welcomed the job of Hilary Styles, representing the soldiers. He knew the woman had to try and discredit Mrs McNulty but he was surprised by the aggressive way she went about it.

"How old are you, Mrs McNulty?"

"Eight-eight!"

"Do you know how many passengers were on the aircraft?"

"A lot." She was not in the slightest intimidated by Styles.

"Over two hundred, in fact. Don't you think it's rather strange that you are the only one who believes the men were all soldiers?"

"It's because I'm the only one who's not frightened or who's not been bought off."

"Oh, I see, so someone has managed to frighten or bribe all those people, but not you? What is your memory like, Mrs McNulty?"

"Good enough to remember a face – like their faces." She pointed to the public gallery. "They know what I'm talking about – yes, you three, I remember your faces. You know what I'm saying's true, don't you?" The three women she was pointing at were immediately identifiable by their embarrassment. "Your boys have been killed and what are you doing about it...?"

"Mrs McNulty, I must ask you to restrain yourself. Simply answer the questions put to you by Ms Styles." The coroner's polished tones sounded artificial alongside the old lady's strong London accent.

"Answer her questions? Why should I? She just wants to make me out to be a stupid old woman who doesn't know what she's talking about – well I'm not and I do. And they know it's true as well, don't you?" Again she turned to the women in the public gallery. They rose and quickly exited from the chamber, their heads held low. "You might well run away..." Emily McNulty shouted after them.

Hilary Styles turned to the coroner with a look of annoyance on her face, and said, "No more questions."

Mike had briefed Louise and taken her new statement, not Tom. In fact, Mike had insisted on it – and when the coroner called her, Louise identified the photographs of the burnt rifles. It seemed extraordinarily strange to Tom, not having spoken properly to Louise for years and then having had two short meetings with her over coffee, both fraught with wordless emotion, to now be questioning her formally.

"Have you subsequently had those pictures analysed?"

"I have."

"With what result?"

"They are, of course, badly damaged but the overall scale of them fits accurately with a self-loading rifle in current use."

"Current use by whom?"

"The British Army!"

"Your newspaper investigated the political situation that existed in Nigeria at the time of the crash – and it was Nigeria which was the aircraft's destination. Would you outline it for us?"

"There is a huge oil development—"

"Ms Watson, I don't wish to hear any more. It is completely irrelevant!" Lady Galsworthy addressed Tom. "I have been extremely lenient with you, Mr Harrison, but you will not continue with this line of questioning. Not only is it irrelevant it is hearsay..."

As Tom was about to reply, Louise's voice cut across him, loud and insistent. "Is it irrelevant that the biggest investor in the Nigeria oil development is Barcroft Holdings, the parent company of Varsity Aviation...?"

"Thank you, Ms Watson!"

"They have killed and tortured to keep that oil concession and that plane was carrying troops to defend their installations..."

"You will step down – now, Ms Watson and the jury will disregard your evidence."

That night, Tom sat down to write a letter to Louise but he stared at the screen for long minutes not knowing what to say. Ostensibly, his reason was to thank her for her contribution in court but even something that simple would not take form. He then realised that there was another, more profound reason for writing and it had nothing to do with the inquest. He wanted to set out his feelings for her but his emotions were so tumultuous that he could not extract meaningful words to describe them, only disconnected phrases.

And then he allowed his mind to wander to the end of the inquest and what he would like to do immediately afterwards, and suddenly his fingers flicked across the keys with little bidding. Tom was aware that he was writing a letter of particular importance – the first love letter he had ever written.

Dear Louise,
When this is all over I want to take you to a warm and peaceful island I know and leave behind the pain and confusion of

soured relationships. There is a palm-fringed terrace overlooking the sea where we will watch the evening sun disappearing. We'll have dinner at a restaurant on the old harbour wall and gaze at the lights of the village reflected in the moving surface of the sea. I will try to persuade you that we are not different people but the same ones to whom different things have happened. When we are replete and content, we will walk home along the sandy half-moon beach below a tiny promenade inhabited by lovers. I will hold your hand in the evening warmth and I will whisper to you, "I've missed you Louise, oh how I've missed you."

As if his courage might suddenly desert him, Tom pushed the letter into an envelope, attached a stamp, addressed it and walked out into the night's rain to post it.

The inquest had entered its fifteenth month when the coroner called Christopher Chandler, Home Office forensic scientist who had been at the scene of the crash. He was a surprise witness and the coroner explained her decision to call him so late in the proceedings.

"We have had allegations of army personnel on board the aircraft, arms and ammunition, explosives – and I think it important to establish what was found on the ground."

Chandler's statement was released to Tom and he could see immediately there was nothing of importance in it. It was a non-committal, bland and extremely short account of Chandler's findings. Tom immediately got Mike to put a call through to Janet Moyes to ask her to come to court. Lady Galsworthy led Chandler through his anodyne statement line by line and at the end of it she looked at Tom as if to say, *Told you so!*

There was an air about the man that was evasive. Tom was sure he knew something but he certainly would not volunteer it.

"Did you carry out any field tests for explosives?" Tom asked.

"Yes, I did, but under those circumstances it is very easy to get false positives. There is such a cocktail of chemicals around, particularly when a fire is involved."

"But you did get positive readings?"

"Yes, but they were eliminated by more sophisticated laboratory tests."

"What additional tests did you subject them to?"

"The usual GCMS tests."

"And all these tests proved negative?" The man was not at ease, Tom could see that.

"Yes, they did eventually."

"Eventually? You make it sound like you kept going until you got the results you wanted."

"It's important to be thorough."

"Was there anything, any explosive substance you didn't test for?"

"I tested for all the usual compounds."

"That isn't the question..." Mike pulled at his sleeve and pushed a piece of paper into his hand. Tom continued, furious that Esther should choose this moment to continue her games. "Were there any compounds you didn't test for?"

"I tested for anything which might be in common usage."

"So you didn't test for all explosives?" Tom could feel his frustration growing but caught a sudden movement in the corner of his eye and glanced at the press benches. Louise was waving her notebook at him as subtly as she could. She held out her screwed-up hand, opened her fingers and pointed at the palm with her other hand. Tom was no longer listening to Chandler. Louise then pointed at Tom's hand and realisation dawned. He unfolded the piece of paper which Mike had passed him and read it.

Ask to see his original notes. He had a notebook – I saw it. Louise.

Tom turned back to his witness who stood silently waiting, a worried look on his face.

"Mr Chandler, you obviously obtained a lot of information on that dreadful evening. What kind of record did you keep?"

"I'm not sure what you mean."

"Notes, Mr Chandler, notes. Did you take notes?"

"Er … yes."

"And where are those notes now?"

"I really can't remember, there's no reason why I would remember after all this time but I am confident they would have formed the basis of my original statement."

"I presume you would not be in the practice of throwing such notes away – in fact, they would not be *your* notes, would they, but the property of the Home Office? And notes of such a momentous event would not be thrown away, would they? It would be a serious disciplinary offence to do so, would it not?" Tom was afraid Chandler might try this ruse and he wanted to make it too difficult for him even to consider reaching for this particular lifeline. But Tom also knew without doubt that Chandler was looking for an escape route of some sort and that meant he was afraid.

Tom continued. "Mr Chandler, the one thing about Government departments you can entirely rely upon is their procedures. What are the procedures in the forensic science department for filing away notes – notes of the kind you took on the evening Flight 469 came down?" Tom was seeking information from the man's eyes and his demeanour as much as from his words, and they spoke volumes. He was squirming!

"We are dealing here with highly sensitive information, perhaps even classified information, and I wouldn't necessarily know where it was filed –" Chandler rejoined with sudden enthusiasm as though an exit sign had suddenly been illuminated ahead of him – "and I might not even have access to it."

Tom shook his head and tutted theatrically. "Oh dear, dear, I think you're going to have to do better than that, Mr Chandler. You're a scientist and part of your work – part of every scientist's work – is to identify similarities, trends, patterns. They do that by comparing one incident with another, by juxtaposing one set of notes with another, by accessing their past work in order to inform their current work. Or are you different, Mr Chandler – are you the only scientist who is denied access to his past records?"

Chandler was blustering – floundering – once again. "Of

course not, no, of course not, I'm not saying that..."

"So you do have access to your notes?"

"Yes, well, yes, for a certain period of time but ... this was such a long time ago, who knows what's happened to them now."

"Is there a time limit on how long notes are kept?" Tom was playing with him and enjoying it but he could sense by the atmosphere in the courtroom that many others were as eager as he was for some straight answers from Chandler. "Before you dig yourself into an even deeper hole, I would like you to answer a simple question to which I know you know the answer – what is the filing system used to store the notes of your various investigations, including that into Flight 469?" Tom tried to deliver the question in a manner that gave Chandler no choice but to answer – a mixture of demand, irritation, disbelief and ridicule. Even Chandler knew the game was over and looked down, speaking softly.

"Of course, they were filed as paper copies with duplicates so they could be accessed under different headings – a standard, cross-referenced filing system..."

"And anyone accessing those files would need to sign them out and in again...?" Tom asked.

"Yes, and with the authorisation of a superior in many cases. It's a huge filing system and very complicated," Chandler declared, almost in desperation.

"Complicated but not impossible," Tom answered with a smile. "Would you please provide for the court the details of where these files are kept and how they can be accessed?"

Chandler looked to the coroner pleadingly, almost in desperation.

"Well, Mr Chandler?" was all she replied.

Tom turned to the coroner. "Please, madam, I request a twenty-four hour adjournment for the files to be searched by the coroner's officer and the Treasury solicitor instructing your counsel. May I also request that a solicitor representing the relatives, and who is particularly well qualified in matters of this kind, accompany her – his expertise might prove invaluable."

Lady Helen Galsworthy looked back at Tom but did not immediately reply and he was certain he could detect a tiny smile at the corner of her mouth. "Any other reason why you might like him to be in attendance?" she enquired.

"No, my Lady," Tom responded with a straight face.

"Very well then, I will grant your request!" She understood perfectly Tom's distrust.

As the court was adjourned Mike said, "I presume I'm the geezer with the expertise?"

"Of course!" Tom replied with a smile.

The jangling tones of Status Quo's *Irene* interrupted Tom's reading and he reached for his mobile and checked the display. "Mike!"

"You're gonna love this, squire! We got in there and we accessed the files and it was all apple pie except for one set of entries...!"

"Oh, let me guess – the Harrow crash files!"

"Spot on – all removed, every one, and do you know when?" Mike didn't wait for a reply. "The day after the resumed inquest was announced. There's a record book of authorisations and who's done what but the initials for this little lot are completely indecipherable. No wonder chummy wasn't very chatty on the stand..."

"... and we now know what the PIIs were all about," Tom added.

"Where the fuck do we go from here, mate?"

"I'll have another go at Chandler tomorrow and hope I can crack him!"

When the inquest resumed, Tom continued once more to bait Chandler.

"Mr Chandler, would it surprise you to know that all the files relating to the Harrow crash have been removed – from your very complicated, cross-referenced filing system? And would it also surprise you to know that those who signed them out left completely indecipherable signatures?" Tom no longer felt like playing games with the man.

"I had no idea," he replied without conviction. "Well, it was a long time ago."

"Not really, not that long ago, considering the date they were signed out was the day after this resumed inquest was announced, just a matter of a few months ago. I would call that recent, very recent, so recent that it must still be fresh in someone's memory! Is it fresh in your memory, Mr Chandler? Did you sign those files out – files this court has demanded to see but can't because of what appears to be obstruction?"

Tom's implied threat rattled the witness and his response was hurried, garbled.

"No, no, I didn't sign them out, I certainly didn't! He went silent and Tom sensed there was something more to come from this uneasy man. He suddenly burst forth with relief, a forced smile and almost schoolboy enthusiasm:

"Of course, how stupid of me, I'd totally forgotten. Yes, of course! We've had an extraordinarily expensive IT system installed – cost millions, even billions – and I received a directive that all original documentation had to be scanned and entered into a computerised databank. It had completely escaped my mind!"

Tom's words were laced with scepticism. "Yesterday a mental blank, today the gusher of truth erupts. What happened in the interim, Mr Chandler? Now let me see? Could it possibly have been my thinly veiled threat of you perverting the course of justice...?"

"Mr Harrison! You will withdraw that remark!" The coroner barked at him from her position on high and he apologised, but not before he had seen the jury trying to stifle laughter.

Before quiet returned, Mike pulled Tom by his sleeve. "Listen, if they're on a Government database, there are strict protocols governing how it's used. There's gotta be records of the scanning, back-up discs and the like; any erasures or deletions can only be authorised at the highest level – and I mean the highest level! The guy's brief is a Government lawyer – he can access this stuff through his laptop. Ask her Ladyship to instruct him to have a go – and for me to sit alongside him just to be safe."

Tom addressed the coroner, explained the situation and without complaint she authorised Chandler's lawyer, the coroner's officer and "Mr Smith" to withdraw to a private room and seek to access details of the scientist's report.

Tom continued to question Chandler but there was little of interest the man could offer and so he sought general descriptions of the damage that had been done to buildings and people and what Chandler thought might have caused them.

Tom was relieved when he saw the trio file back into court and the coroner's officer approach the coroner and speak quietly to her.

Tom abandoned a half-formed question and waited for the coroner to speak but he already knew the result as Mike approached him shaking his head.

"I have to inform the court," Lady Helen Galsworthy announced, "that no trace of the documents that Mr Harrison has requested could be found."

At the lunchtime adjournment, Tom watched Louise leave the court and waited for her to turn her head towards him, to smile or to give at least some acknowledgement that she had received his letter. And then, as she disappeared, he thought, why the fuck should she? Why would one stupid, juvenile outpouring by an emotionally immature, selfish dilettante, repair the emotional damage he had wreaked over years? What an arrogant arsehole he was, what a self-deceptive moron to think that his few pathetic words would suddenly renew him in Louise's eyes. She had probably laughed and tossed the letter into the bin, dismissed it as a meaningless gesture by a desperate failure who simply didn't like to lose.

Even as the insults tumbled around in his head Tom knew that he was rehearsing his worst fears whilst in his heart he was yearning for Louise to understand that the love she had once invested in him had not been entirely wasted. It had taken root and matured and whether she ever looked at him again or not, whether she ever considered him again or not, he desperately wanted her to know that he had loved her, did love her. He had no right to expect anything from her but that one thing at least he wanted her to know. It would not provide what he wanted but it would at last allow him to face her with some contentment. And the need to know how she felt about his letter was to grow with each passing day.

"It's a stitch-up, Tom, a bleedin' monumental stitch-up – but they can't get away with it that easily."

Tom was wrenched out of his introspection by Mike's anger. "What do you mean?"

"Computers are totally unforgiving – they remember every key stroke, everything you put into them and everything you delete from them. They're a bit like a pissed-off girlfriend when she's got the hump and suddenly she's got total recall... Anything that's been on that database can be tracked – it's a kind of audit trail. And what's more, it'll be backed up somewhere, probably more than one place. Nothing ever disappears entirely. If her Ladyship will give me a crack at it I reckon I've got a good chance of finding what we're looking for!"

Tom grabbed Mike's head in both hands and kissed him on the forehead. "You're a cocky bugger but you're a clever cocky bugger. Don't tell me that all those IT courses that cost an arm and a leg are finally going to pay off? How long do you reckon it will take?"

"Hard to say but to be safe I reckon I need a week – and of course I'll need all the necessary permissions and the co-operation of Chandler's brief."

"Oh shit, here we go again. Helen of Croydon is not going to like my request and neither is anyone else but I'll do battle as soon as we reconvene."

With little enthusiasm, Lady Galsworthy did approve his request.

When the court did reconvene, it was an excited Tom and a very relieved Mike Smith who waited for Chandler to re-enter the witness box. When he did so, Tom posed his first question with gravity, a question he had thought about long and hard.

"Mr Chandler ... we now have your notes..." He punched the words out and waited just long enough for the drama to build and for Chandler to absorb them. "We know when they were transferred to the computer, we know when they were deleted and we know who did it – and so do you, Mr Chandler!

What is more, we know why you did not want the court to see those notes!"

The look on the witness's face was one of almost unadulterated misery and Tom had achieved exactly what was intended. Yes, he did have Chandler's notes but what they meant was utterly incomprehensible. Mike had sweated long days before finding them. A man who normally shrugged off worries and pressure like oil off Teflon had become obsessed, irritable and self-doubting. And then, when Chandler's original notes suddenly filled his screen, without fanfare or fuss, it was almost anticlimactic. When they read through them that sense of deflation became acute because there was nothing in there that provided any tangible answers as to why he was afraid and why the Government wanted them hidden. Janet Moyes also went through them and what at first had appeared bland and unremarkable began to yield sufficient bait to make Tom's fishing expedition worthwhile.

"Mr Chandler, it isn't so much the technical detail of your notes that interests me but your personal comments. For instance, what does this mean here, where you've written, 'Oh God, bad news.'?"

Chandler was still deathly white and spoke in little more than a whisper.

"I can't remember."

"Okay, we'll forget that for a minute. What did you mean when you wrote, 'This must not be leaked'?" Tom offered the notebook printout to Chandler. "You seemed pretty concerned, because if you count them you'll see there are seven exclamation marks."

Chandler hung his head and was trembling but did not reply.

"It was explosives, Mr Chandler, wasn't it, military explosives?"

Chandler stood with his head bowed and the whole of the court concentrated on him. When he spoke it was in a thin and reluctant voice.

"No, it wasn't military explosives..." His pause seemed to last for minutes.

Tom was convinced he was lying. "Come on, Mr Chandler,

tell us the truth. It was explosives, wasn't it?"

"Not military explosives... I suspected it might be a bomb!"

Tom was thrown. This was one scenario he had not even contemplated. He needed to know exactly what Chandler meant. "Can I be clear about this, you are saying you suspected there had been a bomb on the plane, a bomb which had caused it to crash, a bomb which was separate and apart from any other explosives – bullets, hand grenades and so on. Is that what you're saying?"

"Yes, that is what I'm saying."

"And were your suspicions confirmed?"

"I'm not sure."

"What do you mean, you're not sure?"

"I found no explosive traces consistent with a large, conventional bomb."

"You're pretty sure a bomb exploded but you couldn't find any traces of it, is that what you're saying?"

"I'm not sure."

"You're not sure. Why aren't you sure, Mr Chandler? Is it because you don't want to be sure? Is there such a thing as an explosive that doesn't leave a trace? A bomb that detonates murderously and then disappears like the invisible man?" Even as he was delivering the question, Tom recalled his conversation with Janet Moyes many years before – unstable, undetectable bombs favoured by some terrorist groups.

Chandler nodded. "Yes, I believe that is possible."

Tom had to quickly marshal his thoughts, as the last thing he had been expecting was agreement with his attempt at scathing humour. The only thing he could do was continue in the same vein. "And is that what you suspected in this instance – a disappearing bomb?"

Chandler's concerns were growing by the second and he stood before the court as a man on the point of collapse. His voice was faint and with little more substance than the breath which carried it. "I did have some suspicions, yes!"

Tom was out of his depth on traceless explosives and so moved on. "Does the number in the right-hand margin help your suspicions in any way?" Tom posed the question with a confidence he did not feel and directed Chandler to the location of the number on his printout. Tom had no inkling as to its import but he did not want Chandler to know that.

"What is it? What does it refer to? Why was it important enough to write down and what does it mean?" Tom's delivery was designed to give Chandler the impression that he already knew precisely what the number meant and they were now merely going through the motions. A simple denial of any knowledge would leave Tom floundering but Chandler's demeanour indicated that Tom had achieved what he had intended.

"It was on a piece of debris I found at the scene."

"A piece of debris? A remnant of the bomb, perhaps?"

"Yes, possibly."

"Now tell the court, Mr Chandler, what does that number signify? Is it an identification number of some kind?"

There was a long pause before Chandler replied. "Yes."

Tom could feel every nerve in his body tingling and had to force himself to breathe more deeply, for although he had no knowledge of their destination he knew he was on the right road and Chandler desperately did not want to go there. The man would only make the journey if he thought that Tom already knew the route and where it would terminate. "What do you think it's from – what does it identify?" The words were patronising, as though the entire world knew the answer to his question.

"I believe it's the number from a printed circuit board."

"You obviously identified it immediately for what it was – your notes tell us that. But how were you able to identify it so immediately? How did you know that number so readily? What does it signify? What was it attached to? Where was it produced?"

Chandler looked to be on the point of fainting and beads of sweat stood out on his now pallid face. "It belongs to a subcontractor of the Ministry of Defence!"

Tom could hear the noise in the chamber beginning to swell and fought hard to maintain his composure as the disclosure stunned him. But he knew the end to a fourteen-year-long journey was clearly in sight and that was all he needed. "I'll ask you again – how did you instantly recognise it?"

Chandler shook his head from side to side almost as if despairing. "They are made in very limited numbers because of the need for high security – please, could I have a glass of water?"

The court usher immediately passed him one and the man sipped it, struggling to recover his composure. But Tom was not finished.

"Is such a piece of equipment available to anyone other than a Government employee?"

Chandler looked straight at Tom as though appealing for help. "No!"

That was it – the journey was at an end and Tom was almost overwhelmed but still he felt the need to maintain the pretence that none of this was new to him and he now wanted the final chapter and verse. "Precisely, Mr Chandler, precisely!" Even as he posed the next question Tom was still trying to assimilate the importance of what the man had said.

"So, Mr Chandler, you are telling this court that you believe Flight 469 carried a bomb manufactured for the Government, with Government materials, and could only have been in the hands of a senior Government employee and that this bomb exploded on board and resulted in the crash of the aircraft and was responsible for the death and destruction that was visited on Harrow?"

There was a long delay before he answered. "Probably, yes!" very faintly. Tom had to read his lips as noise in the court had swelled to a crescendo. The coroner tried to restore order but Tom wanted the final confirmation heard by every member of the jury.

"I'm sorry, Mr Chandler, your reply was inaudible. Would you please speak up so the whole court can hear you."

"Yes!" He almost shouted the word and the noise swelled again and this time there was no likelihood of it soon abating.

Lady Galsworthy called an adjournment, fighting to be heard above the din. Chandler remained in the witness box seemingly frozen and incapable of movement.

*

Participants poured out into the corridor and Tom was surrounded by relatives. Vicky was the first to congratulate him and threw her arms round his neck and planted a kiss on his cheek. "Christ, what's all that about?" He could feel hands patting his back, voices calling to him and laughter as his clients gathered round. He found Mike and they first shook hands before hugging each other. "You little old rascal, you! Would you Adam and Eve it?" Mike said with a huge grin before marshalling their clients into the relatives' room. Tom saw Ailey for the first time since the opening days of the inquest. She had clearly got the message that today might be worth attending.

"Congratulations, Tom. May I…?" She indicated towards the relatives' room.

The mood was one of triumph and Tom shouted for order. "We haven't won yet, okay? The jury has still to return a verdict." He heard a cry of, "Did you see their faces?"

Tom sought out Janet Moyes. "Why didn't he find traces of explosives? Or was he lying?"

"Not necessarily. There's an explosive called TATP – been around for a couple of decades or so. It's made with common or garden household substances – acetone, hydrogen peroxide, sulphuric acid – well, almost any acid, even lemon juice. None of the existing tests would detect it and there are no metallic compounds so it can go straight through airport detection. If you were going to find it, you'd have to know what you were looking for. It's highly unstable and much beloved of fringe groups."

"So what the hell was a terrorist bomb, made by the MoD, doing on an aircraft full of camouflaged soldiers…?" Even as he asked the question a possible answer began to form in his mind.

Janet shrugged. "If you wanted it to look like terrorists…?"

Ailey stepped into their circle. "As the only fully paid-up cynic in the room, can I give you my opinion? Even way back when this whole thing started, there was a battle going on in Ogoniland, as you know, Tom – Nigerian elite plus big oil companies against the indigenous people. Extra-judicial killings, trumped-up executions and environmental disasters.

There's a lot of sympathy for the rebels in both our countries so sending troops to try and quell the sabotage and protests would be political suicide. On the other hand..."

Tom took over. "Have a plane full of Brits crash in the oil fields, cast the rebels as the terrorists and—"

"... You can whip up public sentiment and officially send in troops to protect 'our vital interest'." Ailey tried to mimic a ruling class British accent but it sounded like Dick Van Dyke's chimney sweep.

The explanation was almost fantastical and Tom shook his head in disbelief. "The fate of Flight 469 was sealed before it took off from Northolt with a bunch of sacrificial soldiers and no one would have ever known had it not been for a dodgy cargo door."

"A word of caution, *compadres*," Mike threw in. "That was then and do you know what? It's also now! They're still destroying Ogoniland and have even stretched further out into other states, they're still dispossessing locals and they're still killing innocent people and all the same players are still in place – different names but same *modus operandi*. And British companies are still pumping the oil and we're still buying it from them. THAT's why we've been tearing around getting nowhere like a bumper car on speed. THAT's why the Government issued PIIs and that's why I ain't sure it's all over yet, not by a long chalk! Too many arses in the firing line."

His words were followed by silence.

Tom shook his head, more in despair than doubt and threw out a general question.

"How many of you buy into this scenario? How many believe our own Government could act as cynically as this?"

There was general murmuring of assent with few dissenting voices.

Tom sat down almost wearily. "And I'll tell you something, I believe it too, but I'll never be able to prove it."

When the inquest resumed, it was only for Lady Galsworthy to instruct the jury in their duties and to send them off to consider their verdict. And the waiting began in the family room. Esther spent most of her time sitting with an unlit cigarette in her mouth, Tom and Vicky paced and had to keep avoiding each other. Mike exuded calm and related silly stories from his book-making days in a strategy of diversion. Most remained silent, just occasionally reminding each other that it had to go their way, didn't it? It was four hours later that the usher summoned them back into court and they filed into the chamber and took their places silently.

Lady Helen Galsworthy turned to the jury. "Have you nominated a foreman?"

One of the women, the black woman, stood up. "Yes, it's me."

"Have you reached a verdict?"

"Yes, we have."

"Is it unanimous?"

"Yes."

"What is it?"

"We have found this case very complicated, madam. Can I outline to the court our findings?"

Lady Galsworthy nodded. "Yes."

The forewoman continued. "We believe that many of the deaths – and we've made a list of those we know about – were contributed to by the lack of decent emergency services. We want to make some comment on that because we feel the Government should be called to account, but we weren't quite sure how to describe it."

Tom realised he was barely breathing.

"And what of the other deaths?" the coroner asked.

The forewoman suddenly stood erect as though she felt entirely confident with what she had to say. "We have unanimously decided they were the result of unlawful killing but I'd like to expand on that, if it's allowed." Again the coroner acceded.

"We believe the helicopter played no part in the crash – its position and height were irrelevant. It was the plane that was responsible for the death of the helicopter passenger. We believe that the records of who was on the aircraft – the type of person, that is – and what it was carrying were not accurate and that the cargo probably included explosives and contributed to deaths on the ground." The forewoman refreshed her memory from the notes she carried before announcing each of the jury's findings.

"We believe the aircraft company did not modify the cargo doors and it was this that started a chain of events that led to the crash. We are very concerned about the length of time it has taken for this inquest to be held and we are also concerned by various Governments' attempts to withhold information that was vital to establishing what happened."

The forewoman looked up, paused and looked around the courtroom whilst Tom held his breath. Had she finished? Was there more to come? She cleared her throat.

"We also believe that someone, we don't know who, but with official support from someone in the Government, placed a bomb on that plane and it was this that was ultimately responsible for all the deaths on the aircraft and on the ground."

There was a momentary, almost stunned silence as the import of the forewoman's words sunk in. She remained standing, her face set, solemn but determined, almost confrontational, Tom thought. And then a murmur issued from his clients, from the court as a whole, and quickly swelled as face turned to face, seemingly needing to share what had been said, to confirm that they had heard it correctly. Quite involuntarily, Tom had also stood as the verdict was announced and remained standing, barely able to believe that they had succeeded. The Coroner called for order but had to do so several times before she was able to speak.

"There are many aspects of this inquest which are extremely worrying and I intend to refer all the papers to the Director of Public Prosecutions. I also have to tell the court that I will be recommending, with all the authority at my disposal, that a public inquiry is established forthwith."

Tom had not known what reaction to expect from his clients and was surprised at the dignity he encountered once they were all back in the relatives room. The realisation dawned that this was the end of a long, long battle for them and while that fight had continued, their loved ones had metaphorically stood alongside them, urging them on, constantly in their thoughts. Now it was official – they were dead, had been killed and now determination was replaced by acceptance – and grief. But he knew it was not all over and so waited until the tears and conversations had started to abate.

"Well, my friends, what do you want me to do?" He could see the confusion on their faces. "Do we call it a day, accept the verdict and move on or do we continue?" Confusion spread like a contagion. "There is still more we could do, perhaps should do, because it isn't over yet, not by a long way. The DPP might bring charges against some of the players in this obscene drama; on the other hand he might not. A public inquiry might make recommendations which we like – but on the other hand...!

"So what do we do? We can't touch the Government so my suggestion is ... corporate manslaughter, that's what I think! If the DPP doesn't charge anyone, I believe we should commence proceedings by summons against specific companies and their legal executives! So, let's make sure the DPP knows we're watching him, let's do everything we can to promote a public inquiry, but before you make a decision, I want you to listen to Ailey." She climbed on a chair so she could be seen, perched precariously on her ridiculously high heels.

"I'm going to make some predictions. Varsity's stock will have collapsed by midnight and the company won't be worth a light." There was a mumble of concern from relatives. "They will go into liquidation within the month." More cheers. "And I'll tell you what else will happen. Mr Andrew Goddam Glennister – oh yes, he's still there – will be thrown to the wolves by the board of Barcroft and he will be looking for a job by this time tomorrow. Barcroft will put the whole thing down to rogue management at Varsity and wash their hands of it.

"The big problem for you is – there'll almost certainly be no money from Varsity because their creditors will clean them out. But the good news is, I'm pretty certain that Barcroft will put their hands in their pockets to show what a kind-hearted, responsible company they are. For those of you who haven't yet settled – it's your birthday!"

"Who's a lucky boy then? Fell in the shit and came up

smelling of roses!" Mike's grin spread from ear to ear but Tom's face indicated he had no idea what he was talking about. "Disclosure, mate, or lack of it. You're a jammy bugger and you might just keep your job – I don't think anyone would dare drag you to the stocks after that little performance." He took Tom's face in his hands and kissed him on the forehead. "Well done, Tom. I really don't think you have any idea of just how fucking brilliant you are."

"Drinks are on you then." Tom tried to make light of Mike's praise but his face glowed with appreciation. He made his way to the door and stepped out into the corridor to find the loo and he felt Vicky's hand on his arm. "Before I leave I just wanted to say thanks – again, and I will support any action you decide on but I won't take an active part. That's it, Tom!" There was a mixture of regret and finality in her words. "Take care, you dear, dear man," she said as she offered her face up for what they both knew would be their last kiss. With that final gesture she was gone, her heels click-clacking down the marble-floored corridor as Tom watched her go. She did not look back – he did not want her to.

"Thought I might get an exclusive from you?" Louise's voice made Tom start. She was standing in the corridor behind him. "So you won, then?"

"Yes, I think so."

"Looks like Vicky won too."

Tom could see sadness in her eyes and understood exactly what she was implying.

"That was goodbye."

"Until the next time?"

"That was goodbye." Tom did not elaborate.

"It was a beautiful letter, Tom. Thank you. It made me blink for most of the morning."

They stood in silence.

"Did you mean it?"

"Yes." Again Tom felt no need to elaborate.

"I'm married, Tom, I have a husband."

"I know."

"I have children."

"I love children."
"I don't trust you."
"I don't blame you."
"It didn't work before, why would it now?"

Tom hesitated for just a moment or two before replying. "Because I love you." The words came out with ease and he smiled.

ABOUT THE AUTHORS

Michael Mansfield QC was called to the Bar in 1967 and established his own set of Chambers in 1984 and became Queen's Council in 1989. Michael has represented defendants in criminal trials and appeals, and families of the bereaved in inquests and inquiries in some of the most controversial legal cases the country has seen, particularly where issues of civil liberties have arisen.

Amongst the most recent are: the Hillsborough disaster; Dr Abbas Khan, unlawfully killed in a Syrian prison; Jean Charles de Menezes shot dead by police; Dodi Al Fayed and Diana, Princess of Wales; Stephen Lawrence in the private prosecution for murder, inquest and Public Inquiry; the Bloody Sunday Inquiry in Derry and London; the Marchioness Disaster; James Miller and Tom Hurndall, killed by the IDF; Deptford/New Cross Fire; the Lockerbie/Omagh/Dublin Monaghan bombings and many more.

Michael's past clients include: the Orgreave miners who were unjustly accused of riot during the miner's strike in 1984; the Birmingham Six, released after nearly sixteen years of wrongful conviction; those in the ABC Official Secrets case and the Operation Julie drugs trial; James Hanratty, hanged in 1962 for murder; 'spy' Michael Bettany; Frank Critchlow and the Mangrove; the Bradford 12 and the Newham 7 against the National Front; the Knightsbridge Heist accused; Colin Wallace; the 'Camberwell', 'Torso', 'Big H' and M25 murder trials; Judith Ward; Barry George; Iraqi dissidents fleeing Saddam Hussein; Turkish and Kurdish exiles; Palestinians charged with the Israeli Embassy bombing in London; Angela

Canning, the mother cleared of killing her two babies and Ruth Ellis, the last woman to be hanged in Britain. He has also appeared in European Courts and represented Fatmir Limaj who was acquitted of war crimes in Kosovo.

Michael has served for the past five years on the international jury of the Russell Tribunal on Palestine; he is President of the Haldane; the founder of Amicus, a charity that offers free legal representation to those on Death Row. He is Patron of numerous organisations including Viva! a Professor and Honorary Fellow of many universities as well as being a regular contributor to TV radio and public debates on legal issues and human rights issues.

Michael has five children from his first marriage: Jonathan, Anna, Louise, Leo and Kieran. He has been married to Yvette Vanson for thirty years and they have a son, Freddy.

Tony Wardle was christened on the day the second world war broke out although he claims that the two events were not related. He is a print and TV journalist and writer and the associate director of vegan campaigning group, Viva!, which he helped to found in 1994. He edits and produces their highly-acclaimed magazine, *Viva!life*.

Through their TV production company Vanson Wardle Productions, Tony and producer/director Yvette Vanson, made documentaries for most of the big broadcast channels, winning a Royal Television Society award and an RTS nomination. Their Channel 4 documentary *The Battle for Orgreave* was chosen for screening at the Edinburgh TV Festival. Issue-based videos have won gold and bronze medals at the New York Film & TV Festival, two bronze medals at the Prague Ekofest, a PR Week Public Relations Award, an IVCA Golden Reel Award and an ITVA Award of Excellence.

Book credits include *Presumed Guilty* (with Michael Mansfield QC) and *The Battle for Orgreave*, which accompanied the film.

He also wrote *The Silent Ark*, *Born to be Wild* and the *Livewire Guide to Going, Being and Staying Veggie* (all with Juliet Gellatley). In 2014, Tony completed his novel, *POD*.

He is the only British journalist to have won an Hibakusha Travel Grant to visit Japan and research the medical, social and psychological after effects of the atomic bombings of Hiroshima and Nagasaki.

He has a daughter Niki by his first wife, Christine, and grandchildren Max and Olivia. He was also married to Juliet Gellatley, founder and director of Viva!, with whom he has twin sons, Jazz and Finn, born in 2002.

About the editor

Yvette Vanson was for twenty years an independent producer director of contentious award winning documentaries, her work has been described as "television of a high order, well crafted and aimed unerringly to engage both intellect and emotions" (*Financial Times*). In 2000 she won a BAFTA for a film about the murdered Stephen Lawrence.

In 2009 Yvette co-authored the *Memoirs of a Radical Lawyer* by Michael Mansfield, QC which still remains a number one best seller.

Yvette also edited *The Home Lawyer*, by Michael Mansfield, 2003 and wrote *The Lawyer's Tale* a short story published in 2011.

Yvette first picked up a paintbrush in 2004 and since 2012 has been a professional artist. She is motivated by a strong political commitment to tackling injustice, by exploring and exposing exploitation and inequality and then communicating these abuses and ways to overcome them through her work. Yvette's exhibitions include:

MINERS: an artist's tribute for the 30 anniversary of the great strike of 1984 January 12 – April 26 2015 at the National Coal Mining Museum of England, Caphouse Colliery, Wakefield, Yorkshire.

BREAKING THE BARRIERS TO FREEDOM: November 2013 at the Peltz Gallery, Gordon Square, London. The paintings were derived from her work as Honorary Research Fellow/Artist in Residence at Birkbeck, University of London.

FACING THREAT: February – April 2013 at Maestro Arts, Putney, London, drew on her experiences from a trip to Tar Sands, Alberta in Canada.

Yvette has been married to Michael Mansfield for thirty years and they have a son Freddy, who is a primary school teacher and poet.

Read more & see examples of her paintings, articles and films at www.yvettevanson.com

Printed in Dunstable, United Kingdom

71456279R00258